Unforsaken

by

Cassie Laelyn

The Fallen Guardians, Book 1

Unforsaken

Cover Art by *Diana Carlile*

The Wild Rose Press, Inc.
PO Box 708
Adams Basin, NY 14410-0708
Visit us at www.thewildrosepress.com

Publishing History
First Black Rose Edition, 2019
Print ISBN 978-1-5092-2389-3
Digital ISBN 978-1-5092-2390-9

The Fallen Guardians, Book 1
Published in the United States of America

Raven raced through the forest, focusing on his connection with Tayla to guide him. Her heart hammered and adrenaline pumped through her veins.

He leaped over a fallen branch, half-sprinting, half-flying, his feet pounding against the dirt, snapping twigs. Their connection guided him to the left, back toward the bonfire, growing stronger and clearer the closer he got. He rounded a wide trunk and, at last, he spotted her.

He clenched his jaw.

Tayla stumbled backward, eyes wide, her hand held out in front, holding off a fucking Fallen.

His feral crimson wings spread wide, blazing red eyes glowed in the darkness. The revolting stench of choking ash filled the air.

The Fallen stalked toward Tayla, taunting her with words Raven was too furious to comprehend. Both wings curved around, and the piece of shit aimed poisonous talons straight at Tayla's heart. One scrape would end her mortal life in a split second.

Big fucking mistake.

Dedication

For you,
for shining your light in the darkness,
so I could find my way.

Acknowledgements

With immense gratitude to my readers—thank you for taking a chance on a new author! I hope this is just the beginning of our relationship and you'll stay with me for many, many years to come.

Thank you to my awesome street team, for your hours and hours of reading, brainstorming, designing, and honest feedback—I couldn't do this without you. The bus is just around the corner!

Lara, my editor extraordinaire, thank you for your patience and guidance—you rock!

And to my wonderful family and dearest friends—thank you from the bottom of my heart for your endless support, countless pep talks, and always encouraging me to follow my dreams.

Chapter 1

Fate was a bitch. And man, did Raven know it. Thanks to Fate, he found himself hunkered down amongst the dark shadows, several stories above a shady university courtyard, watching *her,* his assigned Chosen.

The weathered building provided the perfect cover; chipped midnight concrete tiles lined the pitched roof and tall twin Gothic spires stretched toward the cloudless sky, their shadows extended past him like long ghostly fingers reaching over the edge. Fatigue cramped his thighs from the two or so hours he'd tortured himself in this position.

God, he was weary of it.

Of all of it.

He'd lost count of how many hours he spent perched in this very spot, protecting her. While she ate lunch at the wooden benches, nestled between the ancient pine trees or curled up on a rug reading one of her many novels. Countless times, he'd longed to stretch alongside her as she basked under the warm rays.

Today, she said farewell to her colleagues and life as she knew it. Put the horrors of that night in the courtyard behind her.

Having her closer was gonna make his job a

helluva lot easier. A bonus not to have to fly so goddamn far.

Now the hard work began, for both of them.

If only he could shake the nagging ache in his chest. He should want nothing more than for her to follow her destiny. As a Chosen, it was what she was born to do. A rare mortal created by Fate to fulfill an extraordinary destiny, one who would succeed in tipping the scales back in Fate's favor, contributing to her greater plan. Whatever that was.

And he was the Guardian Fate had assigned to keep her alive so she could fulfill her Chosen path. His number one task was to protect her against the Fallen; those pieces of shit dark angels who chose to fall from the Heavens and reside in the fiery pits of Hell. Their sole mission: Capture the brightest souls and lure them into the darkness. Each soul taken tore apart Fate's plans, and there was no brighter soul than one of her Chosen mortals.

No way would that happen on his watch.

But lately, this pull, this unfamiliar tug in his chest grew. And it clouded his judgement.

Time spent hiding in the shadows, watching over her, had only consumed him with the need to know her; her likes, dislikes, what she thought as she twirled a strand of chestnut hair between her delicate fingers.

Hunger to touch her consumed him. To step free from the shadows and let her see him. Truly see him.

Raven massaged the back of his neck, again, not that it helped. He couldn't stop the heat scorching through his veins each time he spotted her, the pounding in his chest at the mere mention of her name. His inability to focus without her near.

No. He couldn't risk causing a ripple in her path, prolonging—or worse, altering—her destiny.

Pissing off Fate wasn't wise; he'd learned that lesson a long time ago.

After this long, he was thankful to have a Chosen to protect, a distraction from the centuries of fighting the Fallen.

Snap the hell out of it, Raven.

Raven glanced down at the courtyard; an oversized space covered in brown-green grass that didn't know whether it should grow or prepare to die off for the coming winter. Paved pathways weaved between ancient pines like a maze one had to decipher before being granted entry to any of the three buildings.

Raven's pulse quickened as sunlight glistened in her hair. Today, she'd tied it up in a messy ponytail, like she'd put it up as a last-minute thought and loose wavy strands fell across her face. He cursed his hand for reaching forward to tuck them behind her ear. A pair of rust-colored skinny jeans and a navy short sleeve blouse framed her slender figure with a matching silk scarf tied round her neck.

His mind wandered—again—imagining his fingers releasing her ponytail, gliding slowly through her silky hair as it cascaded over her shoulders. In unhurried motions, he'd untie her scarf, nudge her closer, press the heat of her body firmly against his—

A familiar *swoosh* interrupted his daydreaming, quickly followed by a series of creaks as the roof tiles protested the weight of another Guardian landing on them.

"Knew I'd find you here." Aric edged down the steep incline to crouch beside him.

Raven greeted him with a nod, without diverting his gaze from her.

"Today's the day, huh? Will be nice for you to have her closer." Aric tucked his jet-black wings tightly behind his back.

Raven massaged the back of his neck. *Why isn't it helping?* He should be bouncing with energy after the hours he'd spent healing under the sun this morning. Maybe that connection was dwindling away, too.

"Oh man, I know that look." Aric slowly shook his head. "It's written all over your face."

"It's fine. I'm handling it." *No, I'm really not.*

"Whateva you say, man." Aric's strong hand briefly squeezed Raven's shoulder. "Anyway, I came to see if you needed anything. Caffeine, bourbon? Maybe a night out on the town to let off a little steam?" Aric tilted his head at Raven and frowned. "Exactly how long's it been since you got any action, that didn't involve your sword in a Fallen's chest?"

Like he needed a reminder of his record-breaking drought, but the suggestion of a seedy mortal club and a one-night stand coming from Aric was just comical.

Raven peered back at Aric and raised an eyebrow. "Is that the remedy *you* use?"

Aric's lips thinned. Case closed.

After all these centuries, maybe Aric regretted the decision to join him. Would he have chosen differently had he known the consequences?

Maybe they all would've.

Aric settled in beside Raven, planting his ass on the cold concrete roof tiles and folded his forearms on top of his bent-up knees. "EJ had another vision this morning."

Great. That was all Raven needed.

He glanced across his shoulder at Aric. "Anything new?"

Aric shook his head. "Nah, same as the last however many. He must be getting sick of foreseeing nothing but destruction and end-of-the-world shit. Bet he's silently wishing he got the tranquil vision of a Chosen assignment, instead of you," he chuckled.

"Doubt it," Raven scoffed. "Might interrupt his busy social calendar."

Aric roared with laughter. "Yeah, he's definitely taken full advantage of our exile, that's for sure."

Raven leaned his head back and peered up at the bright blue sky as comfortable silence stretched between them.

What the hell was he doing there? He should be out fighting Fallen, leading his brothers in the never-ending war to rid Earth of those scumbags. Not to mention the impossible mission Fate tasked him with in the first place.

Now was not the time to crouch on a roof like a stalker, fantasizing about his female, risking ripples in her path.

His assigned Chosen.

Christ, Raven, she's not your *female.*

The sun peeked out from behind a lonesome cloud and Raven scooted backward to remain in the shadows.

Aric softened his voice. "We're here for you, man." He continued to stare at the mortals below, weaving around the university courtyard going about their daily ritual. "You've just gotta keep the faith."

That's the problem, isn't it?

Raven returned a fake smile. He and his comrades

were tight, to be honest, they were brothers more than comrades. The reason he couldn't stomach telling them the truth, wedging a knife between the three of them forever.

His confused feelings for this Chosen were nothing compared to that bombshell.

Raven rose; his knees cracked and joints popped, voicing their complaints as he straightened his legs. The burning in his calves cleared his head a little.

He turned to Aric. "Let's get outta here. I'll meet you back at the house."

Aric stood and gave Raven a brotherly handshake before Aric crept to the rear of the roof and stepped off the ledge with grace that didn't match the size of his body or wings.

As a Guardian, Aric had a warrior's build; over six feet of solid muscle and raw strength. He kept his jet-black hair short on the sides, longer on top, and spent all his free time maintaining the narrow, thin line of three-day growth trailing his square jaw, up the cleft of his chin to his bottom lip.

Raven returned his gaze to her.

Tayla.

The thin strap of her chocolate leather satchel crossed the front of her body and she leaned in, embracing a female colleague. After a friendly kiss on the cheek, the colleague turned and cut across the courtyard toward a parking lot, where a few cars remained.

Tayla stood still.

What is she thinking?

After a few minutes, she continued her unhurried stroll to the front gates of the university, but at the end of the pathway, she paused and turned around.

Raven tracked her every move. Her gaze roamed the courtyard in front of her and her hazel eyes dimmed with a wash of sadness. He ducked his head to peer under a thick weave of branches to catch a better glimpse. The ache in his chest intensified in time with the deep rise and fall of her chest.

His arm absently reached out to brush his thumb over her dusty pink cheeks, even though he couldn't reach her. Or touch her.

Tayla straightened her shoulders and her beautiful smile returned. She twisted around to leave, but stopped midway to glance over her shoulder as though something had caught her attention.

She leaned forward, narrowing her eyes as though trying to focus on something. Or someone.

The drumming of his pounding heart echoed in his ears.

She stretched her neck and her gaze lifted, up and over the top of the trees, directly toward the roof he crouched on.

Raven double-checked his position. Without the ability to mask his presence, he needed to remain hidden. Too many lives were at stake for him to screw this up. He sank farther back in the shadows. She couldn't know he watched, but at his movement, she turned and looked.

His breath caught, trapped while their gazes locked.

Shit. Had she seen him?

Chapter 2

Tayla's Cabin
Cedar Lodge, Snowy Mountains
Two months later

I made it!
Tayla grinned and stared out the panelled window to the wintery landscape beyond. In just over two months, she'd not only quit her old life but felt more in control of her future than she had in, well, as long as she could remember. And that was beyond liberating.

The hidden treasure she'd stumbled on was exactly what she needed and came at precisely the right moment. The moment she'd been suffocating and at the same time drowning in fear at the thought of leaving her room. Something had to change.

So, she seized the first chance to escape her mess of a life—and encroaching crazy-cat-lady doom—and adopted a new motto: Out with the old and in with the new.

She thought back to the moment when she'd shuffled down the stuffy, dimly lit halls of the teachers' dorm at the university, her head down, books tucked closely against her chest, feeling sorry for herself in the lead-up to another lonely, depressing Christmas period. Never before had she bothered to glance at the rows of noticeboards overflowing with pinned colored pages, but that day had been different. Out of the corner of her eye, she'd spied the bland flyer, half tucked behind another generic pamphlet for poetry-reading nights at the local bookstore and self-defense classes—been there, done that, got the T-shirt.

The plain beige flyer seemed to call to her in some strange way, almost as though she was meant to find it.

Believing in a higher purpose had always resonated with her, like each person was destined to follow a path and the universe dished out signs along the way to guide them. But after taking so many hits, there was only so much faith one could summon before doubt crept in and trust in the universe slowly dwindled away.

So, in the end, she'd presented herself with two options.

One: Continue on her current self-destructive path; work a mind-numbing nine-to-five job at a university campus that made her jumpy as hell, develop a serious case of OCD for dead-locking doors and fork out a fortune in counselling fees that didn't make a difference. Until she was old and grey, retired in one of those nursing home villages, playing cards each morning and eating dinner at four pm. With her twenty-three cats.

Or two: She could kick her butt into gear, take back control of her life—after that monster attacked her—pack up her stuff and ditch that town once and for all, leave it and her old life for dust. Start somewhere new without the whispers, without the judging eyes, without the history. Plus, this option was a heck of a lot cheaper than years of useless therapy.

Filling the hole in her heart would be an added

bonus.

Put like that, the choice was easy.

Plus, the lure of gigantic snow gums dusted in powdery white snow and an old red-brick fire place stocked with burning redwood proved too hard to resist.

So, she'd ripped the flyer free from its pin, said farewell to a handful of colleagues, piled all her belongings into the trunk of her car and embarked on her new life.

Dipping into her sizable inheritance, she paid in advance for six months' rent for a self-contained cabin on the grounds of Cedar Lodge, nestled amongst majestic pine trees in the heart of the Snowy Mountains.

And cabin it was.

A middle-aged lady, Ellen, had managed Tayla's booking and set her up in a one-bedroom cabin segregated from the main lodge, where she could enjoy greater privacy. Ellen had been a godsend in helping her arrange the necessities. In a few short days, Tayla had brochures on the local town, Summit Creek, forty-five minutes' drive down the mountain, a fully stocked fridge, and a map of walking trails in the local national park. Plus, she set up a mission-critical Wi-Fi account. A bummer the Wi-Fi was as sketchy as it was cheap, and continued to drop out during her Friday night eye-candy of her favorite vampire brothers—a crime carrying the heaviest penalty.

Tayla peered around the log cabin and grinned. Compact, but hey, it was a lot bigger than the teacher's flat she'd occupied for years.

The open-plan lower level had three sectioned spaces; a main living area to the right, a small dining space on the opposite side and a galley kitchen to the rear. A narrow winding wooden staircase led to a loft containing the main bedroom and elegant bathroom with oversize tub.

Although it came fully furnished with rich timber furniture, the twin floor-to-ceiling panelled windows filled the room with natural light, creating a sense of tranquility as she peered out at the lush dark green foliage of the pine forest beyond.

Tayla opened the solid redwood front door and stepped out onto the veranda. With her gratitude diary in her hand, she reclined in one of the white-washed Adirondack chairs—her absolute favorite spot. She'd fallen in love with the cabin the moment she stepped onto the wide veranda and spotted the chairs, basked in warm orange rays. The chairs reclined at the exact angle to lean back and put her feet up and stare out at the forest.

That had been her second sign from the universe. And a firm sign her old life was dust.

She opened the journal and turned to the next blank page—it had been the combined parting gift from her university colleagues and really hit the mark. What better way to be more positive than to be thankful? Finally, something from those countless therapy sessions put into practice.

These chairs are incredible. She jotted down the first item for today.

The golden afternoon sun burst through the pine trees like trying extra hard to conceal the fact that winter fast approached. But the breeze failed to get the memo and even though it tried to be discreet, goosebumps continued to sprout over her exposed ankles. Not cool enough for a jacket, but enough to have it close by in case the sun ducked behind a cloud.

Until now, the first color change of the leaves, signifying autumn's arrival, made her shudder. She'd always dreaded winter, but this year, in this picturesque setting hidden amongst the protection of ancient snow gums and scented pines, the thought of winter brought a smile to her face. Lying on a shaggy sheepskin rug in front of the crackling fire, book in one hand and a glass of red in the other while the powdery snow fluttered between the branches, sounded like absolute bliss.

Her cell phone pinged on the side table and she grabbed it, swiping the home screen to view the calendar reminder. *Shoot!* If she didn't get a move on, she'd be late for hot yoga, the class kindly suggested by Ellen. And while in town she could swing by the local store and grab some groceries for dinner and a nice bottle of wine for her Saturday night in.

Tayla closed the journal and slid the pen down the spine before ducking inside to lock up. She snatched her satchel from the back of the dining chair, and grabbed her yoga bag and car keys from the side table at the front door.

Her fingers brushed over the creased leather on the strap of the satchel and her heart ached at the memory of her parents gifting it to her after one of their many overseas trips.

Something positive, Tayla...

Right.

The satchel held bittersweet memories and also the perfect size, fitting all her essentials without becoming too heavy or bulky. There. Nailed it.

She closed the door and jogged down the steps to

her car. She opened the driver's door and tossed her yoga bag between the middle of the seats to land in the back and placed her satchel on the seat beside her, like a VIP passenger tagging along for the ride into town.

Gripping the steering wheel, Tayla gazed out the front windshield toward her cozy log cabin and grinned. Finally, it felt like she could suck in a lungful of air after being submerged underwater for so long.

Better watch out, she warned herself. If she settled here anymore, she might end up convincing the owner to sell her the cabin outright.

Then I'll never have to return to the real world, she thought with a mischievous giggle.

Chapter 3

Guardian Mansion
Concealed location deep in the Snowy Mountains

Sweat poured down Raven's spine and any minute now his sneakers would gift him with a face-plant over the side of the treadmill. Lactic acid burned his thighs and the machine whined loudly with each heavy thump of his feet, as though it screamed for him to take out the little red tag and force things to a halt.

But he wouldn't give in.

His mind still raced, even though his limbs throbbed.

And to top it off—if that was possible—someone had messed with the songs on his iPod, switching them for shitty dance versions, torturing his ear drums with a techno-mix of songs he, until now, enjoyed. One bloody guess as to the identity of the culprit.

Like right now, why did whoever-it-was feel the need to dance-up Ed Sheeran? Weren't his songs dancey enough? And what the fuck was Ed Sheeran doing on his playlist in the first place?

He should just bite the bullet and learn how to upload a playlist on his own.

Although, the remixes did get his legs pumping, which was the whole point. Not that he'd admit that to

EJ.

"Screw this," he groaned, ripping the earbuds out as some young punk blasted through the tiny speakers.

Calling it quits, Raven pressed the stop button on the treadmill and rejoiced in the slow wind down, much to the machine's relief.

He snatched a faded gym towel and bottle of water from the holder on the machine and sucked in a breath of clean, cool air as he exited the sweaty gym.

His room was on the third floor of the mansion he shared with Aric and EJ since they'd settled here roughly a century ago. Right after EJ had received his first vision. Although they'd made modern improvements, an underground garage being the most recent, the exterior remained largely unchanged. Even with the countless rooms and loads of privacy, the three of them still preferred to congregate in the common areas.

Raven strode along the hardwood floor of the main hallway toward the front of the house, separated from a sunken living room by a few solid timber posts and railing. He paused and peered over at the oversized painting consuming the far wall. A scene of a world similar to this one all but destroyed, silver-winged angels carrying mortals away from the destruction etched out with heavy strokes.

Did the painting predict the future if Fate's plan failed?

Maybe it represented the past, and this realm was a direct result of the Guardian's triumph over evil.

If only the latter was true, he'd at least have some proof that good could prevail.

Strokes of golden light along the top of the canvas

made his heart ache for the Heavens. God, he'd been in the mortal realm for so long, the memories of his home began to blur.

He clenched his jaw and his foul mood briskly returned thanks to that stupid painting.

Raven turned away and stomped up the first flight of stairs. Aric and EJ's banter traveled down the hall from the entertainment room—or bachelor pad, as EJ called it.

Bar was more accurate.

Raven leaned his shoulder against the arch of the open double doorway and crossed his arms. EJ leaned over the pool table, his sandy blond hair peeking out beneath a dark grey beanie, a tight expression of concentration on his face as he nudged the eight ball smoothly into the right corner pocket.

"Bloody hell, man. You beat me again," Aric grumbled from across the table.

"You're gonna need more than your remaining centuries on this earth to win, Ric." EJ flipped the balls from a pocket back onto the table.

"Man, you have an unnatural ability with a pool cue."

"Among other things."

"You know what? It just became my new mission in this realm to kick your ass at pool."

EJ roared with laughter. "Bring it on."

Aric shook his head and placed the final ball in the rack at the end of the table and lined it up for another game.

Those two had the same brotherly banter since the day they all found themselves permanently kicked out of the Heavens.

EJ stood slightly shorter than Aric, but possessed the same sculpted warrior's build they all did. The main difference was EJ could pass for late twenties, a good five or so years younger than Aric and himself could get away with.

And yes, EJ had a natural gift for pool since the game's creation.

Both males glanced his way.

"Hey, man." Aric nodded at Raven, chalking the tip of his cue. "You work off some steam?"

"Tried." Raven threw his iPod to EJ, who caught it in his palm. "What the fuck did you do to my music? Swap it out for every shitty remix you could find?"

EJ raised a brow. "So shitty you listened to it for over an hour?"

Damn it, good point.

Raven bit the inside of his cheek to stop from smiling. "Regardless, it still sucks."

EJ threw his head back and laughed. "All in good time, Rave. Eventually, you'll submit to the dark side."

The smile dropped from Raven's face and his heart sank; EJ's comment hit way too close to home.

"I'm off to shower and hopefully, scrub those torturous sounds from my skull. Let's meet in the study after and we'll go over our plans for tonight."

"You got it, man."

"Roger that, Rave. And don't forget, we can hear you singing."

Raven flipped EJ the finger as he turned and headed up the last flight of stairs to his room.

He had the whole third level to himself; a master suite, an oversized en suite bathroom and a private study. At the time of their arrival—*banishment*—on

Earth, all those centuries ago, the two had declared Raven their leader. He was, after all, the one who created their mission, and Aric had convinced him the leader should have their own quarters.

Even now, he didn't give a shit about his space, the rooms on the second floor were just as luxurious.

Swinging open the double doors, Raven crossed the lush carpet to the bathroom on the far side and wasted no time showering—without singing.

Stepping outside the shower recess, the image of a worn-out version of himself confronted him in the mirror above the basin.

His shoulders sagged.

Even after his past few mornings under the sun's rays and a full seven hours sleep—loads more than Guardians needed—his skin was dull with decent size bags—no, suitcases—under his eyes. Raven pinched his cheeks, hoping for the skin to react, awaken and brighten somehow. It didn't.

As he turned toward the door, he glimpsed the small patch of crimson feathers on the inside of his right wing, standing out like splatters of blood against the black.

Concealing them was becoming harder. Each day he woke, hoping they'd turned back to black, that there'd been some kind of sick mistake.

But they didn't change. There was no mistake.

He'd sensed the moment his faith in Fate began to slip away at the exact moment his first crimson feather appeared.

Bet Fate's enjoying this twist, he thought bitterly.

Unless this was her twisted plan all along.

Raven threw his towel at his reflection and tucked

his wings back inside the thin slits in his flesh as he stomped to the walk-in closet. He grabbed a pair of faded black jeans and navy tee, and shoved them on. He stormed out of his room, heading to the main study, on the ground floor.

The war room.

Upon entering, Raven rounded the oversized mahogany board table in the center of the room, striding toward the rear and grabbing a bottle of water from the bar fridge.

Maybe a little early for bourbon.

He took a gulp before sinking his ass into the soft leather seat at the head of the table. On his right, EJ fired up two laptops and Raven mentally rolled his eyes at Aric, sitting to his left, as he not-so-discreetly slid a coaster under Raven's bottle of water.

"So, where're we at?" Raven prompted.

Second thought, maybe it wasn't too early for a bourbon.

Aric leaned in, his elbows on the table, interlacing his fingers under his chin. "Seems you're still the only one with a Chosen assignment on your plate."

EJ lowered the screen on the laptop in front of him. "I wonder why, after all these centuries in this realm, Fate suddenly decided to assign one to you. I mean I just presumed she'd taken that role away too, you know, after she threw us out. Even though she said we'd remain Guardians."

Raven shrugged. "Dunno. I couldn't even begin to understand the decisions she makes."

"Maybe she's finally gotten over her little tiff and letting us back in the circle of trust." Aric grinned.

Raven laughed. "I seriously doubt that."

Leaning back in his chair, he took another sip of water before placing it back on the coaster. Wouldn't want Aric losing his shit over condensation rings on the table.

He turned to EJ. "How's the Fallen tracking coming together?"

"I reckon by the end of the week I'll have all the data from those oversized, ancient maps transferred onto the laptop."

"Still don't get what's wrong with using the maps. At least they don't need power…or a degree to operate," he grumbled.

EJ smirked but, apparently, had the sense not to reply.

Aric swiveled his chair to face Raven. "Speaking of Chosen, how are things going with Tayla?"

EJ leaned back in his chair. "Damn, Rave, if only all Chosen were as pretty as her, it would sure make protecting them a helluva lot more…"

Raven slammed his palms on the table. "She's not some piece of meat put on Earth for your entertainment, EJ."

EJ held his palms up in surrender. "Hey, I didn't mean any disrespect."

Raven dropped his head in his hands. "Fuck."

Aric leaned over and squeezed his arm. "You have some serious rage rolling off you, man. What's going on?"

Raven lifted his head. "Nothing."

By the frowns on both their faces, he knew they didn't buy his bullshit and the subject wasn't case closed.

Raven cleared his throat. "Tayla's fine. She's

settled in and seems to be following along her path. Whatever that is. God, I'd forgotten how frustrating it was not knowing where a Chosen's path led."

EJ nodded. "Or how their path would tip the scales back in Fate's favor."

"Yeah, that, too," Raven scoffed. "Anyway, things have been quiet, but I'll head out tonight and do the rounds, just to be sure."

It had been almost a week since he'd seen her, and his body was so tense he could snap someone's head off.

Duh, he just did that, didn't he?

After centuries of no Chosen to protect, he wasn't satisfied with relying on the spiritual tether they shared. He had to see her with his own eyes.

Aric pushed away from the table to stand behind his chair, leaning his forearms on the backrest. "Any sign of your brother lately?"

Raven shook his head. "Haven't seen or heard from him for almost a month now. But as we know, that doesn't mean he isn't lurking in the shadows."

It would be so much easier if that connection was still operational.

The three Guardians finalized their plans for the evening and wrapped up the meeting. Tonight, Raven planned to swing past Tayla's cabin before catching up with EJ and Aric in town to patrol for Fallen. They'd rendezvous back at the mansion prior to dawn, for check-in and a nightcap. Or three.

Standard routine.

Leaving the study, Raven trailed behind Aric and EJ as they headed to the dining room, chatting away to each other. Although only a step or two behind, he didn't take in any of the conversation. As though his body went through the motions, but his soul was MIA.

He sensed distance between the three of them.

No, disconnect.

The worse the situation got, the sooner he'd have to come clean and tell them. He wasn't naïve enough to think they didn't suspect something wasn't right, but he didn't know how the hell to raise the subject. *Hey man, just so you know, I have some crimson feathers...*

Yeah, he could imagine how well that conversation would end.

Entering the dining room, Raven spotted Ellen placing steaming hot food in the center of the enormously long dining table.

Aric and EJ sat in their usual spots and dove straight in.

Ellen wasn't an angel like Raven and the other males—not that he referred to himself as an angel. She was mortal. Well, used to be a mortal. He smiled, remembering the moment he'd swung open the front door to find her standing patiently on the porch, her hazel eyes lit with joy, silvery grey hair fresh out of curlers and tied in a loose bun, and a warm caring smile on her face. She'd politely introduced herself, stating she'd been sent to ensure they took care of themselves. In the absence of contact with the Heavens, he'd taken her word for it and invited her in.

Years later, she mentioned one night over a few too many ports, Fate had offered her the task of taking care of a brotherhood of immortal warriors, in exchange for immortality in the mortal realm. She'd agreed without hesitation. He'd thought the idea was ridiculous—why the hell would a brotherhood of immortal warriors need taken care of? But as it turned out, they kinda did.

Although Ellen employed a handful of mortals to help, she prided herself on cooking their meals. Tonight, she'd prepared a smorgasbord, a combination of succulent grilled meats, steamed fresh vegetables and sweet-smelling pastry filled the air.

But all his stomach did was churn.

Pouring bourbon from the crystal decanter, Raven butted against the side table, content to observe Aric and EJ fill their plates with mashed potatoes, baby carrots and homemade chicken pie, while praising Ellen.

Ellen appeared beside him and glanced at his liquid dinner. "You're not eating again?"

Raven sighed. "I just don't have an appetite."

She turned, fiddling with the glasses on the side table. "I dropped in to see Tayla the other day. She's doing well. I told her about this yoga class in town and I think she's going to try it tonight."

Raven twisted toward her. "Thanks, Ellen."

Ellen possessed a grace and beauty that made her easy to warm to, which was exactly why he'd accepted her help to settle Tayla into her cabin a couple of months ago. He couldn't exactly do it himself, as revealing himself to a Chosen was forbidden, and no way would he trust a mortal to give Tayla the care and attention she deserved.

Raven had hung back in the shadows. As always.

Ellen smiled, straightening her blouse and adjusting her long, beaded necklace. "I'll put a plate together for you and leave it in the fridge for later."

He nodded. "Thanks."

Ellen turned, briefly chatting with Aric and EJ on

her way back to the kitchen.

Raven peered back at his brothers, filling their plates for the third time, the two bodies seeming out of place at the large table. Would more Guardians arrive eventually, or would it be the three of them until they somehow completed their impossible mission? His chest ached at the thought of a house full of Guardians, a family away from home, all living under the same roof. Where everyone crammed around the dining table, several different conversations happening at once, chatting and passing food to one another, laughter echoing off the walls.

Where meal times were chaotic but filled with countless memorable moments.

Moments he hadn't realized he longed for, until now.

Didn't matter anyway. It wasn't as if he'd be around to enjoy them.

Chapter 4

Disgusting warm beads of sweat trickled between Tayla's breasts, soaking into the band of her sports bra as she toweled off her arms. *Ewww!*

For the past hour, her body had oozed perspiration while her muscles stretched this way and that until they'd became loose and relaxed. Her first hot yoga class and already she was an addict.

Total. Bliss.

Her legs were jelly as she crouched down and rolled up the yoga mat before collecting her belongings from the cubed shelves at the rear of the room. Waving goodbye to the instructor—who hadn't even broken a sweat—Tayla exited through the sliding glass door out to the foyer. She slipped on her flip-flops and wiped her sweaty palm on a towel draped over her shoulder before grabbing a pen to sign up for the same class next week.

Ellen had been right, this was exactly what she needed; complete serenity for her mind and soul.

Tayla trotted down the single flight of stairs and pushed open the main door to outside. Her breath caught as she lifted her head. Her heart sank. Not only had night unexpectedly fallen, but the only light visible came from the dimly lit closed shop fronts and scattered street lamps along the road.

Crap.

Tayla stood on the pavement in a tiny pool of light and zipped her hoodie all the way up.

Her stomach growled, nauseated with hunger.

She'd parked her car about two blocks away outside the local store. Easier to grab her wine and groceries after class. Plus, the stroll would wind down her achy muscles. But walking in the dark, the time of day that haunted her most, and alone…

Stupid. Stupid. Stupid.

Nestling her yoga bag closer to her chest like it would somehow keep her safe from the Big Bad Wolf, she swallowed the lump in her throat and…

Slam!

Tayla jumped, heart leaping from her chest as another classmate exited the studio, the door closing hard behind him.

Calm down, Tayla.

Maybe she could ask him for a lift around the corner? Now she was being silly, plus, she didn't know him. Just because he did yoga didn't mean he wasn't a serial killer. Surely serial killers had to keep fit so they could lug all those dead bodies in and out of the trunks of their cars. Maybe yoga was the place they selected their innocent victims.

Oh my god, I'm losing it.

Her heart hammered inside her chest so fast it would surely vault out of her ribcage. Her pulse pounded in her ears, her palms sweaty again.

This was how people ended up on crime shows. Exactly the situations the self-defense instructor told her to avoid. Not to mention the expensive lectures from the therapist.

No, she could do this. She was a strong and

independent woman, who demonstrated she could kick ass when needed; even if it was in the controlled environment of a self-defense class. With a colleague. Who may have been smaller than her. So not the point right now.

She inhaled a deep, steady breath. Inhale and exhale…

The second her thumping heart slowed a notch, Tayla stepped off the edge. Which felt like she just leaped off the edge of the world rather than the pavement.

She dashed in an I'm-not-freaked-out-at-all manner along the concrete sidewalk toward her car and the local store.

About halfway up the street, a prickly sensation fluttered down her spine, that awful sense of someone following her or more precisely, someone watching. She turned her head in both directions. All she spotted was darkness and creepy shadows from the street lamps. Her ears became hypersensitive, compensating for her limited sight. Either the person watching was super quiet or she was being paranoid. Again.

The stupid technique of positive self-talk—*you're okay…there's no one behind you*—did nothing to shake the uneasy feeling.

She picked up the pace, practically running along the pavement until she reached the street light at a deserted intersection.

She spotted her car in the distance, across the road to the far end of the now empty parking lot.

Almost there.

Another quick glance over her shoulder.

Nope, still no one following.

She dashed across the road and bolted down a stretch of closed boutiques. Her ribcage caved in on her lungs, squeezing out any oxygen she managed to suck in. The pulse pounding in her ears disorientated her other senses.

She raced around the corner of the final deserted store, swung a left and…

Her heart sank. *Oh no.*

The entrance to the local grocery store glared back at her.

Lights off.

Dark and empty on the inside.

No! Hastily, she ran to the sliding glass doors that refused to open and double checked the closing time on a white rectangular sign. *Crap!* It closed an hour early on weekends.

Stupid. Stupid.

The ten-minute dash had fried her nerves. She gripped the safety of the straps on the yoga bag in her shaky hands.

Turning around, she braved a peek at the empty parking lot.

Everything looked so creepy at night. If only she was one of those sensible people safely tucked away in the comfort of their homes. Why the heck had she agreed to a late afternoon yoga class?

She just had to make it to her car. Then she could lock the doors and sit there for however long it took to calm down enough to drive. She didn't want to freak out while trying to drive home through that forest in the pitch black.

Tayla lifted her chin and took another deep breath before scurrying toward her car.

About four empty spots away, she shot a final glance over her shoulder...

Her step faltered. Behind her a huge guy dressed all in black stared at her.

Unconsciously, she spun to face him, gripping the straps on her yoga mat so tight her knuckles turned white.

She tried to retreat a step, to turn and run, anything, but her legs froze.

Her heart sank. *No. No, no, no.*

The man took a step toward her and tilted his head slightly to one side. "Well, hello, love," he said, in a surprisingly curious tone.

Her mind went to mush. Blank. Useless. All that self-defense training gone *poof* the minute she needed it.

Her stupid legs wouldn't move, cementing her feet to the road.

The man took another step toward her. His broad shoulders straight, chin slightly tilted up.

Lifting her gaze, she memorized his features for the police report. No way she'd mess that up a second time. *If you make it out alive to file one...*

Arrogance and pure power rolled off him in waves, his strong, solid frame towering over her. A striking jawline with dark stubble, a pointy nose and his worn leather jacket and unlaced black combat boots completed his serial killer look.

But the burning gaze of his smoky black eyes made her shift uncomfortably as though they stared straight into her soul.

He smirked. "Well, this is new. Never in my whole existence, have I gotten this..." He circled her face with his finger. "Freaked out reaction from a female before. You all right there, love? I'm not that scary, am I?"

No.

Wait, what?

He took a final stride toward her; now close enough he could reach out and grab her. A smoky coal scent filled her nostrils, like the smell of an extinguished bushfire lingering in the air. It reminded her of the night…

Her mind went blank as the memory took over. The horrific night in the university courtyard she'd forced herself to forget.

The menacing figure stalked toward her, blood red eyes glowing in the darkness, his wicked snarl sent a chill down her spine.

It's happening again…

No. She had to focus if she wanted to make it out alive.

Tayla shifted her yoga bag around to cover her front, not that it was much use as a weapon.

She cleared her throat and straightened her shoulders, praying her fake confidence would be a deterrent. "Um, yes." She shook her head. "I mean no. Ugh! What do you want?"

It failed miserably. Now she couldn't even speak properly.

His lips turned into a mischievous grin.

And that was the moment she realized she was doomed.

****

A sharp sting stabbed at the back of Raven's neck. His knees buckled under the intensity. His hand out to grip the banister to prevent himself from tumbling down the stairs.

"Fuck!"

His heart hammered inside his chest. No, wait. That wasn't his heartbeat, it was…

He sucked in a breath. "Tayla."

He bolted up the remaining stairs, two at a time, and threw open his door. He crossed the room in a second flat, unfurled his wings when he reached the balcony and shot to the sky.

Tayla's adrenaline spiked in his veins; terror, panic, dread, all collided together in one gigantic blender of emotions washing over him.

The sharp sting stabbed at the base of his neck and he pushed his wings harder to soar higher and increase his speed. *Faster!*

Something was seriously wrong.

The sensation, the feeling…was entirely different than the connection he'd shared with countless Chosen before.

A whole other level.

And now he was in a race against time to reach her.

He flapped his wings again, spurring them on like a jockey on a racehorse. Higher and higher he flew. The frigid wind slapped his face, stung his cheeks and burned his lungs as he drew rapid breaths.

If only he hadn't been moping around at the house, feeling sorry for himself, he could have already been there.

Would have already been there.

Raven shot through the dark sky as fast as his wings would take him, and then pushed them harder. Every muscle and tendon burned, cramped and knotted together, but he ignored the pain. He would use his wings until they fell off, if that was what it took. And after that, he'd pump his legs faster than ever before until he reached her.

Raven spotted lights in the distance, the small town of Summit Creek illuminated the darkness. He flapped his wings harder. *Not far now.*

He'd gained so much altitude to increase his speed that his body tightened from the coldness and the drop in oxygen created ice crystals on the tips of his black feathers.

Stabbing pain exploded down his spine.

"Fuck," he roared.

Faster!

He'd made it to the perimeter of town, soaring above the sleepy houses and puffs of smoke drifting from the chimneys.

Now to find her.

He descended rapidly and scanned the deserted streets below, focusing his attention on his spiritual connection to Tayla; trusting it to guide him. But he couldn't focus enough to grasp it. His frantic mind couldn't distinguish between her panic and his own. Thank Christ it was a small town, it shouldn't take him long.

Where the hell is she?

Raven circled the center of town for a second time before hovering midair over a playing field, searching for the bloody yoga studio.

A moment before he mentally called his brothers for backup, he caught sight of Tayla out of the corner of his eye, over to his left. Standing frozen, alone, in an empty parking lot. Why was she...

Wait a minute.

Raven frowned and leaned slightly forward to zero in on a dark shadow directly in front of her.

What. The. Hell?

His vision blurred, and he blinked.

Tayla retreated a step. The male tilted his head toward the sky. Recognition slapped him in the face and sent his blood boiling.

No way would that sonofabitch lay a finger of Tayla.

He tucked his wings tight like a rocket as he plunged toward the parking lot.

Chapter 5

Tayla's shaky legs retreated a step. The guy was too close.

Raw power illuminated his scorching gaze, boring into her soul as though with one glance he had stripped her of not only her clothes but her skin as well.

She had to get away from him. Turn around. Run for her life.

"There's no need to be afraid, love," he chuckled, matching her step with one of his own.

Said every serial killer ever.

She swallowed the bile rising in her throat. "I need to go."

She retreated one more step. And another.

Just as she turned to bolt, he sniggered, a haunting wicked sound which sent her heart plummeting to her feet. He *was* the serial killer she suspected, and he was about to embark on an evil adventure.

"It's okay to find me attractive, all the females do."

Seriously?

Tayla spun back and gaped at him. How could he be so full of himself to assume her reaction had something to do with his looks? The whole dark knight vibe he had going only scored him points on the creepy scale.

No reason to engage him further; it would only

feed his incredibly overinflated ego. Plus, he likely used it as a tactic to lower her defenses, making her feel comfortable…before he duct-taped her mouth shut.

"Look, whether I do or don't find you attractive has absolutely nothing to do with why I'm leaving," she snapped. "I have someone waiting for me and if I'm late, they'll know something's wrong and come looking for me." She prayed the lie would warn him off.

No such luck.

Engaging in conversation did exactly what she feared.

He smirked as though trying not to laugh and took another step closer.

She matched it, in the opposite direction.

"Hmmm…" He tapped his chin with his finger. "Is that right?"

Tayla nodded, not trusting her shaky voice. *Damn it*. If only she was better at lying.

"Sure you're not telling me a little fib?"

She shook her head.

He mulled this over for a moment. "In that case, you'd better run along, hadn't you? Chop-chop. Don't wanna be late." He shooed her away with his hand.

What? He's letting me go?

Who cares? She turned on her heels and bolted to her car before he had a chance to change his mind. Or decided to grab her.

Crap! Maybe this was his plan and he wanted her to run so he could chase.

She glanced over her shoulder and internally cheered to find he wasn't in pursuit. In fact, he stood in the same spot she'd left him, grinning as though he'd discovered a massive secret.

Almost there!

A few steps away from her car, Tayla fumbled through her yoga bag in search of her keys. She shoved aside her purse, dug under the water bottle. The keys jingled as she gave the bag a shake, but she couldn't grip them.

Where the heck are they?

Her heart rate rose another notch, her shallow breaths quickened.

Another check over her shoulder—nope, he still hadn't moved.

Yes! At last, her fingers clenched the key chain and she ripped them out of her bag with so much force the keys flew out of her hands and landed on the ground.

Tayla rushed over and snatched them off the ground as a deafening roar blasted her ears.

Her flight response kicked into overdrive.

She bolted the remaining steps to the car while simultaneously pressing the key fob to unlock the doors. As she jerked open the door, she froze, glancing back at the parking lot. Serial Killer stood where she'd left him. As though in slow motion, he tilted his head toward the dark sky, a split-second before another guy crashed into him.

From the sky?

Her first impulse was to run and help, but she was the one who needed help, not either of those creeps. Jumping into the driver's seat, she slammed the door shut and engaged the locks. *In, shut, lock.*

Finally, something from self-defense class decided to click.

From behind the safety of the windshield, she gaped at the two men, now engaged in a vicious standoff, as they circled each other.

The second guy leaned in, one fist balled in a striking position, his mouth moving as though shouting, but she couldn't hear him.

The dimly lit parking lot worked against her. She couldn't make out the second guy's face. He circled Serial Killer but both kept to the shadows. She leaned forward over the steering wheel and squinted as though the motion would somehow make her vision sharper. She focused on the second guy, the way his powerful body moved…

Wait a minute, what was behind his back? A sword or two? No, too large for a sword, and it didn't shine in the patchy light. A backpack?

Suddenly, the second guy lunged at Serial Killer, and knocked him to the ground.

A whole car space away.

What the…?

His fierce display of aggression frightened her, yet, bizarrely thrilled her at the same time.

She gaped as Serial Killer rose to stand, rubbing his palm along his jaw while he grinned, not at all affected by having his body smacked onto the bitumen by a guy with superhuman strength.

Her breath hitched as Serial Killer straightened his shoulders and turned to face her. Twin dark shadows unfolded from behind him and stretched wide at his sides. He swung his right arm up and out to the side in a regal manner and bent at the waist in an exaggerated low bow.

'Til we meet again, love—the words drifted in her mind as though he'd whispered them directly in her ear.

Her eyes widened when he launched himself

upward, disappearing into the cloudy night.

What. The. Heck?

Her spine prickled, and she turned her attention to Superhuman. His searing gaze burned her skin as he stalked toward her car.

No way was she hanging around so Superhuman could turn her into minced meat.

But, for some strange reason, she wasn't afraid.

Superhuman crossed into a patch of light under a lamppost. The instant she met his gaze, a weird sense of connection travelled through her blood, drawing her in. Calmness washed over her like a thick warm blanket wrapped around her body on a cold winter's night.

The urgency to flee faded away.

Her heart rate steadied, breathing calmed, and a sense of protection grounded her.

Superhuman continued his long, slow strides toward her.

She focused on his features as he crossed under a closer street light. He was around the same height as Serial Killer, with the same strong, broad shoulders. He wore an open black military-style bomber jacket with the collar folded up at the back, a dark muscle tee stretched firmly over his chest, and faded black jeans with a pair of black combat boots.

He had dark rugged hair but she couldn't quite make out his face.

Her gaze traveled over his muscular torso once more, and her breath hitched as she caught sight of the same twin black shadows.

Were they…wings? *Yes.* Stunning enormous dark glossy wings, extended above his shoulders out to the side in a wide arc.

This night couldn't get any weirder.

Another unhurried step toward her, before Superhuman-with-wings halted in the shadows between two street lamps. He extended his right arm in a slow measured movement toward her, palm up and he lowered his head.

Her thoughts blanked the moment a subconscious connection formed between them, as though he'd plugged into her mind. A brief sense of sorrow washed through her before a wave of calmness, followed by a weird tug in her mind like Superhuman reached in with his hands, gripped a part of her memory and pulled it out. A strange yet not painful sensation.

What the heck is going on?

Her anxiety from the night lifted, drifted away, replaced with that same calming, warm blanket.

Her memory of Serial Killer gradually became blurry until…Wait a minute, who?

Tayla squinted at the intriguing guy surrounded by darkness in the empty parking lot, but couldn't quite focus on his features. Urgency to stop him screamed in the back of her mind.

Stop him from what?

Tayla squeezed her eyes shut and opened them again, but he was…gone.

Through the windshield, she searched the lot, craning her head left and right. Hang on, what was she looking for?

Another wave of calmness flowed over her, and she inhaled a deep cleansing breath.

Her shoulders sagged, her mind cleared. Must be the result of the yoga class.

She grabbed her yoga bag off her lap and threw it

between the two front seats to land in the back. She could've sworn someone else was in the parking lot, but her mind clearly played tricks on her, using the creepy dark shadows to its advantage.

Cold air blasted through the vents when she started the car, and she quickly faced them away from her body until they warmed. She released the parking brake and drove out of the lot.

Something compelled her to glance out the window to an empty patch of pavement illuminated under a street lamp.

Nothing there.

Wow, that was one heck of a weird night.

But she couldn't remember why.

****

Raven lowered his arm to his side and, from his vantage point on the roof of the local store, tracked Tayla's car as it eased onto the street.

Fuck.

He'd let that situation get out of hand.

He slammed his fist on the roof beside him. Blaine knew just how to push his buttons and by how much, and Raven had fallen headfirst into his snare. Not only was he already skating on thin ice when it came to Tayla, but now, he'd demonstrated how much she truly affected him.

Raven ground his molars. God, he'd lost count of the number of rules he'd broken tonight alone.

Fate's gonna have my frickin' head.

He leaned forward and snatched his cell phone from the rear pocket in his jeans and hit EJ's number.

EJ answered on the second ring. "Hey, Rave. Getting the hang of your phone, I see." EJ laughed.

Raven ignored the dig. "I need you to follow Tayla from a distance, make sure she arrives back at her cabin safely," he ordered into the handset.

"Sure thing. What happened?"

"I had to…" He lowered his voice and scanned his surroundings, not that there was anyone listening on top of the roof. "Erase her memory. Blaine was here, and she saw his wings."

"Shit. You all right?"

Not by a long shot. "Don't worry about me. Just make sure she makes it back. We both know what the side effects can be like." Raven sighed. "We made an oath to use it as a last resort for that exact reason."

"I know, but there are times where it's unavoidable." EJ paused. "Hey, Rave, you sure you don't wanna see her get home?"

He lowered his voice. "She saw me, too."

EJ cursed under his breath. "Gotcha. I'll make sure she's safe. Talk soon."

"EJ?" Raven rushed out before he hung up.

"Yeah?"

"Thanks."

"No need. I'll be in touch."

Raven ended the call and dropped the cell phone beside him and stared out toward the dark parking lot, where Tayla had stood. Ominous clouds built in the distance as though they, too, sensed the change and prepared for battle.

God, Blaine made his blood boil.

His stomach churned at the thought of erasing Tayla's memory of him, but he'd been left with no other option. He had to. If he hadn't, there'd be no way to prevent her from going to the mortal authorities and reporting the incident, sending them searching for another nonexistent attacker.

Exactly like last time. Only last time, he'd killed the attacker.

Goddamit. The first time she truly saw him, and he fucking erased it.

Raven stood and followed the beams to the edge of the roof. He scanned his surroundings for a final time before he leaped off the roof and landed with a thud on the concrete.

He'd screwed up tonight. Big time.

What he needed was some space to clear his head, figure this shit out. Remind himself of the risks he took.

The risks he'd already taken to land him and his brothers here in the first place.

Chapter 6

Tayla pried open her sleepy eyes to warm orange rays streaming through the oversized window, reflecting golden light across her bedroom. There was something magical about the sun's rays, how even on a chilly winter's day it could gift her body with warmth from the inside out, heat up and nurture her bones, skin, and mind. How the sun energized and rejuvenated her soul as though it was nature's very own offering of caffeine.

Today, the golden light burst across the pale wood floors, over the plush white duvet, ending in a final stretch up the wall behind her head as though it were long wiry fingers stretching out and awakening her.

Tayla smiled. Moments like these she was truly grateful for, feeding her soul each morning, preparing for the day ahead. Hands up to the self-confessed sun-chaser. She grinned, recalling how Mom used to joke Tayla was cold-blooded, like the lizard who used to hang out in their backyard, constantly preferring the solitude of basking in the warmth of the sun over anything else.

Mom was so right.

Not the cold-blooded part, but the fact she was *that* person. The one who chose to sit at a bench bathed in sun when eating lunch, while everyone else sought shaded areas under the protection of large umbrellas.

Today, she planned to take advantage of those last remaining warm rays before winter well and truly arrived. Chase the chill from her bones and clear her mind. Maybe it would also ease the butterflies fluttering in the pit of her belly. Last night, she'd tossed and turned the whole time the moon silently crept across the night sky, tortured by an eerie dream of a man with glorious black wings staring at her from the shadows between the trees.

Probably the aftereffect of driving home in the dark. Even with no other cars on the road, her jittery nerves were a tangled mess by the time she reached the cabin, having had the sense someone followed her the entire way. Not the first time she'd experienced the feeling.

No more late afternoon yoga classes, that was for sure.

Raising her arms above her head and pointing her toes in the opposite direction, she stretched and lengthened her body before sliding out from under the covers to pad off to the luxurious bathroom.

She turned on the shower, waiting until the glass fogged over before quickly undressing and entering the blissful cocoon of steamy serenity.

Showered and refreshed, she dressed in tan cargo pants which zipped off at the knee, a pale blue button-down, and a pair of tan hiking boots. Not quite the attire for a trek to the summit of Mount Kosciuszko, but sufficient for the short hike she planned.

Wrapping her hair in a loose braid down one side, she headed downstairs for breakfast.

She pulled her phone off the charger and did a final

weather check, making sure there weren't any storms or cold fronts predicted. The Snowy Mountains were notorious for sudden weather changes, and although winter hadn't arrived yet, the possibility of a massive cold snap coming through at a minute's notice always existed. She triple-checked the contents of her backpack before heading out the front door, locking it behind her.

Outside, the stunning autumn day greeted her and invigorated her senses. A light crisp breeze tickled her exposed nape, carrying an earthy scent of pine needles, and the waking sun warmed her cheeks.

Retrieving her folded map from her back pocket, she held it in front of her—north facing upward like Dad had taught her—and hiked down the gravel drive to the main lodge, which linked with her chosen trail.

Her boots crunched the gravel and, less than ten minutes later, a slight burning sensation spread over the back of her heels from where they rubbed against the inside of her stiff boots.

Great. Probably should have broken them in first.

The hiking trail, highlighted in pink on her map, commenced at the west end of the main grounds and wound its way up and over the mountain. At the top, she had a choice of following the same route back or taking an alternative to follow the river, wrap around the base of the mountain, and join back with her starting point.

The decision depended on the pain level of the blisters building on her heels.

Just before the main lodge, off to the right, Tayla spotted her turn, a weathered log sign confirming the trail, and she entered the forest.

Immediately, the tall ancient guards of the forest

surrounded her, towering over her like giants, blocking out a majority of the sunlight and leaving eerie coolness in their wake. The moist air dampened the vegetation, moss blankets draped over fallen trees, and lifeless leaves and twigs littered the forest floor. Smaller, more delicate plants dotted the trail, thankful for the protection of the towering knights above. The decaying wooden boardwalk she followed sank into the earth, like quicksand.

An hour or so into her hike, the path gently inclined up the side of the mountain. Not too steep to use a cane or ropes for support, but subtle enough her heart rate increased and the front of her knees tightened under the pressure. The path gradually curved around to the south, and every half hour, Tayla double-checked her position on the map.

Winding around a sweeping bend, the trail veered Tayla out from under the protection of the forest canopy and into a small grassy clearing, on a gentle slope on the side of the mountain. A rickety wooden bench sat in the center of the clearing, so the occupant had a panoramic view of the town below—the ideal place to rest and have lunch.

The wooden slats bowed as Tayla perched on the bench, grabbed her sandwich container and water from her backpack, plus a couple of bandages for her heels. She took a deep inhale of clean, fresh air, and tilted her head toward the sun to warm her cool cheeks after being in the shade for so long.

Tayla gazed at the town below.

The small town of Summit Creek, at the base of the Snowy Mountains, was the adventure hub for year-round activities. In the summer months, adrenaline junkies flocked to the region for mountain biking, hiking, and kayaking, and in the winter months for snow, skiing, and snowboarding.

This time of the year, the town was between tourist rushes. The summer period had ended, but it was too early for the winter activities.

Tayla peered down at the dam and the town surrounding it. According to local tourist brochures, the town was relocated to its current position when the river was dammed, leaving the remains of the original town submerged under the lake, like a miniature version of Atlantis. In times of drought, hikers could view the rooftops of the old town, peeking above the water. But not today.

Tayla surveyed the surrounding mountains in the distance and followed a lone car along the main highway winding up the mountain to the ski fields—the same road she traveled to and from town.

She rested the back of her head on the back of the bench and closed her lids, basking in the sun…

A devastatingly handsome man stood in the shadows of an empty parking lot…

Tayla shot upright and snapped open her eyes, but the vision disappeared as quickly as it came. No, not a vision, a snippet of memory.

But from when?

Curiosity gnawed at her and she slowly closed her eyes once more. Again, the man appeared in her mind…*Heart-breaking ocean blue eyes stared back at her, glorious black wings arched behind his back…*

She tried to focus on the scene, on the man's features, but before she could get a hold of it, the memory retreated again.

It must be the guy from her vivid dream last night.

Otherwise, she was going mad. *Wouldn't be the first time…*

Opening the lid on the water canister, Tayla took a gulp. The cool water slid down her parched throat.

She gazed around the small clearing. A lush green blanket of gum trees hugged the side of the mountain, stretching their limbs wide as though opening their arms to welcome visitors.

Another memory flashed in her mind but again, only snippets, not clear enough to focus on the details. *A lethal, dangerous man faced her…wings unfolded from his back…he stretched his arms wide in a regal bow…*

Tayla laughed out loud.

Yes, she remembered her dream from last night. Her man-drought had conjured wicked dreams of not one, but two winged men. Gosh, she needed to get out more.

On that note, she packed up the empty container, returned it and her water to the backpack, and applied bandages to her stinging heels. Rest stop over, she slung the backpack over her shoulders and departed the clearing to re-enter the dense forest to continue her hike.

She made good time and although the burning on the backs of her heels continued, she became accustomed to it, and the occasional sting no longer made her grimace.

A half mile later, Tayla veered off and commenced the second trail to descend the mountain toward the river below. But the promise of waterfalls caught her attention.

Over to the right, hidden behind a low-lying branch, barely noticeable, she caught sight of another weathered log sign. This one indicated waterfalls at the end of a side track. Tayla unfolded her map, but couldn't find the trail—maybe it was too small to mention?

She weighed her choices. Continue following her current track and forego the waterfalls. Better safe than sorry on a solo-hike. Or, take it as a sign and hike to the waterfalls.

What to do…what to do?

The allure of waterfalls proved too much. No biggie if the path wasn't on her map. Once at the end, she would turn around and follow the same route back, connecting with the trail she was on now.

They'd better be good!

Mind made up, Tayla stepped onto the side trail. Though the farther she walked, the harder the path was to recognize. Without the aid of a boardwalk, she had to rely on a subtle indentation in the forest floor, which after a few yards, narrowed as the branches and shrubs caved in from both sides.

Continuing on, the trail narrowed again, leading straight through an enormous twin-trunk mountain gum. She eyed the trunk of the majestic giant, craning her head back so much her body threatened to topple backward. Magical. The tree stood high, like a living skyscraper taking pride of place in the center of a bustling city. Its giant arms stretched out, forming an umbrella for the vegetation below. She took out her phone and snapped photos of the tree, having to take several in a row to capture the entire height.

Tayla studied the base of the giant and how the

trunks weaved together to form a cave. Or a doorway to a magical land.

The path lead through the trunks and out the other side.

She stepped closer and peered inside the belly of the giant, stretching her arms across the entrance, but she needed three or four more people joined together to hug the tree completely. Tayla placed her palm on the cool bark, giving it a silent blessing before carefully wading through the long grass to join the path on the other side.

No way she'd go through a creepy, spider-infested hollow trunk.

On the other side, the track narrowed again, to less than a foot wide, with entire sections covered by fallen limbs and vegetation. She stepped over a broken branch and ducked her head under another, and continued on, trying to remain on the almost nonexistent trail.

A thick winding vine stretched between trees in front of her. She lifted it slightly to duck underneath before curving around another wide trunk.

Her breath hitched at the sight before her. Directly ahead, between the parted vegetation, were the falls.

Water gently cascaded over two levels of smooth rock, elegantly sliding down before falling into a large circular pool, landing with the smallest amount of splash as if from an Olympic diver.

Her body gravitated toward the falls. Kneeling, she lightly waved her fingers through the crystal-clear water. The tips of her unpolished nails instantly turned a shade of dark pink. Even on a day like today, where the sun shone brightly in a cloudless sky, the water hadn't captured any warmth through the tree canopy.

Perched on the bank, Tayla closed her eyes and splashed the refreshing water over her heated cheeks before leaning back to take a few long, deep breaths...

Tayla woke with a start, her body jolting upright into a sitting position.

When did she lie down?

Spinning around, she spotted her backpack nestled on the ground behind her, where her head had rested moments before. Looking up, a kaleidoscope of deep blue, light pink, and orange peeked through the canopy of the trees.

Oh god, I fell asleep.

She bolted to her feet and brushed away the dirt from the back of her cargos.

"Damn it," she cursed.

Falling asleep in the middle of god-knows-where when she still had hours remaining on her hike.

"So stupid."

Tayla snatched her backpack off the ground and slung it on her back. She spun around to hike back along the narrow dirt track, but her step faltered when she stared ahead.

Her heart sank.

She saw no sign of the path.

Chapter 7

Raven had had too many. A hundred or so too many.

His shoulders slumped as though balancing a team of acrobats on top, yet, his body was as light as a feather, floating gently in a breeze. The giveaway was his vision; taking a few seconds to catch up each time he turned his head.

So…eyes forward from now on.

He glanced at the glass of bourbon nestled in his rough palm. Condensation dripped around his fingers as the cubes of ice bobbed up and down in the sweet golden liquid.

What the fuck was he doing here?

He should be at home in bed or passed out on the lawn or some shit. Even that would be better than the seedy bar he'd ended up in. Cheap booze and over-the-top cologne filled the air while mortals got it on in every dark corner.

Hours ago, he'd stormed in with one mission in mind: put an end to the agony inside his chest.

Epic fail.

Things had rapidly spiraled out of control.

For centuries, an unholy need to fix Blaine consumed him. Not just Blaine, but the whole freaking world around him. But after that stunt in the parking lot, the only thing that consumed him now was the desire to tear Blaine into tiny pieces for being within Tayla's vicinity. And the intense protective impulses floored him.

His instincts were rusty, out of practice that was all, given this was his first Chosen assignment since their banishment. He was probably losing his edge. Or…missing something.

If only another Guardian could be assigned to Tayla, but the mere thought made him clench his jaw. Nope. Not an option.

Raven took another gulp of the magic liquor in his glass. Not so magic it eased the heaviness in his chest, but so far, it removed the impulse to fly back to Tayla. Christ, allowing her to see him again wasn't an option either, no way could he erase her memory a second time in one night.

Once was risky enough. Once hurt enough.

A young bartender appeared in front of Raven and motioned to his empty glass. "Another?"

God, Raven hadn't even realized it was empty. Again.

He shook his head and slid the empty glass out of his reach. "Nah, I'm done."

Raven swivelled the stool and slid off, dropping his feet on the ground. The world took a spin, and the pit of his stomach went right along with it. *Fuck.* He couldn't fly home at this rate. He'd more than likely fly into a goddamn tree or something. He'd have to hoof it.

Raven stumbled past a small group of tables littered with empty glasses. A drunk female tugged his arm, begging him to join her in some dark, sleazy corner, or a filthy bathroom. He shrugged her off.

He rammed his shoulder against the entrance door and all but fell out onto the street. His breath hitched as frigid air smacked him in the face, burning his nostrils with each inhale. He tilted his head and squinted at the blend of soft dusty pink and fluorescent-orange peeking above the horizon.

If he walked, he'd be home in time for breakfast. Or lunch.

Raven slung his bomber jacket over one shoulder and crossed the deserted street to fade into the shadows of the trees.

For what seemed like hours, he stumbled through the pine forest, up the mountain, away from the main road in hope of avoiding company. Nothing good would come from a mortal finding a tanked six-foot four male wandering along the edge of the highway in the early hours of the morning. Plus, the route he'd taken, or thought he'd taken, was long enough to walk off the booze before having to face the pity-party from his brothers.

A familiar landscape came into view, and Raven sighed. First stop, shower.

Raven rounded an ancient mountain ash and…

What. The. Hell?

He gaped at the cozy log cabin in front of him, blinds drawn over the windows, lazy puffs of smoke coming from the chimney.

Tayla's car parked out front.

This wasn't where he thought he headed, but apparently his body had other plans.

His heart quickened when he glanced up at the loft, and the morning sun streamed through the oversized window where Tayla slept. Great, now he was a frickin' stalker.

He should turn around and go. By now, he should've walked off enough bourbon to fly. Instead, he retreated a few steps into the shadows of the forest and his legs flopped out in front of him. He slid down the rough trunk, landing his ass on a pile of damp brown leaves.

His head lolled against the tree, tilting to the right to peer at her cabin.

He rubbed his sternum with his palm as though the action would lift the heavy weight off his chest.

It didn't.

Eventually, he gave up and dropped his hand back to his side.

The landscape swirled around him as though he were on a merry-go-round, his blinking slowed, and his lids struggled to hold themselves open.

A moment later, it all came to a crashing halt. His lids gave in, head fell forward and his body went nighty-night and passed the fuck out.

Chapter 8

Where the heck is the trail?

Tayla glanced in every direction. She spun around in circles, searching for any sign of the path she'd followed.

It wasn't there.

As though, in the short time she'd been there, the vegetation had grown at an alarming rate and covered it, trapping her in its lair.

She wiped her clammy palms down the front of her cargos. The trail had to be there somewhere.

Inhaling a shaky breath, Tayla steadily followed the edge of the forest in a wide circle, searching for a break in the vegetation. The trail leading to the waterfall had been longer than she anticipated. She couldn't waste any more time searching. She needed to make her way down the mountain before it got too dark.

Shadows stretched along the ground as the sun gradually sank toward the horizon. She rubbed her hands together to stop them from shaking.

Tayla knelt and spread her map over the dirt to roughly pinpoint where she'd deviated from the original trail. She could guess how long it had been to the waterfall but she had no clue which direction.

How could I have been this stupid?

She ripped out her phone from the backpack to access the GPS. No signal. Nothing.

Double crap.

Bile rose in her throat. She had no idea where she was. No one did. She hadn't told anyone because she didn't have anyone to tell.

How could someone find her if no one knew she was missing?

She stared up at the deep purple sky peeking through the thick canopy of intertwined branches, and a conversation with Dad replayed in her head.

"Did you find the hikers, Dad?" she asked.

Dad shook his head. "Not yet."

"Maybe they headed down the mountain, once they realized they were lost."

"It's such an unforgiving landscape, Tayla. One wrong move can lead to disaster. Or worse. When you're lost, the safest thing to do is stay where you are until help arrives. Always."

Tayla raised her brows. "Even if it means starving?"

His jaw tightened. "It's a whole lot better than never being found."

Great. Now she was one of those irresponsible hikers.

Tayla folded the map and stood. This time her options were grim.

One: Stay there for god-knows how long, waiting for the emergency services to send a search party.

Or two: Attempt to make her way down the mountain and meet up with the river. Following the river downstream would lead her back to Summit Creek.

I'm sorry, Dad.

Ignoring her better judgement and the screaming voice in her head, Tayla turned her back on the waterfall and crept into the forest.

After almost an hour of hiking in an unknown direction, she halted beside a large fallen branch, big enough to double as a seat. She collapsed on top and surveyed the shadows around her. Nothing had differed. The same dense forest, fallen branches, broken twigs and thick undergrowth had continued since she'd departed the waterfall.

Maybe this wasn't a good idea after all.

Daylight faded rapidly. Dark blue and purple washed the sky, and the forest darkened around her, the temperature plummeting along with it. Tayla grabbed her cardigan from inside the backpack and shrugged it on, buttoning it all the way to her neck.

Not that it made a difference. It did nothing to erase the goosebumps along her legs, but it slowly warmed her chest.

Her fingers ached, paling as the tips turned bright red, the blood rushing to her vital organs. She vigorously rubbed her palms together; she'd prefer to keep each and every one of her fingers, thank you very much.

After a quick sip of water, Tayla stood and continued to trek to…who knows. *Somewhere*. The tips of her toes tingled and her feet throbbed inside her boots with each step. Still, she continued on.

Another thirty minutes, a thick blanket of darkness covered the forest, taking away any remaining warmth. And light. If she had a thermometer, the little red line would have instantly slid all the way to the bottom.

The tips of her ears ached and her cheeks stung; she clenched her teeth together so tight her jaw ached. She fumbled with the zipper on her backpack and managed to grab her flashlight.

At least she'd remembered something useful. If only it was as powerful as a row of spotlights.

Navigating by a tiny circle of light, Tayla ducked under a thorny twisted vine stretched from one giant tree to another. Her feet wobbled as she stepped over another fallen branch, and the trees swayed around her.

Wait, had she seen that tree stump before?

A twig snapped to her right and Tayla crouched, gulping down a breath to stay quiet.

She flicked off the flashlight. Hugged her arms around her legs. Held her breath.

Her oversensitive ears picked up every nearby rustle. Every scurry. Every snap.

Soon, she would have to give in, concede she was lost and prepare for a freezing night in the elements…and eaten alive by the creatures around her.

A growl to her left snapped her to attention. In one swift movement, she turned the flashlight back on, jumped up and bolted forward.

She was not going to die. Or lose fingers or toes.

A sharp branch scratched her numb cheek as she dashed past, and warm liquid trickled down her chin. Her pulse echoed in her ears. Her breaths heaved the cold air in and out. The crunch of her boots on the forest floor boomed in the darkness as though plugged into loudspeakers.

Satisfied the growling creature was far behind her, Tayla slumped against a prickly pine tree and wiped her sleeve over her torn cheek while she sucked in gulps of air.

If she was going to have any chance of surviving, she needed to find shelter. One night. That was all she needed to endure. Tomorrow, in the daylight, she'd navigate her way down the mountain to the river.

Come on, Tayla. You can do this.

First, she needed shelter. Tayla steadied the flashlight with both hands and shone the light in front of her while turning in a tight circle. The trees and thick vegetation made it impossible to see more than a few feet away. On her second twist, Tayla squinted at something in the distance. Without any other options, she crept closer.

The flashlight revealed a mound of large boulders, stacked on top of each other as though they'd tumbled down the side of the mountain together to land in a heap. Trees stretched between the narrow gaps in the boulders, creating the illusion of a small hill.

She crept closer. The light revealed a gap between the boulders, forming a cavity of sorts; the width of her outstretched arms and high enough to step through—but should she?

Not like I've got much of a choice.

She either ventured into the cave or stayed out in the open with the growling creatures.

Tayla grabbed a nearby rock and threw it into the cave. The sound of the rock colliding with others echoed back to her. She waited a few minutes more. Satisfied no animals waited inside the entrance, Tayla ducked her head and crept in.

Facing inside the cave, she roamed her flashlight around the sizeable space. The ceiling stretched twice her height, covered in thick grey spider webs, two sides of the cave were solid rock with delicate mossy green ferns peeking from the crevasses, and nothing but pitch blackness directly in front of her, for as far as the light could illuminate.

Those spotlights would come in handy right about now.

This might be better than spending the night outside, but no way would she move past the entrance. No telling what kind of creatures inhabited the cave—in addition to the mutant man-eating spiders above her head—or what creatures might arrive during the night.

Safer at the entrance to enable a quick escape.

With shelter sorted, she now needed a fire for warmth and extra light. She rummaged through her nearly empty backpack. Nothing. Even if she found some dry kindling outside the cave, she had nothing to light it with. Pretty sure even Bear Grylls would struggle lighting a fire out of a map, a bottle of water, and an apple.

Tayla's shoulders slumped. *No, he probably wouldn't.*

Well, she couldn't check off building a fire anytime soon, but at least she was dry.

Third task, food and water but she ran low on both.

She hugged her backpack close to her chest and slid down the damp mossy wall, landing softly on the cool dirt of the cave floor. From this position, the sloping boulder on one side protected her body, but she could still view the cave's entrance.

Reclining her head against the wall, she briefly closed her eyes and took a few deep breaths. It didn't help. The frigid air burned down her throat into her lungs, and a cloud of fog escaped her lips when she exhaled.

She grabbed the rapidly depleting water canister and her apple dinner. She clenched the apple between two shaky hands to take a bite, but it wasn't worth it. It tasted like cardboard, and her stomach lurched as the first chunk traveled down her throat.

Giving up, she placed it back in her backpack and blew puffs of warm breath into her cupped hands before tucking them under her armpits for warmth.

Shivers racked her body, numbness spread over her lips and she frequently had to wipe her dripping nose. Her bones ached underneath her skin.

Tayla hugged her legs tightly to her chest, wrapping her arms around them and rested her stinging cheek on top of her bent knees.

This is going to be a long night. She sobbed.

****

Raven peeled his eyes open hours—or days—later. Could have been weeks for all he knew.

The front of his skull pounded like tiny minions using sledgehammers trying to break free. Sharp needles stabbed his eye sockets each time he opened his lids, the glaring sun burned a hole in his brain, and the motion threatened to heave up his guts.

Searing pain ripped down the side of his neck when he tried to straighten it.

Served him right for entering a bourbon-induced coma while leaning against a stupid tree trunk in the woods beside Tayla's cabin.

Creepy much?

After blinking a few times, Tayla's car came into focus, parked in the driveway where it had been when he passed out. His heartbeat took off on a race at the thought of her inside the cabin, preparing to see her any minute now.

Snap the hell out of it.

His joints popped as he rose and stretched his body. God, how long had he perched against that tree? He needed to get home and take a freezing cold shower, clear his head and get back on track. Reaching down, he grabbed his jacket off the ground and brushed off the wet leaves stuck to one side. He grabbed his phone from the inside pocket where he'd stashed it last night—or whenever—and turned it on.

Damn thing instantly sang a chorus of chimes with each missed call notification.

Ping! Ping! The exact reason why he'd turned it off in the first place. *Ping!*

All of them from Aric and EJ. *Duh! Who else would contact you?*

Ping!

Oh, wait. That one was from Ellen—god, they were pissed for Ellen to call. Probably 'cause he'd shut down their mental link and turned the damn phone off.

He didn't want to explain his decision to them, nor did he want the company. They'd only try to talk reason to him, and he didn't want to hear it. With all the other shit he had going on at the moment, what he needed was a little time out. Time out, pass out, same thing. Not that his bourbon coma resolved anything, but it had been damn good to feel nothing but numbness for a while.

He sent a basic text to Aric and EJ to check in and their replies quickly followed. They'd probably be standing on the door step when he returned, stern looks on their faces like they were the parents of a troublesome teenager who'd arrived home hours after curfew. Great, couldn't wait for that conversation. Keeping his mental wall up for a tiny bit longer was a smart move.

Raven peered over at the cabin, and a prickle spiked at his nape. He straightened, scanned the surrounding forest but nothing seemed out of place.

Leaning forward, he tilted his ear toward the cabin.

Nothing.

Maybe the aftereffects of the bourbon binge caused havoc with his senses.

He shrugged off the sensation and unfurled his wings, stretching them over his shoulders and out to his sides in a wide arc. The motion lengthened and loosened his tight muscles.

After a final glance at the cabin, Raven silently took to the sky, heading home to face the music.

****

His boots slammed down on the dewy grass in front of the mansion, sinking into the soft ground. He stood there for a few minutes and took everything in.

The box hedges grew in perfect unison, framing the sandy gravel drive all the way up to a circular turnaround near the entrance. A weeping maple took pride in the center of the turnaround, its leaves turned a deep crimson before gracefully falling to their final resting place on the lawn.

Nothing was more beautiful than watching that tree shed its leaves at the onset of autumn.

Well, one thing was more beautiful, but he couldn't think of her right now.

The mansion wrapped around the turnaround at the end of the driveway. Three stories of stone with two distinct wings stretched from either side. Old Victorian windows trailed the length of each level, peering out at the landscaped grounds beyond, and several chimneys stretched high into the sky. A triangular pointed roof extending from the center of the house covered the main entrance.

He'd been here so long now, had explored every inch of the grounds and house. It had become his home.

Their home.

And it all started with EJ's vision of that damn maple tree.

Raven shoved his hands in the pockets of his jacket and trudged up the drive, his head held low as though the weight of the world lay upon his shoulders.

Well, it kinda does, doesn't it?

His brothers would be pissed. And to make matters worse, his campout under that tree had done nothing to rid the cheap booze and cigarette stench clinging to his clothes. He longed to hit the shower and scrub the putrid smell from his hair.

Raven halted halfway up the drive as power radiated to his side, the air rippled like a pebble dropped into a still pond.

"Gabe." Raven sighed, sensing Gabe's presence a moment before he materialized on the lawn.

"Good evening, Raven," Gabe replied with a curt nod, strolling over to him.

"Nice suit. As usual."

God, could Gabe's obsession with fancy suits get any more ridiculous?

Of all the styles Gabe could create with just a thought, why did he insist on wearing those? Like he was constantly prepared for a pop-up royal ball or some shit. Today was no different. A steel-blue three-piece suit with trousers pressed so crisply he could cut his finger on the crease, a coordinated three-button vest and crisp white shirt, along with a burgundy and cream striped knotted tie and a matching pocket square. A pair of fancy brown leather loafers pointed at the tips topped it off.

Raven rolled his eyes. Talk about overkill.

Bet Gabe couldn't keep up the Ryan-Gosling-in-Armani style if he lived in the mortal world, having to dry clean clothes all the frickin' time.

Gabe stood beside Raven, gazing toward the house. "You look like shit, my friend."

Raven scoffed. "Tell me something I don't know."

For several moments, both angels stood side by side in comfortable silence, as they had thousands of times before.

But staring at the entrance to the mansion wasn't going to solve Raven's problems. "Look, Gabe, it's always good to chat, but today hasn't exactly been my finest. Do you have a message, or did you just drop in to say hi? 'Cause if it's the latter, consider it done. I've gotta get inside and sort some shit out."

His tone was snappier than he intended, but right now he had neither the patience nor the time to deal with anything else. His body ached like he was a hundred-year-old mortal, he stank, and he needed to get this chit-chat with his brothers over and done with before he chickened out, again.

Pissing off Gabe, though, was something he didn't want. Not only was Gabe the Archangel of the Guardians, one of Fate's seconds in command, but also Raven's oldest friend. They'd known each other since the beginning of time, and over the centuries in the mortal world, Raven had come to rely on Gabe's wisdom and matter-of-fact approach.

Gabe smiled, though it didn't reach his chocolate-brown eyes.

Raven could almost hear Gabe's brain ticking like trying to figure out how to say something. Something bad.

Raven pinched his forehead. "Spit it out, Gabe. Couldn't possibly make things any worse."

After another long moment of silence, Gabe finally replied, "Just stopping by to see how things are going, my friend."

Raven sighed. *Yeah, right.*

One guess why Gabe was here. Of course, he knew what was going on; no point trying to hide it, but that didn't mean he was gonna blurt it out either. His stomach lurched at the thought of facing the Guardians waiting inside the house, the angels who'd had his back for centuries, shared a home, and whom he treasured as family. His brothers. Each of them had made an enormous sacrifice to stand here beside him. And instead of rewarding their loyalty, he'd dragged them into his hellhole punishment for the rest of eternity.

If he couldn't stomach confessing to them, how was he supposed to admit it to his oldest friend?

Raven faked a smile. "S'all good, Gabe."

The prickling at the base of his neck returned. What the hell was going on? Tayla was at her cabin, he saw her car there. How could she be in danger inside her cabin?

Raven rubbed the center of his chest with his palm. His own nerves were freaking out about explaining his situation to his brothers.

Gabe pursed his lips and nodded, thankfully choosing not to open that can of worms right now.

Turning to leave, Gabe glanced over his shoulder at Raven. "You need to listen harder, my friend. Choose the right path."

The air around Gabe shimmered and rippled a moment before he disappeared altogether.

What the hell did that mean?

Could this day get any worse?

Raven forced his legs to move, one foot in front of the other crunching on the loose gravel up to the house. He trudged up the stone steps and crossed the entrance to the heavy front door.

He hesitated for a second before gripping the brass door handle. *Here goes.*

Raven pushed open the front door to find Aric standing right in fro—

Crack!

Raven's body flew backward landing on his ass.

What the fuck!

Aric shook his clenched fist before stepping forward, hand out to Raven.

Raven accepted, allowing Aric to tug him to his feet. He rubbed his pounding jaw. "Guess I deserved that."

"Sure did," Aric snapped. "Too hard to check in, man?"

"You had us worried this time, Rave." EJ strolled over with Ellen by his side.

She passed him a wash cloth filled with ice, and he pressed it against his throbbing jaw.

"I'll go fix you something to eat." She patted his

arm before turning on her heels, back inside the house.

Leaving him to face his brothers.

EJ cocked his head to the side. "You'd better get in there before she starts shovelling food in your mouth out here on the bloody porch."

"And between mouthfuls, you can tell us what the hell's going on," Aric grumbled.

Raven accepted the deal, not like he had much choice in the matter, and stalked inside to the kitchen, the other two following close behind.

Fessing up to his brothers would be the hardest thing he'd ever had to do. Besides having to leave them.

The stinging intensified at the base of his neck as though a thousand sharp pins attacked his flesh. His pulse raced.

A cold shiver ran across his back.

Raven froze mid-step.

Holding his breath, he concentrated on the sensations.

"What's wrong, man?" Aric gripped his shoulder. "You look fucking pasty."

Raven frowned. "You guys cold?"

"Cold?" Aric tilted his head slightly and frowned. "Ah, nope."

"Rave, you think it has something to do with Tayla?" EJ glanced at his watch.

Aric leaned around Raven to address EJ. "It's getting close to dusk. Maybe you should tell him?"

Raven glared at EJ. "Tell me what? I'm in no mood for games."

EJ slid a feather from inside his leather jacket and handed it to Raven. A bright crimson feather with flecks of black at the quill. Only one Fallen had that unique combination.

"Where'd you get this?" he growled.

EJ rattled off an explanation, but nothing registered. His lips moved, but Raven's brain didn't comprehend any of the words. The volcano inside him spat warning bursts of scorching lava, threatening to erupt.

"Fuck." Raven grabbed the spot where imaginary pins stabbed his nape.

He hurled the washcloth. The ice flew out and shattered against the wall like fireworks exploding in the sky.

Beside him, EJ froze, his eyes glazed over.

Raven grimaced, waiting for EJ's vision to cease. "EJ, tell me what you see."

A second later, EJ jolted and blinked several times. "Concentrate on the feeling, Rave. You can't sense her if you're frickin' losing it." The urgency in his voice matched the sensations racing through Raven's veins.

A shiver raced through Raven's entire body, his feet stung, and his toes tingled with numbness.

Feeling cold wasn't even possi…

EJ's words hit him like a freight train. It wasn't him at all. He wasn't cold.

Tayla was.

"Something's wrong." Raven spun and bolted for the door, Aric and EJ hot on his heels.

Chapter 9

Raven touched down on the loose gravel in front of Tayla's cabin with his brothers landing close behind him.

The sun sank below the horizon, taking the remaining warmth along with it. Long shadows cast by the ancient gum trees stretched across the gravel drive. His body shivered uncontrollably, and he clenched his jaw to silence the annoying chatter of his teeth.

Raven surveyed the area. Nothing had changed since he'd been here only an hour before.

Except for one thing.

Blaine.

That sonofabitch stood on the veranda, leaning on his elbows on the railing, a smug look on his face.

"Well hello, brother." Blaine smirked.

And that was the final straw. The lid on Raven's volcano exploded, fiery lava erupted out the top, and he took off at a dead run toward Blaine.

"What have you done to her?" he roared.

His feet skidded to a halt, his torso yanked backward by an invisible force. He ripped at his jacket, but EJ's strong arms locked tight around his chest.

"Let me go," he snarled, fighting to get free.

Aric stepped into his spotted vision. "Don't make me punch you again. No good will come from fighting him, trust me."

"It'll make me fucking feel better," Raven snapped.

EJ tightened his grip.

Aric turned to face Blaine. "What have you done this time?"

Blaine lifted his palms in surrender. "Nice to see you too, *friend*." He shifted his sinister gaze to Raven. "Easy there, brother, she's not here." Blaine strolled to the front door and placed his palm flat against the surface as though sensing Tayla's presence. "She hasn't been here for some time."

"What do you mean she isn't here? Her car's in the driveway," Raven shouted back, shoving again against his captor. "EJ, let me go."

Aric glanced across his shoulder at Raven and raised his brows. "Will you play nice?"

"Not likely," Raven snapped.

Aric half-shrugged. "Fair enough."

The second EJ loosened his grip, Raven shoved out of his arms. He stalked toward the cabin.

Aric kept pace with him, within arm's reach.

Raven glared at Blaine. "Where is she?" he growled.

"You know, this look…" He circled Raven's face in the air with his finger. "Kinda suits you, brother, you should give it a go full-time."

More than you know.

"Fuck you, Blaine. This is your last chance. Where is she?"

Blaine shrugged, unfazed by the threat. "No idea. Like you, I just got here."

Blaine leaned his forearms on the railing and tilted his head slightly to one side. "Why is she so important to you, anyway?"

"She's a Chosen. Of course, she's important to me."

Blaine narrowed his pitch-black eyes. "No, I suspect she's more than just your Chosen, brother."

Raven growled, transforming Blaine's smirk into a full-blown sadistic smile.

"While you're here, care to explain this?" Raven pulled the crimson feather from the back of his jeans and held it in the air.

Blaine gaped and pressed his palm against his chest. "What? Are you following me?"

Raven ground his molars and stalked forward another step. "Exactly how many times have you been here?"

"Oh, I don't know." Blaine half-shrugged. "Nice little place though, for a tiny cabin in the middle of a forest. Bet it's quiet, being so far from the main lodge and all." He clapped his hands together and strolled along the veranda before descending the creaky steps. "Anyhoo, be sure to say hi for me if she makes it back."

Blaine unfolded his sinister wings, the crimson feathers bright as if dipped in fresh blood moments before. Only a handful of black flecks remained. "Nice to see you all again, it's always a pleasure." He bowed his head curtly to Raven before he shot to the moonless sky.

"What was that about?" Aric muttered.

Raven craned his head back and stared at the billions of tiny sparkling stars, filling the sky with warm yellow glitter. Goosebumps popped over his arms as a chill traveled down his spine.

"She's somewhere out there, and she's freezing," Raven mumbled, rubbing his chest with his open hand.

He glanced across his shoulder at each of his brothers. "EJ, stay here, see if you can find something that'll give us a clue to her whereabouts. Aric, you and I will check the mountains; she couldn't have gone far on foot."

EJ nodded, already marching to the front door of the cabin.

Aric stepped closer and squeezed Raven's shoulder. "We'll find her, man."

****

Raven hovered several feet above the thick canopy of trees, scanning the ranges. He peered over his right shoulder and zeroed in on the expansive grounds of Cedar Lodge and the smattering of log cabins. No sign of Tayla. His gaze drifted further out to Summit Creek Dam, the still water glossy and black in the darkness of the night, the town's lights illuminating the banks. He turned. More blackness. A gloomy canopy of darkness covered the mountains.

Aric hovered next to him, silently flapping his wings, waiting for a hint on which direction to head.

"She's shivering," Raven muttered.

"Concentrate on the connection to her. Feel past the physical symptoms." Aric motioned to the gloomy mountains. "That's a frickin' lot of ground to cover with just the two of us."

Raven pictured Tayla behind his closed lids, her wavy chestnut hair swaying in a gentle breeze, her fresh spring-rain scent filling his nostrils. Her hazel eyes bright with excitement…

Got it!

Like a fluorescent orange flare shot into the black sky, Raven latched onto their connection. He turned and sped toward the dark mountain range.

The pit of his stomach quivered, and his shoulders tensed. The frigid wind howled over the tree canopy, stinging his cheeks and burning his throat with every gasp of air. He knew this terrain like the back of his hand, had flown over it thousands of times, but he couldn't pinpoint her exact location. The spiritual tether connecting them dropped in and out as though in a black spot or some shit. Which was not fucking helpful.

Aric pointed to his left. "The falls are over that way," he yelled above the wind. "Maybe she hiked there? Or there's the summit trail following the river."

At that moment, the beacon flashed on, and Raven shot toward it, his gaze glued on the location in case it dropped out.

"I can't see a thing up here," Raven bellowed over his shoulder. "I'm going down on foot."

He plummeted through the trees, not giving a shit when branches ripped and tore his flesh. Dead crunchy leaves flew up around him in a frenzy as he landed. Wasting no time, he bolted straight ahead, tucking his wings behind his back.

Aric's heavy footfalls caught up to Raven and he cast him a quick glance. "Rough landing?" He smirked.

Without slowing, Raven used the sleeve of his jacket to wipe the thick warm blood gushing down the side of his face.

They raced ahead, effortlessly leaping fallen trees and shoving overhanging branches to the side, clearing a path. Smaller twigs and ground cover crumbled and snapped under the pound of their boots.

Keep going, nearly there. Faster!

He swiped again at his cheek…

Raven's heavy combat boot stubbed a rock, camouflaged under a pile of leaves. A sickening *crack* echoed through the forest a second before searing pain shot through his ankle. He stumbled forward, flailing his arms in the air, unfurling his wings just in time to prevent face-planting in the dirt.

Righting himself, he balanced on one leg and peered down at his left combat boot, bent in an unnatural way. He swallowed the vomit rising up his throat. He didn't have time for this; he needed to get to Tayla.

He clenched his jaw and pushed his broken foot down on the ground and—*One…two…three*—snapped it in the opposite direction.

The bone popped back into place.

Vomit rose again, and this time he leaned to the side and hurled it up. Trees swayed before his eyes as though he were on that merry-go-round again.

Aric gagged beside him. "Fuck, man, that was nasty. I'll get her. You wait here."

"No," Raven grunted, wiping his mouth with the back of his hand. He pressed his "fixed" ankle lightly against the ground, testing the weight-versus-pain ratio. "I'm good."

Aric grimaced and scrunched up his face. "Providing you don't fucking pass out."

"I won't. It's already healing." *Kinda.*

Raven pointed straight ahead, toward a mound of boulders. "She's gotta be there."

He hobbled forward, as fast as he could, which only slowed them down. Numbness crept up his injured leg, making him wobbly on his feet. White-hot pain burned inside his ankle and his body shuddered.

Faster.

The tug inside his chest intensified and he keeled over, struggling to fill his lungs with air. His hands shot forward to break his fall, scraping his rough palms on the dirt.

"G-get her," Raven choked, pointing ahead.

Aric didn't need to be told twice. He kicked into gear and bolted to the boulders.

Raven heaved in and out, gasping for air.

God, her shivers racked his body as though they were his own.

His good foot tingled with pins and needles and his ears stung so badly they might just snap off.

Latching onto a tree trunk beside him, Raven clawed himself off the ground and stumbled forward.

"She's here," Aric shouted in the distance. "And alive."

Raven sagged against the tree.

Aric rounded the far side of the boulder and strode to Raven, cradling Tayla in his arms. His expression tight. "She's gotta get warm, man. Stat."

The sight of Tayla's head falling limp over Aric's arm snapped him into action. He rushed to Aric, pushing aside his pain and, as gently as he could, transferred Tayla's pale, shivering body into his arms.

Aric stripped off his leather jacket and laid it across her torso.

Raven nudged her closer to his chest. Her head lay in the crook of his arm, against his beating heart. And damn, if it didn't feel so right.

Tayla murmured words in her semiconscious state, but he couldn't make them out.

Raven stretched out his wings and curled them

around his body to gently encase Tayla's slender frame in a warm cocoon of silky feathers.

Heat instantly flooded his body from the center out, traveling along his veins and transferred through their connection. It chased away the numbness. Color returned to Tayla's cheeks and she snuggled her head closer to his chest. Her warm breath tickled his skin through his cotton tee.

God, he had to figure out this connection between them.

But this was not the time nor the place to attempt to process whatever the fuck was going on. His first priority had to be to get her warm without being naked. Although, that was a proven method to increase body temperature. Nope. Nakedness led to other activities, and as much as he wanted to, those activities were forbidden between a Guardian and a Chosen.

Fate had punished him enough for one eternity.

He tore himself away from his thoughts and glanced at Aric, who met his gaze with a slight furrow of his brows as though he saw something Raven didn't.

"She's not out of the woods yet, man, no pun intended. You gotta get her to a mortal hospital."

His stomach churned at the lack of protection at a hospital and her cabin. Blaine had been there, for fuck's sake. But could he risk the consequences for him and his brothers bringing her to the safest place on Earth?

He had to. There was no other option.

"She's coming back with us," Raven said with an air of authority. Suddenly, something inside he couldn't explain, shifted. Locked into place.

He stared hard at Aric daring him to argue.

Instead, Aric nodded before turning away.

Raven peered down at the beautiful mortal nestled between his wings. Her lips had returned to their usual rosy color, her cheeks a healthy dusty pink. The violent shivering had ceased.

Aric returned to his side. "EJ's meeting us back at the house." He jerked his chin at Raven's ankle. "You right to fly, man?"

"Yep. Wings are still attached."

Didn't matter if they weren't. No way would he hand her over to anyone else.

Ever.

Aric pursed his lips, about to argue but didn't. Thank God.

Raven slowly folded back his wings and squeezed Tayla closer to his chest. Shifting her weight into one arm, he tossed Aric's jacket back to him. As gently as he could, he maneuvered Tayla back into position, tucking her tightly against his torso.

Tayla moaned, snuggling in closer. His heart pounded inside his chest.

This wasn't the best idea. *Jesus.* He needed to get her back to the house and out of his arms.

Aric cleared his throat. "Ah, you good, man?"

"Let's go," Raven replied in a thick voice.

Aric wasted no time arguing and shot into the sky in one swoop, skillfully avoiding stray branches. Again.

Raven leaned his head forward and tenderly kissed her warm cheek. He gently reached out with his mind into Tayla's subconscious and eased her into light sleep. Better than her freaking out if she woke on their flight home.

"You're safe now, Tayla," he whispered. "I'm not letting you go, again."

He glanced skyward before taking off—carefully navigating the trees like Aric had—with his mortal safely tucked in his arms.

Chapter 10

Something warm and velvety bobbed under Tayla's feet as she flexed her toes. She poked around a little more and discovered two hot water bottles with her under the covers.

Bright light danced behind her lids and her cheeks hummed with the sun's warmth while she snuggled beneath luxurious bed linens. Her body heavy, yet, relaxed as it sank into the cushiony pallet.

Peaceful silence filled the room and an earthy pine scent lingered in the air, like her body lay nestled deep in the middle of the forest. Her muscles ached as they awakened, as though she were a princess waking for the first time thanks to a spell-breaking kiss from her prince.

Tayla rolled onto her side and the layers of cozy fabrics rolled with her, but the motion tangled her shirt around her torso. She wriggled, adjusted her position and tugged at the shirt which only caused her pants to twist around her waist.

Hang on…Why was she wearing pants and a shirt?

Memories flashed in her mind, like a movie trailer playing behind her lids. Hiking the mountain. The trail to the waterfall. The sickening realization she was lost. Shivering so violently she feared her body would snap in half. Struggling to breathe. Sudden…heat. Soft fur cocooning her aching muscles, whispers of reassurance in her ear and strong warm arms pulling her close.

The sensation of floating off the ground.

What the heck?

Tayla peeked open her heavy lids. Glaring light burst through uncovered French doors in front of her, spilling across the wooden floor, onto the light grey duvet draped over her body.

This wasn't her room. Or her bed.

A sensation stirred in her gut. She wasn't alone. Tayla launched into a sitting position and threw the layers of fabric to the side. The room swayed, and she squeezed her head at the sudden pounding in her temples.

A flash of movement in the corner of the room grabbed her attention. She blinked a few times before the room came into focus. And the man in it.

He leaned forward with his elbows on his knees, perched on an antique wing-back chair in the far corner. Her gaze roamed over the faded black jeans covering his long legs, the crinkled black button-up shirt with the sleeves rolled up to his elbows. She lifted her gaze across his lightly tanned face, god-like chiseled jaw with straight pointed nose, and briefly over his dark brown, perfectly styled hair.

Time paused the moment his unearthly deep blue eyes locked with hers.

Familiarity danced in the back of her mind.

The corner of his mouth lifted in a forced smile. "Good morning." He glanced at the cell phone nestled between his palms. "Well, technically it's afternoon. How are you feeling?" he asked, like it was totally normal to find her waking in this bed.

Wait…was this his bed? Her cheeks heated.

Silence stretched between them until he lifted his eyebrows, prompting her to speak.

What was he talking about?

"Sorry, what did you say?" she asked.

"I asked how you felt. Are you warm enough?"

Tayla chuckled, poking the hot water bottles with her toes. "Yes, thanks to my companions."

His lips curled in a grin, but it didn't reach his eyes. "Good. They were Ellen's idea actually."

Okaaaay…could this situation be any weirder?

Tayla leaned forward and grabbed the duvet, folded it back over her legs, and smoothed her fingers over the soft fabric. "So, I should get up, I guess."

He rose from the chair. She craned her head back to maintain eye contact.

"I've placed some toiletries for you in the bathroom and a few clothes in the closet. Hopefully, there's something you like." He pointed behind her.

"Okaaaay." She briefly glanced over her shoulder at an ajar door.

She glanced back at him. A muscle ticked in his jaw a moment before he gave a curt nod and strode toward a different door.

"I'm Tayla, by the way," she blurted out as he gripped the door handle.

He paused, still facing the door. "Nice to finally meet you, Tayla. I'm Raven."

He exited and softly closed the door behind him.

She tilted her ear toward it, holding her breath waiting for a *click* engaging the lock from the other side as it did in those crime shows on TV.

Nope. *Phew!*

Raven. Tayla waited a few more minutes, snuggled in the bed, rolling his name around on her tongue.

Taking her time, she peered around the oversized bedroom. It comfortably fit the large four-poster bed she currently occupied, along with a few pieces of antique furniture. Thick charcoal curtains were drawn open on the oversized windows, and through the French doors she spied a balcony.

Folding back the layers of bedding, Tayla slipped out of bed and padded to the door Raven indicated. It creaked as she nudged it open, revealing an expansive walk-in closet; rows of shelves and hanging space ran parallel down the entire length of the walls. She moved in farther and brushed her hand along the collection of women's clothing neatly gathered at one end. Dark denim jeans with designer fades and rips hung beside soft cotton button-downs. She took the caramel leather jacket from the rack and inspected it front and back. Her eyes bulged at the price tag hanging over the collar and she shoved it back on the rack.

On the far end, Tayla pulled open several drawers and peeked inside to find folded shirts in various colors, a good chunk of scarves and, she gulped, more revealing lacy underwear than a lingerie model needed.

Is this all for me?

This situation seriously messed with her head. If only she could remember how she got here in the first place…and where exactly here was.

And while she was at it, figure out what kind of person filled half a closet with expensive outfits for someone they'd just met.

Someone planning on having me stay for a long time.

Sudden heaviness pressed against her chest.

Raven didn't look like a serial killer, but then again, what did a serial killer look like? All she had to go off were the countless episodes of crime shows her colleague had subjected her to. Coupled with her own traumatic experience, she'd quickly doubted the intentions of every single man.

Tayla caught a glimpse of a bathroom at the end of the closet. The shower beckoned her. She closed her eyes, snatched a bra and panties—*is there even enough fabric to call them panties?*—and chose a soft cream shirt and a pair of black jeans on her way to the bath.

The natural stone flooring cooled her feet as she bee-lined for the shower, stripping off her hiking clothes on the way.

Reaching in, she flipped on the hot water, waiting for the steam to rise on the clear glass before stepping on the bamboo slats directly under the enormous shower head. Steamy bliss cascaded over her body, soothing her achy muscles. Making use of the products in the nook of the tiles, she thoroughly washed her hair and body. Fresh green tea and mint filled the bathroom air, chasing away the butterflies in the pit of her stomach.

She stood under the water for longer than she probably should have, letting it gush over her body. Finishing up, she turned the cold water off first to get a quick blast of hot across her shoulders before shutting off the water completely.

After drying off, Tayla peeked inside the drawers of the dark wood free-standing cabinet. There were enough toiletries and makeup to keep her locked up for years. The churning in the pit of her stomach returned with a vengeance as she rubbed the towel through her hair and dressed.

What now? Should she wait in the bedroom for Raven to return? Go try to find him?

Climb out the window and make a run for it?

Toughen up, princess.

No, she should at least thank Raven for finding her. Inhaling a deep breath, she forced her heavy feet to the door Raven had exited. Clutching the doorknob, she paused, biting the inside of her lip, her ear tilted toward the door, listening for sounds on the other side. After several heartbeats of silence, Tayla twisted the knob and snuck out of the bedroom.

She peered in both directions down the long narrow corridor.

Phew! No one waiting to throw her back in the room.

The deep rumble of male voices echoed from her right, and with slow, measured steps, Tayla headed toward them, following the plush dark red carpet down the hallway to a staircase.

She inched down the carpeted stairs, one careful step after another until she reached the bottom.

The voices ceased.

She gawked at the grand sunken living area before her. Lofty ceilings with exposed timber beams, floor-to-ceiling shelves lined two of the walls, crammed with dusty books. Two chocolate brown chesterfields sat in front of an oversized hearth with three guys seated on them.

What century do these people think they're in?

Tayla stepped forward and the floor board creaked, making her jump.

She glanced in the living room again and spotted Raven striding toward her.

Her pulse quickened as she watched him cross the room. He stopped across the hall from her, at the top of the landing.

He'd changed into a dark striped long sleeve tee with the arms bunched up to his elbows, the soft fabric stretched across his wide chest. An earthy, masculine scent mixed with fresh pine needles filled her nostrils, making her head swim and her veins heat.

"Find everything you need?" he asked in a deep, gravelly voice that reverberated through her body, warming it a notch.

Oh, this is so bad.

He stuffed his hands in the pockets of his worn, black jeans.

"Ah, yes, thank you."

Tayla peered past Raven, but the other two guys had gone.

"Are you hungry?" he asked.

Her stomach growled. No, she should get back to her place. For one, she barely knew him and two, more importantly, she didn't know where she was.

Tayla shook her head. "No thanks, I really should be getting back. I appreciate everything you've done." A sudden ache filled her chest.

Raven smirked. "You're free to go whenever you please. Let me feed you first, though. You must be starving."

Well, she was hungry. Maybe she could have something quick to eat, then leave.

Raven grinned and motioned to the doorway to her left.

Oh, what the heck!

Tayla nodded and accepted his invitation. And in that single moment, something pivotal inside her shifted and locked into place.

Chapter 11

What the hell have I done?

Raven still couldn't believe his eyes. She sat right in front of him, at his dining room table, in his fucking house.

The situation had spiraled way out of control. Bringing her back to his home wasn't one of his best decisions. And to make matters worse, as soon as he'd arrived with her in his arms, Ellen had fussed around like Tayla was permanently moving in or some shit.

He allowed his mind to wander back to last night. He'd used a touch of mind control to put Tayla to sleep within seconds of taking to the sky; she'd been cold, exhausted, and no way her mortal mind could've processed what was happening. An unfamiliar need had consumed him, screamed to get her to safety.

He'd gambled with Fate yet again and brought her to the mansion. If he was going to keep her safe and alive, there was no safer place.

But that still didn't explain the unfamiliar urge to keep her close to him.

The whole night and following day, he'd slumped in that damn century-old chair waiting for her to wake. At one point, EJ had suggested moving her to Raven's room, so he could get some sleep in the adjoining study. No fucking way. The thought of Tayla in his room, in his bed, twisted in his sheets, lit up his body like a Christmas tree smothered in thousands of fairy lights. In a guest room, on a straight-back chair, he had better control of his thoughts.

Of his actions.

Last night, he'd been so confident with his decision. This morning, not so much. This consuming need to atone for his failure to protect her last time clouded his judgment.

Raven pressed his palm on the sharp pain in his chest. *God, what if I hadn't gotten to her in time?*

What if bringing her here screwed up her path? Fingers crossed Fate had learned a sliver of forgiveness in his absence.

Bringing himself back to the present, Raven glanced across the oversized table at Tayla, her head down while she picked at an uneaten sandwich. Chestnut waves carelessly fell across one shoulder and her porcelain skin glistened with that after-shower glow. Her sweet, fresh spring rain scent drifted in the air, making his head swirl.

Tayla glanced up, catching his stare, and it sent wild sparks through his veins.

The corners of her mouth lifted in a shy smile. "So…" She glanced back at her plate. "Do you mind me asking how I got here? I don't remember much."

He tracked her delicate hands as she picked a piece of crust and lifted it to her lips, only to change her mind and return it to the plate.

"I found you," he croaked. *How much do I tell her?* "I brought you here to recover."

Tayla lifted her gaze to him and another shockwave coursed through his body.

"Is this your house?"

Raven nodded, his throat suddenly dry.

"How did you find me?"

"I was…near where I found you." His stomached churned at the almost lie. God, what he'd give to be able to tell her the truth. The whole truth.

He should've listened to Aric. Acting like a psychopath who'd just kidnapped his victim—not his finest moment.

Tayla sighed and slid her plate forward. "Seems I'm not hungry after all."

Shit. He hadn't thought about what would happen beyond this point. But now she was here, the desire for her to stay consumed his soul.

Raven cleared his throat. "Would you like to take a walk or something?" *A walk? What the fuck?* Insert mental forehead slap.

Tayla smirked. "I don't know if that's such a wise idea. The last time I went for a walk I needed rescued."

Raven's jaw clenched at the memory of her lost and alone, of not knowing if he'd get to her in time.

The smile dropped from Tayla's face. "It's fine. I'm just kidding."

His grinding molars echoed in his ears. *Chill, man, she's safe.*

Raven pushed his chair out to stand. With unhurried steps, he stalked around the table, gaze locked on Tayla the entire time while he trailed his fingertips along the top of the chairs until he reached her seat. She didn't turn as he stepped behind her chair and lightly gripped the backrest. Electricity sparked where he touched her soft shirt.

Tayla sucked in a breath. Did she feel it, too?

Without thinking, he twirled the ends of her silky hair.

Tayla's pulse spiked, racing through his veins as though it were his own. *Maybe it is mine.*

His heart pounded against his ribs as his gaze drifted to the smooth, lily-white skin of her neck, filling his mind with wicked thoughts. He swallowed. With a shaky hand, he moved her hair to one side, folding it over one shoulder to expose her nape. Tayla tilted her head slightly to one side, as though silently encouraging him to proceed.

Ah, fuck.

In a slow and delicate motion, he traced the pad of his thumb along the protruding vein down the side of her neck, across the top of her shoulder, halting when it snuck under her shirt. Tayla shuddered, and tilted her head further. Her sweet arousal drifted through his nostrils, making his vision swarm, driving him into a frenzy.

He moistened his bottom lip and lowered his head to her neck, lost in a trance he was helpless to escape. His warm breath rebounded off her neck and his mouth watered for a taste. Just one taste. His body heated with the countless fantasies tempting him...*Lightly brushing his lips along the soft skin behind her ear, before gently nibbling on the lobe. Using his tongue to trace her smooth, delicate neck down to hook his thumb under her shirt to nudge it wider, trailing sweet kisses along her shoulder...*

He leaned closer, hovering millimeters from her intoxicating skin.

His conscience balanced on a rickety footbridge suspended over a raging gorge. The bridge creaked with each step, threatening to snap the weathered ropes connecting it to the other side. He had two choices. Step back and retreat to the safety of solid ground. Or continue forward, into unknown territory, and risk plummeting into the abyss below.

If Fate forced the bridge to snap, would he survive or drown? Would Fate notice if he reached the other side and basked in the warm sunlight, just once?

About to cross the line, Raven. A distant warning echoed in the back of his mind.

Raven inhaled deeply, his eyes rolling back in his head as her delicious scent consumed him. Heat spread through his veins as though he lay under the scorching midday sun.

Who the hell was he trying to kid? He'd well and truly left that line in the dust the minute he brought her here.

Fuck it.

Fate can go ahead and snap the damn ropes. He was one helluva swimmer.

****

Oh, god. A complete stranger, whom she'd known for less than an hour, was going to kiss her. And she ached for him.

What the heck was she doing?

Who cares!

Raven's warm breath heated the side of her neck and her body prickled with sensations, anticipating his next move. *My god!* Her needy breasts ached, her nipples hardened, warmth flooded her body, pooling in the pit of her belly. Each touch of his rough palm sent shivers down her spine, awakening parts of her body dormant for what felt like forever.

The pad of his thumb drew lazy circles on the top of her shoulder. Her chest tightened, squeezing the air from her lungs, but she tilted her head further to the side, desperate for his mouth to make contact with her skin.

Begging him.

Moments ago, she'd thought of ways to escape…now, she silently prayed for this moment to never end.

Why does it feel so good? So…right?

In an unhurried motion, his thumb traced the outline of her jaw. She jutted her chin and he guided his palm down the front of her neck, pausing in the V of her shirt.

She gasped in short breaths, inhaling his intoxicating earthy scent and her body burned from within, with a need only he could slake. How could someone she'd only just met have this effect on her?

Raven's free hand moved her hair further aside.

Make this ache end. No, keep it going.

His moistened lips grazed the sensitive area underneath her ear lobe and her body exploded with heat. Every bit of air expelled from her lungs. His hot breath rebounded off her burning skin as he steadily trailed down her neck, making her back arch.

His thumb tugged her shirt slightly to the side and cool air tickled her shoulder. He brushed his lower lip over her skin, back up to her neck. She couldn't take it anymore. Her fingers twitched to touch him. She hesitated for a split second before her hand reached behind and slid around the base of his neck, drawing him closer. But still he held back, and his restraint maddened her.

His palm slid along the outside of her shirt, over her shoulder and down her upper arm, leaving a scorching trail of heat in its wake. The soft knitted fabric suddenly irritated her skin as though made of prickly bushes.

Kiss me already!

Raven's lips stilled. His palm tensed on her arm.

No. Don't st—

Raven's head jerked back and his body straightened a split second before the double doors swung open and two massive men, caught up in conversation, barged in.

Tayla jolted. She jerked her head toward the door, and her hair fell back into place.

The two men skidded to a halt and the one behind collided with the first.

"Sorry, man, we didn't know you were in here," said the dark-haired one in front.

Raven's hands gripped the back of her chair and it moaned under the pressure.

I know how it feels.

"We…" Raven cleared his throat and stepped back from her chair. "We were just leaving." His voice raspier than a few minutes before.

Goosebumps erupted over her bare shoulder and she tugged her shirt back into place.

The dark-haired guy glanced between her and Raven, and her cheeks burned like a teenager whose parents had caught them making out on the couch.

The two men filled the doorway, both wearing sweatpants with half empty water bottles gripped in their hands. Sweat dripped along the side of the dark-haired one's face and the blonde one leaned on the door jamb, earplugs hanging from the top of his hoodie, the faint beats filling the silence.

Tayla pushed her chair out from the table and stood beside Raven.

Blonde Guy gave a quick wave. "Hey, I'm EJ."

Raven moved his body slightly in front of her and she peered around him to address EJ.

"Hi. I'm Tayla."

Raven glanced at her over his shoulder, his eyebrows bunched like something puzzled him but he couldn't figure out what.

EJ nudged the dark-haired guy with his shoulder.

"Aric," he grumbled.

Raven twisted slightly and slid his hand around the small of her back to nudge her close. Fresh waves of heat washed over her, and she sighed. *Just when I started to cool down.*

He glanced down at her with a scorching gaze. "You wanna take that walk now?"

She nodded, not trusting her voice.

Without removing his hand from the small of her back, he escorted her out of the dining room, past the two guys who stepped aside as they walked between them. Aric's gaze met hers and she didn't miss the flicker of pain hidden behind his amber eyes.

Along the hall, heading to the front door, Raven suddenly halted and turned toward her. "Can you give me a minute? I'll be right back," he said, before heading back to the now closed doors of the dining room.

She drowned in the hardness of his body as he strode to the doors. The way his shirt stretched across his broad shoulders, perfectly framing his upper body, the sight of his muscular legs filling out the faded black jeans with each long stride. A soft moan escaped her lips when he pushed open the double doors, and his arms bulged beneath the tight fabric, stretching it across his shoulder blades. At that moment, two parallel slits gaped open in the back of his shirt.

She drew back slightly. *That's weird.*

Tayla shrugged it off when Raven disappeared, and the doors swung shut behind him.

Oh, this guy is bad news.

Shaking her head, she turned and strolled out the front door.

Chapter 12

"What the hell am I doing?" Raven leaned against the closed doors, mentally prepared for a grilling from his brothers.

Aric stared back, half a sandwich shoved in his mouth. "Man, you're so far gone." He took a bite, chewed and swallowed. "I mean I thought you brought her back here because it was safer?"

"I did."

Aric raised an eyebrow. "Then…what exactly did we interrupt?"

"I don't know what the hell came over me. It's like something keeps pulling me toward her. Something I can't frickin' shake."

"It's called a Chosen connection, man."

Raven pinched his forehead. "No…it's much stronger than I remember, more powerful than I've ever experienced."

EJ strolled into the room from the kitchen, a plate stacked high with sandwiches in one hand and a can of soda in the other. "What'd I miss?"

"Oh, you know, Raven's catching me up on all the shit he's got himself into."

EJ laughed. "With Tay-Tay, no doubt."

"It's not funny," Raven snapped.

Aric snickered. "Kinda is."

Raven pushed off the door. "EJ, have you seen anything that might suggest something's different with her?"

EJ put his plate on the table and his soda hissed when he opened it. "You wouldn't believe my vision even if I told you."

Probably not. "Maybe I will this time."

Aric leaned back in his chair. "Yeah, right."

EJ took a gulp of soda. "Rave, you gotta trust in Fate."

"Like hell I do. Not one of the visions she sent you has us back home. Assigning me to Tayla is probably her brand new form of torture." He stepped forward. "And you know what? I'm not going to give that bitch the satisfaction of watching me fail. Nor will I give her any ammunition to punish us further."

"Whatcha gonna do?" Aric said.

"Stop things before I get dragged away by the current," Raven grumbled as he pushed open the doors and stormed out.

He hadn't made it to the other side of the river; that suspension bridge had well and truly snapped and sent him plummeting into the wild abyss. Now he was destined to spend eternity fighting to keep his head above the raging current, forever gasping for breath. His only way out was to grab a low-hanging branch, pull himself to the bank, and heave himself out of the raging river.

Then he needed to summon the strength to hold on.

Raven's breath hitched as he swung open the front door and caught sight of Tayla perched on the bottom step, staring toward the landscaped gardens, the afternoon rays glistened in her tied-up hair.

He stared at her exposed neck, where his lips had traced moments before.

Touch her again. No, reach for a branch. Get to the bank.

Tayla twisted to face him. Her radiant hazel eyes caused his knees to buckle and he gripped the door frame for support.

She stood and brushed off invisible dirt from the front of her jeans.

He cleared his throat. "It's probably a bit late for a walk." *Get to the bank.* "I can drive you home if you're feeling better."

She frowned for a moment before answering. "Okay. Sure."

Was she relieved? Disappointed? Why did either bother him so goddamn much?

Tayla ascended the step and halted in front of him, but her warm gaze averted his when she tucked a loose strand of hair behind her ear.

Look at me. Tell me you want to stay. He clenched his palm to prevent it from reaching out to touch her face.

She peered back at the gardens.

"I'll go get the car then." His chest tightened.

"Okay."

Damn it. Hanging his head, he trudged back through the door and softly closed it behind him.

Veering left, he ventured through a door off the hallway, descended the steps and followed a long passage to the underground garage.

Maybe she should stay for one more night, just to be sure she was safe. He shook his head. *No.* He'd grabbed the branch, now he needed to heave himself onto the river bank and he was home free.

If only it would rid the ache in my chest.

Punching the door code into the keypad, Raven disengaged the lock and entered the garage, crossing to the far side where he'd parked his black Jeep Wrangler. He climbed into the driver's seat and started the engine.

Easing out of the garage, he drove around the driveway, pulling up in front of the house. He left the engine running while he jumped out and opened her door.

His body stiffened with a jolt of electricity the moment her soft fingers gripped his hand as he boosted her into the passenger seat.

Back in the driver's seat, he peered at Tayla out of the corner of his eye. She stared toward the house and absently rubbed her thumb over her palm where their skin had touched.

Did she feel it, too?

Ask her to stay. No. He was at the bank about to climb out.

"You ready?" he asked in a thick voice.

"Yep." She peered at him with a half-smile.

And he fought the urge to cup her face and kiss the hell out of her.

Painful silence on his behalf, filled the drive to her cabin.

To distract himself and keep from going frickin' insane, he focused on anything other than her, the fading light, counting the limited number of cars they passed on the windy road, tracking the white lines along the center of the road.

Anything except the fact she sat next to him in the confined space of the Jeep, which felt as if it closed in by the minute, compressing around him while the pressure in the car sucked the air from his lungs.

The ache behind his ribs sharpened as they turned onto the gravel drive and rolled up to Tayla's cabin. He put the car in park and peered over at Tayla, who stared through the front windshield.

His thumb ached to trail the exposed vein in her neck and his lips burned for her taste…

No.

He pushed aside the thoughts for the millionth time and exited the car. He adjusted the front of his jeans and trudged around the rear of the Jeep to open her door.

She leaped down to stand in front of him.

"I can't thank you enough for finding me, Raven." She glanced up at him.

His pulse quickened at the sound of his name on her lips. *Touch her.*

He cleared his throat. "You're welcome."

Their gazes locked, and Tayla stared back through hooded lids. Sexual tension sparked between them, and his pulse sped at the same rapid pace as hers. A low growl rumbled in his chest when he caught her tongue slide over her lower lip. He wanted to moisten her lip, he wanted her to nibble his lip. No, bite.

His knees weakened, and he placed his palm on the warm hood of the jeep, a huge fucking mistake; fantasies instantly filled his mind…*gripping her slender hips as he lifted her onto the hood, nudging her close against his body. Cupping either side of her jaw, he'd tilt her head ever so slightly, to leisurely press his lips against hers in sweet slow kiss. She'd squeeze her legs around his waist, firmly press against his swollen shaft—*

Raven cleared his throat and shoved his hands into the pockets of his jeans so he wouldn't reach out to touch her.

Tayla blinked a moment before she pursed her lips.

And his heart sank.

"Thanks for the ride home." She exhaled a long breath and strode to the cabin.

He silently screamed for her to turn around, to come back to him, but each step she took toward the cabin was a step closer to the shore for him.

He had to let her go and return to protecting her from the shadows. It was the right thing to do.

If only my chest didn't feel as though a blunt blade sliced it open.

He forced his feet to remain cemented to the gravel driveway until Tayla locked herself safely inside.

He did it. He made it to the river bank and climbed out of the raging river to stand on solid ground.

At that moment, he released a deep shuddering breath before getting back in the Jeep.

Chapter 13

Tayla leaned against the inside of the front door, holding her breath until the roar of the engine and the tires crunching gravel disappeared into the distance. She exhaled and slid down the wooden door, landing on her butt with legs stretched out in front.

I can't breathe.

She sucked in shallow breaths and her heart hammered so hard her chest thumped with each beat. A far cry from her common panic episodes.

No, that titillating, gorgeous man she'd spent the last thirty minutes with was the cause of her inability to draw breath. He'd so effortlessly awakened parts of her body which lay dormant for so long. Never had such delicious desire flooded her thoughts…and body.

Tayla trailed her palm down the length of her neck, recalling Raven's hot breaths, his rough fingertips, his scorching kisses, and the ache between her legs intensified.

If the other guys hadn't interrupted them, she would have been helpless to deny Raven, even if he'd lifted her onto the table and had his way with her.

She sighed, lost in the delicious sensations roaming her body. If she responded like that to the touch of his fingertips on her neck, she could only imagine how good it'd be if his rough fingers caressed her breasts, pinched and rolled her nipples, or ventured south to explore between her legs.

It had been forever since she'd enjoyed the touch of a man, way too long, going by the ache in her core. Clearly. Her last relationship—if she could call it that—was far from the all-consuming passion she craved, the touch of excitement with a little danger. Thinking back, she could sum up her experience with sex in one word, meh. Never once had she felt a life-altering connection, a toe-curling kiss, a mind-blowing orgasm.

"Ugh. It's all their fault," she grumbled, recalling the soul-deep love her parents had shared for each other. Not to mention damn Jane Austen setting the soulmate love-standard unattainably high; no man could ever measure up to Mr. Darcy.

With the tingling in the pit of her stomach going nowhere, Tayla rose and headed to the kitchen in search of food. And by food, she meant wine. She filled a glass with a good chug of red and took a swig; delicious warmth spread through the inside of her chest as the wine traveled south. Glass in one hand and bottle in the other, she padded to the lounge to light a fire.

Damn it!

One measly log stared back at her from the wire basket beside the hearth.

She either needed to wander down to the main lodge and refill it or suffer through another freezing night.

Her shoulders sagged; no amount of wine could chase the coldness out of this cabin. She downed the rest of the glass before placing it on the table.

Cursing, she tossed the last log in the fireplace, snatched the empty wire basket in one hand and her coat in the other, and stormed out the front door.

She took off down the narrow gravel drive leading to the main lodge.

A beautiful array of reds, oranges and blues mixed together on the horizon, and the first stars appeared low in the clear sky; skies that beautiful during the day promised freezing nights and heavy frost, the kind that required scraping an inch of ice off the windshield of the car.

Soon, powdery white snow would replace the frost.

The crunch of gravel swapped for smooth bitumen as Tayla connected with the main driveway and Cedar Lodge came into view. The modern timber-clad two-story lodge curved around one side of a man made lake, several stacked stone chimneys stretched up the outside with lazy puffs of smoke drifting to the sky, and narrow floor-to-ceiling windows covered the entrance in front of a wide circular drive. To one side, a few cars scattered the parking area.

If only she'd chosen to stay on site in one of the luxury rooms, she wouldn't have to remember to stock pile wood. But that meant having to socialize every evening at dinner.

Tayla passed through the lofty foyer and waved at the lone receptionist, exited the glass sliding doors at the rear, and crossed to an open wood shed stacked high with logs. She nestled the wire basket atop a small metal wagon and tossed logs in the basket.

"Ouch," she grumbled, pinching the tip of a splinter before ripping it out. *First of many, no doubt.*

Her fingertips stung, and puffs of warm breath fogged in front of her face with each exhale.

Toughen up, princess.

Once the basket was full, she tilted it onto the wheels and lugged it behind her, back the way she came.

Did she have to stay in a cabin at the rear of the estate? The one farthest up the mountain?

She grunted as the stupid wheels jammed on another large piece of gravel. She tugged it to jump the wheels over the stones.

"Need some help there, love?"

Tayla jolted at the male voice behind her. Halting the wagon—not that it was going anywhere—she glanced over her shoulder and spotted a guy strolling toward her.

A prickling sensation sprung over her nape.

"No thanks, I've got it." She gripped the handle and gave the wagon another kick and heaved it behind her.

"Women of this era," the guy scoffed. "Always needing to prove they can do it on their own."

"Well, we can," she countered without turning her head.

Most of the time. When it didn't involve lugging a wagon packed with logs up a steep gravel driveway.

Next time bring the car.

The wagon caught on a large rock for the millionth time and she gave it a yank—

It flipped onto its side, spilling the logs over the gravel.

"Far out." She grunted.

The guy, now only a few steps behind, stood watching with a stupid smirk on his face.

Tayla righted the wagon and gathered the wood. She had half a mind to stomp right over to him and slap that smug grin off his face. *Ugh!*

Full once more, Tayla gave the wagon a softer, more controlled tug and recommenced her slow trudge up the drive. She glared over her shoulder to the guy as if to say, "See! I can do it on my own."

The guy smirked again and resumed his casual stroll, his long strides quickly catching up to her.

The damn wheels caught on another rock and she dared a glance across her shoulder at him. He raised his brows with a look that shouted, "Sure you don't need my help?"

Ugh! She would not give in.

Her shoulder began to burn so she swapped arms and kept going. Kind of. More struggling than going.

The wheels jammed in a pothole and jerked to a halt. *Again*. But this time, Tayla joined it. Her breaths heaved in and out and she wiped her sweaty palm along the front of her jeans.

She peered over her shoulder toward the lodge. She'd made it about halfway, maybe a little more, but still a heck of a ways to go. Uphill.

She sighed to herself and...conceded? Gave in? Fed the guy's ego? *Whatever*.

She peered over at him, now standing a few steps to her side. "Okay, you win. Can you help?"

He cocked an eyebrow. "Only if you ask nicely, love."

What? *Argh!*

She glanced up the never-ending drive to her cabin, *still* nowhere in sight. She could do it if she had to. Really, she could. But did she want to?

Through gritted teeth, she mumbled, "Please. Will you please help with the wood?"

"Why, of course, it would be my pleasure." He extended his arm in a regal bow.

A flicker of recognition whispered in the corner of her mind. Had she met this guy before?

Tayla stepped aside as he pushed in the extendible handle, picked up the entire wagon, and strolled up the drive.

She rolled her eyes. No need to flaunt his strength. He probably expected her to put on some lip gloss and giggle along behind him like a helpless woman.

Yeah, so not happening. Instead, she picked up her pace to catch up.

"Told you we'd meet again." He glanced over his shoulder and…winked.

Jeez. Cocky much?

Her mind raced to place him. She closely examined his features as he casually strolled beside her. He nailed the bad boy demeanor with black ripped jeans and black leather jacket, a dark hoodie poking out the top. But his styled black hair and dark stubble gave mixed messages of being well groomed yet rugged, gentle yet dangerous. And his accent? She could never distinguish between those British accents, so who knew which part of Britain he came from?

Where have I seen him before?

"Are you staying here at the lodge?"

She hardly interacted with other guests, preferring solitude, but this guy didn't strike her as the type to stay here. No, he probably lived in an ancient Gothic castle complete with spooky mist drifting across the driveway and gargoyles guarding the front.

Maybe he's a vampire? She smirked to herself.

Bad Boy abruptly halted and turned to face her. His

smoky black eyes stared straight into hers like he tried to peer into her soul or read her mind or something.

Yep, totally a vampire.

She swallowed the lump forming in her throat.

"Well, that's a bit of a buzzkill." He half shrugged and continued strolling, still carrying the wagon load of wood like it was a basket of feathers.

Tayla maintained her pace alongside him, her mind raced to process what was going on. A buzzkill?

"So, you're staying here?" She pressed.

"Nope."

Okaaaay, not helpful.

The two of them continued along the remaining length of the drive, the crunching gravel echoing in the silence. Tayla rubbed her palms up and down her arms as the last rays of light sank behind the mountains.

Arriving at her cabin, Bad Boy stepped onto the veranda and eased the wagon down beside her front door.

Did his arms ache after that lengthy display of masculinity? *As if he'd admit it anyway.* Maybe lugging random people's wood was how he maintained his wide chest and broad shoulders.

"Sorry, I can't seem to place where we've met." She desperately tried to solve the puzzle.

He turned to face her, and the prickle at her nape sharpened.

His jaw clenched, and red flames flashed across his pupils, so quickly she could have imagined it. Raw power rolled off him in waves, and she retreated a step. Suddenly, she got the sense Bad Boy was *Evil Guy* who could snap her in two without breaking a sweat, and give her a wicked smile while doing it.

And I just led him to my home…

A split second later, Bad Boy's evil demeanor vanished, replaced with the same cocky expression he'd worn since the beginning of the drive.

"That's a tad unfair, love. It would be loads more fun if you remembered. Why don't you ask your Guardian Raven where we met? And while you're at it, ask him why you don't remember." He winked at her.

Again!

Hang on…Raven? What did Raven have to do with her not remembering Bad Boy? She'd only just met them both today. Well, she met Raven yesterday, if him rescuing her counted. And what did he mean by Guardian?

She pinched her forehead as a headache threatened to rise.

"You know Raven?" she asked.

"Oh," he snickered, in an evil-raise-the-hairs-on-your-neck kind of way. "We go way back."

Still not helpful.

He took a menacing step toward her, but she stood her ground. Her heart thumped against her ribs and she held her breath.

He leaned down and whispered in her ear, "You need help carrying that inside, love?"

Tayla jerked her chin up and squared her shoulders. "Nope, I'm good."

He straightened, curving his lips in a devilish grin. "Of course, you are."

He brushed past her and leaped off the veranda, missing all three steps. "Be sure to tell him Blaine said hi," he called out as he casually strolled down the driveway, back the way they'd come.

What. The. Heck?

She stood frozen on the veranda, staring along the driveway until Bad Boy—Blaine—disappeared around the bend.

What a crazy twenty-four hours.

Chapter 14

Three agonizing days had passed since he'd touched her soft, delicate skin and Raven's body still thrummed with energy.

He did his best to distract himself, mind and body, but rapidly lost the battle. He yearned to trail his fingers along her delicate neck, trace his tongue over her swollen breasts down to the sweet spot between her legs. The constant throbbing in his groin was a painful reminder of the line he'd crossed and yet another rule he'd broken.

Fuck.

Raven slammed his fist into the wall of the study, and the plaster cracked and crumbled to the floor. Blood seeped from the tear in his knuckles before the skin around the wound began to tingle and heal.

What the hell was he going to do? He didn't trust himself to see her. He'd tasked EJ with dropping off the clothes she'd left at the mansion. If he'd gone there, his sliver of self-control would've vaporized the second she opened the door. He would've stepped inside and taken her mouth in a hot desperate kiss, pressed her up against the wall and wrapped her legs around his waist...

Where the bloody hell is this coming from?

Raven braced his palms on the mahogany side

table and gazed out the window for a new distraction. Curled brown leaves piled up beneath the trees, a few stragglers lifting into the air and tumbling over the manicured lawn.

He imagined the satisfying crunch as he trampled the shriveled leaves. Nothing was more enchanting than witnessing nature batten down the hatches and prepare for winter's arrival, only to be reborn full of vibrant life once more in spring.

No, again Tayla won. Heaviness lifted from his chest as he slipped into a daydream of Tayla lying under the bare branches, her hazel eyes sparkling as the crunchy leaves swirled around them, giggling when he plucked stray leaves caught in her silky chestnut hair.

Goddamn it.

His concentration level, on anything other than her, had disappeared out the frickin' window, along with his appetite. And sleep. Only a matter of time until Ellen called an intervention and forced him to plant his ass at the table, refusing to let him leave until his plate was empty.

Raven turned his attention to a clearing at the far side of the grounds, where a shirtless Aric swung the axe over his shoulder before using it to annihilate a helpless piece of wood. Headphones in his ears, the glaring sun glistened against his glossy black wings extended in a wide arch behind him. The intricate willow tree tattoo on his bicep came to life with each flex of his arms as though the branches swayed in a gust of wind.

Aric slammed the axe down and split a log in half in one smooth motion. He threw the wood into a waiting wheelbarrow and grabbed the next victim.

Chop and repeat.

Heaviness returned to Raven's chest. Exactly how long would Aric punish himself? He and his brothers had made the same choice that day, yet each one of them had been unprepared for the consequences. The gravity of their decision—agreement to Fate's twisted deal—sank in after Gabe misted them to the mortal realm and none of them were able to mist back.

Raven's heart ached, recalling the price Aric paid, what he had walked away from. For *him*.

An eternity wouldn't be enough time to repay him.

Raven crossed back to the table and shut down the laptop. Avoidance was best when it came to technology. He snatched his glass of bourbon and knocked back the remainder in one gulp, not that it helped take the edge off, and slid the empty glass into the center of the table before he strode out of the study.

He followed the laughter echoing along the hallway all the way to the open double doors to the entertainment room. He braced his palm against the door frame and spotted EJ lying on the three-seater leather couch, silver laptop open and nestled in his lap.

EJ nodded at Raven. "Hey, Rave. Did you know there's a dedicated social media page for those who fucking hate coriander?"

Raven chuckled. God, EJ came out with some weird shit. "Sure you didn't create it?"

"Nup. Can't take credit, but I'd sure love to meet the mortal who did. Thank them for their contribution to humanity. Now, if only they'd rid Earth of that poor excuse for an herb, the world would be a better— Run! Run!" EJ shouted at the TV hung on the wall to his right. Raven peered over in time to see some guy slide on the dirt feet first toward a white square.

EJ fist pumped the air. "Yes!"

He reached over and swiped a glass from the coffee table. Ice clinked as he took a swig, somehow managing not to swallow the ridiculous amount of limes and other green bits floating in the glass.

Raven rolled his eyes. *It's meant to be a drink not a frickin' salad.*

"You wanna drink, Rave?"

Raven shook his head. "Nah, just came by to…"

"What?" EJ waved his arm at the TV. "How'd you bloody miss that? C'mon!" Attention back on Raven, EJ sat up and placed the laptop on the coffee table. "Sorry, Rave, what'd you say?"

"S'all good. I'll catch you later."

Raven rapped his knuckles on the door as EJ leaped off the lounge, shouting profanities at the TV.

Why did it suddenly feel like there was a gaping cavity the size of the Grand Canyon between him and his brothers? Instead of protecting them, all he'd managed to do was drive a wedge between the three of them. And he had no clue how to fix it.

Raven slammed open the door to his room and ripped off his clothes on the way to the bathroom. Avoiding the big-ass mirror, he stalked into the double shower recess and flipped on both taps. His chest and back took the brunt of the icy jets before it gradually warmed.

Planting himself in the center, he twisted his body and unfurled his wings, stretched them wide from one shower head to the other. The steamy water cascaded along his feathers, falling from the tips like a gushing waterfall, vibrating through his body and lightening the tension in his tight shoulders.

Snatching the soap off the shelf, he worked a lather between his palms and washed every inch of his exhausted body like some kind of cleansing ritual. Like it would magically rid him of the forbidden thoughts of Tayla currently taking up residence in his head. He gritted his teeth and focused on the mundane task of washing.

Scrub.

Rinse.

Repeat.

Shower done, Raven flicked off the water and stepped free of the recess. Steam rose from his arms as he snatched a towel and wrapped it around his waist. He caught his reflection out of the corner of his eye and froze. His heart hammered against his chest and he inched closer to the mirror until he stood directly before it. He held his breath. He arched his right wing, silently praying they were gone…

Nope.

The handful of crimson feathers, tucked close to his torso, stood out like fresh blood splattered over glossy white tiles. Like his own fucking murder scene where the blown apart victim's head had sprayed bits of brain, bone, and blood across the wall. Only his wings were the wall and his failure to protect his family was the splattered pieces.

He clenched his jaw and leaned closer.

Goddamn it. There were more.

What the hell was he doing wrong? Deep down, he knew the answer so he shouldn't keep torturing himself with the same stupid question.

Again, he considered giving in. Being a Fallen

would be a helluva lot easier than this self-inflicted torture.

It'd be the safer option for his brothers and Ellen.

It'd be the safer option for Tayla.

The line between light and dark began to blur. Lately, he'd doubted how protecting fragile mortals fit into Fate's grand plan for this realm. He doubted there even *was* a grand plan. Knowing his luck, Fate had him running around for her own personal shits and giggles.

He rubbed at the ache in his chest, recalling everything he'd given up, thrown away. After centuries in the mortal world, all he had was the fact he still drew breath.

And now insert...Tayla.

He peered back at his reflection. Dark circles hung under his eyes like droopy wet tea bags. Had Fate sent Tayla so she could watch him plummet over the edge and into the darkness?

He glared at the ceiling. Bet she was having a good ol' laugh now.

Bitch.

Raven threw the towel at his mirrored self. The collision seriously lacked the destruction he desperately craved. He stormed into the bedroom to find Gabe kicking back in the armchair in the far corner, steepling his fingers under his chin.

"Damn it, Gabe, couldn't give me some warning?" He stormed past Gabe and snatched a pair of black jeans and a black collared shirt from the closet.

"You have some serious conflict going on there, my friend."

"Yeah, well, welcome to the mortal world," he snapped.

Raven rolled up the sleeves of his button-down and stood in the doorway facing Gabe. Today's suit was likely by some fancy Italian designer; all black, even down to the silk dress shirt underneath and glossy pocket square.

Raven cocked an eyebrow. "What, no tie today?"

The corner of Gabe's mouth lifted slightly, but he didn't react.

"What's the deal, Gabe? Why am I the only one assigned a Chosen? After centuries of Fate completely fucking forsaking us, why the hell now?" He was in the mood for a good showdown, not that Gabe would engage.

He never did. Might mess up his fucking suit.

"Fate assigns her Chosen when the time is right."

Raven's voice deepened. "What's her endgame? 'Cause we're all getting a little fed up being her puppets down here. Does she still have a plan for this world?"

Probably wasn't a wise move to vocalize the fact he doubted a plan existed.

Gabe studied him closely, dark eyes boring into Raven's similarly dark soul. "We are all part of her plan, Raven. Fate ensures the scales continue to balance in our favor. Her greater plan for this realm will reveal itself in time."

Blood filled Raven's mouth as he clamped his teeth on the inside of his cheek. He needed to get the hell out of there before he said something he'd later regret.

Again.

"So you keep saying," he sneered. He snatched his jacket off the bed and stormed toward the door.

"You must listen to your instincts, my friend. Fate will guide you down the correct path." Raven halted.

Enough with the cryptic bullshit. For once, he wanted a straight answer. Fuck Fate and her so-called correct path.

He ached to scream exactly that to Gabe but instead, he held his tongue. He ripped open the bedroom door.

Stop fighting your path, my friend, Gabe whispered in his mind.

"Get outta my fucking head, Gabe," he roared back as he stormed out, slamming the door behind him so hard the edges splintered from the impact.

Following his pointless chat with Gabe, Raven stomped downstairs. He told EJ he needed some fresh air and quickly declined EJ's offer to come with. He didn't need hand-holding; plus, he didn't even know where he was heading. All he knew for sure was he had to put some distance between him and Tayla.

Listen to your instincts. What the hell did that mean?

If he relied solely on his Guardian instincts, his tether connecting him to Tayla, he'd be free to stand back, to put distance between the two of them before he did something stupid that got them all in shit. Maybe that was what Gabe meant.

Except that reasoning lasted about three fucking minutes.

Resisting the pull to her, he jumped in his Jeep, tearing out of the garage and heading in the opposite direction. Destination unknown.

He drove along the narrow windy roads ascending the side of the mountain, the sinking sun cast long dark shadows across the deserted road. He focused on the feel of the car beneath him, the roar of the engine, leaned in and out of every curve, left and right, every acceleration and brake, the smooth shift of each gear change.

That should have been enough.

But two hours later, a journey across the top of the mountain to the farthest ski field not yet open for business, and back down the other side, he unconsciously—yeah right, who was he trying to kid—made his way here.

And now, he found himself perched on a hard, numb-your-ass log guard rail, lining the edge of the forest around Tayla's cabin. Waiting for her to come home, like a fucking lost puppy.

Even the wind emphasized how pathetic he was, laughing at him as it howled through the towering trees.

Tilting his head back, he peered at the clouds slowly building above as they thickened and expanded, becoming darker and more ominous. A large icy drop smacked his face and the cold blast briefly numbed his skin, as though upstairs warned of the dangers to come.

He didn't listen. *Again.*

He rejoiced in mortal moments like these. How the warm sun restored his ancient body, the freezing snow briefly numbed his fingertips, the frigid wind burned his nostrils on each inhale—

Raven sensed Tayla a moment before her car rounded the driveway, the tires crunching on the gravel. His stupid heart fluttered and his pulse quickened as the car came to a halt in front of him and Tayla stepped out.

He rose, blood returning to his numb ass and stepped forward, shoving his hands in his pockets as a reminder her body was out of bounds.

Tayla waved and slung a gym bag over her

shoulder. He greedily drank in her curves as she strolled to where his feet refused to budge. A pair of black and orange patterned tights clung to her slender legs, curving around her hips. Shame she had the grey hoodie zipped all the way up to the collar as if determined not to let any warmth escape. He wouldn't mind slowly unzipping it with his teeth—

"Hi." She smiled, halting an arm's length in front of him.

He cleared his throat. "Hey."

"Thanks for dropping my things off the other day."

"No worries." *God, get yourself together, man.*

Thunder rumbled in the distance a split second before a heavy drop splashed against the gravel at his feet.

He briefly glared at the gloomy sky. God, those bloody angels wouldn't give him a break. Surely they had more important tasks.

Tayla wrapped her arms across the front of her body and rubbed her palms up and down.

Like all angels, he didn't feel the cold; even if he did, he doubted he would in her presence. His blood pumped so goddamn hot he should be more concerned with overheating. But for the second time in his entire existence, goosebumps exploded over his arms, timed perfectly with Tayla's shivers.

He frowned at his open palms when his fingers stung as though hundreds of tiny needles pricked their tips. Tayla blew into her cupped hands before vigorously rubbing them together in front of her face.

What the hell was going on? It was as if...no, it couldn't be. Could it? He recalled the last time his body suffered a dramatic drop in temperature—the time when Tayla had been freezing in the forest.

Was it even possible for their bodies to be in sync? He'd never experienced it or heard of it happening between a Guardian and Chosen before.

He was no stranger to the invisible thread binding a Guardian and their assigned Chosen together; the one-sided gravitational pull like a tiny dark moon orbiting a planet full of human life, whose sole duty was to collide with stray meteors threatening the planet's existence. Only with Tayla, the thread was more powerful, more intense, like she was not an Earth-sized planet but rather an enormous, blazing sun, and he was helplessly being drawn into her solar system.

Right now, that fiery sun was slightly pale with pink cheeks and lips a dark shade of purple.

"S-so," Tayla stuttered, interrupting his thoughts. "You wanna come inside before it rains or are we going to keep standing out here in the freezing wind?"

Yes. No, not a good idea.

But, he didn't want to leave.

She blew into her cupped hands again and made the decision for him. "Just come in already." The words barely left her mouth before she raced up the steps to the protection of the covered veranda.

When he turned to follow, the clouds opened up and dumped their icy payload right on his frickin' head.

"Give me a fucking break," he muttered under his breath as he trudged to the veranda.

Tayla bobbed on the spot, fumbling with a jingling set of keys. Her shaky hand struggling to insert the key into the lock.

Raven stepped up beside her. "Here, let me do it."

He gripped the keys in her cold hands. A blast of

heat scorched his fingers as they connected. Tayla gasped, but didn't pull away.

Helpless to resist, his thumb traced light circles over the back of her palm. Waves of warmth flowed along his skin, traveled up from his palms, and chased away the numbness in his fingers.

Gradually, her shivering ebbed. She lifted her gaze to meet his. Bright hazel eyes darkened, building with desire with each stroke of his thumb.

In the far corner of his mind, he faintly registered a warning.

He ignored it. *Obviously*. Sent that thought packing, never to return.

His racing heart pounded in his chest so hard it could have leaped out his skin and fallen flat on the wooden deck. He hardened behind the scratchy zipper of his jeans, lengthening toward the waistband. Her desire oozed into him through their connected hands as though it were an IV bag slowly dripping life into his veins.

He inhaled deeply, and her spring-rain scent filled his nostrils—

Stop.

Something registered in the far part of his mind. This time he listened.

He jerked his hand from hers and mentally threw a bucket of freezing ice cubes over his head.

He was supposed to keep his distance, not mentally strip off her many layers of clothing while they stood on the veranda.

Clearing his throat, he leaned in front of Tayla, unlocked the door, and motioned for her to enter first. She did.

He released a long breath and…followed her in.

Bad. Fucking. Idea.

Raven softly closed the door behind him, but remained stationary on the entrance mat, not knowing what to do next.

Tayla flipped off her runners and dropped them in a wicker basket before shuffling to a narrow built-in cupboard at the foot of the stairs—he tried to not stare at her ass, he really did.

A plush towel smacked him in the face and landed at his feet.

Should've been paying attention.

"I'm gonna take a quick shower to warm up. Make yourself at home," she called over her shoulder as she raced up the stairs to the loft.

Again, with the ass staring.

He should join her. Strip off his damp clothes and storm into the steamy shower; show her how talented he could be at warming her up.

But did she want him to? Or was that his wishful thinking?

Raven squeezed his forehead. So much for keeping his distance.

The water came on upstairs. To keep himself distracted—rather than imagining the shower trickling over her perfect breasts—he put the towel at his feet to good use, drying his clothes.

Raven hung his wet leather jacket on the door handle, water dripped from the hem onto the mat. He added his shoes to the wicker basket before ruffling the towel through his unruly hair.

He slung the used towel over the balustrade and considered, for the tenth time, ascending the stairs. No.

He couldn't risk venturing on that rickety suspension bridge again. He'd only just managed to pull himself from the raging current last time.

Instead, he'd hang out on the torturous shore line and dream of the glorious world on the other side, out of his reach.

Raven turned and headed to the stacked stone fireplace. He crouched down and piled a few logs on the dying embers.

The shower turned off upstairs and a few minutes later, Tayla descended the stairs in a pair of sweatpants and navy hoodie with some logo across the front.

She looks sexy even in those.

Once again, her movements mesmerized him; the delicate sway of her hips, how her hand lightly brushed along the wall as she swung around the corner into the kitchen.

"You want a drink?" she called out.

Man, did he want bourbon, but smarter to keep a clear head. "No, thanks."

He planted his ass on the couch directly in front of the fire and stared at the crackling logs.

Tayla joined him, facing him with one leg curled under the other and a mug cradled between her hands. Having her sit beside him, in close proximity, only heightened the twitch he had to touch her, kiss her. He needed to summon better control or the night wouldn't stop there.

She gently blew over the rim. "I didn't know if I'd see you again."

Raven angled his body to face her, resting his right arm along the back of the couch. "Why would you think that?" *Did she miss me?*

"We didn't exactly make plans."

He couldn't stop his left hand from brushing her bent knee, trailing lightly along her thigh. "How could I *not* see you again?"

She smiled shyly, and his stupid heart skipped a beat.

Subtle crackling of logs on the fire filled the comfortable silence between them, and he admired the flickering light in her chestnut hair as she lazily sipped the contents of her mug. His fingers continued to lightly stroke her leg back and forth in a slow, delicate motion, and he didn't miss the hitch in her breath each time he ventured a little further upward.

He could do this all fucking day.

"Oh, I almost forgot." Tayla jerked back, and the contents of her mug spilled down the front of her hoodie. "Crap."

He was beside her in an instant. "You all right?" He took the cup from her hands and placed it on a table beside them.

"Yeah." Tayla laughed and she shook the bottom of her top. "I'm such a klutz."

He clasped her hands and turned them back and forth, inspecting both sides. "Did you burn yourself?"

Her gaze lifted and locked with his. "No, I'm fine."

Tayla's breaths became heavier. Without breaking eye contact, he slowly lifted her hands and pressed his lips against each palm, lingering for the briefest moment.

His willpower dwindled away when he heard a moan escape her breath.

Still holding her hands, he leaned in and hovered inches from her mouth. "It spilled all down your top."

She drew in her lower lip. "I should go change."

He leaned closer. "Need help?"

Her lips parted.

Letting go of her hands, he smoothed his palms along her outer thighs until he reached her hips. When he slid her toward him, she squealed and jumped off the couch.

"Oh no, it's all over the couch too," she gasped.

He chuckled at the decent sized wet patch on the leather where she'd been sitting.

He rose. "Why don't I clean this up while you go change? That wet top is becoming distracting."

She smirked. "How distracting?"

"You have no idea." He shooed her away. "Off you go, I've got this."

Tayla paused for a moment with a sexy grin on her face before she darted upstairs.

He wandered into the kitchen in search of a paper towel, which he found on the bench and returned to the couch and patted down the wet patch.

God, talk about mood kill. Just as well, anything to keep his thoughts from wandering into forbidden territory again. He well and truly sucked at keeping his hands to himself around her.

"What I was trying to say before I stupidly spilled my tea…" Tayla called out from the loft. "Was I met a friend of yours the other day."

That was strange, he didn't have friends. He dumped the sodden paper in the trash and returned to stoke the fire.

He glanced over his shoulder as Tayla descended the stairs with a replacement hoodie.

"I can't remember his name," she muttered.

"Blake? No…"

Raven's jaw tightened. He clenched the fire stoker in his hand so tightly, warm trickles of blood seeped from the indentation of his nails.

No fucking way.

Tayla rounded the couch to face him and her eyes widened. "What's wrong?"

He jammed the fire stoker back in the metal holder. "Who was it?" he growled.

She frowned. "I can't remember his name. Why?"

"Tell me what he looked like."

"I dunno…tall, black hair, freakishly strong. Pretty darn full of himself to be honest."

If that sonofabitch so much as laid a finger on her, he would rip him to shreds with his bare hands.

"Um, Raven, your eyes—"

"Blaine?" he spat. "Was his name Blaine?"

Tayla's face lit up. "Yeah. That's it. Anyway, he said to say hi."

Raven shoved his fingers through his now dry hair and paced the suddenly too small room. His clothes itched against his skin like made of synthetic shit and about to burst into flames from the heat of his boiling veins.

"Was he here?" he snapped.

"Yeah. Well, kind of. He helped me with a wagon full of wood from the main lodge. And by help, I mean, carried it the whole way in his arms like channeling Hercules or something," she chuckled.

He stopped burning a track on the wooden floor and stood before Tayla. A spooked look passed over her face, but she quickly recovered.

"How do you know him?" she asked.

How the hell do I answer that? "We have history," he grumbled.

"Yeah, that's what he said." Her shoulders drooped.

The last thing he needed was to try to explain exactly how he and Blaine…

"You know, he said something strange I just can't figure out." Tayla lifted her chin and met his gaze. "He said he and I had met before, but I can't seem to remember when, or where for that matter. He said to ask you about it. About why I can't remember."

Raven's heart sank all the way to his feet, smashed through the rough wooden slats, through the hard earth below and into the fiery pits of hell.

Skidded to a halt alongside his brother's.

The room swayed, and his stomach lurched.

He rubbed the base of his neck with a hot clammy palm. He'd never regretted wiping a mortal's memory as much as he did right now. But he'd had no choice. Keeping their existence hidden was necessary, and he had to follow the rules. No way would he allow his brothers to suffer again as a result of his decisions.

Fucking Blaine. He must've peered into Tayla's mind and figured out what Raven did. Set him up to fall.

Raven rubbed the sharp pain in the center of his chest. "Maybe he mistook you for someone else." Where had all the oxygen gone?

"No, I don't think so. He acted as though he knew exactly who I was."

And back to wearing a track in the floor boards. What was he supposed to say? *You have met him, I just wiped your memory of that night.*

He needed to get the hell out of there before the

walls caved in around him, pressed his body from all directions, and squeezed the remaining air from his lungs.

"What aren't you telling me?" Tayla whispered.

He froze. This wasn't what he had in mind when he stepped inside the cabin. Far from it.

He turned to face her. "What do you want me to say?"

"The truth." Her eyebrows bunched together. "I know it sounds weird...but I feel like there's some kind of connection between us. Something I can't explain. For some strange reason, I feel as though our paths were meant to cross." Tayla stepped in front of him. "All I'm asking for is the truth."

Goddamn it. Tayla had no idea how right she was. There was a connection between the two of them, and Fate had made damn sure their paths crossed, back at that university courtyard just over six months ago. But no way would he reveal that.

"I can't," he choked.

How had he let things get so out of control? *This is what happens when you get too close.*

Tayla inched closer. Close enough he caught the golden specks in her irises, the pale freckles across the bridge of her nose. He wanted to step back, keep the distance. He'd have more control that way. But his feet refused to budge.

"Can't or won't?" She reached out her hand.

He battled against his feet, begged them to retreat a step, but they remained cemented to the floor.

If she touches you, all control will be lost...

He watched intently as her shaky hand reached his upper arm and lightly touched his shirt. Heat scorched through the cotton to his skin underneath. Warm tingling sensations traveled through his veins, and his mind balanced on a tightrope, using every ounce of control not to fall.

Back on the fucking suspension bridge…

Step forward, kiss her…Step back, snap the hell out of it.

"Raven, tell me what's going on. *Please.*"

Please.

One single word. One single touch. That was all it took for his control to come crashing down like a building demolished in a single explosion.

"Last week," he murmured.

Tayla dropped her arm. The loss of contact snapped him awake like heavy curtains ripped open to blinding sunlight.

He retreated a step, but too late. The words had already fallen from his mouth.

What the hell have I done?

Tayla frowned. "Last week? What happened last week?"

His throat tightened, his mind raced to come up with something that wasn't the truth…but given he couldn't speak a lie he had limited options.

"Raven?"

He had only one way out of this, and if he had any remaining shred of decency he'd take it and cough up the truth. *Kind of.*

"You saw him last week," he sighed. Breathe in…and out. "You saw both of us last week."

Later, Raven would recall his choice to walk into the cabin; the catalyst that spun his world upside down and ripped apart life as he knew it.

Chapter 15

What?

Tayla scrambled for a memory. A snippet. Anything. But came up empty. If she'd met Raven and this Blaine guy before then she didn't remember.

"Why don't I remember?" she demanded, her voice elevated along with her pulse.

As if she could forget meeting him.

Instead of answering, Raven shoved his hands in the pockets of his black jeans, shifting his weight between his feet.

"Raven?"

"I…" His deep blue eyes darkened, swirling with clouds of black. "Maybe you forgot."

Forgot? "You're kidding, right?" she snapped. "I'm pretty sure I'd remember. Unless, you drugged me or something?"

She was joking. Kind of.

Hang on, could he have drugged her?

Her chest tightened, denying the inhale of oxygen while she waited for his answer.

Raven lowered his head and stared at the floor beneath his bare feet. His jaw clicked several times like he clenched his molars together so hard they were about to pop out the sides.

His expression remained tight. No smirk. No

laughter at her outrageous accusation.

No denying it, either.

Oh my god. She staggered back. "You drugged me?"

Another step back.

He lifted his head. His eyes darkened further, all traces of the deep blue replaced with black likening the deepest depths of the ocean. Hands still squeezed into his pockets, he stepped toward her.

She matched his step with one of her own...backward.

He sighed heavily. "Tayla, I didn't drug you. I..."

How could I have been so stupid? She'd let her growing attraction to him cloud her judgement, her fantasy of the knight-in-shining-armor who rescued her from the forest. Just because he caused her belly to clench and desire to burn through her veins, didn't mean he was one of the good guys. She didn't know this man, he could be anyone, she'd only met him mere days ago.

Or so she thought.

He's in my home.

Her gaze darted to the front door. Self-defense rule three? Or four? *Whatever*—always be closest to the exit.

Tayla sidestepped to her left, narrowing the distance between her and the front door. *Check.*

Raven's stormy gaze tracked her movement. Did he know what she was doing? Was he going to try to stop her?

How could she have been so stupid? *Again?* Lead a strange man to her doorstep and, days later, let another waltz inside?

"Tayla." His breath hitched as if trying not to spook her.

She mentally cursed herself for softening at the mere whisper of her name. *Pull yourself together. Focus!*

Tayla lifted her chin and squared her shoulders. "I want to know what's going on. Now."

Raven took that as an invitation to sneak a step closer to her.

Nope, not happening. She was onto him. "Stay where you are." She raised her palm to him.

He stopped, raising his hands in surrender.

"I can't tell you how sorry I am," he choked. Hands shoved back in his pockets.

"Sorry for what? Tell me what you did."

She sensed the moment she'd pushed too hard, the moment his wall shot up. His eyes swirled back to their usual deep blue color as he glanced at the door and back at her.

His hands slid out of his pockets.

"I think I should go," he said with a voice as emotionless as his expression.

"Fine. Go then," she snapped.

Backing to the door, she ripped it open and stood to the side for him to exit. She stared outside even though the landscape didn't register. Anything to avoid looking at him.

She stiffened as he strode to the door and snatched his shoes from the basket. She held out his jacket with a trembling hand; his earthy, pine scent drifted from the leather, weakening her restraint.

Raven's massive body towered in front of her, way too close, and she made the mistake of making eye contact. She needed him to leave before she reached up and brushed her fingers along his strong jaw. Then, it would all be over. Heat simmered beneath the surface of her skin, traveling downward.

Great. That was all she needed.

Focus, Tayla.

Raven tilted his head slightly and his lips parted as though about to speak.

Let him go, Tayla, he's lying to you.

She broke the burning connection and turned her head away, focusing on the rain water pouring from the overflowing gutters. But she didn't miss his shoulders drop as he accepted his jacket and stepped out.

As soon as he cleared the threshold, she slammed the door shut and leaned against it.

For the second time this week, she sank to the floor.

Only this time it felt so very different.

Chapter 16

Raven stomped through the dense forest, ramming his muddy shoes down on defenseless twigs, the satisfying snap echoing through the trees.

What have I done? Screamed over and over in his head.

Spinning left, he slammed his fist into the trunk of an ancient gum and a wicked snarl curved his lips. Blood burst from his knuckles and sharp pain shot up his forearm.

"Fuck!" he roared.

He smashed the trunk again. The skin ripped open, bone and tendons staring back from the deep gashes.

Red and black spots flickered on the trunk before him.

He bashed again and again, like the punching bag hanging in the gym. Over and over again. Harder and harder.

The tree creaked in protest, bark and wooden splinters exploded to the sides, scattering over the muddy ground. His blood splattered the wide trunk. Bones crunched in his long fingers, and tiny splinters stuck out of the ruptured skin like hundreds of toothpicks. Repeatedly, he slammed his fists until finally his hands surrendered, falling limp as blood poured from the gaping wounds.

He clenched his jaw, remembering his cursed existence. Too soon his bones would fuse, tendons rejoin, skin stitch itself back together.

And when that happened, the crippling agony in his chest would return.

Raven sank to his knees. Tilting his head back, he glared up at the stormy night through the thick canopy of the trees.

If only the punishment would end.

Icy rain pelted his face, stinging his eyes. The downpour washed away the bark and blood like a miniature flash flood. His legs formed a trench where they sank into the mud, transforming his black jeans to a filthy brown.

Fire ignited in his torn hands as the bones fused back together. His skin itched as it stretched and tightened, seamlessly closing the wounds as if they'd never existed.

What he'd give to be mortal. *Just another reason I can't be with her.* After Tayla completed her path, she would die and leave him behind, waltz on through those pretentious gates to the other side, where they could be together…if he ever returned.

But he wouldn't return.

Fate had stripped that privilege away from him. Sent him to bring back a godforsaken fallen Guardian who didn't want saving in the first place. Raven cradled his head in his hands, the memory of that horrific decision centuries ago springing forth as if it was only yesterday…

Raven charged into Fate's sanctuary, slamming open the white-paneled double doors.

"Fate! Where the hell are you?"

He stomped over the pristine white floor. Wishing like hell he trampled in mud before arriving. God, what he'd give to smash each and every perfectly cut diamond embedded in the tiles to pieces with a sledgehammer, then hurl it through those towering stained-glass windows.

He marched around the base of a crystal fountain, its jeweled tiers stretched up to the glass dome ceiling. The echo of slow trickling water pounded in the back of his skull, as though someone tapped a pencil on a desk. Right next to his bloody ear.

"Fate!" he screamed, again and again until his throat burned like fire.

A bottomless dark abyss ripped open in the center of Raven's chest and his legs collapsed.

Gabe materialized and crouched beside him, gently placing his palm on Raven's shoulder. "Let him go, Raven, I beg of you. Let him go."

Raven shook his head. How can I let him go?

He gagged as the sickly-sweet stench of cherry blossoms filled the air a moment before Fate entered through a hidden door. Her silky gold summer dress swayed in the gentle breeze as she casually approached, not a care in the universe.

"Raven," she greeted him.

Her soft angelic voice was out of place in his crumbling nightmare.

He glanced up at her crystal-clear blue eyes, sparkling like the water trickling in that stupid fountain.

How dare she look as though nothing had happened.

"Bring him back." He begged her. "He didn't mean what he said."

"Blaine has chosen this path, Raven. I cannot bring him back."

"What?" He rose to his feet and scowled down at her. *"How could you do this? How could you just let him go? This is all your fault. All he ever wanted—"*

"Raven." Gabe's stern voice interrupted him.

He glared across his shoulder at Gabe, who slowly shook his head.

There will be consequences if you challenge her, my friend, *Gabe whispered in his mind.*

He glanced back at the almighty Fate; Queen in the universe's game of chess. The most powerful piece on the board, capable of making any move in any direction to fulfil her objective.

Including luring vulnerable pieces into her trap.

And in that single moment, with the glint in her eye, he no longer felt like the Knight he was created to be, but rather a tiny defenseless pawn about to be crushed into a million pieces.

He staggered back.

"I will excuse your tone only once, Raven." She lifted her chin. *"As I said, I cannot influence his path. Only Blaine can choose to return."*

With the back of his hand, he swiped away the pathetic tears streaming down his face. His whole existence had crumbled to dust.

Gabe stepped forward. "We're sorry to intrude, Your Grace. I'll escort Raven ba—"

"What if I convince him to come back?" Raven blurted out.

Fate's eyes flickered silver, and she waved her hand for him to carry on.

"What if I go to the mortal realm and convince him

to return? Once I talk to him, he'll see his mistake and choose to come home. I can get through to him."

Out of the corner of his eye, he glimpsed Gabe lower his head and his shoulders slump.

Fate smirked.

Oh, shit.

"Very well," she announced. *"From this day forth, you will continue as a Guardian of the Chosen, permanently in the mortal realm, until your brother Blaine chooses to return to the Heavens."*

And in one swift move, Fate annihilated the pawn.

Raven lowered his hands and opened his eyes, returning to the present. He wiped at the soaked hair plastered across his forehead.

He'd let Fate trick him, and now he and his brothers would pay the price for eternity. His only consolation was he was still a Guardian, albeit a fallen one. But in the end, Blaine was never going back.

None of them were.

Nice choice of words, Fate.

And now the Ice Queen had thrown in Tayla. Like he needed more added to his personal hell.

Raven slumped against the thick trunk he'd beaten. His ass sank into the cool mud and he flopped his legs out in front of him, letting his head fall back on the rough bark. He didn't bother closing his eyes while the rain pelted his face.

No need to relive another godforsaken memory.

Without the distracting pain of his torn apart hands, his thoughts drifted back to Tayla.

If only he could figure out why the connection with her was so different.

Why, after centuries on Earth, had he allowed a

mortal to see him? What was the driving force behind his burning desire to be in her presence, to caress her delicate skin, kiss her rosy lips? To worship her very existence.

And while aboard the blame-train, why did he insist on acting like a frickin' ass back at her cabin?

Goddamn it.

Bet Fate's having a good fucking laugh while he stumbled through this vicious game of hers.

Pity he had no desire to compete. All he wanted was to make it out with his soul intact.

Raven squished his hands in the mud, pushed himself up off the ground, and peered down at his filthy clothes. He sure rocked the post-mud-obstacle-course look. Using his palms, he cleaned off a majority of the mud covering his saturated jeans.

He had to make the right choice here. For once.

He had to let Tayla go. She didn't belong in his dangerous world. She needed to continue along her fated path, even if it meant leaving him behind to drown in his sorrow. No way would he risk further punishment to his brothers for his mistakes. All he had to do was spin her some tale that he was going away or some shit. And stay the hell away.

He was all too familiar with personal hell; this just added another torture to the lethal combination.

He would lock away the memories of her; his fingertips stroking her soft skin, her intoxicating spring-rain scent, her breathtaking smile when it lit up her hazel eyes. Never would he experience something so heavenly again.

Even if, by some twist of Fate, he did return to the Heavens.

He snatched his jacket off the wet ground and gave it a hard flick out to his side, ridding it of soggy leaves and rain, before sliding his arms back in.

Turning around, he stalked back in the direction he'd come, through the dark and drenched forest, heading for Tayla's cabin.

Chapter 17

Tayla sucked in a breath. *There's someone on the veranda…*

Thump, thump, thump.

Heavy boots stomped up the stairs and thudded along the veranda. The wooden slats creaked with the weight.

Thump, thump—

The thuds came to a halt between the twin floor-to-ceiling panel windows directly in front of her. Luckily, the drawn curtains hid her existence from the intruder.

Tayla leaned forward. She eased her glass of wine onto the coffee table slowly, to prevent making a sound. Holding her breath, she inched off the couch and crouched low behind the protection of the table.

She closed her eyes and focused on the sounds around her.

Eerie silence echoed in her oversensitive ears. Her heart pounded as adrenaline spread through her veins, preparing her body for fight-or-flight mode.

More likely flight.

Screeeeeeeech.

She jolted and almost knocked over the glass on the table.

"Crap," she breathed. A glass smashing on the wooden floor would give away her position.

Instantly, her mind flooded with images from all the horror movies she'd watched in her teens…a masked killer lazily dragging an axe on the veranda behind him…a bloodthirsty vampire preparing to attack the second she peeked out from behind the heavy curtains…or a scarred man tugging the body of her friend by one leg, to dump at her front door…*Focus, Tayla!*

Oh, god, this was not the time to allow her imagination to run wild.

She tilted her ear toward the windows and held her breath. Her mind raced to figure out the source of the screech. It almost sounded like wood scraped against the wooden slats.

At least that ruled out a body.

She leaned closer as though it would give her superhuman hearing or something. She mentally listed the items on the veranda. Only two Arlington chairs, nestled against the wall between the windows.

Where the boots had ceased stomping.

Creeeeeak.

Wait, she recognized that creak from the chair on the right. The one she didn't sit on in case it collapsed and she landed on her butt.

Why is a masked killer sitting on my veranda? Unless it was Raven? Her heart skipped a beat.

It had to be.

She smiled to herself. He came back to apologize for not telling her the truth.

But why didn't he just knock?

Because he's a man and men don't know how to apologize.

Tayla exhaled. Poor guy was probably sulking in

the chair. Which was kinda cute.

All at once, jittery nerves vanished and her body heated with desire. Which wasn't helpful. If she wanted answers, she needed to focus.

Grabbing her sweater off the end of the couch, Tayla slipped it over her head as she opened the front door and stepped out onto the dimly lit veranda.

"I'm still upset with you..." She slammed on the brakes.

Not Raven.

Sprawled out in the rickety chair was Blaine.

"Upset, love?" He glanced over his shoulder with a sinful grin. "Why on this earth are you upset with me?"

"I..." She shook her head to try and clear her thoughts. "Sorry, I thought you were someone else."

The chair creaked when he leaned back. "Eager to see him again?"

Her cheeks heated. *Busted.*

"Why are you sitting on my veranda?" She motioned to the darkness beyond the veranda. "In the middle of the night."

Blaine pouted and exaggerated slumping his shoulders. "You're not happy to see me then?"

"No, it's not that. Your visit is just, well, unexpected." *And super creepy.*

Blaine snickered.

She followed his gaze as he stared out toward the pitch-black forest, which was creepier with Blaine currently sitting on her veranda. Dark shadows of towering giants replaced the ancient pine trees, their spooky skeletal arms stretched wide as though luring victims into the darkness. Sweet bird tweets gave way to the haunting wind as it howled between the branches.

At least the rain had silenced the rustling leaves from creatures scurrying along the forest floor.

"Thought I'd see how you got on with my brother." Blaine turned to face her. "Did you ask him?"

Brother? Is Raven his brother?

The corner of Blaine's mouth lifted in a smirk. "You didn't notice the family resemblance? Well, clearly, I'm the better looking one. And way more wicked, for that matter."

"He never told me you were brothers."

Tayla leaned in and softly closed the front door, locking in the heat. She crossed the veranda and leaned against the railing to face Blaine. Cool mist from the pouring rain tickled the back of her neck and she crossed her arms over her chest.

"I'm sure he didn't tell you much at all, love."

"Not really, no."

Blaine patted the seat beside him, motioning for her to sit.

She pursed her lips.

"I won't bite." He teased, with raised eyebrows. "Unless, of course, you want me to."

God, this guy's ego is out of this world. Tayla shook her head, and Blaine's exaggerated pout returned.

"Why are you really here, Blaine?" she asked. She'd filled her quota today of weird strange men she barely knew.

"Curiosity, love. That's all. So, did the good brother own up to what he did?"

She frowned. "What do you mean?"

"Why, the reason you don't remember." Blaine threw his arms in the air. "Geez, Tayla, catch up already. Chop chop!"

Wait, she didn't recall giving him her name.

"Listen, Blaine, I think you should—"

"Oh goodie!" Blaine clapped his hands, interrupting her. "You can ask him now."

His sinister smile widened as he held his palm out, motioning to the forest, as though offering her some twisted gift.

She slowly turned around to peer into the darkness. Nothing.

She squinted her eyes. Still nothing.

Wait. What was that?

A large figure stalked between the trees toward them. Her heart skipped a beat as the figure's features revealed themselves.

Raven.

Her gaze drank him in as he exited the tree line. The closer he tracked, the clearer his features became. Menacing possession filled his onyx eyes and a low growl rumbled from his chest. That dark burning gaze bored straight into her soul, mentally ripped off her layers of clothing like he planned to stake his claim on her, right then and there on the veranda.

A shiver ran down her spine and warmth pooled between her legs. Ugh! She mustn't allow this hot, powerful man to affect her.

"Wondered when you'd drop by, brother," Blaine said. "Although, you might wanna stand out there a tad longer and take advantage of the free shower. Have you forgotten how to wash?"

Raven ignored him. Muddy water flew from the sides of his shoes as they slammed onto the soaked ground. She found herself inching backward until she bumped against the wall beside the front door.

Raven's intense gaze locked with hers as he stamped up the steps to stop before her, just inches away.

Mud, earth, and his delicious pine scent filled her nostrils. His clothing soaked to the core, his dark tee stretched tight across his broad chest.

"Did he hurt you?" he growled.

Tayla frowned, gazing at Blaine and back at Raven.

Blaine answered instead. "Relax brother, we were just chit-chatting."

"Shut the fuck up, Blaine."

Tayla jolted as Raven roared at his brother. She pressed her palms against the wall—would that help her get away quicker if she needed to?

Raven's heavy breaths fogged between them and his body towered over hers. He narrowed his intense eyes like waiting for her answer.

Wait. What had he asked? Oh, right.

"No," she whispered. "He didn't hurt me."

Raven released a breath and broke his stare to swiftly position his body between her and Blaine.

"Why are you here, Blaine?" he sneered.

Blaine casually stretched his legs out in front of him and crossed them at the ankles. "Was curious to see what you told her."

"About what?"

"Why she doesn't remember me, of course." Blaine leaned his head back to peer at Tayla from around Raven. "Why don't you ask him, love? And given he can't lie, I'm dying to hear his answer."

Raven froze. His jaw clicked.

Now or never… "Tell me, Raven," she whispered.

On second thought, maybe she didn't want to know anymore.

Raven shook his head without turning to face her. "Don't do this, Blaine."

"Oh, come on, tell her. She asked so nicely."

Tayla stepped from the safety of the wall and placed her hand lightly on Raven's arm. There were too many unknowns. She had to find out the truth, no matter what.

"I want to know, Raven, please."

He pivoted to face her, his brows knitted. "Tayla, please. Let's discuss this later."

"Tell her about that night in the parking lot. You know when you wiped her memory." Blaine's eyes widened and he slammed his palm to his mouth. "Oops. Did I say that out loud?"

Her heart sank. Did he say wiped her memory?

Raven reached for her, but she sidestepped. "Tayla, please, let me explain. It's not what you think."

Her heart pounded in her chest. "What does he mean?"

He lowered his head and muttered, "I…erased your memory."

They can't be serious. "Oh, right, I get it. You used mind control from your spaceship?" she snorted.

Phew! Gosh, they nearly had her, she could have sworn they were being serious.

She stopped and peered up at…a stone-faced Raven.

He wasn't laughing along with her.

Or smiling.

She glanced past him to Blaine. He winked at her, his lips turned in that sinister smile she began to associate with him.

Her breath hitched, and the smile dropped from her face. She staggered back.

They were serious.

"Please let me explain," Raven pleaded, stepping toward her.

"Stay where you are," she snapped, reaching behind her to grab...an umbrella. Great, how was an umbrella going to help defend her? Whatever, something in her hand was better than nothing.

She pointed the useless weapon at Raven. "What did you do to me?"

Raven looked at the umbrella and smirked, but it quickly disappeared. "I have...the ability to erase memories."

"And you did this to me?"

"Yes."

Surely, this isn't real.

"And I've regretted it every day since," he breathed.

"And that's my cue." Blaine rose from the chair and straightened his leather jacket. "It was so lovely to see you again, Tayla." He leaned forward in an exaggerated bow before turning to smirk at Raven. "Brother."

Bracing himself with one hand, Blaine leaped over the balcony and whistled a tune as he strolled toward the forest.

Leaving her alone with Raven.

She turned her attention back to him. "You didn't drug me," she whispered.

Raven shook his head.

Okay, let's say he was serious—and he acted like

he was—how did someone erase memories in the first place? And then act like it was no big deal.

Her blood heated. Shouldn't she get to choose whether he erased her memories or not? What gave him the right to take them away from her?

"I want them back," she snapped.

"Tayla…" He cleared his throat. "There are things in the memory you won't understand."

"Like what? They're my memories, damn it!" *How dare he.*

"I can't tell you."

"Stop with the bullshit, Raven. I want to know what's going on." She stepped forward, poking the umbrella at his strong chest. "I deserve to know."

Raven pursed his lips, ignoring her useless weapon. "I never thought things would go this far." He squeezed his forehead with his fingers.

"Never thought what would go this far?" she snapped.

He dropped his arm back to his side and stepped back. Under the outside lamp, she saw his irises flicker, returning to a dark blue as his expression tightened.

She matched a step toward him. "How did you erase my memory?"

Raven shook his head. "I can't tell you."

"Why the heck not?"

His hand reached to touch her, but she stepped out of reach, and he lowered it back to his side.

"I'll never forgive you for this," she fumed.

A low shot and she knew it. But she desperately wanted the truth. He had no right to erase her memory, if that was even possible.

Silence stretched between them and time seemed to

slow. Even the rain eased like it also awaited his answer. Her heart raced so fast it could have won an Olympic sprint.

She needed some kind of answer. Anything.

After what seemed like an eternity, Raven finally spoke, his voice void of emotion, "That's a chance I'll have to take."

Not at all the words she longed to hear.

She peered up at him, at the torment in his eyes. How could things have turned out so badly? Why couldn't he tell her what was going on?

She didn't believe he'd erased her memory, and that was what hurt the most. Why make up some stupid lie to cover up meeting or not meeting him and Blaine?

"I think you should go," she choked out.

She glanced away the moment her eyes began to sting, and she bit the inside of her cheek to prevent the tears from falling. She would not give him the satisfaction of knowing they were for him.

The gripping pain intensified in her chest, as though Raven had ripped her heart in two with his strong bare hands.

"I'm so sorry," he murmured.

Out of the corner of her eye, Raven turned away and retreated down the steps, his head hung low, and disappeared into the forest. Leaving her standing on the veranda. Alone. With a stupid umbrella in her hand.

Breathe in, hold...release. In, hold...release. In, hold...release.

Her hands trembled as her adrenaline level plummeted and the gravity of what happened slowly sank in.

The umbrella fell from her hand, its wooden handle

thudded on the decking at her feet.

Countless emotions spiked inside her, competing for airtime, and threatened to send her mind swirling out of control. And she was helpless to stop it.

Tayla forced her numb limbs to the steps and sank down on the top one, lowering her head into her hands.

Breathe in, hold...release.

After her carnival ride of emotions gradually slowed to a stop, the crippling pain in her chest remained. One thing was certain, for a reason she couldn't explain nor understand, she shared a connection with Raven. Though at that moment, the connection felt like a weathered rope fraying at the edges, threatening to snap.

He'd betrayed her by not trusting her with the truth.

He'd betrayed her by walking away.

Tayla lifted her head, straightened her back, and wiped her cheeks with the sleeve of her wool sweater. Doing what she did best, she made a mental list of all the things she knew so far.

First up, Raven.

One: He rescued her from the mountain when she'd gotten temporarily misplaced. Without him, she would have died alone, her body found weeks later under a foot of snow. Well, maybe that was a tad dramatic. She may not have died, but she would've been dehydrated and starving, with blisters the size of balloons by the time she made it down the following day.

Two: He'd been nothing but kind and tender toward her. Maybe a little intense. *Let's not mention the touching.*

Three: After days of radio silence, he arrived at her cabin and her heart had exploded at the sight. But then he did everything he could to avoid telling her the truth.

And finally, four: The undeniable connection between the two of them, well, on her side anyway. The intense way her body reacted to his touch, the fact he'd effortlessly awakened parts of her dormant for what seemed like forever. She felt this unfamiliar *need* to be near him and she couldn't shake the sense their lives were somehow connected, entwined and Raven knew a heck of a lot more than she did.

Now to Blaine.

One: She'd met him the other day near her cabin…or so she'd thought.

Two: He made the hairs on the back of her neck stand on end, easily flipping from a serial killer vibe to a stylish bad boy. The politeness covering the lethal man beneath didn't fool her one bit. And the way he so easily baited Raven had Blaine sliding up the creepy-guy scale.

Great, that got her absolutely nowhere.

Maybe she had some sort of hero worship for Raven because he'd rescued her. But since meeting him, whenever that was, she'd experienced a sense of peace, and, weirdly enough, safety.

Her first sense of belonging since she lost her parents.

But now her heart panged, recalling the pain in his eyes when he turned away from her. When he walked down the steps and out of her life.

With her heart firmly clutched in his hands.

Chapter 18

Raven flew. As fast as his wings would take him.

Frigid rain burned where it smacked his face and his open jacket flapped against the underside of his extended wings.

He fought the desperate urge to turn back, to go back to her. To cradle her safely in his arms and confess the truth. Spill his soul to her. Finally, he would have someone to confide in, someone to hold at night, someone to share his world; a yearning he hadn't realized he possessed.

A soulmate.

He scoffed at himself; soulmates were for mortals. Half the time Guardians protected their assigned Chosen mortals so they could find their soulmate. He'd never forget the love in their eyes, the tenderness in their embrace and how two mortals could be so swept up in each other's gaze that the world around them ceased to exist. And that weak, sappy, pansy part of him had always checked back years later to ensure things turned out right; that the connection hadn't fallen apart.

Which it never had.

Who the hell was he kidding? He knew the real reason he checked back, though he'd never admit it out loud.

"Fuck!" he roared up at the Heavens.

Doubt they're even listening.

He flapped his wings harder, as if the motion alone would release the burning rage inside him.

Why was he so goddamn bothered by Tayla's reaction and the pain behind her eyes? His job was to protect her; she wasn't his soulmate. For all he knew, she was one of those Chosen mortals destined to find her mortal soulmate and live happily-ever-fucking-after.

He clamped his teeth together. There'd be no happily-ever-after when he tore the other male's throat out.

There was only one angel capable of pulling him out of this mess.

Shielding his eyes from the onslaught of rain, Raven spied his destination ahead; an opening in the tree canopy jutting out from the side of the mountain.

He curved his wings together in a V behind his back and rapidly descended, not bothering to slow as he neared the ground. He couldn't give a damn how rough he landed. It would do him good to switch the lights off in his brain and drown in a puddle of freezing rain.

Pity he wouldn't be out for long.

He flicked his wings out wide at the last second, and his muddy shoes slammed on the slushy ground. A violent jolt shuddered up his spine. Mud and rocks flew out to the sides as he skidded to a halt.

Curving his wings behind his back, Raven did a quick search of the area, even though he knew no mortals ventured this far up the mountain, especially in this weather.

"Gabe," he roared to the heavy black clouds.

Nothing. Only rain, blurring his vision as it gushed down his face for the second time that night.

He stomped around the clearing, counting each second that followed by a grind of his teeth. Red spots flickered in his vision as the fire in his soul fought to take control; rising like the inside of a building volcano, lava crept up the walls, anticipating the coming eruption.

"Gabe! Get the fuck down here!" he roared again.

A shimmer of energy buzzed behind him. *About fucking time.*

Raven spun around. "Assign her to someone else," he barked, the instant Gabe appeared.

The nails on his clenched fists sliced the skin on his palms and blood trickled to the soggy ground beside his shoes.

Gabe held his composure. "Raven, my friend, you need to calm down." An air of authority boomed in his voice.

"Don't tell me to calm down," he spat, taking a menacing step toward Gabe.

Gabe shook his head and faced his raised palm at Raven.

Buzzing energy seeped into his veins and a wave of calmness scratched at the center of his mind.

No fucking way.

Raven's volcano erupted. White dots swarmed his vision and raging fury consumed his mind. "Get the fuck outta my head," he roared, leaping in the air at Gabe—and landing flat on his face in the mud.

"You won't get a fight from me." Gabe's voice sounded from the far side of the clearing.

Raven lifted his head and glared at Gabe, who

leaned against a boulder, crossing his arms in front of his chest.

Being able to mist must be nice. *Another thing Fate took from me.*

Raven exhaled a long breath and rolled onto his back to stare up at the ominous clouds. Rain beat down steadily, washing away mud from the front of his body and his face—again—cooling the lava in the process, so only ash and drifting smoke remained.

He massaged his forehead with the base of his palms. *What the hell is wrong with me?*

"Shit. Sorry, man," he grumbled.

In an instant, Gabe stood by his side, hand extended. Raven accepted the offer and allowed Gabe to pull him off the ground. As always.

Gabe removed a piece of linen from his breast pocket and wiped the mud from his hand. "All is forgiven, my friend."

No doubt he'll send me the dry cleaning bill.

Raven cleared his throat. "I'm begging you, Gabe, assign her to someone else. Please."

"You know I can't do that."

"Aric. Give her to Aric."

The mere thought awakened the lava, and he clenched his jaw to stop from growling. He lowered his head to stare at the mud and wet grass covering his previously black shoes, anything to distance himself from this conversation, to remove his emotions from the task at hand.

Ellen's going to have a fit when she sees these shoes.

"Raven, she is your Chosen."

Raven jerked his chin up. "What do you mean

my?"

Gabe's face twitched for a split second before he regained his composure. "You are assigned to protect her."

Hmm, standard line there, Gabe.

"I'm pretty damn sure any Guardian could do the job. Anyone but me."

Raven closed his eyes and tuned into the rain pelting through the pine trees, on the ground beneath him, and the thunder rolling in the distance. God, the agony inside his chest wouldn't go away.

"I can't do it," he choked. "I can't be her Guardian."

Gabe remained silent for so long, Raven pried open his eyes to make sure he was still there.

Yep, still there.

"What troubles you the most, my friend?"

He mentally searched for the root of the pain. The fact he broke the rules and risked further punishment for his brothers? *Not really.* The fact he and Tayla couldn't be together? *Kind of.* They all stirred dark emotions inside him, but it wasn't what hurt the most.

Then it came to him.

"I betrayed her trust," he sighed. "God, I hate not being able to tell her the whole truth."

Gabe nodded, like he knew the answer before he'd even asked the question. "And why does that bother you so much?"

Raven scowled at Gabe. "What, are you my fucking counselor now?"

"Is that not why you sought me out? You don't truly want another assigned to her. What you seek is confirmation that this is the correct path."

Raven shoulders sagged. Gabe knew him too frickin' well. "So, what do I do?"

Gabe squeezed the top of his shoulder, a tight expression on his face. "Do what you must to make it right, my friend. You must fix this. It is imperative that she completes her path."

Raven lowered his head, and Gabe's body shimmered in front of him. Flesh and bone swirled into energy before dissolving and disappearing into the air.

Do what you must to make it right.

God, if only there was a manual for deciphering Gabe's fucking riddles.

Right. First step in fixing this mess was to check in with his brothers, own up to the shit he'd created with Tayla. Then, he needed to figure what the hell to do about her and get this situation under control. *Fix it.*

Sort his shit out once and for all.

****

Raven entered through the rear of the Guardian mansion and stripped off his muddy jacket, shirt, and shoes, and dropped them in the laundry chute. If he was lucky, Ellen wouldn't roast his ass until tomorrow.

Now to track down his brothers before he lost his nerve.

Striding down the hall on the second floor, Raven caught a glimpse of EJ in the entertainment room, stretched over the pool table, his cue aimed at a single black ball. He paused outside the room and leaned his bare shoulder against the door frame.

EJ nudged the ball so gracefully it rolled across the table and slipped into the corner pocket without a sound.

EJ peered over at him. "Hey, Rave."

"Hey. You know where Aric is?"

"Just ducked out. Probably washing away his loser tears." EJ straightened and stood the cue upright in his hand. "Going for the caveman look now, are we?" He smirked.

Raven rolled his eyes.

EJ's laugh echoed around the large room.

"When Aric gets back, and you stop fucking laughing, can you both hang tight? I'll be back in a minute."

"Roger that. Be sure to wash thoroughly, will you? You've even got it in your frickin' ears."

Raven gave EJ the finger as he pushed off the doorway and continued along the hall. EJ's laughter trailed him as he jogged up the carpeted stairs to his room.

In record time, he stripped off the remainder of his clothes—shit, even his boxer briefs were caked with mud—and washed every inch of his filthy body like a car going through a car wash.

Enter grimy, dusty rust bucket; exit sparkling brand new ride.

Avoiding the mirror on the exit, Raven crossed to the closet and tossed on another pair of the same black, faded jeans and muscle tee. He threw the wet towel toward the bathroom, scoring a landing on the edge of the vanity, and descended the stairs two at a time.

Pausing just outside the entertainment room, he rested a palm on the closed double doors. His chest felt lighter somehow, as though the decision to tell his brothers lifted a weight.

Forcing his legs forward, he twisted the brass knob and opened the door. He spotted Aric first, across the room, perched on a black leather bar stool. His forearms resting on the bar with a neat glass of golden liquid cradled between his palms.

Aric peered over his shoulder as Raven trudged in and pulled out the bar stool beside him.

"Thanks," Raven mumbled, planting his ass on the stool.

EJ stood behind the bar, as usual, and by the grinding motions, making his standard concoction of squished limes in the bottom of a glass, topped with glugs of top-shelf vodka. Way too much work for a drink.

With perfect precision, as though rehearsed a thousand times, EJ slid a glass of bourbon along the bar toward Raven. He caught it neatly in his hand.

"So, Rave." EJ dropped a sugar cube in his own glass before squishing it with the lime quarters. "What's going on?"

Raven took a long, slow sip of bourbon. His shoulders sagged as the familiar burn traveled down his throat and warmth pooled in his belly. "I honestly don't know where to start."

Aric squeezed Raven's shoulder. "From the beginning, man."

Raven stared down at the glass as though the bobbing ice cubes gave him the confidence to let the words spill from his mouth. He laid all the shit he'd gotten himself into on the bar for them both to see. Well, most of it. The important parts. Him rocking a handful of crimson feathers had nothing to do with Tayla and his assignment to protect her. No need to worry his brothers about that just yet.

"He said I need to do what I must to fix this mess

I've created. Whatever the hell that means." Raven pinched his forehead between his fingers.

As the silence stretched between them, EJ grabbed the bottle of bourbon and refilled Raven's glass before plonking it back on the bar.

Good chance they'd be there for a while.

Finally, Aric broke the silence. "Watcha gonna do, man?"

"I have no idea."

"You gotta tell her who you truly are," EJ piped up, "As Gabe said, you've gotta fix this."

Raven jerked his head back. "You can't be serious. It's forbidden." He glanced over his shoulder to Aric.

"Don't look at me," Aric grumbled to his whiskey. "Do I need to remind you that I'm still paying for the last decision I made concerning a female?"

Yep. Not going there.

EJ grabbed his glass, strolled out from behind the bar, and sank down on the leather lounge.

"Rave, come on. Fate drafted those laws at the beginning of frickin' time." EJ held a palm up in defense. "I'm not saying they don't have merit; all I'm saying is maybe, just this once, they can be broken. We can't keep tiptoeing around, forever worrying Fate might throw another bloody grenade our way. She hasn't since she banished us all those centuries ago, why would she start now? Plus, there's a good chance Tayla will understand if she knows what's really at stake."

Aric swiveled around to join the conversation. "He's got a point, man, times are changing, and maybe it's about time we start taking control."

Raven squeezed his temples, but it did nothing to

cease the pounding in his skull. He wouldn't be surprised if that OCD bitch threw a bomb on them and blew them to bits for the mere mention of taking control.

Taking control of their own destiny? What a joke.

"Even if I agree, and I'm not saying I do, telling her the truth is a big risk. What if she doesn't believe me? What if she freaks out and leaves town altogether? Then what the hell would I do?" Raven scoffed. "If that happened, Fate wouldn't bother throwing a grenade at us; she'd set off a fucking nuke."

Aric cleared his throat. "Show her then."

Raven glared across his shoulder. "What? You've gone frickin' mad."

"Why, Rave? She has to believe you if you show her. Have you considered that maybe this is all part of her journey? Knowing the real you, I mean."

He narrowed his eyes at EJ. "Why? Have you seen it?"

EJ took a swig of his liquid salad, avoiding Raven's gaze. "Was just a thought."

Raven sat there for god knows how long, mulling over the conversation in his head. For some twisted reason, the idea of showing Tayla his true self appealed to him. No longer would he need to hide, deceive her, or pretend to be someone he wasn't.

But the thought of her freaking out and telling him to leave, again, or worse, fleeing town, made his chest ache.

Raven slid off the bar stool to stand. With his glass cradled in his palm, he paced around the room, pausing in the center to peer up at the extravagant bronze chandelier suspended from the high ceiling. One of only a few original chandeliers remaining in the mansion following the installation of modern lighting.

Was he clinging to the past? Abiding by the archaic rules and structure that had forever governed his existence, in the mere hope it prevented further punishment and maintained his last thread of faith. That one day he and his brothers would exit this hell and the sacrifices he'd made along the way, the golden stars for his performance, would grant them access back to the Heavens. Back to their home.

But as with everything, change was inevitable.

What if meeting him was part of Tayla's path?

Or could this be another one of Fate's twisted plots to torture her defiant angels?

He turned back to face his brothers, who waited silently for him to decide his next move. Yet again, they had his back.

He made up his mind; he would tell Tayla the truth and risk the consequences.

Can't get any worse.

He took a final swig of bourbon. "I'll go see her, then."

His stomach knotted and twisted.

Aric raised his glass to him. "Whatever happens, man, we've got your back."

EJ nodded. "Just give her some time to calm down, Rave. She'll see things clearer if she's not still pissed at you."

Good point.

Now, he just had to make it through the night.

Chapter 19

Tayla stretched her neck to the side, reaching behind to massage the knot of tension burning in her shoulder.

Gosh, she'd crouched in the back corner of the library for so long, she started to smell like the dusty books surrounding her.

She'd come here seeking answers. Anything.

Sure, she could have searched the internet, which she had, but the more her fingers typed and searched, the more and more confused she became. So much information in one space made it almost impossible to drill down on a topic. And that was after she'd deciphered which results were kind of legit and not a complete load of rubbish.

Given her search topic, a majority of the results were rubbish.

Not the internet's fault. Searching phrases like erasing memories, abnormal strength, and sexy hot man with the ability to erase memories was bound to bring out the crazy side of the web.

In the end, the results got silly, secret government experiments and psychological techniques. She didn't have any knowledge of secret government experiments—which government agencies did those anyway? None of the psychologists she'd previously worked with had ever mentioned using techniques to erase memories.

So back to square one, and time to turn to the good old-fashioned library.

The elderly lady at the front counter—who reminded her of her late grandmother, with blue rinsed hair fresh out of tight curlers and small rectangular reading glasses hanging from a silver chain around her neck—directed her to this section.

She started to feel like the girl in that movie, who scoured the internet for clues on a hunky, mysterious guy at school. Already in crazy-land, she mentally compared the fictional guy to the mysterious whatever-their-surname-was brothers she'd just met. Recalling Raven's palm on her shoulder, his warm, slightly rough lips on her neck had caused her blood to sizzle. *Nope, Raven's definitely not cold.*

But the jury was still out regarding Blaine's ridiculous strength.

Plus, Raven's ability to erase memories and of course, the weird sense there was something the two of them hid from her.

No point in pursuing the vampire path anyway, Raven clearly wasn't a blood-sucker, otherwise, he would have sunk his sharp fangs into her neck during their little session at the dining table. Unless super-self-control was another one of his special abilities.

And so, the plot thickened, at the top of the small metal staircase in the far corner of the library in the Mythology and Folklore section.

Who knew that was even a section?

But there she sat, cross-legged on the faded brown carpet, back pressed against the end of the row, her bum numb with pins and needles, a pile of books on either side of her and one in her lap.

The stack on the left for books she'd leafed through but held no clues. One on the right for books which had potential for answers, and a small pile in her lap she hadn't yet examined.

The aim for today's visit was to collect as much information as possible before embarking on an all-nighter of reading, like a last-minute cram session for an exam.

Not like she was getting much sleep anyway.

It'd been days of silence from both the mysterious brothers, and she wanted to be prepared to confront Raven the next time they crossed paths. Which might be never, considering how she'd left things between them. After all, she did say she'd never forgive him.

Stupid move, Tayla.

Back to the research.

In the take home pile, the books covered ancient mythologies—Greek, Roman, gods and heroes—books on werewolves and a bunch of Grimm fairy tales. The hardcover myths on mermaids and vampires were among the dud pile to her left because she'd already figured out Raven wasn't a vampire and come on...mermaids? *Pfft. Doubt it.*

Was she going overboard? Raven acted so freaked out when Blaine pushed him for an answer, gloating in front of her that he already knew.

No. She needed to solve this puzzle.

Tayla sighed, adding the *Egyptian Book of the Dead* to the growing dud pile and let her head fall back against a shelf, staring up at the pitched ceiling.

From the outside, the old red brick library still held

the characteristics of the church it had once been; a steep, pointed slate-tiled roof, tall rectangular paneled windows and wide concrete steps leading up to the entrance. Inside, aisles and aisles of towering dark wood bookshelves filled the space, overflowing with majestic book collections. At the rear, a narrow-grated metal staircase wound up to a loft.

Now that was a place she could hide away for hours.

The crackle of the burning fireplace at the opposite end of the loft, echoed down the aisle and the flames flickered light on three armchairs around the hearth. She sighed. Probably should have sat on those instead of the rough, prickly carpet.

Her shoulders sagged when she glanced at the piles of books surrounding her. God, she'd somehow lowered herself to a creepy detective—borderline stalker—motivated on finding answers to questions she didn't even know.

And it drove her crazy.

She snatched the Grimm fairy tale book off the top of the take home pile and thumbed through its pages; vampires, witches, werewolves, all living in plain sight, disguised as ordinary humans. Closing her eyes, she imagined Raven belonging in those worlds. Him as a witch with a creepy black cat purring at his feet, a crooked wand in his hand, chanting over a boiling cauldron. Maybe as a werewolf, his thick warrior body transforming into a majestic fur-covered beast, howling up at a full moon.

Tayla chuckled out loud. *Now you're being ridiculous.*

"What's so funny?"

Her gaze shot up as her breath hitched.

Raven. Standing at the top of the staircase with a dark, broody expression on his face.

Her chest tightened so hard it made it impossible to reply.

He took a step toward her.

She quickly hid the stupid book, turning it upside down.

Raven took another slow step. His intense gaze bored into hers right down to her very soul.

How did he do that? Not daring to look away—not wanting to—she leaned on one hand and rose off the carpet.

She cleared her throat. "Hi."

Another step forward. "Hey." He nodded to the pile of books at her feet. "Searching for something in particular?"

Her cheeks heated. *Busted!*

She half shrugged. "Just some research." No need to mention she researched him.

"Tayla…" He shoved his hands in the pockets of his black jeans. "I wanted to apologize about the other night."

The roughness of his voice vibrated deep in her belly. Was she still angry with him? Was she ever angry with him? How could she be angry at someone who had the unfair advantage of making her heart skip at the mere mention of her name?

But he'd hurt her. More to the point, he'd refused to tell her the truth. Did she want to be around someone who could lie so easily?

Raven trudged forward until he stood an arm's length from her. His earthy, masculine scent filled her nostrils, and her body responded wildly like an addict who'd just gotten a hit after an excruciating period of abstinence.

"I'm sorry about the way things ended." He reached his hand to touch her, only to stop midway and shove it back in his pocket.

She found her voice. "I need answers."

He nodded, a pained expression flashed across his face. "Let me show you."

Show me? Her heart speed, thumping wildly against her rib cage. What could he show her to explain his lies?

"You have nothing to worry about," he assured her, like he knew her thoughts.

Maybe he did. *Let's not rule anything out.*

Tayla inhaled deeply. Now or never. And she did want answers.

"Okay." She crouched down to gather the books she'd placed in her take home pile.

Raven bent down beside her, and sparks of electricity shot through her body as he gently touched her forearm. Her skin scorched at the connection point. *Will it always be like this?*

"You won't need those," he said with a mischievous glint in his deep blue eyes.

Okaaaay then.

Raven took the books from her arms and placed them on the return trolley. He turned and held out his hand to her.

And she took it.

Never releasing her hand, Raven led her out of the library. He said farewell to the librarian behind the ancient box-like computer on their way, who smiled dreamily back like Raven was some kind of rock star.

Cold autumn air burned down her throat as they exited the warm cocoon of the library and the damp, fresh scent of rain tickled her nostrils. Raven released her hand to curl his arm across the back of her shoulders and nudge her closer. She nestled into the crook of his arm, the heat radiating from his body a constant source of warmth. Arriving at his Jeep, he opened the door and helped her inside.

Where was he taking her? And why were the front seats so far apart?

Concentration was nonexistent during the drive to their unknown destination, not until the Jeep veered off the main highway onto a dirt path leading farther up the mountain.

An underused goat track.

Overgrown grass stretched from the sides and brushed the Jeep as Raven skillfully dodged tree branches scattered randomly across their path. The car constantly bounced in and out of ditches, so much she probably should've worn a sports bra for better support.

Without warning, the track ended in a small turnaround space that would require a seven-hundred-point turn to drive out the way they came, unless he planned to reverse the whole way.

She smiled as Raven opened her door, helping her down. *Mr. Darcy might exist after all.*

Hand in hand, Raven navigated them through the dense scrub, silently lost in thought. Which was fine with her. She was too nervous to form a sentence anyway.

Never slowing his pace, Raven guided her around the base of a wide tree, gently gripping her hips to effortlessly lift her over fallen trunks, raising low branches for her to duck under. She tried unsuccessfully to focus on the damp vegetation around her rather than the tingling sensations on her skin every time he touched her body. But it was no use. Even the wet pine needles blanketing the ground reminded her of Raven, his rugged intoxicating scent somehow belonging out here in the wilderness.

Focus, Tayla!

In the nick of time—much longer and she would've pulled him in and smashed their lips together—Raven brushed aside a tangled vine, holding it for her to duck under as she stepped into a clearing.

Oh, my goodness.

Tayla halted at the breathtaking view before her. A clearing about half the size of a tennis court, tucked away on the side of the mountain where no one could find it.

Except them.

Enclosing the space on one side were large grey and silver boulders of all different shapes and sizes, like they'd dropped from heaven with the sole purpose of closing in the clearing. A thick growth of trees and scrub edged the remaining sides in a semicircle.

Tayla crossed the patchy wet grass to the ridged edge where the earth sharply plummeted, creating an uninterrupted panoramic view of the Snowy Mountains before her. Braving a quick peek over the edge—and instantly regretting it—she caught glimpse of the massive descent and the sharp jagged rocks of the steep cliff face.

Her knees wobbled, and she backed away as the contents of her stomach threatened to rise.

She didn't do heights.
Nope. Not. At. All.

Chapter 20

Raven hung back at the entrance to the clearing, content to admire Tayla exploring the space for the first time.

Nothing could be more breathtakingly beautiful than her.

He drank in her movements, focusing on their internal connection, to experience her emotions as if they were his own. Searching for any slight warning she might flee.

He snickered as she peeked over the edge of the cliff and his stomach lurched along with hers.

Tayla turned to face him. His knees nearly buckled when their eyes locked and she returned to the center of the clearing. Loose strands of chestnut hair fell from her braid, brushing over her dusty pink cheeks. God, he thought he'd witnessed beauty in the Heavens, but no angel compared to her.

His chest tightened when her lips curved in a sweet smile, so mesmerized he forgot, for a moment, how to perform the basic functions of inhaling and exhaling.

What he'd give for another touch of her skin. To experience the taste of her soft lips.

No. He was there to make things right. Explain her unique role, then get her out of his system.

Outta his head.

Great, now his pulse was racing.

He swallowed the lump building in his throat and wiped his sweaty palms down the front of his jeans, even though the temperature was luckily in double digits. He forced his legs forward until he stood in front of her, so close he caught the clouds of her warm breath and the slight tremble of her body.

Concentrating on their connection went out the window when he caught a spike in her heart rate.

She glanced up. "What did you want to show me?"

You can do this, man.

"I honestly dunno where to start." *Or what the hell to say.*

Goddamn it. This seemed like such a good idea in the beginning. Now he was too freaked out about her reaction to form words.

What if she didn't want to see him again? *That would solve everything, wouldn't it?* Yeah, and tear his fucking heart in two.

Electricity sizzled in his palm, and he peered down to find Tayla's hand entwined with his, her warmth seeping into his body. His thumb lazily circled over the back of her hand.

"I'm not afraid. I want to know," she reassured him.

He'd brought her there for a reason. He'd brought her to show her his true identity, the real Raven.

He retreated, allowing Tayla's hand to slip from his. The break in physical contact jerked him from the daze. Good. Now he could focus on the task at hand, rather than the too many layers of clothing they both wore.

He trudged to the edge of the cliff and peered at the

adjacent mountain. The uniform pine trees slid down to the valley below, a flowing river weaved between the break in the canopy at the bottom, and icy water cascaded over the rocks scattered underneath.

He'd been here so many times.

His spot. His hidden gem. The escape from reality to clear his head, the first place he'd found true sanctuary after his exile. In some ways, it reminded him of his pad back in the Heavens. Elevated above a valley, safely nestled against the mountainside, the surrounding forest provided comfort and peace with a constant shine of bright rays through the open canopy.

Okay, not that last part. It rained here more often than not.

He recalled when he'd first discovered the clearing. A clear summer night with a warm breeze drifting up the mountainside. The stars so bright and big he could almost reach out and touch them.

So close to home.

He'd found Blaine for the first time in almost a century. He'd been so hopeful of their reunion, so sure Blaine would realize his mistake and want to go home. God, how wrong he'd been. Blaine was so fucking arrogant and smug about his choice, his bitter laughter echoed in Raven's ears when he'd begged him to return home.

I'll never give her the satisfaction, Blaine had spat at him.

But back then, Raven had been too naïve to see what was right in front of him. Too focused on the task at hand—which seemed so simple at the time.

Too simple.

He never would have imagined he'd stand here

now—how many centuries later—no closer to returning home, no closer to saving Blaine, and in fact, more lost than he'd been in the first place.

Bringing himself back to the present, Raven turned to face Tayla, who sat cross-legged on top of a small boulder, her hands folded in her lap. The larger boulders reached up behind her like a protective shell, ready to pounce should he step out of line.

She nodded, encouraging him to speak.

"Okay." He inhaled deeply. "I guess I'll start from the beginning."

Still not sure what the hell to say, he hoped the words would fall out in some logical order. Tayla leaned forward, her elbows on top of her knees, chin resting on her interlaced fingers.

He held her gaze. "I'm…a Guardian."

She frowned. "Like a bodyguard?"

"Yeah, kind of." He shoved his fingers through his hair. "You see, since the beginning of time, Guardians have been sent to Earth…Well, I guess we reside here now. Anyway, our duty is to protect rare Chosen mortals, keep them safe so they can fulfil their destiny, and follow the path paved for them by Fate. That's the short version."

He held his breath waiting for her to speak, react, do something.

"Sent from where?"

"The Heavens."

There, he said it. No taking it back now.

She titled her head. "And you are one of these Guardians?"

He nodded.

"What do you mean by Chosen mortals?"

"They're mortals, humans, whose destiny will make a difference in the world. They'll do something extraordinary to restore the balance in Fate's favor, contribute to her greater plan for this world."

Her forehead creased. "Balance of what?"

He kicked some dirt with his shoe. "I guess you could call it the age-old good versus evil, light versus dark, if there is ever such a clear distinction. If the balance is in favor of the Fallen, the dark side, then the world suffers mass destruction, murders in the street, terror attacks, train derailments, plane crashes."

"Earthquakes and tsunamis?"

"No, Ariel are a whole other division."

"Okay. So, which side are you on? Light or dark?"

He chuckled at her candidness. "Light. Kind of." *For now.*

What would she say if she knew the truth? If she knew it was only a matter of time until he was on the dark side, the cause of all that destruction?

"You say the word mortal as if…as if you're not."

No turning back now.

"I'm not."

God, so tempted to tap into her mind to know her thoughts, just for a sneak peek, but the idea of violating her trust like that—again—knotted his stomach. She deserved to process this in her own way. All he could go on was their connected emotions and, at the moment, she wasn't the least bit scared.

Her strength made him want to go all king of the jungle and beat his chest.

"What are you then?" she asked, lifting her chin as though preparing herself for his answer. "Show me."

Raven craned back his neck to stare at the thick

grey clouds, for once giving him a break and holding back the rain. Never, in his entire existence, had he revealed his true nature to a mortal and let them walk away with the memory intact.

But this was why he'd brought her here. Convinced by his brothers this would make things right.

Let's hope they're right.

Without another word, he pivoted, his back to her. He unzipped his jacket and slid it off his arms. It fell to the dirty ground at his feet. One by one, he undid the buttons on his shirt, his hands shaking so badly it made it almost impossible to slide the stupid button through the ridiculously tiny hole. He sighed as the last button popped free. The shirt slid off his shoulders and dropped on top of his jacket.

This is it.

He lowered his head to stare at his shoes. And inch by inch, as slowly as he could so he didn't freak her out, he unfurled his wings through the two slits in his back, stretching and extending them to their full capacity in a high arc over his shoulders, out to his sides.

Tayla gasped from behind him, her heart hammered inside her chest—or was that his?

He didn't dare move, not even when he heard her shoes crunch across the dirt toward him.

For agonizing moments, he stood there, the weight of her stare like a laser beam on his back. But he couldn't face her yet. Couldn't bear to see repulsion in her eyes.

His breath caught the moment her warm, soft fingertips brushed the outer edge of his right wing.

"Raven," she breathed.

In an unhurried motion, her fingers glided down a single feather. Her touch fueled a flame in his body he hadn't been able to extinguish since he'd first laid eyes on her. His hands trembled with a desire to touch her, caress her body as if she was his.

He gritted his teeth and pushed down through his heels, forcing himself to remain stationary, to give her the time she needed to process this.

He didn't mind her roaming hands one bit.

Eventually, it became too much. He had to see her face, had to know if it had been a mistake.

The moment Tayla removed her fingers from his wing, he glanced over his shoulder before pivoting to face her. She stared at her hand and absently brushed the tips of her fingers with her thumb.

Through long brown lashes, her gaze lifted to his. She stepped closer.

His heart rate shot up, pounded in his ears, drowning out the panting of his shallow breaths.

Tayla drew in her bottom lip. Her chest rose and fell at the same rapid rate as his.

No longer could he deny touching her. A distant warning screamed for more self-control, that this was a mistake. No way could things end well between the two of them.

But in that split-second, he didn't give a shit.

All he craved was the breathtaking woman standing inches from him. Craved her more desperately than anything else he'd ever wanted.

Closing the distance in one swift motion, he reached out and gently cupped her face between his palms. He leaned down and paused at her sweet lips, waiting for her to pull away, wishing she would pull back and make the decision for him.

"I'm not afraid," she breathed.

Her warm breath exhaled onto his lips, and hunger growled inside him.

"That's what scares me the most," he rasped.

He closed the distance between their lips and took her mouth with his. Heat and passion exploded through his entire body. He gently kissed her moistened lips, but her cherry lip gloss sent him into a frenzy. He needed more. Tilting her head slightly to the side, he kissed her deeper, easing his tongue forward, searching for hers.

Tayla groaned, opening her mouth wider to accept him and entwine her tongue with his. Her scorching fingers gripped his bare waist, pulling him closer. Quickly their kiss became fierce and desperate, both helpless to deny their hunger any longer.

Her intoxicating taste swarmed him with fantasies of exploring every inch of her curves with his tongue.

Tayla nudged closer, pressing her body hard against his. He ached to rid the barrier between them, needing more of her each second their mouths remained joined, like she was oxygen and he desperately choked for air. Her moans sent a shudder through his body as her hands slid around his waist and she splayed her fingers wide on his lower back. Inch by inch, she crept up to the base of his wings. The moment her fingertips connected with his feathers, his body exploded in sparks.

Fuck.

He groaned, which only spurred on her exploration of his wings. Her splayed hands brushed against the inside of his wings, scorching a path as they moved. His shaft throbbed as it lengthened, pressing against the inside of his jeans. He eased her closer; any closer and she'd be on top of him.

Now there was an idea.

She breathed a soft moan into his mouth, a moan he wanted to hear escape her sweet lips every day for the rest of his existence.

A moan he needed to hear.

Screw the fucking plan.

Chapter 21

Oh my god!

Tayla pressed against Raven's hard chest, desperately seeking every ounce of pleasure he delivered.

How could her body be this responsive with just one kiss?

Oh, but it was.

Burning heat scorched through her veins, so hot she was at risk of combusting right then and there. Her core was a delicious wet mess, aching and burning for the hardness pressed against her belly.

His wings, so strong and masculine yet at the same time so delicate and soft, each thick black silky feather extended out from a muscular base, a multitude of colors reflecting in the fading light like oil spilt in water on a sunny day. She couldn't stop touching them. And boy did they fill her head with wicked images of the two of them—*his wings wrapped around her while he lazily explored every inch of her body.*

Raven's rough palms angled her head, gaining better access as he thrust his tongue inside her mouth, entwining with hers. A low growl rumbled from deep inside him, and her heart hammered so hard behind her ribs she wondered if he felt it beating against his bare chest.

Her tight nipples stung beneath her loose-fitting shirt, the fabric suddenly too constricting, the merino wool scratching at her chest as if made of steel.

She brushed her hands along the inside of his wings, and her fingers burned as though each feather branded her skin.

Oh god, she craved another glance at the magnificent tattoo extending down the length of his spine, accurately etched between his majestic wings. A chance to trace the black swirls and thick straight lines forming an ancient-looking sword with her fingers…or better yet, her tongue.

Too soon, his mouth slowed and their kiss came to a devastating end—sadly, without taking off any clothes. His hands relaxed their hold on her jaw as he hovered close to her face, his eyes closed. Her lips tingled like static electricity sparking between them.

Raven opened his lids and their eyes locked. His irises swirled with black like paint poured over a blank canvas.

Still cradling her face, Raven retreated half a step and she shivered as frigid wind rushed between them. He lowered his forehead to hers and clouds of warm breath collided between their mouths.

Raven tucked a loose strand of hair behind her ear, an action so tender it made her chest ache. How could he be so strong and powerful on the outside yet so gentle with her? He lowered his arms and took another half a step back, never once breaking their stare.

At the break in contact, countless questions invaded her mind, threatening to explode out the top of her skull. *Oh god, his hot lips pressed against mine…Wow!* If only she wasn't so torn between the desire to ask the questions and a hunger to have his lips against hers.

She cleared her throat. "I, ah…wow."

A smile hinted at the corner of his mouth. "Yeah."

She needed to clear her head, focus, this might be the only chance she got to squeeze answers out of him.

Ugh! Focus, Tayla!

She squeezed her forehead. "So, you're an…angel?"

A pained expression washed over his face. "Sometimes I don't feel like one."

Might leave that topic for next time. She paced around the clearing for a moment before turning back to face Raven. "Your brother told the truth. I saw him before."

Raven nodded.

"You did erase my memory," she gasped.

Another nod.

"Why? *How?*"

"Mortals can't know we exist. It's forbidden."

Okay, fine, maybe it was some angel rule, but did he regret it?

He glanced away. "I regret it every single day."

"What? You can read my mind, too?"

"I try not to." He turned back to her. "But sometimes your thoughts are loud, like screaming at me."

"Oh. Sorry."

His lips curved. "It's not your fault."

Wow, the conversation just shot into the red on the weird-o-meter.

Right. Back to pacing and thinking of questions.

She paused again and glanced across her shoulder.

"Can you give it back? The memory, I mean."

Raven gave a clipped nod. "Are you sure you want it back?"

She pursed her lips. "I think so."

He crossed to stand before her, raised his arm, and pressed his thumb lightly against the center of her forehead.

Her heart pounded inside her chest, this time for an entirely different reason. The moment her eyes slid shut, images—no, memories—of the night outside the closed local store played behind her lids. The night she'd first seen Blaine and Raven.

She slowly opened her eyes as Raven lowered his arm and stepped back.

She exhaled a long breath. "I get it…I understand why you needed to erase the memory. It's a lot to take in."

His shoulders sagged, but his lips tightened in a firm line. "Doesn't make it right though."

"Maybe. Maybe not. But how were you to know how I'd react? Plus, by the time you arrived, I'm pretty sure I was freaking out about Blaine." She interlaced her fingers with his. "For what it's worth, I forgive you."

Their eyes locked again. "You shouldn't."

"But I do. So…What happens now?"

More kissing?

A wild glint flashed in his eyes making her squirm and brace for another bout of hot kissing, but it quickly disappeared, replaced by Raven's I'm-not-giving-away-how-I-feel expression.

A bit unfair the mind-reading didn't go both ways.

"I'll continue to protect you," he said in a thick

voice.

"Protect me?"

"You're mine, Tayla. My assigned Chosen."

His? Oh man did that word fire up her body all over again.

" 'Assigned Chosen?' " she scoffed and took a step back. "What greatness am I supposed to achieve? I quit my job and moved into a cabin in the middle of nowhere. I'm still trying to figure out what to do with my life, and all I've done so far is make a half-assed attempt to escape my dismal reality while sitting around enjoying the change in seasons. I haven't even made any friends."

Raven stepped toward her. "I don't know what your path is. It doesn't work that way. All I do know is you're my Chosen."

"How does that work then? And what are you supposed to protect me against, anyway? Or don't I want to know?"

Raven's face tightened. "Against Fallen, like Blaine. Angels who chose to fall from the Heavens and now reside in Hell. Their sole objective is to corrupt mortal souls, turning them into a Devoid when they arrive in Hell. The brighter the soul, the greater the power derived from it. With every turn, they tip the scales back in Hell's favor, and the age-old war between the Heavens and Hell rages on. Though, since Blaine's arrival, it's gotten a helluva lot messier. I suspect he's not only out for souls…he's also out for blood."

She softened her tone. "Blaine? But isn't he your brother?"

Raven turned away and peered out to the valley.

"It's a bit more complicated than that."

A cell phone rang—a totally inappropriate and inconvenient time to ring. Raven ripped the phone from the back pocket of his black jeans.

"What?" he snapped into the handset. "There's a reason I didn't reply."

His face turned grim and he stalked past her to the opposite side of the clearing, out of earshot.

She stared after him, mesmerized by his magnificent wings as they shrunk and folded in on themselves as though sucked back into his skin by a slow vacuum. The slits covered over and the flesh sealed back together like nothing had ever been there.

She ogled his bicep as he held the phone to his ear, ropes of muscles that bulged and tightened with the action. He should probably put his shirt back on before she started panting.

Eventually.

Maybe tomorrow.

God, she needed to get a life.

She broke her stalker-like leering and spun to face the mountains, to give him some privacy, even though she desperately wanted to hear the conversation. How could she not? She'd just discovered Raven was an angel—Guardian—and curiosity gnawed at her. She tilted her ear in Raven's direction, but she couldn't make out a single word. If only the breeze would stop swirling through the pine trees.

Maybe she should tiptoe closer?

Shoot! A second later, the phone call ended, and she missed her opportunity.

Raven returned to her and snatched his shirt from the ground, and put it back on.

"Sorry 'bout that. Shitty timing," he said, buttoning up his shirt.

Her fingers ached to button it for him. Okay, that was a lie, unbuttoning more like it.

She swallowed. "Everything okay?"

He avoided eye contact. "Yeah, s'all good. We should head back now, it's getting late." He grabbed his jacket from beside his feet.

Was it? It didn't seem late. Maybe he was needed somewhere else, and that was his excuse. Did he have another Chosen to protect? Her fists clenched at the thought. Were all his assigned Chosen women and did he kiss all of them like he kissed her?

Raven stilled, one arm inside his jacket and frowned at her. "You all right?"

"Fine," she snapped. What the heck was wrong with her? She softened her voice. "Sorry, I'm fine." As long as you're not kissing other women, she added in her head.

Raven didn't press any further, instead choosing to finish putting on his jacket.

She took his offered hand, and he led them back to where he'd parked his Jeep.

Awkward silence filled the drive back to her car parked at the library, giving her the perfect opportunity to fill her head with doubt. *What do I do now? Will I see him again? Does he* want *to see me again? Am I just a job to him?*

Ugh!

Next thing she knew, the Jeep pulled up beside her lonesome car in the empty parking lot. Why was the return trip always quicker?

"Where's your phone?" he grumbled.

She frowned at his grumpy tone, but slid her phone out of the back pocket of her cords, and waved it at him.

"I want you to save my number."

She punched in the numbers as he rattled them off. Was it inappropriate to save his contact under Hot Angel?

Raven left the car running as he opened the passenger door, and offered his hand for her to climb out.

"Text me when you're home safe," he said the moment her shoes touched the ground.

"Okay."

When will I see you again? She wanted to ask, but didn't get the chance. Raven reached around her and slammed shut the passenger door before stomping back to his side and climbing in. The Jeep's engine revved as it reversed and skidded onto the road, speeding off into the distance.

Leaving her standing in the freezing parking lot.

Alone.

Okaaaay, that was totally weird.

She rubbed her upper arms and glanced around the empty lot. The library had closed for business and its customers and staff were long gone for the evening. Pink and orange peeked over the grey clouds on the horizon, and goosebumps popped over her legs as the wind swirled in the vacant space, cutting straight through her many layers.

Tayla unlocked her Audi and locked the doors again the moment she landed on the freezing seat. She started the engine and cranked on the heater for her drive home.

Maybe then, she could figure out what the heck just happened.

Chapter 22

Raven turned the Jeep dangerously around corners, at a speed excessive even for him, screaming past frustratingly slow cars as they cursed at him from behind the protection of their closed windows.

His emotions ran in sync with the Jeep, a racing hot mess.

How the hell had he let things get so out of control? Again.

Telling her the truth and apologizing for the whole mind wipe thing did not involve kissing her soft lips or nudging his swollen shaft against her body.

Again, he'd taken advantage of her. And now, his punishment was gonna be so much frickin' worse than before.

Images rose of her lips, swollen from their kiss, her long thick lashes framing her hazel eyes, strands of chestnut hair cascading down her shoulders.

God, he could touch her hair all fucking day, twirl the silk strands between his fingers while she lay beside him. Naked...in his bed, their exhausted bodies tangled between the sheets, fresh from a day of making love.

Oh, he'd fucking done it now.

Not only had he failed in his one task to make amends and step back into the shadows, but now he'd amplified the fantasies playing on loop in his mind.

Nope. He'd made everything a helluva lot worse.

Thank Christ Aric had called, interrupting his little session with Tayla. Otherwise, there was no telling what would've happened. Who was he trying to kid? He knew exactly where things would've went, and it didn't involve wearing clothes.

Raven slammed his fist on the steering wheel.

For Christ's sake. He needed to remind himself of the kind of future they could have. Or more accurately, couldn't have. They had limited time together on Earth, be it five or eighty years, it didn't matter, it would eventually end. Once Tayla completed her Chosen path, her life in the mortal realm would cease and their paths would splinter off in opposite directions. Opposite dimensions. Fate would grant Tayla access to the Heavens, through the invite-only pearly gates, where she'd spend her eternity like all other Chosens before her, surrounded by majestic gardens, balmy breezes and pristine waters.

And his unrelenting reoccurring day would resume its continual loop for the rest of his fucking existence.

The tires slid around the final turn, dirt and rocks clanking up under the mud guards. A light layer of dust coated the side windows as the Jeep skidded to a halt in front of the Guardian mansion. The garage could wait.

Given his lack of concentration and erratic driving, it was a miracle he and the Jeep arrived in one piece.

Aric stood at the top of the porch steps, arms crossed over his chest, a tight expression on his face.

Raven kept his ass planted in the driver's seat and stared out the front windshield, focusing on the inhale, exhale thing.

He shouldn't be surprised it'd happened. EJ had

seen this day and, until recently, Raven had eagerly awaited its arrival. But now, the timing couldn't be worse.

Another responsibility to add to his already overflowing plate.

Exiting the car, Raven peered at the blank screen on his phone; no surprise he beat Tayla home, given his rally-worthy session.

Aric crossed the gravel drive. "EJ's with them in the lounge. Ellen's in a spin."

"I bet she is. Thanks, man," he replied, as they both marched up the steps.

"How'd things go with Tayla? You sort it out?"

Raven shook his head. "Fucking disaster."

Crossing the threshold, Raven hesitated for a split-second. Was he capable of leading this team? Was he fit to lead?

All you focus on is that Chosen, his inner voice taunted him.

God, he at least needed to act like he had his shit together.

He pushed aside the doubt—it'd come out and play again later anyway—and lifted his chin and continued inside.

Aric silently followed and nudged the door closed behind them.

Striding down the hall, Raven snuck another glance at his phone, still cradling the stupid thing in his palm like receiving a text from her was more important than breathing. Why wasn't she home yet?

He cursed to himself and continued along the landing, rounding the banister before they descended into the lounge room.

EJ rose off the chesterfield and crossed to give Raven a brotherly handshake. "Hey, Rave. How'd it go with Tayla?"

Raven sighed. "Don't ask."

Thankfully, like Aric, EJ didn't push the issue. Instead, he nodded and stepped aside to reveal two angels standing behind him.

The male stepped forward and shook hands with Raven. "I'm River." He nodded to the female beside him. "And this is my sister Raine."

The sister remained silent with an I-don't-give-a-shit-who-you-are glare. Okay then.

"I'm Raven. And you've already met EJ and Aric."

Raven motioned to the lounge for them to sit. He parked his ass in the single arm chair while Aric and EJ sank into the chesterfield across from the newcomers.

Raven sat his phone, screen up, on the arm rest. Still no text.

Was something wrong? Fuck it, he'd give her five more minutes before he called.

Yes, he had her number. And her previous addesses, work places, and info on her family and close friends, not that she had any living relatives since the death of her parents. The standard bundle of intel EJ collected, he was handy like that, all FBI agent-like with his assortment of computers and IT gadgets. Without it, finding a Chosen would be impossible, given they couldn't mist like they could when they were in the Heavens.

Raven studied the brother/sister combo. Both angels had the same rich olive skin, high cheekbones and lean bodies, but that was where the resemblance ended. The male, River, had bright moss-green eyes with dark brown hair, all shaggy with a wild mess of curls piled on top. While the female, Raine, had deep violet eyes with platinum blonde hair, pulled back in a severe bun with something resembling a chopstick poking through it.

Their personalities, so far, chalk. And. Cheese. No, scrap that. Only one possessed a personality.

River peered around the room. "Wicked setup you've got here."

"Thanks. Apart from Gabe, we've never had visitors. What sent you down?"

River glanced at Raine as though he expected her to answer, but she didn't. She continued to slouch with her arms crossed, glaring at everyone around her like a sulky mortal teenager forced to attend a family gathering. What the hell was her problem?

As long as she chose not to use the daggers strapped to her thigh and ankles, they'd all make it to dinner.

River shrugged off his sister's death-stare and leaned forward to rest his forearms on his thighs. "From what we hear, you're in need of Raine's mad skills. Plus, well, although she might look all friendly and innocent, Raine ruffled some feathers upstairs and needs a…time out. And not in a good way, if you know what I mean." He smirked and raised his eyebrows.

Raven's phone pinged on the armrest and he peered down at the lit-up screen. Finally, Tayla was home. Just as well since only twenty-seven seconds remained on the clock.

Now capable of diverting his attention from the phone, Raven flipped it face down and peered up to find River offering him some sort of metal arrow.

What the hell?

Raven inspected the arrow in his hand. An ordinary looking metal arrow, likening the countless ones he'd seen over the centuries. What was so special about this…

A glint of metal—no, more a crystal-like substance—caught his attention. At the arrowhead, four blades folded together as one to form a point, shining and shimmering as though made from…

"Is that what I think it is?" EJ gasped and leaned forward in his seat.

River clapped his hands. "Sure is. Raine's been experimenting with *Purah*, seeing how she can freeze and shape it, testing its strength and durability, how light or flexible she can make it. And, well, this is the result. Cool, eh? She's managed to forge a few different weapons. No longer will you need to rely solely on those big-ass swords." He glanced at Raine. "Show them your stars, sis."

Raine tucked one hand inside her black leather jacket and, quicker than any of them could track, flicked a throwing star at the couch in front of her. It lodged in the leather neatly between Aric's knees.

"What the fuck?" Aric shouted as he jumped off the couch.

EJ snorted and leaned across to dislodge the throwing star. He held it up to inspect the work, and nodded to himself before tossing it to Raven.

The Purah cooled the center of his palm as he examined the star, forged entirely from the water in the Eternal Fountain. Five perfectly pointed miniature blades extended from the small center hole, a blunt semicircle, big enough to fit a finger or thumb, curved each blade together.

Raven glanced at River. "Are you both Kutiel?"

"No, no, we're not forgers. Believe it or not, Raine over here—"

"I made them and showed Gabe." Raine cut off her brother.

River peered at her, and she scowled back.

What aren't they telling me?

River shrugged and looked back at Raven. "Anyway, Gabe thought you could use some, what'd he call them? Oh yeah, modern weapons."

"So, you're here to deliver them?"

"Ah, not quite. You see, Raine told Gabe she'd only make them if she could do it outside the Heavens." He smacked his thigh and laughed. "Should have seen the look on Gabe's face."

"I can imagine," Raven sighed.

River held his arms out. "So, here we are. We've come to permanently join your crew. If you'll have us, of course. Pretty wicked, eh?"

Aric perched on the arm of the couch. "Let me get this straight…you plan to forge these weapons here? How is that even possible when the Eternal Fountain is in the Heavens?"

River nodded. "Yep. Well, no, not me, Raine will. Dunno how yet. Hopefully, it won't take too long for Gabe to figure out. What's the time difference down here anyway?"

They all looked at Raven for an answer. "We don't know, Fate took away our ability to mist back and forth."

River half shrugged. "Yeah, we had to give that up, too. Whatevs."

Aric raised his eyebrows at Raine. "Can you use them? On anything other than a sofa?"

Raine glared back. "Wanna see?"

River grinned. "We're good. Gabe's been training us since he made his little deal with Raine."

Raven leaned back in his chair and twirled the throwing star between his fingers. This could be a game changer. For the first time in God knows how long, he felt lightness in his chest.

But why hadn't Gabe said anything? Especially if he'd been training them. Then again, he was so caught up in his own bullshit even if Gabe had mentioned it, it wouldn't have registered.

Raven cringed. God, the last time he'd seen Gabe, he'd taken a fucking swing at him.

The inside of his clenched fist stung, and he quickly opened his palm as a trickle of blood dripped onto his jeans.

They were definitely sharp.

He wiped the throwing star on the denim to clean off the blood and placed it on the armrest.

Now he needed to figure out where exactly Raine was going to forge the new weapons. They had a small stash of swords and daggers, which they'd had on them when Fate exiled their asses. Over the decades, Gabe had replenished their stock, but they'd never had an abundant supply that warranted a dedicated storage room. Plus, each of them preferred to store spare weapons in their rooms for easy access. How much space would Raine need? And exactly what did she need?

This could finally put them on the front foot. For so many years, he'd wanted to ask for help but didn't want to see the disappointment in Gabe's eyes. Again. Now, finally, this could give them the break they needed, the weapons to give them the upper hand in fight against the Fallen.

With nothing but their word, Raven rose from the armchair and spread his arms wide. "Welcome to your new home." He tossed the throwing star to Raine and she slipped it back inside her jacket. "Raine, whaddaya need to get set up?"

Before she could answer, Ellen gracefully entered the room. "Sorry to interrupt, Raven. I thought your guests may like something to eat after their long journey?"

Raven nodded. "Of course. Thanks, Ellen." He turned to the newcomers. "Why don't you choose a bedroom and grab something to eat? We can meet in the study in an hour to work out all the details."

"I'll give you the grand tour along the way," EJ offered.

River gathered the arrows and slid them inside a long brown quiver. "That'd be cool. Thanks, boss."

The newbies followed EJ out of the room and headed up the staircase. Once out of earshot, Raven glanced at Aric.

Aric screwed up his face. "I know what you're thinking. She's one piece of work."

Raven smirked. "Not exactly the most astonishing news of the day."

He shoved his fingers through his unruly hair. The thought of Gabe not trusting him, the friend he'd stood side by side with since the beginning of time, left a bitter taste in his mouth.

"Wonder why Gabe hasn't said anything," Aric

said.

"I was just thinking the same thing."

"Regardless, it's a game changer, man. And totally in our favor."

Raven nodded. "I just have trouble believing Fate agreed to this."

Aric grinned. "Maybe she didn't?"

"What? You think he snuck them out? No, something else is going on here. Nothing gets past her, you know that."

"True, but there are some choices even Fate doesn't see coming."

"Yeah, but after Blaine, I doubt she'd let another one creep up on her."

"I don't know, man. It all seems like a bit of a coincidence, and we both know coincidences don't fucking exist. Let's just roll with it and see where it leads."

Raven nodded, even though he wasn't sure he agreed. "Go join the others. I'll be right behind you."

Aric hesitated a moment before he stood. He squeezed Raven's shoulder and leaped up the steps.

God, after so many centuries in the mortal realm, filled with the same routine over and over, then out of nowhere, in the space of a couple of mortal months, his whole existence flipped upside down. EJ had seen the day two more joined their ranks, which meant bloody Fate was involved somehow. Why would she add more angels to his forsaken band of Guardians? Did those two read the fine print?

He was convinced Fate had forgotten him and his brothers, like the unsavory cousins tossed aside and ignored at family gatherings. But the niggle inside his gut wouldn't ease. Something was brewing, he just didn't know what.

Heavy thumps accompanied the deep voices of EJ and River as they traveled down the staircase, and Raven's heart ached at the sound of their easy banter. Raven turned just in time to catch a small rectangular wooden box tossed at him over the banister.

EJ stood with his palms resting on top of the banister, with River beside him, leaning over the rail as though he considered jumping. Aric stayed behind them, arms crossed, while Raine halted on the third step from the bottom.

"It was in the study, sitting in the center of the table." EJ nodded toward the box in Raven's hand. "Open it."

Raven inspected the dark mahogany box and bounced it up and down in his open palm, testing the weight. There was a small golden clasp on the long side and two miniature golden hinges on the back. Besides those, there were no other identifying markers as to the sender or what might be inside.

As if clipping one of the colored wires on a ticking bomb, Raven slowly lifted the clasp and eased open the lid. Wrapped in a maroon velvet cloth was a gold antique key with in a small piece of parchment, which read, "An offering in good faith."

Raven removed the key to inspect it closer. He held it up to the others. "Anyone have any idea what the key's for?"

River nodded. "It's for the forging equipment, I guess. She said it would be here."

Aric jerked his head up. "She?"

Raine glared at her brother. "He means he. Gabe.

Still a bit fatigued from the journey, brother?"

Raven scrubbed his hand through his disheveled hair. "Any idea where the forging equipment is?"

EJ tilted his head. "It could be in the basement. I doubt the wood shed is big enough to store it all, plus, it's out in the open, not exactly secure."

Raven closed the box. "Let's check it out."

The others followed closely behind—except Raine, who held back a few paces.

The air thickened with each step down the stairs to the basement, the stone walls dampened as they neared the bottom. The basement was the perfect place to store weapons, a windowless solid stone room running the length of the house with only one entry. EJ had thrown around the idea of a wine cellar, but since none of them drank wine the idea never got any traction.

Raven brushed his fingertips along the cool rough stone when he rounded the final corner and halted in front of a solid dark wood door with an antique brass lock. The lock hadn't been there last time he'd ventured down. He removed the key from the box and inserted it into the lock, turned it to the right and heard a *clunk* as the mechanism disengaged. He pushed open the door and entered the basement.

Raven smiled as he roamed the space. Gabe had come through on his end of the bargain, somehow setting Raine up with all the forging equipment she needed. In their home.

Collective gasps sounded as the others entered the room behind him.

He wandered around and took it all in. In the center were three oversized stone tables spread evenly apart along the length of the basement, each topped with various equipment including god-worthy hammers, cutting machines and a collection of tools in different shapes and lengths.

Two leather aprons hung from brass hooks on the wall beside the entrance. Over to one side two steel devices resembled furnaces, with another collection of tools sticking out of a metal tub to the side. But what caught his interest was the waist-height black rectangular stone basin positioned on the other side of the room. The shimmering silver and grey flecks set in the stone drew him closer, as though a spell pulled him in.

As he stepped near, he inspected the long rectangular frame, about the size of a dining table, only narrower. Encased inside was crystal clear water, the black stone on the bottom creating the illusion of a bottomless pit.

Unable to stop, Raven reached forward and ran his finger along the surface. The liquid rippled and illuminated; yellow, pink, blue, and silver reflected off the surface like a high quality crystal caught in the sunlight.

Could it be?

Raven took a step back, mesmerized by the beauty of the crystalline water, watching the kaleidoscope of colors gradually disappear as the liquid stilled once again.

EJ appeared beside him. "No frickin' way." He stepped forward and trailed his finger along the surface of the water which set off another round of shimmering colors. "This is so awesome."

"Yeah. But I thought it was impossible for Purah to leave the Heavens in liquid form, which is why weapons are forged up there."

Aric peered over the edge of the basin. "I don't think this water technically left the Heavens, man. I reckon the basin has a direct link. It's the only way Gabe could've pulled it off."

Raven turned to take in the whole basement…Well, armory now.

Raine had her head inside one of the furnace-looking contraptions, fiddling with something. River stood at the closest bench top, lifting various tools one by one before returning them to the bench.

Finally. Finally, they could operate independently. No longer would they feel cast out and forsaken by the Heavens.

Either Fate had softened—which he doubted—or Gabe tried to influence a path on his own.

Good luck with that, old friend.

This was just the thing to give his brothers—and sister? No, that sounded weird, he'd have to come up with a different term—a boost, a lift in their faith, a nudge to say they made a difference and someone, whoever it was, trusted them to pull it off. Whether the task was protecting a Chosen, restoring the balance, or his own personal battle with Blaine.

Whichever one. Maybe now, they could nail it.

****

Raven left the others to play with the new toys. Raine got straight to work and, by the time he headed out of the basement, she'd fired up the furnace—one for heating and the other chamber for freezing—and stood alone at the far bench, using a tool to scrape along the edge of a narrow piece of frozen Purah. Aric watched from afar, a look of fascination on his face as Raine forged his weapon of choice. River methodically wandered around the room, pen and paper in hand, noting the tools and equipment they had and compiled a list of other items Raine needed. EJ had left the basement long ago, mumbling something about a fingerprint scanner for the door. Guess he didn't trust the antique key to keep out the bad guys.

Not that a Fallen could physically step foot on the grounds due to the heavenly spell cast on the perimeter by a Raziel, but one day they'd devise a way to break through, and they need to be prepared when that happened. Raziel spells had the added bonus of concealing the location from mortals, preventing them from wandering onto the grounds. If they looked closely enough and in the exact direction, all they'd see was a shimmering ripple in the air, not unlike those on the surface of a pool, but the view beyond would mimic dense forest. Walking through the ripple would simply mist them on the other side without them knowing. The protection barrier wouldn't work, though, if they knew what they were looking for and exactly where to find it.

Tayla had been the first outsider to step foot on the grounds.

Tayla.

Shit, so much for trying to get his head in the game.

He'd lasted half a fucking day. Well…that wasn't quite true. He'd lasted about an hour. Forty-five minutes maybe.

So much for believing one kiss would solve his craving to taste her. It'd only succeeded in making it a billion times stronger.

Raven groaned. A run was what he needed to clear

his head and burn off some tension. He dashed up the stairs two at a time to his room, changed into running gear, swiped his iPod and headphones off the dresser and leaped off the balcony, unfurling his wings to soften his landing. The dark night was no match for his immortal vision as he jogged toward the forest. No way he could push his body to the brink of exhaustion and still think of her.

Is that a challenge? his mind threw back.

****

Somehow it worked. Raven ran until every muscle in his body burned with a satisfying ache, and after he showered off, he effortlessly fell into a deep slumber on his bed.

The *ping* of his cell phone made him shoot out of bed like the damn house was on fire.

He snatched the device off the side table and glanced at the screen to find a text message from Tayla. At this hour? Was something wrong?

Instead of reading the damn thing like a normal person, he dialed her number. It took every ounce of self-control not to leap out the window and fly to her cabin.

One ring…he should ring back tomorrow. He needed to put distance between them.

Second ring…flying to her in the middle of the night was not keeping his distance.

Third ring…why wasn't she answe—

"Ah, hi. Sorry, I didn't mean to wake you," Tayla answered, her voice a little rattled.

"What's wrong?"

"Oh, nothing, everything's fine."

He lowered his voice. "Then why aren't you

sleeping?"

God, he would give anything to stand in front of her instead of talking on the phone. He stepped toward the window. *No.* He couldn't go. Especially when the anticipation of seeing her ignited his entire body.

"You didn't read my text?"

What? Oh right, the text. He needed to figure out how to reply to those damn things.

"Nope, sorry. What did it say?"

The phone went silent, and Raven stepped onto the balcony.

After a moment, she softly replied, "I wondered if you had plans tomorrow?"

Why would he have plans?

"Never mind. Of course, you do. Sorry again, I didn't mean to wake you." She blurted before he had a chance to reply.

"Wait…" Desperate for her not to hang up. "I don't have any plans."

Shit. He played with fire, and it wouldn't end well.

"Well, I thought, if your job is to protect me and all…then…wouldn't it make it easier if you were with me?"

He grinned. That was logic even he couldn't argue with. "What did you have in mind?"

"I don't know. Maybe we could have dinner or something?"

Where had all the oxygen gone? *Stop thinking about going to see her.*

But once again, he ignored his better judgement. "Sure. What time do you want me to pick you up?" *Now?*

"Um, maybe six-ish?"

How the hell was he going to fill the time between now and then? That was almost a whole day away.

"Okay," he begrudgingly agreed.

"Well, until tonight then."

He heard the smile in her voice. "Until tonight. Goodnight, Tayla." *Sweet dreams.*

"Night, Raven."

God, the sound of his name on her lips sent his heart rate through the roof.

He leaned his forearms on the balcony rails and stared out into the night. *Damn it.* He had zero self-control when it came to Tayla. All his better judgement had flown out the frickin' window. He needed to work on that before he saw her again.

But, first order of business was to figure out how to speed up time so six p.m. would come quicker.

Chapter 23

Tayla cradled a warm mug between her palms, lifted it to her lips, and blew over the rim, out of habit rather than because the tea was too hot. Curled up on the couch in front of the dying fire, she folded her legs beside her, toes tucked under the chunky knitted throw.

Still a whole sixty-three minutes—not that she was counting—until Raven was due to pick her up.

Tea, a little yoga session, wine, nothing neutralized the jittering in the pit of her stomach, which filled her head with doubt about tonight's date. Wait! *Date?* Was it a date?

Ugh! I can't think properly.

She had tossed and turned all night, recalling that kiss. The delicious taste of his lips, the feel of his smooth feathers, inhaling his intoxicating scent. For some reason, when Raven left her in the parking lot, she sensed he intended to put distance between them, and if she wanted to see him again, she needed to take control. Which prompted her twenty seconds of bravery to text him in the early hours of this morning. Which, of course, led to Raven calling rather than replying. Man, the sound of his deep sensual voice vibrating through the handset had erased all hope of sleep.

The whole day passed in a daze. With her thoughts focused on seeing Raven again, she couldn't even remember what she did until the moment came to get ready.

She'd taken an embarrassing amount of time choosing her outfit, even though it was a stupid and pointless exercise. Considering the weather outside, she needed to cover whatever she wore with a goose down jacket and scarf, but she drew the line at a beanie. No need to look like a snowman.

She brushed her finger along the cover of an unopened book beside her. She'd given up trying to distract herself after having read the same line a hundred times.

Now there was nothing to do but wait. A whole fifty-nine more minutes.

Butterflies fluttered in her stomach as if trying to flee an enclosure. One minute, her heart pounded inside her chest and the next minute, she gagged at the nausea rising in her throat.

Attempting to calm her jittery stomach, she mentally listed all the things she knew concerning the situation she'd gotten herself into.

This wasn't the first date she'd ever been on. Although it had been quite a while, she knew how things rolled. Plus, it wasn't a blind date; she refused to participate in those. She knew Raven, knew him well enough to have already shared a hot, passionate, toe-curling kiss that left her weak at the knees.

And man, did she want him to kiss her like that again, cradle her head in his rough hands and take her mouth with his.

Great, now I'm thinking about that kiss again.

Ugh! She threw off the blanket and it landed in a heap on the floor. It wasn't a date, for goodness' sake.

His job was to protect her. He'd probably spend the evening searching for threats as she rambled on about random stuff, making a fool of herself…

Tayla jumped when a sharp knock thumped on the door.

She glanced at the clock in the kitchen; still forty-seven minutes until she expected Raven…so who was at the door?

Swallowing the lump in her throat, she rose from the couch, and tiptoed to the front door, wincing with each creak of the floorboards. She leaned toward the door and peeked through the security hole to see…

She breathed a heavy sigh.

Raven stood on the veranda, his back to the door.

He spun around as she swung it open.

Her breath caught. *Oh man!* The dark and dangerous black combination, teamed with his I-don't-care hair and sensual dark blue eyes, caused a stir deep inside her belly.

"Hi." She cleared her throat. "You're, ah, early."

He shoved his hands in the pockets of his jeans. "Yeah, I know. I can come back if you'd prefer?"

"No," she said quickly. "It's fine, I'm ready." *And have been for hours.*

"Good. I thought we could get there early to watch the sunset."

Watch the sunset with him? Oh, this guy was bad news. "I'd like that. I'll just grab my coat."

Tayla dashed back inside, snatched her coat and the bottle of red from the table, and locked the front door on her way out.

Her heart raced so fast it tightened her chest, making it difficult to breathe.

Relax, Tayla, it's just dinner…with a drop-dead gorgeous angel.

Raven stood by his car, the engine running, holding the passenger door open for her. She climbed into the warmth of the Jeep and nestled the wine between her thighs.

When they hit the highway, Raven drove in the opposite direction from town.

She glanced across her shoulder to him. "Where are we going?"

He grinned at her. "It's a surprise."

Great. She didn't like surprises, but for some strange reason the universe had sent her down this path, so she may as well try it out.

Settling back, she twisted slightly in her seat to face Raven, allowing the motion of the car to lull her body into a trancelike comfort. He glanced over and met her gaze. She internally swooned when he reached across and took her hand, lifted it to his lips, and kissed the back of her hand.

Cue belly stirring again.

She took advantage of the car ride, and his distraction of driving, to drown in his features. A light dusting of dark whiskers covered his chiseled jaw. He wore the same black military-style jacket with the collar turned up at the neck, which for her wouldn't block out the cold, let alone the wind chill. Underneath, a charcoal crew-neck tee stretched across his chest and he wore the same style black jeans she'd seen him in previously.

Forcing her gaze from him before she ventured into creepy territory—which, to be honest, was pretty damn hard to do—she looked out the windshield. Orange, pink, and red rays streamed through the thick bank of gum trees alongside the road. Wide, gloomy shadows loomed over the pavement, her mind constantly turned them into creepy shapes prepared to jump in front of the car. Dark ominous clouds brewed in the distance, gathering together to form a blanket over the deep blue sky, chasing away the remaining daylight.

Raven eased off the accelerator and turned onto an unmarked, unpaved road. When the Jeep halted at the end, she realized she'd been there before.

She smirked across her shoulder at Raven. "We're not going to a restaurant after all?"

Raven put the Jeep in park and killed the engine. "It's safe here. It's harder to protect you in public places where a threat could come from any direction at any time. Plus…" He half shrugged. "I hate crowds."

She smiled and hopped out of the car. Having Raven to herself for the evening sounded like an ideal date…*dinner*…whatever.

Raven once more guided her through the forest to the clearing, the same clearing he'd brought her to reveal his secret, which now felt like a lifetime ago.

Only tonight, he'd transformed the space into so much more.

Exiting the tree line, her breath hitched at the sight before her. A rectangular tartan rug lay in the center on a soft patch of grass, scattered with plush oversized cushions. A wicker picnic basket sat on one side and a folded fleece blanket on the other. Glass jelly jar lanterns hung from the limbs of trees that edged the clearing. Directly ahead, where the space opened at the cliff edge, a warm glow spilled over the top of the mountain.

She turned to find Raven holding back at the end of the path, his shoulder leaning against a tree trunk.

She motioned to the magnificent display in front of her. "This is beautiful. How did you…?"

He shrugged like it was no big deal. "I had a little help."

Raven crossed to stand before her and took her hands in his. "I wanted to make up for having to leave so suddenly the other day. For ruining our…moment."

She smiled up at him. "I happen to think our moment went quite well."

He leaned in, as though he might kiss her. "As do I."

Raven pulled back and led her to the rug. "Let's see what surprises are in the basket."

She slipped off her boots, grabbed a cushion and settled down on the blanket to ogle Raven as he plated cold meats and cheeses, and poured them each a glass of red. She accepted the plate and Raven relaxed on his side beside her, propping himself up on his forearm.

She fiddled with a piece of salami. "So, tell me more about you."

"Like what?"

"I don't know. Maybe your likes and dislikes. Your family. What you do. Maybe, I don't know, if you, uh, have a girlfriend?"

Her cheeks burned. Did she seriously ask that?

The corner of Raven's mouth lifted. "Was dinner code for a night of interrogation?"

"Sorry. Too much. Maybe start with one?"

She shoved the salami in her mouth to stop herself from talking.

He chuckled. "No, I don't have a girlfriend. A

constant female companion has never fit in with my…work."

Phew!

"And as for your other questions, autumn is my favorite season, watching the leaves change and fall, I hate crowds and that shit called techno music and I consider my family to be the two other Guardians I live with, well, no, now there's four, plus Ellen."

She mulled over his answer and didn't miss the fact there was no mention of Blaine, even though he was Raven's brother—store that question for later.

"Are your parents here also?" She grabbed a piece of bread from the plate and took a bite.

"Angels don't have parents, we're created straight into adulthood. The closest thing we have to family in the mortal sense of the word are siblings, angels created at the exact same time using the same magic. And…you've already met my brother."

"Blaine."

Raven nodded. "Do you miss your parents?"

She nearly choked on the piece of bread. "How did you…? Oh, of course. There's probably some manila folder with my entire life history in it."

Raven chuckled. "Nah, EJ prefers digital files."

"Of course, he does," she grumbled.

She took a long sip of wine as the memories of her parents rose. "Yes, I miss them. Every single day." She peered up at the first sparkle of a star appearing in the sky. "But, I was lucky you know; they were the best parents anyone could've wished for. We were so close. All they ever wanted was for me to follow my destiny." She cleared her throat and glanced back at Raven. "And even though it sucks and still hurts, especially around

Christmas, for them to die together while traveling overseas, doing something they loved, was probably the best way to go, I guess."

Raven's lips thinned, and she took a gulp of wine. That was a bit deep for a first date—dinner.

Tayla waved her hand in the air. "Enough about me, back to you. So, if you're born an adult, do you age?"

He smirked. "No. Although, I feel like I've aged since being on Earth."

"How long ago were you created?"

"Does it matter?"

She bunched her brows. Maybe. "No."

Raven took a sip of wine. "I wouldn't even know. There's no concept of time in the Heavens. Things just are, they simply exist, there's no passing of day and night. Everything just is." He inhaled deeply. "I've only been counting my years in the mortal realm, here on Earth."

She swallowed the lump forming in her throat. "And how many years has that been?"

He frowned and peered inside his wine glass. "A few centuries."

"What?" she squawked, knocking over her glass. "Ugh, I'm sorry."

"Don't worry about it." Raven chuckled.

He grabbed a hand towel from the basket and leaned over her to soak up the wasted red.

"Second time you've had to clean up after my clumsiness," she grumbled.

Raven leaned closer. "Luckily, I'm prepared for any situation."

Tayla laughed, but it abruptly cut off when she

caught Raven's earthy pine scent. Was he wearing cologne? Surely his body couldn't naturally smell that good.

Raven titled his head and smirked.

Whoops. Forgot about the whole mind-reading thing.

Raven tossed the soaked towel in the basket and poured her another glass.

"I'm having a hard time comprehending you're a few hundred years old." She accepted the glass and took a sip. "You must've experienced some amazing things."

He pursed his lips. "Yes and no. I've watched this world rapidly change, witnessed outstanding changes in technology I still baffle to understand, medical advances, and even the way society has evolved. Mortals have gradually become more aware of global issues, focusing on protecting the Earth and its inhabitants, but at the same time I've also seen so much destruction. Mortals destroy themselves time and time again, destroy their homes, villages, fall prey to a Fallen's temptation. After so long, it gets harder and harder to remember the good when there's been so much bad."

She couldn't imagine how it would feel to have lived so long and experienced as much change.

She had so many questions rolling around in her head competing for airtime, but one in particular bugged her. "You keep telling me your job is to protect me from the Fallen, but how can they be so bad if they were once angels, like you? The only one I've encountered is Blaine, and really, he doesn't seem that terrifying."

His jaw clicked. "Never underestimate them, Tayla, they're vile creatures. When they fall, they sever their spiritual connection to the Heavens and...lose their humanity, so to speak. They also undergo a physical transformation; the color of their wings change, plus they grow sharp black talons on the tips with enough poison to kill even an immortal under the right circumstances. And although they retain their ability to manipulate mortal thoughts, without their link to the Heavens they're not bound by the truth, which can be a lethal combination for a mortal."

Holy crap, Raven painted a grim picture of his own brother. "What do you mean by their wings change?"

"All angels have different-colored wings depending on their role in the Heavens, kinda like factions, each responsible for a different part in maintaining the balance. Archangels, the leaders of each group, have golden wings. Guardians, like me, have black. Azrael, the soul collectors, have silvery-grey wings and the list goes on."

"What color do Fallen have?"

He inhaled deeply. "Crimson. The color of blood."

Raven had given her much information to process. A whole immortal world existed in secret around her but still, she wanted to know more.

"So...do all angels have a spiritual connection to the Heavens, even if they're here on Earth?"

He nodded. "Yeah, the spiritual connection is what mortals label as faith; faith in Fate to guide the way. It's the light that burns bright in a soul, and required for a mortal to enter the Heavens when they die. For angels, the light not only prevents them from becoming a Fallen, but it also allows an angel to access magic from the environment around them while in the mortal realm, like the healing power of the sun, for instance."

She grabbed a cracker and a slice of cheese, mulling over the new information in her head. She believed the universe sent her signs to follow. Were these signs of faith like Raven said? Would her own spiritual connection to the Heavens permit her entry when she finally kicked the bucket? Her parents had been strong believers in following fate and that each person walked a paved destiny. Did that mean because of their faith they were now in the Heavens and she would be able to reunite with them one day?

Wow, that was too much to process right now.

"Do you go back to the Heavens regularly?"

"No," he said with bitterness in his tone.

She paused with the cracker at her lips. "Why?"

Raven looked away and stared toward the mountain in front of them.

She didn't want to pressure him into answering, especially if it was something he didn't want to talk about. She chewed the cheese and cracker, constantly reminding herself not to speak. In the end, it got the better of her. "It's okay. You don't have to…"

"I…can't go back," he choked.

Her heart panged from the sadness in his voice. "Why?" she whispered.

He inhaled deeply and continued to stare at the mountain. "I made a deal, and I can't return until I fulfill my end of it."

Wow, that must've been one heck of a deal, if centuries later he still hadn't completed his part. Which was totally fine, it meant he was here…with her.

But for how long? *Until I die of old age and he*

carries on living for the rest of eternity?

She twisted on the cushion to face him. "Do you miss it?"

He turned her way. "I used to."

"What changed?"

Raven leaned forward and brushed his calloused knuckles down her jaw, lighting up her body like a Christmas tree.

"You," he breathed.

Her breath caught. "But...don't you still want to go back?"

He slowly shook his head. "Now I've got a reason to stay."

She held her breath as Raven leaned in, hovering inches from her. Her blood hummed with desire as he closed the distance and brushed his full lips against hers. Sparks ignited, and a rush of pleasure rushed over her, and she leaned in for more.

Raven cupped her face, tilting her head to the side, kissing her with so much passion, so much desperation, as though at any moment it could be ripped out from underneath them.

The pang in her heart deepened and spread throughout her chest. God, she'd fallen fast for this guy, so quickly she also feared the moment would end.

Her tongue entwined with Raven's and he leaned in further, his free hand gripped her hip and eased her closer. Without breaking their kiss, she shuffled over and pressed the length of her body against his. Heat seared through her layers of clothing, boiling her veins.

Raven broke their kiss, and he eased his head back to gaze at her face. "I don't know what Fate's plan is. She'll probably curse me for this, too," he breathed.

"But I don't want to be without you. I don't think I can fight it any longer."

Not knowing how to answer, she brushed his bottom lip with the pad of her finger. *I'm not going anywhere.*

Raven must've heard her thought because his gaze instantly heated, and he took her mouth again in a searing kiss. His hand wandered underneath her jacket…and sweater…and shirt, but his hand tangled in layers of fabric before he reached her aching breasts. In one swift moment, he effortlessly rolled her on top of him, so she straddled his hips.

A twig snapped to her right, but she ignored it.

Raven groaned and slid his palms under her shirt once more. "These layers have to—"

The sound of a rock tumbling down the cliff edge accosted her ears.

Raven rolled her off and shot to his feet faster than her eyes could register. She jumped up beside him. Her heart pounded inside her chest.

He turned to her and held a finger to his lips. "Stay here," he whispered.

She held her breath. Frozen. As he crept into the forest.

Chapter 24

Raven did a thorough search of the perimeter and came up with nothing, but by the lingering ash and smoke scent drifting through the trees, someone had been there.

As Raven turned to head back to the clearing, he caught movement out of the corner of his eye. In one swift motion, he ripped a dagger from his waist and spun to face the threat, but it wasn't within range.

In the far distance, hovering high in the dark night, a Fallen's red eyes stared back at him.

He locked gazes with the piece of shit, and Raven unfurled his wings. Giving chase meant leaving Tayla in the clearing alone, with the hideout compromised; no telling how many Fallen now knew its location.

Tayla was his priority.

The lucky sonofabitch would live another day.

Raven raised his arm high in the air and gave the Fallen the finger. "Fuck you," he growled, knowing the Fallen could hear him.

Pity Raine hadn't perfected forging the Purah bullets. He could use one right about now.

The Fallen spun away from Raven and shot through the night, blending in with the thick clouds.

Raven returned his dagger to its sheath and jogged back to the clearing. Next time Gabe showed up, he'd request for a Raziel to cast a new protection spell.

He exited the forest to find Tayla standing in the same position he'd left her, eyes wide and hugging her arms close to her chest.

"Come here." He nestled her in the crook of his arm and kissed the top of her head. "I've got you."

Her breath hitched. "I hope it wasn't a Fallen."

He remained silent. Now was not the time to confirm the threat to her life.

Tayla leaned her cheek against his chest, and he pulled her in closer to wrap both arms around her petite frame.

Having her that close felt so goddamn good.

In light, slow strokes, he rubbed the top of her arms until her heart rate steadied. They stood there for who knows how long, watching the bright red and orange rays change to deep violet and grey as they streamed through the thick clouds building above them.

His heart swelled so much he feared it would burst, and the almost constant ache returned with a vengeance. He rested his chin on her head, not trusting his voice to work. It'd been so long since he felt at peace, since he'd stopped and immersed himself in a single moment in time and actually paused to appreciate it. A mortal pleasure he'd taken for granted since he'd arrived in this realm.

A thunderous roar bellowed in the distance a moment before a single heavy raindrop smacked the top of his head, as though it served as a split-second warning before the attack.

He glared up at the dark sky. "Give me a fucking break," he muttered.

Damn it, why were they determined to ruin every

moment with her?

He wasn't ready for the night to end.

He leaned down and whispered seductively in her ear, "You wanna continue this someplace drier?"

She eased back and raised an eyebrow. "Where did you have in mind?"

"The safest place in this world."

She smiled, and at the same moment, the sky opened up.

They rushed to gather the blankets and pillows in record time. The candles, having long extinguished, could wait until tomorrow. Actually, he'd leave them here permanently.

By the time he'd turned on the flashlight—for Tayla—rain had soaked through their clothes. He piled everything worth bringing under one arm and over his shoulder, grabbed Tayla's hand, and they raced off to the car.

After helping her safely inside the Jeep, he threw the saturated picnic cargo in the back and started the engine to crank on the heat. Tayla shrugged off her jacket and threw it into the back, and alternated between vigorously rubbing her arms and holding her palms in front of the heater vents. Her chattering teeth snapped him out of his gawking and he hit the accelerator with one destination in mind.

****

The Jeep eased into the underground garage at the mansion. He couldn't catch his breath the whole frickin' drive; all he could think was how her damn saturated shirt clung to her breasts. Halfway there, with every nerve ending tingling throughout his body, he considered pulling over and taking her right then and there in the backseat. It'd be a squeeze, but he'd make it work. Somehow, he resisted. She deserved so much better than sleazy car sex.

Now he needed to get her to his room. Without interruptions.

Although he wasn't on duty tonight, there were no guarantees they wouldn't run into anyone between the front door and his room—three stories up. Aric and EJ would have a frickin' field day if he ran into either one of them. Hopefully, by now, they'd taken the newbies out on patrol.

That left only one option, and he sensed Tayla wouldn't like it.

He took her hand and led her up the ramp to the garage exit. Slushy rain splattered on the exposed concrete.

He strode out into the sleet, but Tayla slipped her hand from his and stood her ground under the protection of the roof line.

She frowned at him. "What are you doing?"

"Taking you to my room."

"Isn't there an internal door, you know, to avoid the rain?" She glanced around the garage.

"Yeah, but the quickest way is up. My balcony is just there." He pointed above his head.

Tayla's eyes widened. "No way."

"It's one quick swoop."

"But…it's raining. I'll get all wet."

His voice deepened. "You're already wet."

Her lips thinned. "That's not the point. Can't we just take the stairs or something?"

"Okay." He feigned agreement and shrugged out of his saturated jacket. It slapped the concrete at his feet.

"But we have to leave all our drenched clothes here. Ellen will have a fit if we wet the carpet."

Tayla smirked. "I see what you're doing, and it won't work."

"We'll see." He stepped closer and brushed his thumb along her jaw. "You're shivering. Let me warm you up."

Her lips curled. "And just how do you plan to do that?"

"Oh, you leave that to me. I'm sure I can come up with something."

God, he sensed her desire from where he stood, even in the freezing rain, and it drove him crazy. He needed her now and he wanted to spend the entire night getting to know her body, every curve, every inch, every sweet spot.

She bit her bottom lip. For the second time tonight, he considered stripping her then and there, but the garage floor was a shittier move than the backseat of the Jeep.

Time to play dirty.

As slowly as possible, he unfurled his wings. The rain tingled his feathers.

Her heated gaze tracked his movements.

He glanced up to his balcony. "Let's go warm up. Together."

The instant Tayla stepped into his arms, he lifted her to straddle his waist. Her core rubbed against him and she moaned, igniting his entire body, as though fire scorched through his veins.

Random strands of soaked hair plastered across her forehead, the drops ran down her face. The scent of the rain hitting the concrete swirled together with her own combination was intoxicating.

He narrowed his gaze on a raindrop hovering on her bottom lip; he had to taste it. A low growl rumbled in his chest as he took her mouth in a frenzied kiss, thrusting his tongue inside to brush hers. She met him with equal passion, gripping the back of his neck to hold him in place. Lost in their kiss, she didn't flinch when he swooped to his balcony, over the railing and barely landing before he slammed open the French doors, retracting his wings as he strode through the bedroom into the bathroom.

Slow down!

Raven eased back and lowered Tayla's feet to the ground. A ripple of pleasure flickered through his shaft as her body slid firmly down his front. She stood before him, her chest heaving in and out as rapidly as his.

He couldn't concentrate enough on their connection to know if the desire coursing through her veins or the fact she was freezing caused her cheeks to flush. Given the deeper color of her lips, maybe the latter.

He needed to get her out of those clothes and warm, his desire to roam over her body with his lips could wait. Providing he made it out of the bathroom fully clothed.

He met her stare and a possessive growl rumbled in his chest, his heart pounding as though he were once again on an ancient battlefield, facing an army of Fallen.

She sucked in a breath. "Have I upset you?"

Raven froze. *What?* "No, why would you think that?"

"It's just, well, your eyes. They changed to almost

black. I've noticed it happens when you're angry."

Is it suddenly hot in here?

"True. They change with intense emotion." *Like now.*

She twirled the hem of her shirt between her fingers. "So, you're not angry?"

He shook his head and swallowed the lump in his throat. "Far from it."

Tayla nibbled her bottom lip as her heated gaze skidded downward, halting at the zipper of his jeans. His shaft lengthened further at the attention.

She glanced back up at him under hooded lids, and their ragged breaths mingled between them. Her pulse quickened through their connection. Or was that his?

"So…what intense emotion do you feel?"

He had to touch her. Craved to taste her. No longer could he deny the urges, the need, the burning desire he had for the woman standing before him. The scent of her sweet arousal scrambled his mind.

"I think you know," he rasped.

"Show me."

Once again, those whispered words were his undoing. He pinched her chin and hovered at her full rosy lips, using every ounce of self-control not to close the distance. He wanted her to want this, too. Once they crossed this line, there was no going back.

Already maddened from a mere kiss, a glimpse of her beautiful body would send him over the edge, far beyond repair. This need to touch her, to consume her, had simmered for too fucking long.

He needed her to assure him it wasn't one sided.

"Tayla, if I kiss you right now, we'll end up naked."

She swallowed and slowly nodded.

"We don't have to do this."

Tayla moistened her lips and his knees buckled. "I want to."

"Maybe you should have a shower, and I'll wait outside." One last attempt to let her change her mind. *Please don't.*

She rose on her toes and pressed her palms flat against his chest. "Raven, stop talking and kiss me already."

Her soft command blasted his self-control to smithereens.

He pressed his mouth against her glistening lips, easing into a smoldering kiss. Though he wanted to devour her, he would take this slow and savor every moment.

She instantly responded, widening her mouth, her tongue reaching for his.

He cradled her head in his palms and tilted it slightly to one side. A soft moan escaped, the heavenly sound heightening his desire.

Tayla nudged closer and pressed her hips against his jeans, the wet denim so fucking irritating it felt like he wore a suit made entirely of rough sandpaper. Their slow burning passion quickly turned desperate, panting breaths and moans mingled in their mouths. He needed to slow down.

God, the connection, the desire, the *need* consuming his mind and soul, so foreign he had trouble reining it in. *It must be because she's a Chosen.* But he couldn't argue with the fact Fate had assigned him female Chosen before, several during his existence, yet these urges had never surfaced.

Bet Fate laughed at his weak display of willpower.

Cold air slapped his face when Tayla broke their kiss and stepped back. She halted on a plush mat, desire burning in her eyes. He held his breath as she reached for the hem of her soggy shirt and tugged it over her head, letting it slap on the floor by her feet.

His legs wouldn't work.

His brain went blank.

Without breaking eye contact, she unzipped her pants, lowered them to her ankles and shoved them off with her feet. His knees buckled as his eyes roamed over her matching dusty pink lingerie with a helluva lot of skin peeking through the lace.

"You're so beautiful," he groaned. He rubbed his palm down the bulge in his jeans. "Look what you do to me."

Tayla responded with a sexy smirk while reaching behind and unhooking her lace pink bra, discarding it with one hand. Her plump creamy breasts sprang free, sitting full on her chest.

Raven stifled a groan when she hooked her thumbs in the band of her skimpy panties and slid the lacy garment down her slender legs.

He stood there, spellbound, while she stepped behind the shower recess and turned on the water. Steam rose on the glass, blurring his view of her naked body.

"Are you joining me?" Tayla's seductive voice snapped him to attention.

Hell yeah.

With lightning speed, he tore off his clothes, not giving a shit where they landed, and entered the steamy shower.

This woman will be my undoing. And the thought excited the hell out of him.

****

Through the foggy glass, Tayla tracked Raven's movement as he threw off his saturated clothes and stalked into the shower like a predator about to devour his prey. Her heart pounded inside her chest, and every nerve ending sparked with electricity the closer he crept.

Steam glistened on his tanned skin, his lips full and swollen from their kiss, his onyx eyes burned with desire to consume her. And man, did her cheeks heat under the weight of his stare.

She couldn't stop her gaze from drifting down his strong, muscular chest to follow the narrow trail of dark hair to the thick display of manhood jutting proudly from his body.

She swallowed the lump in her throat.

The moment he joined her under the water, his steady hands explored down her sides, following the curve of her waist, and moisture instantly flooded her core.

"So beautiful," he murmured while his heated gaze drank her in.

He gripped her hips and gradually turned her around, leaning her back against his strong chest. The steamy water cascaded between their bodies, heating her internal temperature, not that she needed anymore warming up. The heat in Raven's stare when she'd stripped off her clothes was enough to scorch an entire city.

Raven reached past her and grabbed a washcloth hanging from a hook. He squeezed shower gel on it and washed every inch of her skin. With a slow, steady pace, he guided the soapy cloth down her arm and back up, across the back of her shoulders and down the other arm all the way to her fingertips. Her head fell back against his shoulder as he moved the washcloth over the top of her chest, between her breasts, down her stomach to the peak between her thighs.

Oh my god. She moaned, and her hips tilted toward his hand.

He sucked in a breath and the washcloth fell to the floor.

Goosebumps rose on her flesh as he leaned down and hovered at the base of her neck. His warm breath rebounded off her skin while his fingers traveled through her patch of curls and gently flicked her bundle of nerves.

"Oh, god." Her knees buckled, and Raven's free arm wrapped around her middle, supporting her weight.

"You drive me into a frenzy," he groaned next to her ear.

He stroked up and down at the same torturous pace and she rocked her hips, tilting her head to one side while he nuzzled her shoulder. His free hand slid around her ribs to her breast and he rolled a nipple between his thumb and forefinger. The sensations were too much.

"I can't…oh, god," she panted.

He groaned at her words and the sound maddened her, sending another ripple of heat to her core.

The hot water rushed over her breasts, traveling along her stomach and collided with his palm between her legs. Every inch of her skin burned as though on fire. While still stroking with his thumb, he gently slid a finger inside.

"Fuck," he groaned in her ear.

Her eyes rolled back in her head. "Oh, god, *Raven*."

His unrelenting pace continued while her climax built. Raven leaned around and took her mouth in a sinful kiss that sent her careening over the edge. Stars exploded behind her lids, over and over her core clenched, gripping his finger as though he were inside her.

He continued to stroke as the last of her climax rippled through her body, and she leaned her head back while her breaths slowed.

Raven sweetly kissed her shoulder. "I can't get enough of you."

He twisted her around to face him, and the wicked intentions swirling in his eyes had her body heating all over again.

He brushed his knuckles along her jaw. "Now that we've warmed up, I'm gonna slow down a bit."

He shut off the water and led her out of the shower. Taking his sweet time, he towel-dried her hair and every inch of her body, sending her once again to the edge with each skilful brush of the towel over her too-sensitive skin.

When fully dried, his powerful hands cupped her face to guide her mouth to his and their lips pressed together. Although he held her firmly, she sensed him holding back, taking it slow, as he'd promised. But his slow pace was killing her. All she wanted was for him to throw her on his bed and have his way with her.

Lightly, he massaged her breasts, flicking her nipples with his thumbs. Her knees wobbled under the pleasure. Her head fell back when he leaned down and took one in his hot mouth, swirling the peak around with his tongue.

He returned his blazing tongue to the base of her neck, kissing and sucking a trail up to nibble on her earlobe. Her hands roamed over his smooth hard chest, sliding over his broad shoulders to his muscular back, digging her nails where his wings would be. The growl that rumbled from Raven's chest was a mixture of ragged warrior and wild beast, and man, did it make her belly clench.

Her desperate need skyrocketed, the burning in her core intensifying with each lap of his skillful tongue. Tayla tilted her waist forward, searching for the friction she desperately craved and, using her nails, she scraped a path along his sides down to his hips.

Raven jolted when she brushed her finger up the smooth, hard length stretching up to her belly button. For the second time tonight, he effortlessly lifted her, wrapping her legs around his waist, only this time they both wore a lot less clothes.

Which was so much better.

His hard length pressed against her core, and she couldn't stop rolling her hips. He gripped her butt and carried her to his bed, easing her down on the thick duvet.

She leaned back, supporting her weight on her elbows as Raven stood at the foot of the bed, his smoldering gaze consuming her naked body.

"God. You're so beautiful. Heaven sent," he rasped.

She swallowed the lump in her throat and scooted up the bed as Raven crawled between her legs like a lion about to consume its helpless prey. His earthy pine scent filled the air, maddening her senses.

Maintaining eye contact, Raven slid his palms up the outside of her thighs and leaned down to gently kiss her hip. Her body writhed in response.

Oh, man, this was going to be the best night of her life.

****

Raven had been kidding himself this whole frickin' time.

Fucking delusional.

One taste would never dull the burning need for the breathtaking woman lying before him.

An eternity wouldn't be enough.

The touch of their bodies had opened his eyes, awakened his senses, his existence. Not realizing until that single moment in time, he'd been walking around in a haze, a daydream of sorts. A nightmare.

His gaze burned a trail along the slender curves of her body, up to her hazel eyes glowing bright with desire. Her hooded lids, her pink swollen lips, her hard nipples glistening from his wet kisses.

Her cheeks flushed under the weight of his stare, but there was no need for her to be embarrassed. Never in his entire existence had he laid eyes on such beauty.

And we're just getting started.

Tayla widened her legs as he crawled between them, kissing a trail to her ruby-red lips. He nibbled the bottom one, waiting for her to pull back. Instead, she leaned in and took his mouth in a heat of passion. She moaned, sliding her palms around his back.

Then things got blurry.

He barely suppressed bellowing her name as she

grazed her nails over the sensitive slits where his wings exited, causing a surge of pleasure to rip through his body. *Fuck.*

"Raven. I need you inside me," she panted.

His chest heaved in and out. He was so far gone, one slide inside her hot core and he would explode.

He eased back on his haunches and reached for the side table, snatched a foil packet, and covered himself; he'd broken enough rules for one day. Leaning down, he slid one hand under the small of her back and the other under her shoulders to lift her onto his lap.

"I don't deserve you." He brushed his knuckles on her cheek.

The smile she returned caused his chest to tighten, an unfamiliar ache intensifying behind his ribs.

She stroked her thumb along his bottom lip before leaning in to kiss him.

The outside of her core rubbed along his shaft as she rocked her hips, sliding up and down without entering, the pressure and pleasure built to a painful level. Without breaking their kiss, Raven gripped her hips and lifted her to slowly slide inside.

"God. You're so fucking hot," he grunted. "And wet."

Using every piece of self-control, he eased her down slowly, stretched and widened her core to accommodate his size as he slid in, all the way to the hilt. Beads of sweat ran down his trembling arms.

Tayla's gaze heated as he eased out and slid in once more.

She reached her arms over his shoulders. "Unfold them," she whispered.

He frowned.

"I want to feel your wings."

Fucking hell. The suggestion alone sent him spiralling out of control. Helpless to deny her, he unfurled his wings, arching them above his shoulders as he sank deeper inside her.

An all-consuming need gripped him the instant her burning fingers grazed his feathers, and Tayla cried out as another climax rocked her body. She clenched him tightly as he pumped faster, in and out, desperate for more but at the same time never wanting it to end.

She gripped his shoulders. Their gazes locked. Lost in passion, he went careening over the edge, taking her along with him.

"Tayla!" he roared. *Mine!*

On and on, he rocked inside her scorching core until they were a withering hot mess, tangled in each other's arms. As the last ripples ran through them, he softened his hold on her hips and nudged her body closer.

Their foreheads touched, panting breaths colliding in front of their mouths. Raven wrapped his wings around and enclosed the two of them, as tiny aftershocks rippled through her body.

"That was…amazing." She panted while her hands roamed his chest.

He leaned his head back to admire her face, her heavily lidded eyes, her swollen pink lips. "You are amazing." He brushed a kiss over her lips. "You warm enough now?"

She leaned in. "Actually, I've suddenly gotten a cold chill."

He grinned. "Is that, right? Well, we'd better fix that, hadn't we?"

Tayla giggled as he lifted her chin and took her mouth with his.

Chapter 25

Raven couldn't frickin' concentrate, and they all knew it. His mind focused on only one thing—Tayla.

Was she still in his bed? Was she still naked? The feel of her soft breasts in his hands, the way her body writhed with need as he stroked her and slid in and out of her heat.

Countless times, he'd glanced at the mansion and considered bolting straight back to his room to throw her down on the bed. Or lean her over the dresser. Or against the tiles in the shower.

Instead, he'd fought to keep his feet glued to their spot on the grass.

What the hell was wrong with him? This had gone too far. Focusing on his mission should be his priority.

What an epic fail.

Last night, he'd claimed her in his mind—and his body. No way he'd be able to let her go. If she was destined to be with someone else, Fate would have to fucking deal with the fact it wouldn't happen.

He was done for. Tayla had well and truly brought him to his knees, and he loved every minute of it.

He braced his forearm against a tree trunk and scanned the grounds. EJ and River stood at the edge of the forest engaged in target practice with newly forged Purah arrows. River skilfully shot them through the tree line to slam into the center of a large red circle painted on a trunk.

Raine and Aric sparred to his right, and it was a frickin' comedy act.

Raven bent at the waist and laughed as Raine knocked Aric to the ground for the second time. He couldn't help it; it was too damn funny. But his laughing only fed Aric's rage and he launched himself back onto his feet, his eyes turning a murderous shade of black, a low growl emanating from his chest.

Aric was out for blood, but Raven wasn't sure he'd get it.

They'd all made the mistake—big fucking mistake—of going easy on Raine, but she'd showed each of them, not only had she held her own, but she served up their asses on a platter while doing it. A natural warrior; strong, fast and lethal, but her skin-tight leather and long blonde hair gave the illusion of easy prey. *Ha!* Easy wasn't a word a male could use around her and escape with their balls still nestled between their legs.

Raven had pulled his punches while they sparred earlier, he'd felt a bit weird about fighting a female— one who wasn't a Fallen—but she'd gifted him with the fracture in his now swollen cheekbone.

He wouldn't make that mistake again.

Raven had then engaged River in a duel, testing his skill with a sword, while EJ got the same lesson from Raine.

River had been as confident and lethal as Raine, and even though arrows were his weapon of choice, he could do some serious damage with a sword, too.

Raven had let his mind wander at one point—well,

maybe more than once, but who was counting—and River advanced, managing to add some slices to the tops of Raven's arms.

Nothing that wouldn't heal, but it did manage to snap him out of his daydreaming damn quickly.

Raven ducked as a throwing star whizzed past his ear, narrowly missing the left side of his head and lodging in the tree trunk behind him. Speaking of daydreaming...

Aric glared at him. "That's for all the fucking laughing."

"You deserved it," he snickered. "She kicked your ass."

Aric gave him the finger as he chugged down a bottle of water.

Raven dislodged the throwing star from the trunk and bounced it in his hand, testing the weight. The Purah tingled the center of his palm and the five points glistened with a kaleidoscope of colors in the morning rays. He gripped a point and glanced at Aric. The moment Aric lifted the bottle to his lips, Raven drew back his arm and threw the star. It shot through the air with the precision and accuracy of a bullet. At the last second, Aric whipped out his dagger and sliced it across the front of his body, colliding with the throwing star. Raven expected it to shatter but instead, it held its form and slammed point down in the dirt.

Aric slid his dagger into the sheath strapped across his chest and glared at Raven with an as-if-I-would-miss smug look on his face.

Raven smacked his thigh and laughed. Dunno if it was the fresh air, the sun warming his skin or the fact he'd spent the night—and morning—pleasuring a gorgeous woman, but he hadn't felt this good since—

"Watch out!" EJ shouted.

Raven turned just in time to drop to the ground and kiss the grass as an arrow shot passed his head.

His head, goddamn it! "What the fuck?" he shouted.

"Sorry, Rave. I might need some more training with these."

"You think?" Raven grunted to his feet and brushed the dirt from his jeans.

Now Aric laughed at him.

Raven glared back, giving him a piece of his own medicine and flipped him off.

"I think that's enough for this morning before someone gets decapitated," he scowled at EJ. "That's something even the sun can't heal."

The group converged, and Aric threw around bottles of water. "Maybe it's safer if you use foam arrows, EJ?"

"Like the little kid Nerf guns I saw on TV," River snorted.

EJ rolled his eyes, picked up the arrow off the ground, and shoved it in a quiver.

Now was probably a good time to tell them about Tayla—his latest screw-up. Raven's stomach churned as he prepared to come clean.

"Listen, while you're all here." He shoved his hands in his pockets. "I'm gonna ask Tayla to stay here for a bit. It's the safest place to protect her from the Fallen, at least until we figure out her path. I'm guessing it's fucking important, given her previous Fallen attack at the university and my run-in with one last night. Plus, it's hard to overlook the fact Blaine reappeared at the exact same time; he doesn't come out of Hell for nothing."

Aric nodded. "Or maybe those twisted fucks are just excited to have a Chosen to flip for a change, rather than a standard mortal."

"Why would they prefer a Chosen over an ordinary mortal?" River asked. "I mean I know they enjoy messing with Fate's plans, but why is a Chosen so much better?"

Raven cleared his throat. "All mortals are created by Fate, but only Chosen are born with a hint of Fate's power inside them, which means they possess the brightest soul and have the purest concentration of faith for a mortal. Infecting a Chosen's soul would not only put a serious kink in Fate's plan, but also dwindle her power, almost like a piece of Fate was infected as well. Plus..." He ground his molars. "Apparently, Chosen souls reap the biggest rewards in Hell."

No way would he fail Tayla and allow Hell to capture her soul. The thought of her tortured by filthy Devoids awakened a rage in him he didn't know existed.

River slowly nodded. "Righty-o, that is a big draw, isn't it?"

Raven raked his hand through his hair. "Yeah. So, does anyone have a problem with her staying?"

He exhaled a long breath when they all shook their heads.

"You gonna let her out of your room long enough to meet us?" Aric raised an eyebrow.

Raven ignored the dig. Of course he'd have to let Tayla out of his room, he wasn't stupid enough to think he could hide her away. Not that he wanted to hide her away; quite the opposite, he wanted to parade her around as his to the whole fucking world.

But most of all, he wanted their support before approaching Tayla with his proposition.

"I'm cool as long as she doesn't have your taste in movies." EJ smirked.

Raven rolled his eyes. "What exactly is your problem with Jason Bourne?"

EJ raised an eyebrow. *Whatever.*

"Right, that's settled." He glanced at Raine, arms crossed, leaning against a tree with one leg lifted, pushing her heel into the trunk. Not a scratch on her, or even a smudge of dirt, for that matter. "Great work on the new weapons, Raine."

She gave a curt nod while maintaining her damn death stare.

But she did acknowledge him, and that was progress.

EJ lifted his nose in the air. "Mmm, I smell coffee. I'll tell you what, that has to be the best reward for an eternity of banishment."

"I would've thought you'd consider females your biggest reward." Aric smirked.

EJ sniggered. "Females *and* coffee."

The group fell into comfortable banter—except Raine, of course—as they collected the weapons and headed inside through the rear entrance for breakfast.

Breaking off from the group, Raven bolted up the rear staircase to the third floor, mentally listing all the wicked ways he could explore Tayla's body. He burst into the room—

Where the hell is she?

He gaped at the empty bed, sheets remade, duvet

folded at the foot and a small pile of clothes folded neatly at the end. He grabbed a shirt from the top and held it out, recognizing it from the clothes he bought her the last time she'd spent the night. But how did they make it to his room?

He walked into the bathroom. A fresh scent of spring-rain drifted in the air while steamy fog lingered on the basin mirror. *She showered without me*. Pity.

He backtracked to the bedroom and took another glance at the folded clothes.

Damn it. Ellen must've brought them up for her. His heart sank at the thought of her sitting in the dining room for breakfast and four Guardians, covered in weapons, bursting in.

He raced out of the bedroom and leaped down the stairs, racing to the dining room on the ground floor. The smell of bacon drifted through the air as he rounded the corner. Voices rumbled from the other side of the double doors.

Shit. He was too late.

He skidded to a halt at the doors—so he didn't look like a complete lunatic—before pushing them open. The sight nearly floored him.

The bustle of conversation filled the room, the clank of cutlery, plates and dishes served and passed around the table. Exactly what he'd longed for. The previously too-large table somehow now filled the room perfectly.

He froze in the doorway like a complete idiot, taking in the faces around the table. Aric sat in his usual spot on the opposite side, shoveling mounds of bacon onto his plate before returning the tray to the center and moving to the pancakes. River sat opposite him, listening to something Aric said, a glass of OJ in his hands and only a few smears of sauce left on his plate. EJ backed through the kitchen doors, carrying a tray of eggs, laughing as he placed it on the table. Aric's face lit up.

But what caused his chest to swell and his knees to buckle was the sight of Tayla, sitting at the head of the table—in his usual seat—chatting with Raine to her left.

Wait…what? He did a double take. Yep, she chatted with Raine.

God that was it. No way was he letting Tayla go after this. The sight of his woman—yes, he'd admit it— sitting at the head of the table, engaged in a conversation with an angel who had done nothing but throw mental daggers since arriving, absolutely floored him. He had no frickin' idea how she managed it.

Ellen arrived beside him in the doorway. "Good morning, Raven."

"Morning, Ellen."

"Raine seems to like her," she said softly.

He grinned. "How could she not?"

"Almost seems like she's meant to be here."

What? The thought hadn't even crossed his mind but now that Ellen mentioned it, it made a helluva lot of sense…but it couldn't be true.

He glanced at Ellen across his shoulder. "You think her path is meant to involve us, in more than a protective role?"

She smiled. "Perhaps her path is meant to involve *you.*"

He glanced back at Tayla. "You know that meant-to-be crap doesn't apply to us."

"You keep saying that, Raven, but do you truly believe it?"

He couldn't answer. All he knew was the sight before him caused a flutter in his belly, and his shoulders somehow felt lighter. He knew too well how dangerous hope was—powerful enough to bring immense joy, but also capable of tearing a soul to shreds.

A chair scraped the floor, snapping Raven to attention.

"Raven, are you going to join us?" Tayla waved him over.

She slid her plate to the side and pulled out another chair to sit. No fucking way. He was at her side a second later, planting his ass on his usual seat. He gripped Tayla's hips, and she giggled as he pulled her onto his lap. He'd get Ellen to buy a new table so he could fit two chairs at the head side by side. No, scrap that. Tayla didn't need a separate seat; her position was here, on his lap.

Tayla reached forward and piled food on a plate. She slid the plate beside hers and glanced over her shoulder. Her wicked grin only spurred on his raging erection. *Ah, fuck.* Would it ever be satisfied? *Definitely not.*

Twisting around, she hung her legs off the side of his lap and passed him a fork. He wasn't interested in eating—well, not food—but grabbed it anyway and did his best at one-handed eating while his free hand stroked the small of her back underneath her shirt, never breaking contact with her soft skin.

Raine pushed out from the table and slid on her fingerless leather gloves as she stood. "Nice to meet you, Tayla."

"It was lovely to meet you too, Raine."

Raine ignored everyone else in the room, including him, while she stacked her plate and cutlery. Her ridiculously high heels—capable of gouging an eye out—clicked on the wooden floor into the kitchen.

"She's really nice." Tayla smiled.

What the fuck?

Tayla laughed. "What? She *is* nice."

"If you say so." Were there two Raines in the house and he was yet to meet the nice one?

"Is she a Guardian like you?" Tayla whispered in his ear.

EJ chuckled. "No point in whispering, Tay-Tay. We could hear you from the living room."

Her cheeks reddened. "Oh, sorry."

"Ignore them. Especially EJ." Raven tucked a loose strand of hair behind her ear. "We're all Guardians, except Ellen."

She smiled. "Yes. I met Ellen earlier, by the way. Well, I met her again. You know, I kinda feel like you set this all up from the start."

Busted. "I couldn't trust anyone else to help you settle in. It would've been a catastrophe me posing as a receptionist."

She giggled. "It would've been funny seeing you try."

He brushed his fingers along her jaw. "You're not angry?"

She shook her head. "No, how could I be? Ellen has been nothing but kind to me and made me feel so welcome when I moved here, which was exactly what I needed. I'm glad she helped." She frowned. "I know it's silly, but I'm still a bit confused about something."

"Tell me."

"Well, how exactly did you make me move here, to Cedar Lodge? I mean, did you post that flyer and just hope for the best, or did you use your mind-control thingy on me?"

He leaned in and kissed her forehead. "No, that wasn't me, honey. Fate led you here." *To me.*

Hey, man, we're gonna head out now, you still coming? Aric's voice echoed in his mind.

Raven glanced around Tayla to address Aric. "Give me a minute."

"We'll meet you outside." Aric nodded to Tayla. "It's good to have you here, Tayla."

Tayla smiled. "Thank you."

When the others had left the room, Raven gently squeezed Tayla's hip. "Listen, how would you feel about staying here for a bit?"

"As in today?"

His heart pounded inside his chest, and his breakfast churned in his stomach. "More like the coming days. And nights."

Tayla's lips parted.

"Tayla, I don't wanna scare you, but as a Chosen, the Fallen will constantly target you. Your soul is bright and a source of power for them. Plus, Blaine already knows where you live, and although he hasn't hurt you, you can't trust him. It's safe here at the mansion, and you'll be free to roam around as though this is your house, too." He kissed her forehead. "As you said, it would be easier to protect you if I was with you." He wasn't above using her own words against her.

She smirked. "That seems like sound logic."

"So…is that a yes?"

She nodded. "Yes."

He exhaled a breath. "Good. I've got some things I need to get done, but when I'm finished, we'll go grab some of your stuff."

"That's okay, I can go and save you the trip."

His lips thinned. "I can't protect you if I'm not with you."

She smirked. "Fine, Mr Protective. I'll wait for you."

Tayla slid off his lap and stacked their plates on top of each other.

He grabbed her waist and pulled her back onto his lap. "Glad you agree," he grumbled before pressing his lips against hers. Their kiss heated, and he once again considered lifting her up on the table, but instead, he eased back. "I won't be long."

"Take your time," she sighed with flushed cheeks. "I'm not going anywhere."

Chapter 26

Tayla inserted the key into the front door of the cabin, the place she'd called home for almost three months, maybe a little longer. But now, as she pushed open the heavy door, everything seemed unfamiliar, foreign, like she hadn't been there for years.

How could things change so quickly?

She'd been here only yesterday, waiting nervously on the couch for Raven to pick her up for their date. A date that started out so well, had a curve ball, but ended with a spectacular bang. Or three. Recalling their activities in his room sent a delicious shiver through her middle.

Wow.

She stepped through the door and dropped her keys on the small circular dining table, a piece of furniture she'd never used for its true purpose, preferring instead to eat with a tray on her lap on the couch. Far less depressing than eating at the table alone.

Raven stood behind her and rubbed the tops of her arms.

"How long will I stay?" she wondered out loud.

"As long as you like."

How long did she want to stay? Things between them had heated up quickly and progressed faster than she'd ever experienced, but she got the sense Raven wasn't going anywhere. Could this be where her new life was leading her?

Raven wrapped his strong arms around her; a level of protectiveness she found so damn attractive. With him, she felt like she could battle the darkness, chase away the scary monsters, and live her life without fear.

He squeezed a little tighter. "You're safe with me."

"Reading my mind again?"

"I try not to, I really do but when your thoughts are in sync with mine, it's hard not to hear them."

She turned to face him. "Can the others read my mind?"

It'd be good to be prepared, especially if she stayed in the same house as the other Guardians.

"All angels have the ability to read mortal minds when they choose. But for us, we use it as a last resort, only if absolutely necessary. I don't want you to feel as though they're reading your mind twenty-four-seven while you stay with me. The others wouldn't do it; they have more respect for you than that. Blaine, on the other hand, doesn't abide by the same set of morals, so beware."

She nodded. "Good to know."

Raven took her hand in his and surveyed the living room. "So, what's yours and what's not?"

"The books on the coffee table are mine, the wine glasses in the kitchen, and my clothes and some things are upstairs. Plus, the stuff in the bathroom. Not much when you think about it."

"It's all the things important to you."

She smiled. "Exactly."

"Right. Let's grab it all then, just in case you decide to stay longer, you'll feel more at home."

All my stuff? Her stomach flipped. She was about to move in with a sexy Guardian and leave behind life as she knew it. But was she ready?

She had promised herself to listen to the universe, have faith in herself to choose the right path. Plus, Raven said at breakfast fate had led her here, so she must be listening to the right signs.

Her mouth went dry. Would she move her stuff into Raven's bedroom or a guest room? Waking up next to her Guardian each morning would be her own personal Heaven, but what happened if things didn't work out?

She quietly mulled this over for a moment as she wandered the cabin. Maybe, for the short term, she should keep the key to the cabin. After all, she'd paid rent in advance so no need to rush and hand it back straight away. At least until she was a hundred percent sure.

It was a big step. And what if Raven needed to protect another woman? *I'd have to take her out, no biggy.* Actually, she might take Raine up on her offer of self-defense lessons. Raine looked confident in kicking butt, and Tayla could use a little freshen-up. Especially if the creatures whose butts needed kicking weren't human.

Not human. That sounded so weird.

"Hey…" Raven appeared in front of her, leaning his head down to look her in the eyes. "Are you all right?"

Follow the signs, Tayla.

She nodded. "I'm good."

He smiled and pulled her in, wrapping his arms around her, and his heart beat strongly against her ear.

"You don't have to stay if you don't want."

She chuckled. "I thought you could read minds." She reached up and kissed him. "I want to stay."

He exhaled as his shoulders dropped. "Good. Let's start packing."

It took the two of them less than two hours to pack her entire life, again, into cardboard boxes and pile them into her Audi.

EJ had arrived a few moments before and poked his head in to say hi. He and Raven chatted in hushed tones out on the veranda while she did a thorough triple-check of the cabin to make sure she didn't forget anything.

Raven stood at the bottom of the stairs as she made her way down.

"All good?" he asked.

"Yep, all packed and ready to go."

"Did you leave out a jacket?"

She nodded. "It's hanging on the dining room chair. Why?"

"EJ dropped off a picnic basket full of goodies courtesy of Ellen, so we'll never hear the end of it if we don't eat it. He's going to drive your car back, so we can go together."

"You know I saw a flyer at the library the other day advertising a bonfire tonight at the old Alpine property. I heard some millionaire from out of town just bought it and he wanted to host a winter festival on the grounds. We could have our picnic there."

Raven's jaw clicked, and she knew by now that meant his protective Guardian instincts had kicked into gear. Great. He stared at her for long moments and she prepared for his "it's not safe" speech. Moving in with him, under the protection of the Guardians inside the mansion was one thing, she got that, but never allowed to venture out was another thing entirely. No way would she hide away until her Chosen path was over—whenever that might be.

She took a deep breath, ready to argue her point, but Raven spoke instead.

"Okay, let's check it out."

She raised on her toes and planted a soft kiss on his lips. "It's a date."

****

After what seemed like forever, Raven turned the Jeep onto a gravel driveway and parked in a small clearing scattered with a dozen or so cars. He grabbed the picnic basket from the back before opening her door to help her out.

He led her, hand in hand, through an open spiked wrought iron gate and up a long narrow gravel drive lit with iron fire torches evenly spaced along the edges. The whole place dished out all kinds of creepy haunted house vibes. Thank goodness for the flames illuminating the driveway. Without them, she wouldn't be able to see her hand in front of her face.

The wind stung her cheeks and even with a scarf wrapped tightly around her neck and jacket zipped up all the way, her body shivered like she wore only a bra and panties.

Raven pulled her closer. She sighed as she nestled against the walking furnace.

Halfway up the drive, the fire torches veered off to the right and continued along a smaller path, luring visitors across an immaculate landscaped lawn to a large open field in the distance.

At the junction, Raven tensed. His gaze was distant while he frowned, peering ahead along the dark sinister driveway which she imagined led to an even creepier house.

She glanced at him. "Is there something wrong?" When he didn't answer, she stepped out from under his arm. "Raven?"

He snapped to attention. "What? No, it's nothing."

He took her hand once more and led her down the narrow path toward the open field. Electricity sparked in her palm where their skin connected, and warmth seeped along her veins.

As they continued strolling down the path, Raven peered over his shoulder several times as though searching for something. Or someone?

The gravel ended, and they continued strolling over soft, dewy grass before arriving at a giant stack of timber pallets, piled high into the sky. Tayla craned her neck to peer at the wooden snowman sitting proudly on top of the pallets. Three wooden circles stacked on top of each other, black painted eyes and mouth, a carrot nose shoved through a tiny hole, and twigs attached for the arms. A bright red knitted scarf wrapped around its neck.

Gosh, she hadn't been to a bonfire in forever. And by the number of wooden pallets stacked high into the sky, this one could burn for an entire week.

People scattered around the stack with picnic blankets and cooler bags, setting up for a long night beside the open flame, while others chose to mingle around the center, plastic cups in hand. Music sifted through the space from large speakers in each corner of the clearing.

Raven led her away from the main crowd and threw out a blanket on a patch of grass toward the edge of the forest. They were so far from the bonfire she might not even feel the heat.

She relaxed onto the blanket while Raven placed an old-fashioned wicker basket in front of them and meticulously set up an assortment of delights, as he had the night before.

"Yum," she murmured.

"Ellen likes to fuss about these kinds of things."

She chuckled. "Lucky us."

A soft glow from the torches illuminated Raven's strong jawline and his deep blue eyes, and she found herself staring…*ogling*.

Oh, I'm so done for.

She stretched her legs out and tilted her head back to admire the clear night—she couldn't stare at Raven all night. Plus, dark cold nights like these somehow created magical clear skies, and tonight was no exception. Millions of tiny stars and planets scattered across the darkness like sparkly diamonds, the Milky Way Galaxy glowing like a smear of glittering fairy dust thrown from one side of the sky to the other.

The heat of Raven's gaze tingled her skin. Being this close to him was intoxicating. Turning her head, she met the burning gaze of his deep blue eyes swirling with black. He offered her a glass of wine and she took it, taking a gulp before peering over at the bonfire waiting to be lit.

Raven relaxed on his side, propped up by his elbow. "Are you warm enough?"

She grinned. "What would happen if I'm not?"

He shrugged one shoulder. "We'd leave. Go warm

up some place a little less public."

"Let's at least wait until the bonfire's lit."

"If we must," he grumbled.

Tayla grinned and turned back toward the sacrificial snowman as two men walked with metal jugs, pouring liquid around the base. The next minute, one threw in a lit match, and the bonfire ignited. Cheers erupted from the crowd and those closest retreated a few steps as the flames grew.

She peered back at Raven. "So…I've been wondering, how exactly does an angel become a Fallen?"

Raven chuckled. "Another interrogation dinner?"

"Sorry, I'm just curious. I want to know everything."

Raven brushed his knuckles down her arm. "It's fine. I'd be concerned if you didn't have questions." He took a long deep breath and peered up at the sky before looking back at her. "It rarely happens instantly. In fact, it's only happened that way a handful of times in history. Lash was the first; he severed his connection to the Heavens the instant he made the decision to fall. Blaine was another. But for most angels, it happens gradually, over time."

She kept silent, allowing the words to spill from Raven's mouth, greedy for every bit of new information.

"You see, in the Heavens, angels are celestial beings filled with love, joy and faith. They don't need to maintain the light in their soul, it's just there, always guiding, nurturing, and healing. But the longer an angel spends time in the mortal realm, the more influenced they are by mortality, and the harder they have to work to maintain the connection to the Heavens. Over the years and centuries, all that death and destruction, along with the influence of the Fallen, takes its toll. When this happens, most angels return to the Heavens for a period of time, to restore their faith, strengthen the connection, kind of like what mortals call checking themselves into rehab."

Tayla chortled.

"But for some…they choose not to return and instead give in to the influences and in the end become Fallen."

Tayla took another sip as her mind scrambled to take it all in. She didn't expect there to be so much to understand. *Duh, it's a whole other world.* An immortal world.

"Can a Fallen be saved?"

Raven scoffed and peered toward the flames. "I honestly don't know. It's never happened before."

She didn't miss the sorrow in his voice and the fact Blaine was one of those Fallen who may never be saved. She chose that moment to cease her interrogation before she ruined the mood entirely. Instead, she grabbed a cracker with a slice of Brie and glanced at the bonfire. Now in full burn, the flames stretched high like giant fingers reaching up at the sacrificed snowman, its knitted scarf the first to light. Wood smoke and pine filled the air, twigs crackled under the flames, and she found herself mesmerized by the fire before her. The haunting sound of Pete Murray's *So Beautiful* played in the background through the speakers; its soothing tune lulling her body into a state of relaxation.

A strange tingle traveled through her body, beginning in her toes, gliding up her legs and settling in her core. She turned to Raven as fantasies swirled in her mind of the two of them sprawled out on the blanket.

He sat up and leaned in closer to brush his thumb over her bottom lip, causing her chest to tighten and making it difficult to inhale.

Gosh, it was suddenly boiling. She tugged the scarf away from her neck and dropped it in her lap. A gradual fog drifted through her head and everything around her faded away; leaving only her and Raven, in that single moment. And man, he smelled so darn good.

Without taking his gaze off her, Raven slowly unzipped her jacket and used it to pull her closer. Her belly clenched when his lips pressed against hers.

Her breaths came hard and fast, and her body writhed with need. She shuffled closer and shoved the jacket off her shoulders.

Closer. Can't get enough.

Cold air slapped her in the face when Raven retreated, breaking her trance.

"You have to be kidding me," Raven snapped.

What?

Suddenly, he was on his feet, glaring at the trees behind them. "Stay here," he commanded. "I mean it. Do. Not. Move."

Before she had the chance to protest, he bolted into the forest.

What the heck just happened? Did she accidently project the wicked images in her mind and scare him off? No, she sensed his desire in their kiss, in his swirling, black irises.

She glanced at the bonfire, the image before her blurred as though a thin veil of cloud rolled over the entire space. She focused on the couple closest to her, curled up in each other's arms on a picnic blanket, jackets and beanies tossed beside them.

The flames were too hot.

Tayla stood and faced the dense forest where Raven had entered and squinted trying to see more clearly. It didn't help.

Should she go after him?

She waited several minutes, the churning in her stomach competed with the tingling in her blood. Every nerve ending sparked and prickled and she grew more fidgety by the second. Her fingers tapped on her pants, scratched an invisible itch on her chest. Something crawled inside her skin, along her hips, the flames singing her from the inside out.

Okay, time's up. She couldn't stand it any longer, she had to get away from the heat. Crouching down, she shoved everything back in the basket. She'd go back to the Jeep and wait for Raven there…

The snap of a tree branch sounded behind her. She froze. Turning her head, she braved a peek over her shoulder. Nothing.

She stood, grabbed her cell phone from her back pocket and turned on the flashlight, aiming it at the tree line.

A series of clangs, like a sword fight, echoed in the darkness.

She took a step closer. "Raven?" Her voice barely above a whisper.

A male voice shouted through the trees, followed in close succession by another. Her breath hitched. From this far away, she couldn't tell if one of the voices was Raven.

What the heck was going on? Was he in there

fighting…a Fallen?

She bit her bottom lip, trying to decide what to do. What if it was Raven? What if he was hurt? What if he needed help?

She inched closer to the forest. But he'd told her to stay…

Too bad. She couldn't just abandon him, leave him in the forest while she ran to the safety of the Jeep.

With a long deep breath in, she crept into the eerie forest, guided by the light on her phone.

The fog thinned with each step farther into the forest. Her mind cleared as though she woke from a heavy dose of anesthetic. She took another step. The crawling sensations eased, disappearing from beneath her skin as quickly as they came.

Her heart leaped from her chest when a twig snapped under her shoe and the sound echoed through the darkness around her.

Maybe this was a bad idea.

The forest was straight-out-of-a-horror-movie creepy. Thin rays of moonlight broke through the thick tree canopy, illuminating the branches, which stretched out like wrinkly arms creating all kinds of scary shapes and shadows.

They're just shadows, they can't hurt you.

Swallowing the lump in her throat, she continued on, shining the light from her phone on the ground to avoid tripping. But every rustle made her more and more jumpy to the point the pounding of her pulse in her ears drowned out all other noises.

"Raven," she whispered to the darkness.

She halted, holding her breath and waiting for a reply. Nothing.

Tayla jumped when a loud snap sounded to her left, followed by a grunt. Raven? She narrowed her eyes, focusing in the direction of the sound but saw nothing other than never-ending blackness and sinister shadows.

She kept her light pointed to the ground. If she raised it, she may regret what it illuminated.

"Who's there?" she whispered.

Silence.

Another loud snap echoed in the darkness. Closer this time. Followed by heavy thumps as though someone—or something—stomped the forest floor.

She ducked behind a tree and shoved her phone back in her pocket. She couldn't risk discovery. Her heart sank. What if it wasn't Raven?

Tayla poked her head around the trunk and sucked in a breath. As her vision adjusted to the complete darkness, she caught a large shadow between two trees. Stalking in her direction. She moved closer to the tree and her foot kicked a rock. *Yes!* She snatched it off the ground and gripped it in her palm, ready to use as a weapon.

Peeking around the trunk again, the shadow grew larger the closer it came, forming the shape of a tall person. Male or female, she couldn't tell. *Wait!* She recognized the shadow of wings extending over its shoulders. But in the darkness, she couldn't tell what color they were.

She swallowed the lump in her throat. They could be crimson.

She held her breath and gripped the rock tighter. Closer and closer the shadow came. Adrenaline pumped through her veins, her heart at a rapid rate. The shadow would reach her any second.

Deep breath. She squeezed the rock tighter. Three…two…

In a split second, the shadow disappeared and reappeared behind her. The rock flung out of her hand. Her back slammed hard against the tree, expelling the air from her lungs.

A large hand covered her mouth to muffle her scream.

Chapter 27

Raven leaped back to dodge a kick to his side from yet another Fallen. He'd lost count how many he'd taken down, but the line didn't end. More appeared for each one he turned to mist.

Find her and get her the hell out of here.

He prayed Tayla stayed where he left her, but he sensed she hadn't. Her heart raced through their connection and her nausea swirled in the pit of his stomach. Nope, he'd put money on the fact she'd fucking followed him into the forest.

"Ugh!" he grunted, dodging another strike.

He sliced his short blade down diagonally, striking the Fallen across the bare chest. Blood poured from the wound, but it barely noticed. The Fallen lunged forward in a counterattack, rapidly criss-crossing daggers, and Raven again went on the defense.

He needed to get back to Tayla, needed to ensure she was safe.

Where the hell are—

Aric shot through the tree canopy and landed on the ground behind the soon-to-be-toast Fallen. Sensing the threat, the Fallen turned his head, but too late, Aric's dagger punctured cleanly through his back, straight into the Fallen's blackened heart. The piece of shit peered down with gaping eyes as the heavenly water rapidly traveled through its bloodstream, exploding flesh and bone into crystal-like mist before blowing away into the night.

Raven bent at the waist, sucking in quick breaths.

Aric stepped closer. "You need a lie down, old man?"

Raven straightened, hands on his hips with the hilts of his short swords pressed against his sides. "Nice of you to show up…at the end."

"Spoke too soon, man," Aric snorted as he turned to face the new threat, daggers in both hands, ready to engage.

You take the right, Raven said to Aric.

Aric nodded and charged forward.

Blades clanged, and the sounds of grunts echoed through the trees.

Out of the corner of his eye, Raven admired Aric's technique. Daggers in hand, his arms effortlessly jabbed and slashed at a rapid pace, slicing the Fallen across the chest, on the arms, across a cheek, on the tops of the thighs. Only then, after the slow leaking caused the Fallen to waver from the blood loss, did Aric slam his dagger in its heart, sending him back to Hell.

The clang of Raven's sword brought him back into focus, and he ducked in time to save his head from being cleanly removed.

A wave of strength roared to life as he zeroed in on the dark angel before him. He stalked forward, parrying with the Fallen, forcing him to retreat as Raven stretched forward and sliced his blade down diagonally. The Fallen leaned backward to dodge and Raven leaped forward at the same time, catching him off balance. The move worked, and he jammed his blade through the chest, straight into the heart. Raven pulled out his blade and the Fallen fell to the ground before exploding into mist.

He heaved in a breath and surveyed the trees before slipping his swords back into their sheaths at his waist.

He turned to Aric. "Where are the others?"

"EJ took the newbies to the bonfire. I told them to wrap it up and send the mortals on their way." Aric wiped his daggers on the thigh of his jeans. "How'd you know there were Fallen here?"

"I felt the shift in energy. They must've used the bonfire to lure mortals here so they could fucking infect a heap of souls at once."

"From the air, it looked like the forest wraps around a Gothic-style castle. We'll go check it out and see if anyone's home."

"Tayla said some millionaire from outta town bought it. Damn it. I've gotta find her and get her the hell outta here. I left her at the bonfire, but I doubt she's still sitting there."

"You need help, man?"

"No, you go ahead and find the others. I'll touch base once she's safe."

Aric and Raven slapped palms before taking off in opposite directions.

Raven raced through the forest, focusing on his connection with Tayla to guide him. Her heart hammered and adrenaline pumped through her veins.

He jumped a fallen branch, half-sprinting, half-flying, his feet pounding against the dirt, snapping twigs. Their connection guided him to the left, back toward the bonfire, growing stronger and clearer the closer he got. He rounded a wide trunk and, at last, he spotted her.

He clenched his jaw.

Tayla stumbled backward, eyes wide, her hand held out in front, holding off a fucking Fallen.

His feral crimson wings spread wide, blazing red eyes glowed in the darkness. The revolting stench of choking ash filled the air.

The Fallen stalked toward Tayla, taunting her with words Raven was too furious to comprehend. Both wings curved around, and the piece of shit aimed poisonous talons straight at Tayla's heart. One scrape would end her mortal life in a split-second.

Big fucking mistake.

Raven charged forward, his twin blades raised above his head. The Fallen, so consumed in his game, didn't sense Raven's arrival. A second before his swords plunged into the Fallen's back, he burst into flames. Raven recoiled from the heat as the flames roared to life. The Fallen's screams echoed through the darkness around him, wildly thrashing its limbs to extinguish the fire, but to no avail. Within a few short seconds, the Fallen's body disintegrated. All that remained was a pile of ash where it stood moments before.

Raven kicked the ash with his shoe. *What the hell just happened?*

A strangled sound escaped Tayla's lips, and he snapped back into focus. He took a slow and steady step toward her, his hands raised in front of him.

"Tayla, it's me," he softly spoke.

She staggered back against a tree, eyes wide, her trembling hands holding him off.

"You're safe now."

Tayla's gaze darted left and right as though assessing new threats. Her shaky hands still in front of her.

He risked another step, close enough to touch her palm.

"Tayla, it's me, Raven."

Tayla blinked a few times. "R-Raven?" she croaked.

"Yes, honey, it's me."

Her arms fell to her sides and Raven closed the distance between them, embracing her trembling body.

"The red eyes...the smoke..." Tayla mumbled.

"I know, but you're safe now. I've got you."

Tayla leaned against his chest and he lightly kissed the top of her head.

The clanging of swords echoed in the distance. "I need to get you out of here, it's not safe. We're gonna take a little flight."

She leaned back. "*What?*" Her face suddenly pale, her gorgeous eyes wide again.

He held her gaze. "I'm going to fly you home."

"You're what*?*" She retreated from the safety of his arms. "No way. No, no, no. I don't do heights."

"You'll be perfectly safe. I flew you up to my balcony, remember?"

He tried to make light of the situation, but humor had never been his forte. That was EJ's gig. Shit, he didn't have plan B. Well, there was always a plan B, but he didn't want to put her to sleep without her consent.

"It's one thing to whisk me two stories in the air while distracting me with your kiss, but it's another thing entirely to fly me all the way home with nothing but a pair of arms preventing me from plummeting to my death."

"I've been flying for a long time; you're perfectly safe with me. I won't let anything bad happen to you."

She glared at him and retreated another step. "Something bad just happened!"

Raven froze.

"That...*thing* attacked me," she snapped, pointing at the pile of ash.

"It wouldn't have if you stayed put like I told you." He didn't have time for this, he needed to get her to safety. Now.

"I thought you were hurt! What did you expect me to do? Ugh." Tayla threw her hands in the air. "Isn't it your job to keep me safe?"

Bile rose in his throat at her words. It wasn't the first time he'd failed to keep her safe from a Fallen and he refused to make that mistake again.

He softened his tone. "Tayla, I can't tell you how sorry I am, but I need to get you outta these woods. You can scream at me all you want when we're someplace safe."

Tayla stared at him and clenched her fists.

He considered option B again. No, that would land him in deeper shit than he already was.

"Please." He wasn't above begging. "Let me get you out of here."

A moment passed and another. At least the battle sounds had ceased, for now. But that didn't mean they'd eliminated the threat.

Tayla squared her shoulders. "What if you drop me?"

He tried not to laugh—that would get him nowhere. "Tayla." He held out his hand. "I will *not* drop you."

"Can't you just drive?"

"Flying is faster."

"And higher." She shook her head. "No. I can't do it."

Right. Time for plan C.

Raven stretched out his secret weapons and grinned to himself when the distraction worked. Tayla's gaze instantly heated, locking onto his wings, her expression softened. He took advantage of the reprieve in her anger and returned her to the safety of his arms.

He gently cupped either side of her nape and lightly stoked her jawline with his thumbs. "I promise you'll be safe with me."

"You're not playing fair. And just so you know, I'm still angry with you."

"I know." He smirked. "Close your eyes."

Tayla inhaled deeply before she nodded and closed her eyes.

Electricity sparked through his veins as he gently slid his palms down her back and lifted her body to hook her legs around his waist. She followed his lead and wrapped her arms around his neck, nestling her head against his shoulder.

He gave himself a mental slap as her warm breath exhaled on the sensitive part of his neck. Now was not the time or place.

Tayla leaned her head back to peer up at him. "I'm ready."

Me too.

He tightened his grip. "Hold tight."

Tayla squeezed her lids shut again and sucked in a breath as he lifted into the night. She tucked her head closer to his neck, any closer and she'd be inside his shirt.

Do not think of that either.

Instead, Raven surveyed the landscape below, getting his first glimpse of the castle Aric had mentioned. A rectangular stone building at the end of the long narrow drive they'd used to reach the bonfire. Burgundy and black tiles covered the pitched roof with twin chimneys at either end. But there were no puffs of smoke and no exterior lights on, only darkness surrounding the castle. No signs the resident was home.

Why hadn't he seen this place before?

"Do you...have to fly so high?" Tayla's shaky voice broke him from his thoughts.

"Yes," he snickered. "Otherwise mortals would see us."

"Right. It's just, well...really high."

"There's no need to be afraid. I won't drop you."

Tayla nestled back into the crook of his neck. A shiver ran through their connection and he wrapped his arms tighter around her.

She belongs in my arms.

Raven flapped his wings and caught an updraft, using it to stretch out and glide, banking to the left. The mansion came into view up ahead. The front porch light was on, but he didn't plan to go through the front. Instead, he veered around the side and gracefully eased them down onto his balcony. He let Tayla's feet slide to the ground, but kept his arms around her waist until she regained her balance.

She opened her eyes and glanced around.

"Safely delivered," he said, folding back his wings.

"Thank you."

His cell phone pinged and he ripped it from his back pocket to read the text message.

EJ: Gang together. Weird-ass castle clear. No need to come back...finish your night on a high.

At the end was an emoji of a face sticking out a tongue. Smart-ass. Raven shoved the phone back inside his pocket and glanced up as Tayla stepped inside his room and crossed to sit at the foot of the bed.

Now that they were home, she could scream at him all she wanted. He trudged behind like a fucking puppy in trouble for pissing on the floor, and halted next to the bed post.

Tayla shifted to face him. "I'm sorry for what I said. It isn't your fault I was attacked."

"It is my fault. I left you unprotected." *Again.* "I'm the one who should apologize."

"I was stupid. I should've stayed put, like you told me."

He eased onto the edge of the bed beside her. "I shouldn't have left you. We could go back and forth like this all night."

She inspected her hands, nestled in her lap. "Was that a Fallen? It was so different from you. Red wings and eyes that seemed to glow like fire."

He nodded, remaining silent, waiting for her to continue.

Tayla's gaze grew distant as she stared toward the antique dresser. "I think...tonight wasn't the first time I've seen one." She inhaled deeply. "About six months ago, I was...attacked. It was so dark. The deserted path was a shortcut through the pine trees. I knew I shouldn't walk it alone, but I was freezing and I just wanted to get back inside. I'd walked through there a thousand times in the daylight and knew the path well. But…I didn't see him until his hand clamped over my mouth. I remember screaming at two students huddled under a lamppost at the end of the pathway, but nothing came out. It happened so fast. He knocked me to the ground, and I must've hit my head because the next thing I remember was waking up in my room."

Raven's grinding teeth echoed in his ears as he recalled the events of that night. The part where he'd left Tayla unprotected. *And I fucking did it again.*

"For a long time after," she continued, "I had nightmares of this creature with glowing red eyes. I'd wake up coughing like I'd inhaled a lungful of smoke."

Raven held his breath.

"The counselor said I conjured the red eyes in the nightmares, I associated the feature with evil creatures. But tonight…I came face to face with a real one. A creature that exists outside my nightmares."

He took her hands in his and she peered down at them entwined in her lap. "Why do I feel so safe when I'm with you?"

"Because I'll always protect you."

Her lips thinned and she glanced across her shoulder at him. "Because it's your job?"

"Tayla." He brushed his knuckles along her cheekbone, and she leaned her head into his hand. "You mean more to me than just a job."

She smiled, but it didn't reach her eyes.

"I'm sorry I wasn't there quicker." He crooked a finger, lifting her chin to gently kiss her lips.

The pang in his heart sharpened. He couldn't deceive her any longer, he had to tell her the truth about him. She deserved to know.

He cleared his throat. "I need to…tell you something."

She shook her head. "I think I've had enough surprises for one night."

"But I need to—"

"Raven, stop talking and make love to me."

Their eyes locked. He should resist, pull back until he told her the truth.

"Whatever it is, it can wait until tomorrow," she breathed and leaned in.

His restraint fell away the moment her lips pressed against his.

First thing tomorrow, he would tell her everything, including the part where he was becoming one of the monsters from her nightmares.

Chapter 28

Tayla woke, cocooned in Raven's delicious heat, his body pressed hard against her back, strong arms wrapped protectively around her waist. She wasn't going anywhere, even if she wanted to—which she didn't.

She stretched out her legs and flexed her toes, feeling her calves loosen and lengthen. Her body ached in all the right places, thanks to their steamy night together. Just thinking about it caused her belly to clench. Raven had been so eager to please her, and not just once.

Oh, man. The way their bodies joined together had her seeing stars. Absolute bliss. No, bliss wasn't a strong enough word. *Heaven.* Yes, it'd been heaven, and how fitting was that? The strange connection she experienced with him increased the more time they spent together. Could she fall any harder for him? Last night, as Raven climaxed inside her, her mind had claimed him as hers, as though in that single moment she'd bound her entire heart and soul to him, and there was no going back.

Was their connection so strong because she was his assigned Chosen? Or simply because he was an angel?

Tayla pried open her lids and instantly regretted the decision. Laser beams of sunlight shot through the open blinds and burned her sleep-sensitive eyes. She snapped her lids shut and waited until the tiny red flashes disappeared before easing them open once more.

Adjusting to the brightness, she took in the room, still not wanting to remove her body from its warm haven.

This will be our room.

Golden rays streamed through the tall uncovered windows, basking the furniture in an orange glow. Craning her neck, she caught a glimpse outside and spotted fog rolling between the tops of the pine trees. The morning light drifted through the wispy clouds, making it look like they glowed.

Fog equaled cold. Better to be safe and stay in bed, like she needed much convincing.

She lowered her head onto the pillow and dozed off to Raven's soft snoring, the only noise in the peacefully quiet house.

His strong arm nudged her closer.

"Good morning, beautiful," he groggily whispered.

Goosebumps sprouted along her leg. "Good morning to you, too."

"You hungry? I could use some breakfast," he said, pressing his length against her buttocks.

Her stomach grumbled—they hadn't eaten much last night. Well, food, that is.

She giggled like a love-sick teenager. "Really? You haven't had enough?"

"Doubt I could when it comes to you."

She moaned as his lips brushed the top of her shoulder and at the base of her neck, trailing hot kisses up to nibble on her ear lobe.

"Maybe a shower?" he groaned hotly against her

ear.

Raven smoothed his sword-roughened palm down her waist, and his middle finger circled her hip. A shiver ran through her body, heating between her legs.

His fingers sneaked down the tops of her thighs—

Thud! Thud!

Raven ignored the loud banging on the door—had she imagined it—and grazed his hand on the inside of her thigh, easing her legs apart as he lifted one to hang over his.

Her heart thumped loudly as his hot lips caressed her neck...

Bang! Bang!

The knock banged on the door more forcefully this time.

"Raven, man," a guy's voice called from the hallway. "You know I'll kick down the door if you don't answer."

Raven cursed to himself and angled his head away from her ear without removing his wandering hand. "What?" he snapped. "I'm busy."

Her cheeks burned. *Please tell me the door's locked.*

"Good, you're awake. Good morning, Tayla. Raven, we're meeting in five."

Tayla breathed a sigh of relief, the guy no longer at risk of barging in.

Raven took his time replying, inching his hand to the hot spot between her legs. His finger lightly stroked, and Tayla bit the inside of her cheek to keep from crying out.

"Make it ten," he growled to the door.

"Copy that. Have fun in there, you two."

Tayla cringed. Could it get any more awkward? Her shoulders relaxed as heavy footsteps thumped down a flight of stairs before slowing fading out of earshot.

Phew!

Raven carried on as though the interruption had never happened. He slid a finger down her core, easing inside, while his thumb stroked her in a steady rhythm. Her body tingled and ached all over and a moan escaped her lips when Raven resumed his hot kisses on her neck.

Building and building, her body writhed with need. Her hips rocked of their own accord.

"Let go, honey," he groaned.

His command quickly sent her over the edge. Tiny stars exploded behind her closed lids while her core clenched as Raven wrung every last sensation.

"I need to be inside you," he rumbled.

She moaned as he eased his length inside her from behind, sending her body screaming to the edge again.

Raven eased out and slid back in. His hands roamed up the curve of her belly, between her breasts, until he reached her jaw and tilted it to face him. He increased the tempo as he took her mouth in a hot kiss. Her hips rolled back and forth as they found their rhythm, while his rough hands squeezed her nipples, rolling them between his fingers, building her up for yet another release.

"Tell me you're mine," he groaned between kisses.

Oh, god!

"Yes! Raven, I'm yours!" she cried out as a shattering climax ripped through her body, too lost in the spiral to care if everyone in the household heard her succumb to the most intense pleasure she'd ever experienced.

"Mine!" Raven roared as he convulsed with his release.

Eventually, their bodies stilled, their panting breaths and heart rates yet to follow. Raven released his grip on her waist and delivered soft sweet kisses along her shoulder.

"God, I want to stay here with you, forever," he said, brushing his thumb along her lips.

"Be careful what you wish for. Forever's a long time."

"Forever wouldn't be long enough," he said, with a hint of sadness in his tone.

What was his deal? One minute, he devoured her with scorching passion and the next, he acted as though the world was ending.

Cold air drifted over her heated flesh as Raven rolled away. She lay on her back to admire his over six-foot, fully naked, warrior body as he slipped out of bed.

He strolled over to his closet. She traced his back with her eyes, lingering over the tattooed sword etched down the center and along the two faint matching scars running parallel down his shoulder blades, where his sensual wings sprouted. She leered as his muscles flexed when he lifted a black crew neck tee over his head, sadly taking her view with it. He entered the closet, briefly disappearing out of sight and returning fully clothed.

"Why the pout?" He smirked at her.

"You're dressed, but I'm still lying in your bed…naked."

Her breath hitched at the speed he returned to the

side of the bed.

He leaned over and kissed her lips, lingering for the briefest moment. "Our bed."

Tayla smiled up at him, the pang in her chest intensifying.

"I won't be long." He lowered his voice. "And then I intend to fix the problem of me being dressed."

Raven kissed her forehead before turning and striding out of the room, the door softly clicking behind him.

Leaving her a hot, achy mess.

The silence of the room created havoc in her mind instantly swirling with unanswered questions. Was she falling for Raven too fast? *Yes!* Was it too soon to move in with him even though her gut told her to? *Listen to the signs, Tayla.* Should she lay here and wait for him to return? Would Raven leave her once his Guardian job was complete?

Nope, she refused to go down that bunny trail.

Let the universe guide you, she reminded herself.

For a reason beyond her understanding, being with Raven felt right, as though the universe had intentionally collided her path with his and made her a Chosen for a reason. So, for now, she didn't plan to fight it. In fact, she'd embrace it.

Chapter 29

Goddamn it, could this meeting go any longer?

Raven glared at the faces around the table. EJ to his right, laptops fired up in front of him, brows creased as he stared between the screens. Raine stood with her arms crossed, ass against the side table as though she wanted to be there as much as he did. Which was, oh, about zero percent. Aric reclined to his left, chair pushed out from the table, flipping a dagger in one hand, his head tilted toward River, whose lips moved but Raven didn't hear. All his brain computed was a whole load of gibberish.

Some sort of debrief about the events at the bonfire…something about the number of Fallen…*yadda, yadda*…no one home at the medieval castle…*blah, blah, blah.*

Raven drummed his fingers on the mahogany table, hoping to annoy the shit out of the others so they'd get up and leave. And he could return to Tayla, currently lying naked in their bed. Or maybe showering in their bathroom.

His heart swelled, recalling the sight of her clothes filling the closet and a second towel hanging beside his. Simple pleasures he hadn't known he yearned for. And speaking of pleasures—

"Rave? Helloooo, anyone in there?" EJ's voice

snapped him from his wicked thoughts.

Save those ideas for later.

Raven glared up as Aric and River strode out of the room, disappearing around the corner, Raine's mile-high heels clicking a few steps behind them.

Was it finally over? "Sorry, what?"

"Fuck me," EJ cackled. "You're totally in another realm, Rave."

Raven rose from his chair.

"You mind hanging back for a bit?" EJ leaned his forearms on the back of his chair.

Really? Raven groaned to himself. *Of all the days...*

Crossing to the side table, Raven poured a generous whiskey from the crystal decanter. Not his usual poison, but better than that rocket-fuel gin Raine had started drinking.

"Sure, EJ, what's up?" On second thought, EJ hanging back after a meeting equaled a triple-shot.

He turned back to face EJ with what he hoped was a "time starts now" expression on his face...*tick-tock...*

"Just thought I'd see how you were."

What the hell? He didn't have time to discuss feelings, he had somewhere to be. "Fine, why?" he snapped.

EJ stared at him a long while before answering. "Must be nice having Tayla here."

He downed the whiskey in one swig and refilled his glass. "She's safer here."

"And you're finally getting laid." EJ cackled.

Raven rolled his eyes. "Piss off."

"No seriously, what the hell's up? For someone who's let off a lot of steam, you seem to be churning with some serious fucking conflict. And don't feed me any bullshit excuses."

He didn't want to do this now. He didn't want to do this ever. But the sooner he gave EJ an answer, the sooner he could track down Tayla.

He took a deep breath. "To be honest, I'm constantly torn between whether I'm risking her life by having her close and whether I can exist without her by my side."

EJ held his gaze. "Anything else?"

He shot back the whiskey and refilled the glass. "And..." Raven half shrugged. "There's a part of me that believes she deserves better. Better than me."

There. He'd said it.

"Because she's a Chosen or the fact you're undergoing a change of wardrobe so to speak?"

Raven's head shot up. "What?"

"If you ask me, crimson's not really your color."

Raven squeezed his forehead. "How long have you known?"

"The real question is what are you doing about it?"

Raven took another swig of the whiskey that suddenly tasted like ass. "It's under control. I haven't had any feathers change for a while now. Do the others know?"

EJ shook his head. "Not my secret to tell."

Raven exhaled a breath. EJ knowing was one too many.

"Next question, have you told Tayla about it?"

Raven shook his head. "No."

The silence stretched between them. Raven stared down at the glass in his hand, swishing the pale orange liquid around in circles, creating a miniature whirlpool, which would any second now spiral out of control. *Story of my fucking life.*

EJ rounded the table to stand beside him. "Rave, don't you think she deserves to know what she's signing up for? It won't end well if you keep it from her."

Raven's heart sank. "Have you seen it?"

"A mortal's path can always change; you know that. But you have to be up front with her."

Was that a yes or no?

Raven slid the glass onto the table and paced the boardroom. "I can't bring myself to tell her, to see the horror and disgust on her face like last night after that piece of shit at the bonfire. It's bad enough she had to fucking relive the attack at the university. She's almost died—not once, but twice—because I screwed up and didn't protect her." He shook his head. "To admit to her that one day the attacking Fallen could be me? It's too much—"

"What did you say?"

Raven spun to find Tayla gaping back at him from the doorway.

EJ muttered a curse, and Raven could have sworn he uttered the words "too late."

Raven peered at EJ.

EJ tilted his head with a stern look on his face. *Choose wisely, Rave,* he said in Raven's mind before he cleared his throat. "I'll leave you two to it."

Tayla stepped aside as EJ passed her and exited the room.

She glared at Raven. *If looks could kill...* "What did you just say?"

Raven took a deep breath. "Tayla—"

"How did you know I was attacked in a courtyard at uni? Oh wait, that's right, you've got a whole file on my life history, haven't you? Tell me what the heck is going on, and don't try to twist the truth."

Tayla's voice repeating Blaine's words put a bitter taste in his mouth.

He closed his eyes. How the hell would he climb out of this one? EJ's warning echoed in his mind; he had to tell Tayla the truth. Something he should have done last night.

He swallowed the lump in his throat and glanced back at her. "I knew because I was there, I took out the Fallen responsible. I saved you."

Tayla scoffed. "Saved me? What, did you think it amusing to watch that Fallen have some fun with me first before you stepped in all knight-in-shining-armor?" Her voice raised an octave.

"No, it wasn't like that." *Keep it together, Raven.*

"Do tell, Raven. What could possibly have kept you from stepping in earlier?" Tayla held her palms up, facing him. "No, don't bother, you'll probably just erase it from my memory anyway," she sneered.

Raven swallowed the bile rising in his throat. Breathe in…and out. He stepped toward her.

"Stay where you are," she snapped.

He froze mid-step. "I was fighting another Fallen on the other side of campus when you were attacked. I got there as soon as I could."

"Oh, great. I feel so much better." Bitter sarcasm laced her voice.

"Honey, please don't—"

"Don't you dare call me that."

And that was the moment his world crumbled to

dust for the second time in his existence.

****

How could I have been so stupid?

Tayla shook her head.

He's lying to me again. Well, not technically lying, but intentionally withholding the truth. Again. And now he stood in front of her trying to justify why he'd done it.

"How could you do that to me?" she yelled. "The police searched for weeks for the attacker, doubting my story more and more because they couldn't find one. Nor any witnesses. I felt like I was going crazy, like I imagined it. Some people even whispered I did the injuries myself." She glared at Raven. "I spent months in counseling because of those nightmares."

"I'm so sorry," he choked.

"No you're not, Raven. You're just sorry you got caught. Again. God, I probably would've preferred you erase the memory."

"That wasn't an option. There were too many mortals who saw me carry you to your room, I would've had to erase everyone's memory."

She threw her hands in the air. "Then you should have told me."

"The night of the attack, you had no idea this world even existed." He fought to keep his voice level.

"But keeping me in the dark didn't make it right."

"Tayla, I'm sorry. I realize that now. I'll always protect you."

"Protect me?" A sharp pain clawed her chest. How could she have been so stupid? She trusted him and he'd deceived her. Made her believe they had a connection when all that time he hid the truth. He couldn't protect her, not when he was turning into one of the monsters. "How can you protect me from yourself?"

Raven's eyes flickered black, reminding her he was an immortal, capable of breaking her neck with the snap of his fingers. She had to get out of here.

He inched closer. "You're safe here with me."

"The safest place for me right now is far away from you."

A muscle in his jaw flexed as though he mentally counted to ten. "Don't do this. Let me explain."

"There's nothing to explain. For the first time, everything is crystal clear." She backed out the door.

"Please don't go," he choked. "I...love you."

Her step faulted. *Don't stop, Tayla, walk away.*

"Then you should have trusted me as much as I did you." She turned away and raced down the hall, not giving him the chance to reply.

****

Tayla put one foot in front of the other as she crossed the garage to her Audi.

Parked beside Raven's Jeep...

Raven had remained silent the entire time she'd ripped her clothes off the hangers and stuffed them into a duffle bag, piling her toiletries on top, packing necessities only. The rest could wait until she was strong enough to face him without the risk of caving. Her eyes stung when she'd stormed from the closet to find him sitting at the foot of the bed, his head in his hands.

The bed they'd shared. The bed he'd earlier declared as theirs.

No. She had to leave. How could she be with

291

someone turning into one of those monsters? How could she be with someone who didn't trust her?

Unlocking her car, she stuffed the duffle bag on the backseat and turned to find Raven standing in front of her, his eyes puffy, his hands shoved into the pockets of his jeans.

"Tayla, please. Don't leave. I meant what I said."

His earthy, pine scent weakened her restraint. *No, it has to be this way.*

"I can't be with a monster," she said, shaking her head.

Raven didn't fight her when she opened the driver's door and sank down on the seat, and the engine roared to life.

Through watery eyes, she peered in the rear-view mirror as the car screamed out of the garage; Raven fell to his knees and roared her name so loudly it vibrated the car windows.

Keep driving, Tayla, keep driving.

Rounding the bend onto the gravel drive, Tayla silently sobbed as her heart ripped apart into a thousand tiny pieces.

Chapter 30

Tayla sulked alone on the lumpy couch at her cabin in front of a dying fire, a cold cup of tea on the side table and her gratitude journal lying open on her lap.

A blank page stared back at her. Taunting her.

Think of one positive thing…

Peering over her shoulder, she scowled at the bright, cloudless sky through the paneled glass windows. Golden rays streamed through the drawn curtains, as though the sun mocked her, its warmth seeping onto the leather couch and across her lap.

She snatched the pen and scrawled in the journal.

Dear stupid journal,

The sun rose again today, as though nothing had ever happened. As if the entire world hadn't fallen off its axis and gone tumbling into this black hole. I hate it now, more and more each day.

*Its warmth reminds me of…*him.

Chapter 31

Faint buzzing swarmed through Raven's head, his thoughts too foggy to identify the source. Was he dreaming?

Semi-awake, he rolled onto his side.

The buzzing sounded again.

He eased open his heavy lids, his vision blurry. Beside the toppled, empty bourbon bottle, a dim light illuminated the dark room in time with a mini-jackhammer pounding into his skull.

He blinked several times, bringing the light into focus. With a heavy arm, he reached over and grabbed his cell phone as the light extinguished.

Good, saves me from answering it.

About to throw the device across the room silencing it forever, the screen lit up once more.

"What—" Raven barked into the handset.

"Rave, get down here. Now," EJ shouted.

The urgency in his voice snapped Raven to attention.

"Where?" He cradled the phone between his shoulder and ear as he swung his legs out of bed and yanked up his jeans, kicking aside the bourbon bottle at his feet.

"SubZero."

Which explained the shit music screaming in the

background.

"On my way."

Raven stuffed the phone into his back pocket, shoved a smelly shirt over his head, and snatched his jacket off the floor before racing out of the room. He bolted down the stairs, two at a time, unfurling his wings as he sprinted. Once outside, he pushed off the ground and shot into the air, pounded his wings, gaining height and speed. The dark sky remained covered in stormy clouds, making it easier for him to blend in.

Because nothing good came from revealing his true identity.

Raven slammed his wings harder on the downward flap, gaining more thrust and speed. Wind whistled past his ears, the frigid air stinging the tips. At least it had stopped fucking raining for once.

Curving around the base of the mountain, the town of Summit Creek came into view, illuminated in the dark valley like a beacon at the bottom of a ravine. SubZero was in the center of town, a club dedicated to that shit EJ called music—which made Raven's head throb more than a bourbon-bender—and constantly filled with intoxicated mortals practically screwing on the dance floor.

No thanks.

His style was the small whiskey bar on the outskirts, where mortals went to drown in their sorrows. Alone. A place where the only conversation expected was ordering the next drink and, even then, only a chin jerk was required.

For the past four days, eighteen hours and thirty-six minutes, he'd hosted a pity-party for one right in the comfort of his own bedroom.

The neon orange sign at the club's entrance came into view. Raven folded his wings, descending swiftly to touch down in the dimly lit alleyway at the rear of the club.

He took off sprinting the moment he connected with the gravel lot, simultaneously retracting his wings. He rounded the side of the club, up the service driveway segregating it from the neighboring building, and spotted his first Fallen.

And he was more than ready to engage.

The filthy piece of shit dark angel had a mortal female pressed against the dirty brick wall, his arms extended on either side of her head, palms flat against the wall. The Fallen glared over his shoulder, sensing the threat. Pushing the mortal aside, the Fallen turned to face Raven, leaning forward in an attack position. A wicked snarl curved on his lips.

Go home, Raven projected into the mind of the mortal, taking away the short memory of their meeting along with it. She quickly spun around and took off in the opposite direction, out to the main street.

Raven withdrew the twin short swords from the scabbards strapped to his waist and surveyed his surroundings. Double-story, red-brick, windowless walls flanked the alley, running parallel to the main street. Only two ways in and out. One from the direction he'd come, the other in the direction the mortal went.

No time to play. Other drunk, defenseless mortals could wander down the alley or cross the entrance at any moment.

But fuck, he wanted to.

The Fallen smirked at Raven and took a menacing step forward, preparing for battle. Raven caught a glint of metal as it drew a dagger from behind. He narrowed his eyes at the dark angel; rigid scars and thick black tattoos marred his neck, disappearing under the skin-tight shirt. Black tight-fitting leather pants covered thick legs with a chunky silver chain hung loosely from the belt loops.

Raven gripped the hilt of his blades and the coolness briefly stung his palms. He swung his arms in a wide arc, awakening his muscles and testing his grip.

The Fallen prowled forward.

Straight for the heart, he reminded himself.

Raven distributed his weight evenly on both feet, slightly raising on the balls, preparing to engage. The twin Purah blades, both light and cool in his palms, shimmered with heavenly power.

Eager to finish this and aid his brothers inside the club, Raven leaped forward, his blades raised out to the sides. It wouldn't hurt to cleanly detach the piece of shit's head from his body before striking through the heart.

The Fallen collided with Raven midair, swiping a single blade across his body, blocking Raven's attack. Landing back on their feet, the two engaged in a lethal battle of swords. Attacking and defending, the metal and Purah clinked when it collided.

From out of nowhere, the Fallen unfurled his crimson wings and struck him with a poisonous talon, effortlessly slicing through Raven's jacket and gouging his upper arm.

"Fuck," Raven cried out.

He lost his grip on a sword, and it clanged onto the

concrete.

Excruciating agony shot up Raven's left arm as the venom traveled through his veins, heading for his heart. The Fallen didn't get a chance to inject enough to kill him instantly, but if he didn't hurry the fuck up, it would send him to the ground.

Technically, below it.

No way would Raven give that low-life a second chance. His legs wobbled, and the Fallen took full advantage of the momentary distraction. The Fallen lunged forward, both wings curved inward with talons prepared for the fatal strike.

Raven dived to his right, falling on his uninjured arm in the nick of time to avoid the talons. Continuing his momentum, he tucked and rolled, springing up. In one swift motion, Raven raised his remaining sword above his head and slammed it into the back, piercing the Fallen straight through the heart.

The Fallen's blood curdling cry echoed down the alley as his body shuddered before it exploded into mist and drifted away with the breeze.

One down.

Raven snatched his second blade off the ground and slid them back into their scabbards, concealing the hilts with his jacket. The cool Purah traveled through the holders, tingling the top of his thighs.

He took off, exiting the narrow alley out onto the bustling street.

He dodged to the side to avoid colliding with Aric.

"I'm on this one. EJ and Raine are inside," Aric shouted over his shoulder as he sped past Raven, hot on the heels of another Fallen.

For a split second, Raven considered joining Aric

in the pursuit. He shook his head as the rational side of his brain kicked in. Aric could handle himself, especially one on one.

Or one on fifteen. Probably even one on fifty.

He spun around and raced to the club. The beefy mortal bouncer gave Raven a curt nod and released the chunky red rope, motioning for Raven to enter. Pausing just inside at the top of the dirty metal grated staircase, Raven scanned the crowd below for any sign of EJ or Raine.

The foul, sweaty air made him gag, threatening to project his recent bourbon diet, and the deafening thump of shit music drowned out any chance of conversation.

Which was the point.

He peered over the heads of hundreds of intoxicated mortals crowding the dance floor. Different colored lights flickered from all directions, making it impossible to focus on one person. He narrowed his attention to the rear of the building, where he spotted an illuminated Staff Only sign through the smoky air.

Knowing EJ, he would've taken the fight away from open areas and prying mortal eyes. There were only so many things they could write off as drunk behavior before they had to start scrubbing memories.

Raven descended the staircase onto the main dance floor. The thick humid air stuck to his clothes like a heavy weight, and he shoved his way through the drunk, half-naked mortals crowded in the too-small space. One grabbed his uninjured arm and, with a crook of her finger, begged him to join her. Without halting, he pushed the filthy, leather-wearing female's hand out of his way.

With the back of his own hand, Raven wiped away the hot beads of sweat pooling on his forehead. The revolting, stale air made his skin crawl, heating his body temperature like standing in a sauna switched to the max. While dressed in a frickin' snow suit.

More likely the Fallen venom slowly poisoned him with the sick objective of blackening his heart. That would explain the swishing of his brain and the tingling sensation creeping up his left arm as though millions of baby spiders crawled under his flesh. This was not his first brush with the poison, but with his faith so goddamn low, his immortal healing ability was in serious jeopardy. A chill ran down his spine when he thought of the realm where his soul would burn for eternity if he didn't come through this.

Hell was a walk in the park compared to that place.

Exiting the sweat-fest on the other side, a scuffle over to Raven's right caught his attention. Though her back was to him, he recognized Raine, her hair slicked back in a tight ponytail. He stepped in her direction but halted when he focused on the scene. She lurked in a dark corner with a mortal male in front of her, one hand squeezed around his throat and lifting him slightly off the ground while the other gripped his crotch. She leaned forward and said something in the male's ear and he thrashed his legs. Poor guy.

Raine glanced his way and nodded toward the Staff Only door. *Meet you in there when I'm finished with this scumbag.*

Raven turned away and left her to it.

He dodged tables crowded with non-dancing, semi-sober mortals, pausing at the door. Leaning his ear closer, he picked up muffled grunts of battle and the familiar clang of swords, but he sensed no mortals on the other side. Raven drew a blade and silently slipped through the door. His eyes took a second to adjust to the complete darkness. The room came into focus as a bulky shadow lunged toward him from the side.

Friend or foe?

A gleam of metal stabbed his side, below his ribs, and quickly retreated; the shadow prepared for the next strike.

Definitely foe.

"Fuck," Raven roared, swiping his blade out to his side, slicing off the arm of the Fallen who'd bettered him.

First time for everything. Well, second, if the talon incident counted.

The Fallen shrieked, clutching the stump, but he didn't have time to mourn. A split-second later, a Purah blade shot through the Fallen's back and out the front.

The Fallen gaped down at the hole in his chest. Sickening black blood oozed from the crevice before the body shuddered and exploded into mist.

"You good?" EJ came into view from behind where the Fallen had stood moments before.

"Just a cut." *That hurt like hell.* "You?"

"Yeah, I'm good."

Raven assessed the nicks in EJ's shirt and the tiny swabs of crimson staining the material. He lifted the hem of his own shirt and dared a glance at the gaping wound in his side. It was gonna need sutures to stop him from bleeding out before his body could heal.

Black dots danced before his eyes. Exactly how long was it 'til dawn?

"What happened?" Raven grunted as he ripped off

his jacket and shirt to press the fabric on his wound before he bled out all over the floor.

Or passed out from the Fallen venom.

EJ snatched his cell phone from his back pocket, pressing the keypad before putting it to his ear. "They were all over the fucking place when we got here. Inside and out. We tried to lure them out of the club, but there were too many. They were onto us before we could get the upper hand…" EJ turned his attention to the phone, "Where are you, 'Ric? Good. Listen, Rave's injured; can you get a hold of River and get him to grab the car? Roger that, we'll meet him out the back."

Raven held up his palm in protest. He could fly; it wasn't that bad.

EJ challenged him with four raised eyebrows. Or were there six?

Maybe EJ was right. It wouldn't be that discreet having blood fall from the sky and landing on some unsuspecting mortal. Or if he fell from the sky like a winged sack of fucking potatoes.

EJ slipped the phone back into his jeans pocket and stepped closer to Raven. "What the hell happened to your arm?"

Raven peered at the gash. The skin around the wound was dark and rotten, as though it had been festering for weeks, and thick black spider-like veins spread from the tips of his fingers up to his shoulder.

"Ran into one in the alley. I'm fine." *So far.*

"Yeah, right. It's gonna be one helluva wait 'til dawn, Rave. You're gonna need a serious boost from the sun to heal that one."

Yep. Already knew that.

The door eased open and Raine slipped through.

"What'd the poor guy do to you?" Raven asked.

"Checked out my ass then had the nerve to wink at me."

Raven attempted a mirthless laugh, which turned into a grimace as slicing pain ripped through his side. "Argh!"

EJ nodded to the rear of the room. "I compelled the staff to avoid this room, but let's not hang out to see how long it takes to wear off."

Raven winced, sliding his arms into his jacket; any part of the wounds that had begun healing just reopened. A fresh gush of warm blood seeped onto the shirt pressed against his side.

"Where's Aric?" he grunted.

"He ended up on the outskirts of town but managed to get all the runaways."

Raven trailed behind EJ, his vision fading in and out, his legs behaving like he was on a cruise ship in rough seas. With his uninjured arm, he reached out to brace himself against the smooth wall of the long dim corridor EJ led them down.

He sighed as an illuminated Exit sign came into view. Talk about a light at the end of the tunnel.

EJ pushed open a steel door and held it for Raven. A burst of fresh night air brushed his skin as he stumbled up the two steps and out into the alley behind the club, where he'd landed earlier. Raven staggered to a shadowy corner and gave his legs permission to collapse, leaning against the cold metal dumpster.

The frigid wind did nothing to cool his burning forehead.

EJ, daggers gripped in his hands, surveyed the parking lot, while Raven laid a short sword across his thighs for easy access. Not that he could do much with it.

Raine stood before him. "You look like shit."

"Thanks," he grunted. "Why were there so many in one place?"

"Dunno. Their numbers are increasing. Rapidly. And they're getting fucking bolder." EJ crossed to stand next to Raven. "I wonder if it's all connected—"

Why did EJ's voice sound so far away?

His head lolled to the side to peer up at EJ. Black and white dots blinked across his features.

An engine roared in the distance, and EJ disappeared from view. Raine moved into his vision. Her mouth moved, but he couldn't hear her words. She waved her hand in slow motion in front of his face.

Tires screeched.

His body floated up off the ground.

Grunting and swearing echoed in his swishy head before cool leather kissed his burning cheek. His knees somehow ended up under his chin.

I'm frickin' done for, was his last thought before he drifted away into the blackness.

Chapter 32

Tayla leaned her forearms on the wooden railing of the cabin's balcony. Goosebumps sprouted on her skin under the layers upon layers of clothing. She lifted her chin as mist from the rain sprayed her face. It'd been pouring constantly for the past few days, as though the universe had granted her silent plea to take away the sun; its warmth a painful reminder of Raven.

It didn't work.

Now, the freezing rain tortured her with memories of him. Of the time he'd cradled her body against his in the pouring rain and for the first time flew her up to his balcony. The exhilaration and complete sense of safety she'd felt in his arms. Her chest ached recalling that night, when he'd taken her on a date to his secluded spot, where he'd meticulously hung hundreds of tea-light lanterns in the trees, laid out cushions and culinary delights for them to enjoy. He'd been so nervous of her reaction. So eager to please her. So...protective.

Or the first time they'd made love and he'd peered down at her with total adoration and affection in his onyx eyes...

She sighed. She did mean more to him than just a job. Then why didn't he tell her he was becoming one of them? A Fallen.

I didn't give him a chance...

Tayla wiped away the mist on her numb cheeks. For the past few days, her new life had ground to a halt, as though suspended in the ether, hanging in limbo. Like the universe had given up hope. She couldn't shake the feeling she'd made a huge mistake leaving Raven, that somehow amidst all the chaos, instead of listening to the signs she'd for some reason fought them.

Nothing eased the crippling ache inside her chest. Did Raven feel it, too? Did he miss her?

He hadn't bothered to make contact since she'd stormed out of his home. *And left him on his knees, roaring my name...*

Maybe he thought it was better this way? *But he said he loved me...*

Tayla scanned the foggy tree line and froze when she caught sight of a figure, out of the corner of her eye, stepping free from the shadows.

Her shoulders sagged when the figure's face came into view.

"Disappointed to see me again, love?" Blaine's hand slammed his chest in mock horror. "Oh, you wound my blackened heart."

Chuckling, Blaine crossed the soggy driveway and stomped his unlaced boots on the steps a couple of times to rid them of mud before he joined her on the veranda.

How strangely considerate.

Tayla followed his movements, twisting around to lean against the railing.

Blaine, acting like he owned the place, shook off his worn leather jacket and reclined on the Adirondack chair, stretching his long legs out in front of him, unfazed by the water dripping off his jeans onto the floor.

"Things not work out with your Boy Scout?" He ruffled a hand through his shaggy hair, flinging water droplets in all directions.

"Something like that."

He raised his brows. "You finally give him the flick?"

"Did you just come here to gloat, Blaine? 'Cause I'm really not in the mood."

"On the contrary, love. I happened to be in the area so I thought I'd drop in and say hi."

"Why on earth would you just drop in and say hi?"

Blaine gaped and pressed his palm over his heart. "Wounded again. And I thought we were friends."

Friends? They weren't friends. He was Raven's brother, for goodness' sake. Fallen brother.

Tayla squared her shoulders. "I know who you are."

He threw his head back and laughed. "Of course you do, love; we've met before, remember? Don't tell me you're having trouble with your memory again."

"No, I mean, I know what you are."

His laughter turned into a smirk. "And yet, you do not fear me."

Tayla concentrated on the steady beat of her heart, the unhurried inhale and exhale of her lungs…

He's right.

She met Blaine's gaze. His onyx eyes flickered red, like tiny flames igniting from within.

She lifted her chin.

He tilted his head slightly. "Why did you run from a measly little fox when you don't even fear the Big

Bad Wolf?"

What? She mulled Blaine's words over in her head. No way. She'd fled from Raven, from her new life because he was becoming the creature of her nightmares. A creature she'd unconsciously feared since her attack. But in comparison, Raven was a measly wolf on the Fallen scale. Blaine, on the other hand, was the real monster and he sat before her as though they were having a perfectly normal conversation.

Oh no, I have made a mistake.

"Anyhoo!" Blaine burst out before she had a chance to reply. "Do you reckon he's started healing yet?"

"Who? Raven? Healing from what?"

"Oh, I assumed you knew, love."

Back to his tricks again...

"Tell me," she demanded, stepping forward from the railing.

He dismissed her concern with a wave of his hand. "I'm sure it's nothing. He engaged a way-too-cocky Fallen and well, copped a talon in the arm."

Copped a talon? "What does that mean?"

"A talon, you know, a sharp claw at the tip of—"

"I know what a talon is. Why is it so bad for Raven?"

"They're toxic, love. I've heard the poison's agonizing. He's probably wishing for the end right about now."

She swallowed the bile creeping up her throat. Raven had warned her about a Fallen's talons. "When did this happen?"

Blaine half shrugged. "Few days ago, I guess."

That's why he hasn't contacted me.

Her mind raced to process what Blaine said. "Shouldn't he be healing, being immortal and all?"

"Well, that's the tricky thing, love. Seems his faith bucket, his connection to the cloudy paradise, is a tad too low for him to access the sun's power to boost his healing."

What? A talon poisoned Raven, and he wasn't healing because his faith was too low?

She narrowed her eyes at Blaine. "Why are you telling me this?"

This better not be another one of his tricks.

Blaine leaned forward. "There's no coming back from Fallen poisoning, love. Even I can't extract an immortal's soul from the Infernal Pits. And…" He winked. "My cunning plan would have a rather dull climax with one of Fate's Guardians dead."

"Dead?" she squawked.

He exaggerated rolling his eyes and relaxed back in the chair. "Keep up, love. Even immortals can die."

What? Raven could die? Her eyes stung recalling her final words to him…*I can't be with a monster.* Raven must have a sliver of light remaining in his soul. Otherwise, he would've completely fallen by now, that meant there was still a chance he could be saved. Was him having a few crimson feathers enough for her to push him away forever?

He said he loved me…

Long ago, she'd made the decision to listen to the signs from the universe, and for the past few days she felt stranded on a deserted beach with no sign of civilization. Was this the sign she'd been unconsciously waiting for?

Maybe it was about time she listened to her heart and not just her head.

"Oh my gosh, I have to go to him."

Blaine smirked and rose from the chair. "Very well, I'll try not to be offended with you cutting our chat short. Be sure to say hi for me," he said, shrugging on his dripping wet jacket. "On second thoughts, no, don't, I'll see him when I get back."

Blaine gave one of his regal bows before he leaped the three steps and sauntered off the way he'd came.

Drive safely, love, he whispered in her mind.

****

Ugh! Where's the turnoff?

Tayla slowed the car to a crawl as she drove the windy highway up the mountain, scanning the side of the road, searching for the turnoff to the mansion.

Can't see anything in this rain.

The heavy rain pounded against the roof of the car, increasing in intensity the closer she got to Raven's. The wiper blades waved frantically, doing nothing to clear off the water and improve her minimal vision.

She squinted and leaned closer to the steering wheel, tracking her gaze along the curb. Suddenly, a figure stepped onto the edge of the road and motioned toward a break in the tree line. She looked in the direction—*yes*! The turnoff.

Tayla cautiously veered the car off the road, onto the gravel and slowly crawled up the driveway. Without warning, the passenger door flew open and she screamed, slamming on the brakes.

"Chill, Tay-Tay, it's me."

She recognized EJ as he jumped into the passenger seat, slamming the door shut and flipped the hoodie off his head.

"You scared the crap out of me."

"Sorry. Thought you'd need help finding the turnoff."

She frowned at the Guardian dripping water all over her leather seat. *Worry about that later.* "How did you know I was coming?"

He shrugged. "Lucky guess."

Forget it; reaching Raven was more important than figuring out that puzzle.

Tayla eased her foot onto the accelerator and continued along the gravel drive. Her grip on the steering wheel loosened as the Guardian mansion came into view.

"Go, I'll park for you. He's in his room," EJ said.

Tayla put the car in park before bolting out the door and up to the main entrance. Without bothering to knock, she shoved open the heavy front door and raced down the hall and up the stairs as fast as her legs would take her. When she reached the third-floor landing in front of Raven's room, she took a second to lean over and suck in gulps of air, willing her lungs to expand and her thighs to cease burning. Straightening, her shaky hand gripped the door handle, and she quietly slipped inside.

Her heart sank at the sight before her.

Raven lay on his back in bed, twisted in the sheets and groaning in a semi-conscious state. Sweat beaded his pale forehead, even though the temperature in the room matched the artic weather outside. Tayla shivered, vigorously rubbing the tops of her arms. She scanned the tall uncovered glass for an open window or door but found none.

She snatched a discarded blanket from the floor and wrapped it around her shoulders before easing down on the side of the bed to take Raven's clammy palm in hers. Her eyes traveled over his bare chest, pausing on the bloodstained bandage wrapped around his middle. Leaning closer, she inspected the black veins spreading from under the gauze on his biceps and up over his shoulder, as though a spider slowly wrapped his torso in a fine black web from the inside out. Raven sighed as her fingertip lightly traced a thin strand traveling toward his heart.

Toxic…agonizing poison…

"I'm here, Raven," she whispered.

His eyes moved behind closed lids as though he'd heard her voice, and it encouraged her to continue.

"I'm so sorry I left." She placed her cool palm flat against his burning chest. "I'm here now, and I'm never leaving again."

There was so much she wanted to say, so much she needed him to hear. Right now, though, her words could wait. In this moment, she longed to be close to him. To somehow ease his pain and suffering.

Tayla removed the blanket from around her shoulders and draped it over the foot of the bed before shrugging out of her jacket and kicking off her shoes. Determined not to bump his wounds, she lifted the covers slightly and as carefully as possible, slid underneath to lie beside him. Unconsciously, Raven's head turned toward her and she snuggled in close against him, resting her cheek on his uninjured shoulder.

A feeling of peace and love washed through her, chasing away her doubts and her fears. This was where she was meant to be. Here with Raven. And if that meant exposing herself to the world he lived in, then so be it.

No longer would she run from a measly fox. She would once again put her faith in the universe and listen to the signs. She was here to save Raven...if only she knew how.

"I love you," she whispered against his chest.

Moments later, her lids slid closed, soothed by Raven's steady breaths and the rain battering the bedroom windows.

Chapter 33

Slow, steady waves of light washed over Raven's body, like a lazy tide rolling onto the shore before sliding back out again. His breaths steadied, became less labored each time Tayla's distant voice echoed in his mind.

He was hallucinating. The last thing he remembered was the fight at the club before a sheet of darkness fell over his consciousness. He didn't have enough faith to survive. This was the calm before the storm. Any minute now, his soul would arrive at the fiery pits of Hell.

Unless the venom killed him before he turned. If that was the case, he didn't want to face the storm.

The agony in his chest eased a notch as another wave washed over him.

He squinted when a glowing light intensified in the far distance.

The darkness in his mind retreated as the light brightened. It expanded faster, like a massive star on the cusp of one last catastrophic explosion. He covered his eyes with his forearm as the brightness stung, until…

Raven peeled open his heavy lids to find himself in his room, stretched out on his bed. Tayla lay curled up asleep beside him, her head resting against his shoulder.

Had he been dreaming?

Bright lasers of light beamed through the windows, stretching over his body, the glare burned a hole through his retinas into the back of his skull. He shielded his eyes with one hand and rolled onto his side, facing Tayla, and placed his back to the lasers.

Slicing pain ripped through his arm, and the events of the battle came rushing back.

He peered down and inspected the bandage wrapped around his stomach and the dark red/brown stains. And whaddaya know, he had matching gauze on the top of his bicep.

The warm sun streamed into the room and heated his bare back, rejuvenating his body and numbing some of the pain. The familiar tingling of his body healing spread through his veins and focused on his wounds.

He leaned his head forward and lightly kissed Tayla's temple.

"Good morn…" He swallowed, moistening his dry throat. "Good morning, beautiful."

Her eyes opened, and a smile filled her face. "Raven, you're okay." Tayla placed the back of her hand against his cheek. "And the fever broke. Oh, thank god."

He frowned. "It was just a scratch, there's no need to worry."

Her eyes watered. "Just a scratch? Raven, you nearly died."

He jerked his head back. "What?"

"You've been unconscious for almost five days. Your body wasn't healing."

What? He'd been out for five days? He hadn't been dreaming. If that was the case, why was he rapidly healing now?

Wincing, he sat up, taking a moment to adjust to the pain in his arm before he unraveled the bandage around his abdomen. He peeled back the gauze and inspected the fifteen or so sutures running in a straight line down one side. His faith must've been lower than he thought. He brushed his thumb over one of the sutures and it fell from his flesh. The pink skin underneath closed and healed.

He turned his attention to the matching gauze around his bicep. No sutures there. All that remained underneath was a nasty, thick, jagged grey line where the talon had gouged his skin, deeper than he thought.

At least it had healed, and those foul black veins vanished. Fuck, he was lucky.

He glanced over his shoulder at Tayla sitting beside him, her brows knitted together as she inspected his wounds.

"It's kind of you to be here," he muttered.

She took his hand in hers. "I want to be here with you, Raven. I'm sorry I left."

He exhaled and kissed her forehead. "Not that I'm not ecstatic, because I am, but what changed your mind?"

"Let's just say I realized what was really important."

He slowly shook his head. "But it doesn't change the fact I'm still becoming one of them."

"No, but we'll get through it, together. Whatever it takes. I'm not going anywhere." She gave his hand a squeeze. "Why didn't you tell me?"

He lowered his head. "I wanted to, I really did but I was so scared of losing you I just couldn't bring myself to do it. I hadn't even told the others."

She was quiet for a moment. "What happened to cause you to lose your faith? No more secrets," she whispcrcd.

He took a deep breath. No more secrets. "Blaine happened."

There. The dam had broken, and the words he'd held in gushed out. "I couldn't stop him from falling, losing his faith, and severing his connection to the Heavens. I've spent the past centuries on Earth trying to save him, trying to convince him he made a mistake and should return to the Heavens. 'Cause every goddamn year he's a Fallen, the guilt of failing him and the others, chips away at me."

"Did he have something to do with the deal you made?"

He nodded. "Return Blaine to the Heavens or be banished forever."

Tayla lightly kissed his shoulder. "I'll help you. I believe in you, Raven, I see the good in you. We can do this together, and then we'll kick some ass and save Blaine."

She smiled up at him, melting his fucking heart, chipping away more blackness, letting the light seep in through the cracks.

"Show me the crimson feathers," she whispered.

"I don't want to scare you."

"I've faced the Big Bad Wolf and survived. I can handle it," she chuckled.

What did he do to deserve the remarkable, strong woman sitting beside him? Raven inched off the bed and rose to face her. He'd spent the last few decades hiding the growing number of crimson feathers on his wings; it felt strange to show them off. But at the same time, a weight lifted off his shoulders.

As slowly as he could, he unfurled his wings and extended his right wing straight out to the side to reveal the damning evidence.

Tayla sucked in a breath. "Raven…"

"I know, but there's only a handful."

"There aren't any."

Wait. "What did you say?"

She frowned. "See for yourself. There are no red feathers, only black."

Raven peered under his arm, where the path of crimson feathers were just days before. Tayla was right; they were gone. How could that have happened?

He glanced over at Tayla and the realization struck him. All this time, he'd been holding back, closing off his heart, balancing on a tightrope to avoid making a wrong move and putting his brothers in danger. Instead, he'd focused on trying to restore his faith before he became a Fallen. This whole time, the answer, the key to restoring it had been right in front of him. Gabe had told him to listen to his instincts, to stop fighting his path.

Being with Tayla had been his path all along. Gabe had been fucking right, again.

She brushed his cheek. "What are you thinking about?"

He cupped her face in his hands and softly kissed her lips. "It was you. You restored my faith, restored the light in my soul. That must've been your Chosen path."

She smiled. "Maybe it was our path?"

"God, Tayla, I love you."

"I love you, too, Raven. Now kiss me already."

****

Raven refused help from Tayla, even though she hovered like he might collapse at any minute, and changed into fresh clothes successfully without passing out. The pain in his stomach had subsided, though a smoldering fire still burned along his biceps with each twist or lift of his arm.

He padded to the bathroom to freshen up. "You sure I can't convince you to spend the day in bed with me, instead?" he called out.

Tayla appeared in the doorway and his heart skipped a beat. "Not until you're fully healed, Raven, I mean it. There's plenty of time, I'm not going anywhere, remember?"

He drew her in for a quick kiss, to hide the new pain growing in his chest. By the time he'd figured out Tayla's Chosen path, she'd already completed it. No telling at what moment Fate would take her life and recall her soul to the Heavens. The future was yet again in Fate's hands.

Worry about that later, Raven.

He entwined one hand with Tayla's and used the other to grip the banister as they descended the stairs together in search of the others. He silently winced each time his foot pressed against the ground and the vibration shook through his body. They followed the trail of voices to the entertainment room and entered the room.

Raine nodded from beside the pool table, chalking the cue gripped in her hand.

River crossed from the bar and gave Raven's shoulder a squeeze before handing him a bourbon.

"You had us worried there, boss."

"I know. Thanks, River."

"Next time you decide to black out, man, I'm dumping your ass in a spare room on the ground floor. Three fucking flights of stairs is ridiculous," Aric grumbled from the couch.

Raven crossed to Aric. "Nice to see you, too. Thanks for the patch-up and…I'm sorry, man."

Aric rose and slapped palms with him. "It's good to have you back. It might be wise to catch some rays today, while it's sunny." Aric peered around him. "Appreciate you bringing him back, Tayla."

She smiled and gave Raven's hand a light squeeze.

Bracing his weight on one hand, Raven eased his aching body onto the couch and held out his arm, motioning for Tayla to curl up beside him, which she did, right where she belonged.

The smell of freshly baked bread drifted into the room a moment before EJ strolled in carrying a tray.

"De-li-very!" EJ announced with Ellen hot on his heels, no doubt having an aneurysm. EJ peered over at Raven. "He lives."

Did EJ just wink at Tayla?

Tayla chuckled beside him. *What the hell?*

"Anyone for coffee?" EJ asked, in a high-pitched voice while he placed the platter of bread and cold meats on the mahogany coffee table.

"I think you've already had enough," River teased.

EJ tapped his chin with one finger. "Quite possibly. We'll be right back," he chuckled.

"Don't you dare. I can manage." Ellen shooed EJ away before gliding out of the room.

EJ slumped on the couch beside Aric and exploded

in a fit of laughter.

Aric rolled his eyes.

Raven reached forward, swallowing the stinging pain in his arm, and grabbed a plate, piling it with a selection and passed it to Tayla.

"Thank you." She smiled.

Repeating the process for himself, he piled the plate high to avoid leaning forward again unless absolutely necessary. Like if the house was burning down or something. Even then, maybe he'd reconsider.

He turned to Aric. "Catch me up on what's been happening."

"EJ reviewed the chatter while you've been in holiday mode. It seems there's been a large increase in the numbers of Fallen arriving in the area."

"Over the past few months," EJ added. "Whoever's creating them must've been planning it, for the numbers to increase so suddenly."

Raven nudged Tayla closer.

Before he spoke again, Ellen returned with a pitcher of sweet black nectar.

"Thanks, Ellen."

"You're welcome, Raven. I'm glad you're up and about again." She smiled. "Let me know if you need anything else," she added over her shoulder as she exited.

EJ shuffled forward to the edge of the couch and took charge of filling mugs of steaming java, offering the first one to Tayla.

Raven passed. He couldn't stand that bitter shit.

"Thanks, EJ." Tayla cradled the cup between her hands.

"EJ and I think it's all connected," River said from

over by the pool table. "Blaine showing up after being MIA for a decade or so, the increase in Fallen activity in the area, and the frequency of EJ's visions."

Shit. He'd forgotten all about EJ visions.

"Has Gabe given any hints?" Aric asked, glancing at Raven.

"No, but that's not unusual. Since we've been here, he hasn't been forthcoming with much information, Fate's probably got a tight leash around his neck. I'll ask him, though, when I see him next. If he's not still pissed at me."

The conversation effortlessly slipped to casual as they chowed down, sipped hot coffee—or bourbon—and chatted about random topics. Like the fact EJ was finally getting his ass whipped at pool. By Raine.

Sporadically, River leaned over the couch and stuffed some food in his mouth before returning to the pool table. At some point, Ellen refilled the coffee pot and food.

Raven reclined on the couch and peered around the room. The sight made his heart swell. This was it. What he'd longed for. A room filled with family. Guardians he trusted with his life, those he could not imagine living without, and a woman by his side, a soulmate whom he loved more than the Heavens itself.

All of a sudden, his dreary, bleak existence filled with light and, for the first time in millennia, hope.

And he had Tayla to thank for bringing it all together.

Raven sucked in a breath and forced down the shooting pain in his arm as he leaned forward to return his glass and empty plate to the table. Using the chair to brace his weight, he rose to his feet.

The whole room froze, tracking his movements as if he were a frail mortal who might kick the bucket any minute.

"We're gonna go catch some sun," he grunted. He held his hand out for Tayla.

"Remind me not to peek out the windows." EJ smirked.

Raven ignored the dig and wrapped his arm around Tayla's waist. "I wanna meet before anyone goes out at sundown."

A chorus of "yeps" and "copy that's" sounded behind them.

"Take it easy, man," Aric warned.

Raven nodded before strolling out of the room with Tayla nestled beside him and one destination in mind.

Where the sun was shining, and clothes were optional.

Chapter 34

Tayla swallowed a final mouthful of the steamy beef casserole. So mouth-watering and delicious, especially with the darn sexy Guardian feeding it to her. That sensual smile of his beamed and the hardness she currently nudged against while sitting on his lap, grew with each mouthful.

Was he ever sated? *I sure hope not.*

"You're positive you don't need me to stay?" he rumbled, his voice a little hoarser than the mouthful before.

This marked Raven's first night back on patrol following his near-death episode. He would join River and Aric, heading out to fight Fallen, she guessed. He was a bit vague when it came to her questions about fighting. Maybe he spared her the gory details of his job or tried not scare her off.

"No, it's totally fine. EJ just gave me a heap of TV shows to binge on." She smiled over her shoulder at him. "Some hot Guardian has been occupying all my time lately and I'm so far behind."

He tightened his hand on her hips and nudged her butt firmly against his hardness. "Is that so? Well, I'm gonna have to take him out; I don't like to share."

Tayla laughed. *God, this felt so good.* And not only her current position, but the whole darn situation. She was so at home in this house, with his family, in their bed, that sometimes she had to pinch herself to make sure it was actually real.

Yep, sure was.

Her gaze roamed over the others spread out around the oversized dining table as they finished their meals. Aric and River sat beside each other, empty plates in front of them, deep in conversation. Both of them dressed in what she now recognized as their fighting gear: black combat pants, muscle tees stretched tightly across their broad chests, and heavy boots. Were they discussing their strategy for tonight?

What was involved in hunting down a Fallen?

On the other side of the table, EJ stared at the screen of his cell phone, his thumbs frantically punching at the keypad, a wicked grin on his face. Lining up a little catch up of his own? Although EJ wasn't on rotation, he was still heading into town. Two seats farther down sat Raine. She wasn't heading into town with the others, but still wore a black form-fitting top and sprayed-on black leather pants with the highest fiery-red patent heels she'd ever seen, currently hidden under the table.

How the heck does she walk in those?

As though Raine could sense Tayla's stare, she glanced over and gave a curt nod before sliding on a pair of fingerless gloves—also black leather.

A chorus of screeching broke out as chairs slid back from the table and the Guardians grabbed jackets from the backs of their chairs, almost in unison.

Tayla gawked at the weapons strapped to their bodies. *My god.* How many Fallen did they expect to encounter? On Aric alone, she saw two large knives strapped over his chest, some sort of handgun tucked behind his back, plus a belt around his waist with silver stars poking out the top. Those were the visible ones.

Raven interrupted her people watching when he gripped around her waist and effortlessly lifted her body off his, then eased her back on the chair.

"You sure you'll be all right?" he asked, standing before her. "I can stay. They're fine without me."

She chuckled. "Raven, go. I'll be fine. Stop worrying."

"I can't help it." He peered deep into her eyes for a moment like he struggled with his head and his heart—or another body part—and searched for the tiniest excuse to stay.

When he didn't find one, he leaned forward and took her mouth in a hot kiss. Heat instantly flooded her core, speeding up her heart, her breath escaped her lungs, only to be left gasping for air when he pulled back.

"That should tide you over until I return," he rasped. "Make sure you call if you need me."

She nodded, not trusting her voice to work.

Raven gently kissed her again before he turned to face Raine.

"Raine," he said with an air of authority in his voice.

She glanced over her shoulder and gave a curt nod, before pushing in her chair. "I will," she replied and clicked off toward the kitchen.

She will, what?

****

Two hours had passed since the Guardians left to do their thing and protect the town. After giving up ten minutes into the latest episode of her favorite vampire brothers—even they couldn't hold her attention tonight—she'd gone in search of something to do.

If only her mind would relax. A jumble of thoughts raced around competing for airtime, but only one thought stood out from the rest and kept screaming in her head: Take the leap and move in permanently with Raven. The idea had sprung in her mind during dinner and refused to disappear. Not wanting to freak out Raven, she'd pushed the thought aside to work through later.

But it wouldn't go away. The voice constantly whispered in her ear, egging her on.

As a last resort, she'd grabbed her unfinished novel and settled into an armchair in the sunken living room, facing a warm and cozy lit hearth. Despite the soft leather, she couldn't get comfortable. She twisted and turned in every position conceivable, but each new pose irritated her restless body further, her mind unable to concentrate on the words, and she ended up reading the same sentences over and over again. Switching chairs made no difference. Eventually, she'd ended up where she was now, on the rug in front of the crackling fire.

But now, she was too hot.

Ugh!

Her cheeks burned as they faced the flames. Her knitted top itched as if made of sandpaper and every movement scratched at her hypersensitive skin. With a huff she gave up, shoved in a bookmark, and slammed the book closed on the wooden floor beside her.

What to do? What to do?

She pushed the urge to move in with Raven permanently out of her head. Clearly, she struggled with his absence after spending twenty-four-seven with him over the past week and a half. Maybe she should text him to say hi. No, he would take that as a sign she needed him to come home. Since being here full-time, Raven's protectiveness hadn't eased one little bit; in fact, it had increased. He kept going on and on about needing to keep her safe from the Fallen and that her Chosen soul was a prized bounty—which she wasn't too keen to know. A couple of times, she'd heard him mumble something about Fate recalling her soul, whatever that meant. It wasn't like she was unsafe at the mansion. How could she be with all the protection spells Raven told her about? Plus, there was always one Guardian who stayed back…

Raine! Tayla jumped up from her spot on the floor and dashed off in search of Raine. A girly chat would cure her restlessness for sure.

Tayla caught Ellen in the hallway, running the vacuum over the rugs. "Hi, Ellen."

Ellen smiled and pressed the red button on the vacuum with her foot, instantly silencing the noise. "Good evening, Tayla. Is the vacuum disturbing you? I can move to another area if you like."

"What? Oh, no. No, the noise isn't bothering me at all."

She smiled. "What do you have planned for the evening?"

Ellen was easy to adore, in a sweet grandmotherly kind of way, with her immaculate hair in that fresh-out-of-curlers look. She'd changed since dinner, and now wore a simple black long-sleeve dress that reminded her of something out of the 1930s.

Come to think of it, all the clothes Ellen wore

reminded her of the '30s.

"Tayla?" Ellen prompted.

"Sorry, what? Oh, yeah, sorry, I was a mile away. I wondered if you knew where Raine was?"

Ellen nodded. "Of course, dear. She's down in the armory."

"Oh great. Thanks, Ellen."

"If you're going to see her, would you like to take some refreshments?"

"Yes, that would be great."

Ellen moved the vacuum to the side against the wall and hurried off down the hall. She returned few minutes later with a tray full of all kinds of delights.

"Thanks so much, Ellen." Tayla turned away, then realized something. "Ah, where exactly is the armory?"

"It's in the basement, dear. Would you like me to show you?"

"No, no, that's okay. You've done enough." She smiled. "They're lucky to have you looking out for them."

"You included, Tayla. And you are most welcome." Ellen slightly bowed her head before pressing the red button on the vacuum to resume her duties.

Tayla gripped the handles of the tray tightly in her hands as she descended the stone staircase, determined not to have the two sodas fall, resulting in a fizzy explosion when opened. Curving around the last corner, a solid metal military-style door came into view. Tayla sighed with relief.

How did Ellen make it look so easy?

While balancing the tray, she thudded the bottom of the door with her foot. *Ouch!* Note to self, if it looks like solid metal, it's probably solid metal.

Several clicks sounded like a code punched in, followed by a clunk as the lock disengaged. Raine pulled open the door, wearing a leather one-piece machinist apron.

"I come bearing refreshments."

"Good timing."

Raine took the tray from her and motioned for Tayla to enter.

She straightened her arms, and flexed her fingers to revive the circulation.

Tayla heaved the door closed and jumped as the lock automatically engaged. She gaped at Raine. Did she just lock them in?

"Don't worry; you can get out." Raine slid the tray down on a nearby work bench and snatched a can of soda. It hissed as she opened it.

No explosion. *Phew. One crisis averted.*

"You been down here yet?" Raine asked, taking a sip.

"No."

Biting into a sandwich, Raine strolled to the far end of the basement, motioning for Tayla to follow.

Raine explained all the ins and outs of the various contraptions. Tayla's mind boggled at the extraordinary setup, and the fact Raine made—forged—weapons out of water. From a freaking fountain connected with the Heavens.

After a brief tour, Raine placed the plate with her remaining sandwich at the end of the long bench and carried on with her work. Tayla settled on a stool across from Raine, fascinated by the routine of cooling, hammering, heating, bending, cooling again.

Raine wasn't much of a talker so Tayla filled the silence with random ramblings, basically anything that flowed through her mind and out her mouth.

Which, right now, happened to be all about moving in permanently with Raven.

"And so, I want to surprise him and drop my key off. For good," she mumbled, examining her uneaten sandwich.

"Yup," Raine replied, neither agreement nor disagreement while removing a crystal-looking blade from the chamber.

No help at all.

"I've basically moved back anyway…"

Raine held the blade on the workbench and slammed a hammer along the length. *Bang! Clank!*

"…and the thought of being with him permanently…feels right."

"Mmm-hmm."

Ugh! She wasn't even listening. "Raine?" she raised her voice.

Raine paused and peered across the workbench at her. "Tayla. Just because you're a fragile mortal does not mean you can't go out and take what you want."

"Okaaaay. Does that mean you think I should move in permanently?"

"I thought you already had," she said with a deadpan expression before banging the long, thin, silver dagger-looking thing on the table in front of her.

Raine thought she already lived there permanently? She hadn't been back to her cabin since Raven had his episode, and EJ had collected her stuff from the cabin while she'd been at Raven's bedside. Plus, she had thought about how things felt right staying at the mansion, being with Raven, being a part of this house. And she knew Raven would approve.

What did she have to lose? Her pride? Yes. Her heart? Also, yes. But she had so much more to gain. She grinned. Never again would she run from a measly fox or fear the immortal world Raven lived in. Instead, she was going to embrace it.

Tayla jumped off the stool. No longer able to suppress the urge to cut ties with her old, boring life. She would take control and start a new, fresh and exciting one with Raven.

"I'm gonna go drop off my key to the cabin. I won't be long."

Raine froze mid-bang. Tayla spied her jaw flex on either side, as though she counted to ten in her head, trying to simmer a temper. "You should wait for Raven. Do it tomorrow."

"It's only down the road. I'll be back in an hour, tops."

Slowly, Raine shook her head.

"Come on, Raine," she whined. "I can't get the idea out of my head. It's driving me crazy. It's like a compulsion or something making me do it. I have to do it tonight, otherwise, I'm going to run around the mansion pulling my hair out."

"Nope. Raven will have my wings when he finds out."

"So…don't tell him."

As soon as it came out of her mouth, she knew it was a stupid thing to say. She wanted to surprise Raven, but she couldn't keep it a secret from him and she sensed Raine wouldn't.

Raine rolled her eyes, as though impatient for the

conversation to end. "You need to call Raven and tell him you're going first."

"Deal." She grabbed her phone from the back pocket of her jeans. "I'll text him now."

"That's not what I said."

She tried to hide her grin. "I know."

****

Tayla rolled her eyes as her phone rang not even a second after she'd sent the text to Raven.

Raine stared at her, a raised eyebrow and an "I told you so" expression on her face.

Damn it.

Tayla turned her back to Raine to answer the phone. "Hey, Raven."

"Tayla, listen, I know you want to go and I want nothing more than for you to move in permanently, but can't it wait until tomorrow? I'll take you to drop your keys off first thing in the morning."

"I'll be an hour, tops. I'll be careful and keep car doors locked the whole way."

"Locking the doors isn't what I'm worried about, honey. It's late. Plus, you won't be able to spot the turnoff on your way back."

She needed some of Raine's badass confidence to win this battle. "Yes, I know it's late, but it's just down the road. I promise not to pull over for anything and I'll take note of the turnoff when I get out on the highway. I'll remember it. Please, Raven, I feel like I have to drop them off tonight."

She tuned out when Raven started listing all the reasons it wasn't safe for her to be out at night unprotected. She was losing the battle.

Wait. *Unprotected?*

Raine peered up from the dagger in her hand and a lightbulb clicked on in Tayla's brain. She met Raine's gaze; she wasn't ready to give up just yet.

"I'll take Raine with me," she blurted out. "That solves the location and safety points. So…you good with that? If she comes with me?"

She heard Raven's sigh through the phone. *Yes!* "Put Raine on for a minute, will you?"

Tayla passed the phone to Raine. "Raven wants to talk to you."

Raine snatched the phone and put it up to her ear. "Yup."

Gee, now would be a good time to have immortal hearing like the others. She practically bounced on her toes at the thought of closing that chapter of her life and beginning a new one…with Raven.

Raine shook her head, and with her free hand, resumed smooth upward strokes with the metal file. "Nope. I'm busy here."

Tayla leaned closer and whispered to Raine, "It won't take long, I promise."

Raine glared at her. "No can do."

"Please, Raine."

Raine held the phone away from her ear to address Tayla. "If I say yes, will you stop whining?"

Tayla squealed. "Yes."

Raine pressed the phone back to her ear. "Fine. I'll take her…Yup…got it."

Raine handed the phone back to Tayla and she put it to her ear.

"Tayla, I want a text when you get to the lodge and another when you're back safe. Straight there and straight back. This isn't negotiable."

"Deal."

"Listen to Raine and...*be careful*. I don't like this idea one little bit."

"It feels right, Raven. You don't need to worry, we'll be back in no time. Love you."

"Love you, too."

Tayla disconnected the call and shoved the cell phone back in her pocket. "I'm going to run upstairs and grab my coat. Meet you in the garage?" she asked Raine.

Raine sighed heavily. "Yup." She rattled off the code for the door, sliding her tools neatly into the leather satchel before rolling it up and securing it with a tie.

Tayla raced out of the armory.

Chapter 35

Tayla burst into the garage and spotted Raine tapping the pointy toe of her super-high heels on the cement floor. Raine had swapped to a shiny, sleek black pair with a thin strap clasp on the side of her narrow ankle. Tayla glanced down at her brown ankle boots and shrugged. They were better than gumboots.

She pressed the key fob for her car, and the lights blinked.

"I'm driving," Raine snapped over her shoulder, striding to the driver's side.

"Do you even know how to drive?"

Raine glared across her shoulder. "Of course, I do."

"Okay." Tayla dangled the keys in front of her. "But I wanna drive on the way back so I can identify the turnoff for next time."

Raine rolled her eyes. "Fine."

Tayla threw the key fob over the hood, and Raine caught it in one hand. She lowered herself into the passenger seat and strapped in. *Safety first.* Raine slid into the driver's seat, and Tayla gaped at the number of daggers she unstrapped and piled in the center cup holder.

Raine raised an eyebrow. "What? They're uncomfortable to drive in."

Finally, Raine arched her back, pulled out a black

handgun, and placed it between her thighs.

I'm in the car with a crazy, expensive-heel-wearing killer.

Raine pressed the central lock button for the doors, locking them inside before the engine roared to life and they screeched out of the garage into the stormy darkness.

As soon as they were outside, Tayla instantly regretted the decision. Rain fell—no, not rain, icy slush—and the frantic flick of the wipers were useless against the force. Raine twisted the lever to increase the frequency, but it didn't help. Rather than clearing it, each wipe gathered a pile of slush and stuck it together in the center of the windshield. The pile built and built with each swipe.

A few minutes down the highway, Raine pulled the car over to the side of the road to scrape off the slush, all the while cursing about ruining her Jimmy's. Whatever that meant.

Thick fog rolled down the highway toward them; its tendrils stretched out and engulfed the car. Even with the headlights, she was lucky to see more than a car length in front of them.

After thirty minutes of sled driving, they arrived in the carpark of the Cedar lodge. Raine kept the car running as she strapped her weapons back over her body.

Tayla gasped. "Raine, you can't take those in."

"Like hell I can't," Raine scoffed.

"Oh my god, you're going to get us arrested. I'll just run in and drop the key off."

"I do have a jacket," Raine said, snatching it from the rear seat.

Tayla sent a quick text to Raven to let him know they'd arrived before stepping out into the bitter wind. She briefly peered up at the gloomy mountain they'd just descended; stormy, ominous clouds gathered in the distance, several rolling into one another, building in intensity. She had a strange fluttering in the pit of her stomach. Probably nerves. Handing in the keys to her cabin was a big step, but they had to hurry and get back to the mansion before the heart of the storm hit. By the looks of it, they'd only driven through the outer edges.

"Do what you have to do and make it quick," Raine instructed Tayla. "I'll wait out here."

Tayla shielded her eyes, like that would somehow protect her face from the icy blasts, and bolted up the stone steps and through the double glass doors. Raine took post under the eaves, in the shadow of the exterior lights, while Tayla handed her key in at the front desk and organized her checkout. A few minutes later, she exited and raced back to the car.

"Have you seen the weather?" Raine snapped, motioning to the sinister clouds above them. "I'm driving; you can learn the turnoff another day."

"I've driven in weather like this plenty of times, way more than I'm guessing you have. Plus, you agreed."

Raine stood her ground for a moment, and Tayla prepared to argue. But she didn't need to. Raine narrowed her eyes a second before stomping like a small child to the passenger side and slammed herself in the car. By the time Tayla sank down on the seat, Raine had unloaded all the weapons again and stashed the gun between her legs. Tayla cranked the heat and they both tossed their soggy jackets onto the rear seat.

Ten minutes later, they were back on the road, winding up the mountain.

She maintained a slow but steady pace as the icy slush battered down, so fast and heavy the wipers no longer aided. At all. Thick dark grey fog surrounded them, and wind howled up the side of the mountain. Tree branches cracked and tumbled onto the edge of the road, and she had to safely direct the car around them. Leaves and debris flew over the windshield, occasionally smacking into the side of the car. Several times she considered pulling over and waiting for the storm to pass, but on this stretch of road, that wasn't necessarily a safer option. Plus, the blackness extended as far as she could see, a good indication the storm wouldn't pass any time soon.

The wild weather worsened. Icy golf balls dropped from the sky, bouncing off the hood of the Audi.

Tayla's phone lit up from the console with Hot Angel displayed on the screen. Raine snatched it, pressed the green button, and held it up to her ear.

"On our way back," she said to the handset. "Yup, we're right in the middle of it."

Her phone beeped, and Raine looked at the screen. Tayla glanced to see EJ's name flashing on the screen.

Raine rejected the second call and returned the phone to her ear, continuing speaking to Raven. "Sorry, what?"

Out of the corner of her eye, Tayla caught a shape dash between the trees, disappearing so fast she may have imagined it.

"Ten, fifteen minutes tops," Raine said to the handset.

Another phone rang from the backseat. She

recognized Raine's ringtone. They both ignored the call. No way would she reach behind her to answer the phone while driving, regardless of the weather.

Uneasy flutters in the pit of her stomach roared to life.

"Slow down." Raine held her palm up to Tayla while she stared out the passenger window. "There's something out there," she whispered.

Raine had seen it, too. *Not my imagination.*

"S'all good," Raine said, talking to Raven. "We're nearly ba—Tayla!" she screamed.

A split second later, a large shadow appeared from nowhere and landed in the center of the road. Blood red wings splayed out to its sides. Fiery red eyes glared at them through the fog. Tayla yanked the steering wheel to the left, swerving to avoid a collision. She simultaneously slammed on the brakes. All four tires locked up and the car spun out of control along the icy road.

Every following second played out as though in slow motion.

The Audi spun in vicious circles. Trees, rocky mountainside, and the slush covered road swirled past the windshield in a blur. Both of them helpless to stop the inevitable collision just seconds away.

Tayla's heart sank the moment she caught a glimpse of their final destination. She yanked her seatbelt, but the more she tugged the strap, the tighter it got.

Raine snatched a dagger from the console and sliced through her own seatbelt straps in one swift motion.

The car continued to spin, closer and closer to their

end.

Raine unfurled her wings, filling the cramped space. Dagger in hand, she reached across the console and grabbed Tayla's seatbelt, preparing to slice it off.

At the exact same moment, Tayla gaped out the window.

The Audi spiraled past a bend in the road.

Their screams echoed in the car as it plummeted off the edge of the mountain.

Chapter 36

"Raine?" Raven shouted into the phone. "Tayla?"

He squeezed the phone tightly against his ear to catch a hint of their voices. Tayla's muffled screams ripped through his chest. A loud thud, followed by static, echoed through the earpiece. He pressed it harder against his ear and squeezed the handset so tight it creaked under the pressure. He couldn't make out what was happening.

Aric bolted toward him. "What the fuck's going on?"

Raven's chest heaved, but he couldn't suck in oxygen.

Aric squeezed his shoulder. "Man, is it Tayla?"

He nodded, slamming his fist against his chest. *Pull yourself together. You have to get to her.* "Tayla…Raine," he choked. "Crash."

"Where are they?" River stood before him, phone pressed against his ear.

"She said fifteen minutes…"

He roared as crippling pain ripped through his torso, like someone cutting out his organs one by one with a blunt blade and no anesthetic. He crashed to his knees and scratched his chest to make it stop.

"Raven. Snap out of it, man." Aric kneeled in front of him and gripped his shoulders. "Show me where they are. Use the connection. It's the quickest way."

He blinked several times, trying to focus on the fuzzy figure in front of him. "I can't…"

His head jerked back as Aric's fist clocked him square in the jaw.

"Fuck!"

"Get up and focus," Aric barked.

River shoved his phone away. "EJ's following the highway to Tayla's cabin. I can't get a connection with Raine."

That snapped him to attention. Desperation to reach his soulmate consumed him. He would not fail her again.

He jumped to his feet and released his wings in one swift motion, shooting into the blackened sky, with Aric and River behind him.

Flapping his wings hard, he soared across the furious night, the harrowing wind ripped at his feathers. Of all the nights to have a freak storm. *Of all the nights to leave her…*

Closing his eyes, he focused on his connection with Tayla, which grew weaker and weaker by the minute.

Hang on, Tayla, he sent her the thoughts, *I'm nearly there.*

Hovering in midair, he scanned the darkness below for her car as Aric and River arrived on either side of him.

"This is the spot," he shouted above the howling wind. "She's here, I know it. But I can't see a damn thing."

He tucked his wings close together and shot toward the ground.

The Audi's headlights shone in the distance and

Raven sped toward them, not caring about dodging the trees.

He forced down a gag when he glimpsed her mangled car. The metal so twisted he had trouble telling the front from the rear. It had landed on the river bank with the trunk edging into the water, four wheels pointed up to the sky. Glass scattered over the muddy bank from the busted windows, a rear door hung open, and the engine pushed into the front cabin.

Raven's boots skidded on the ground, and he bolted to the wreckage. He spotted EJ on the far side, ripping off the driver's side door.

In his peripheral vision, Raine huddled next to a tree trunk, her arms wrapped around her legs, bloodied wings limp behind her. River crouched before her. In slow motion, River's head turned to Raven, eyes wide. "Raven, no," he shouted.

Thick arms wrapped around Raven's chest and his legs fumbled in the air.

"Let me fucking go," Raven roared.

"Let EJ get…" Aric grunted.

Raven's vision filled with red. He fought against the hold, but the arms wrapped tighter. He had to get to Tayla. His fingers stretched until they gripped the hilt of a dagger at his waist; he ripped it free and twisted it upside down to stab the underneath of Aric's arm.

"Jesus!" Aric shouted, and he released one arm.

Raven twisted, escaped Aric's hold, and shot forward. He hurtled over the wreckage in one swift movement to witness EJ lower Tayla onto the dirty ground, a jacket covered her torso.

He collapsed to his knees beside her.

There's so much blood…

He cradled her cold hand between both of his, his vision blurred. Her head lolled toward him, and the pain in her eyes flattened him.

"Tayla?" he choked. "Stay with me." He smoothed bloodied hair from her face and tucked it behind her ears. "I'm here. We'll get help."

Tayla shivered. Raven ripped off his jacket to cover her legs.

"I love…" She coughed. "…you."

"Oh god, don't try to speak. I love you, too. So fucking much."

She attempted a smile, but it was short lived. Using his thumb, he wiped away the tears falling over her nose. The crippling pain in his chest intensified, squeezing the air from his lungs.

"S-should have stayed h-home." Her teeth chattered.

He inched forward and lifted her head onto his lap.

"Shhh, honey. It's not your fault. Just, hang in there for me, okay, so we can go home together." He brushed her jaw with his thumb. "God, I've loved you since the first moment I laid eyes on you."

"Don't give up…on B-Blaine. He needs…you. I'll w-wait…for you…in the Heavens."

"No." He shook his head. "Don't you dare leave me here without you; I need you. I can't do this without you."

"K-kiss me."

He swallowed the lump in his throat and bent forward to lightly kiss her deep purple lips.

"All this time, all these centuries, I've been waiting…for you," he whispered against her ear. He sensed the others around him, but he didn't give a shit, he needed her to hear the words. "I was so lost before you. So…broken."

Tayla's body convulsed. Her arm lifted slightly before dropping back to the ground. He leaned back and lifted it for her, and held it against his cheek.

He stared into her dim eyes. "You saved me. Pieced me back together and made me whole. Helped me feel again. Showed me how to…love. Truly love. You were the key to my faith this whole time."

He pressed his lips against the inside of her cool palm.

Tayla coughed, harder this time. Her breaths labored, becoming more and more shallow.

"I'll find my way back to the Heavens. To you," he choked. "Whatever it takes, I'll find a way."

The corner of Tayla's mouth lifted before she shifted to stare at the menacing clouds above. Suddenly, the rain ceased, as though the clouds realized there'd been enough disaster for one night and granted them a reprieve. In the wake of the rain, gentle snowflakes danced around them.

"S-so…beautiful," Tayla murmured.

Her body shuddered again, and Raven tracked a single snowflake as it floated down in a slow and delicate motion to land on her pale cheek.

As quickly as it had arrived, the crippling, physical pain in his chest vanished with a *snap*. The realization ripped open his heart.

No. No, no, no…this can't be happening.

"No, Tayla, don't leave me." He lifted her lifeless body to his chest. "Honey, wake up, please."

But it was no use. He felt the moment her heart ceased beating, the exact moment their connection severed.

Scowling up at the Heavens, he roared until his throat scratched like sandpaper rubbed on concrete.

This had to be a dream. He was asleep, and any moment now, he'd wake from this sick nightmare to find Tayla snuggled beside him, her warm body pressed against his chest, her heart beating in sync with his.

Off to the side, a bright white light flashed before it gradually dimmed, revealing an Azrael standing in its wake. Prepared to escort Tayla's soul to the Heavens.

No fucking way.

"Get the hell away from her, Cole," he spat.

He cradled Tayla closer against his chest.

She's gone, Raven, Cole spoke in his mind with a calmness so out of place amid the chaos and pain.

"Then bring her back."

Cole took a long stride toward him. "You know I can't do that."

"Back off," Raven growled.

"Her place is in the Heavens now, brother. Let me escort her there."

He shook his head. This couldn't be happening. How could Fate assign her to him only to take her away so soon? What the hell did he do wrong this time?

Heavy footsteps approached from behind a second before a firm hand squeezed his shoulder. A calming wave washed over him and opened wide the gates for his pain and sorrow to come gushing out, as though a dam had collapsed, and the mighty river came crashing over the rubble.

"Let her go, my friend." Gabe's soothing voice broke through the chaos.

Raven lowered his head. There was nothing he

could do for her now. He knew this day would come. The moment he woke without crimson wings, he knew her Chosen path was complete. But couldn't it have been eighty years from now?

Eight hundred years from now?

With a shaky hand, he gently wiped away the blood from the side of her face and brushed his fingertips over her lids to close her beautiful eyes for the final time.

He cradled Tayla's lifeless body in his arms and he rose to face Cole.

The angel stood before him in his standard dress; a long black medieval tunic, tapered at the waist with gold embossed down the center and on the hems. The silk fabric unaffected by the gusty wind. Cole's silvery-grey wings stretched out wide behind him, shimmering like millions of tiny diamonds twisting and spinning under the sun's rays.

But there was no sun, only darkness in his nightmare.

Cole's lips thinned, and he lowered the hood on his tunic to reveal his short midnight black hair and haunting grey eyes.

Raven leaned down and pressed his lips to Tayla's forehead one final time before transferring her into Cole's waiting arms.

Cole gave a curt nod and summoned the blinding white light around him.

Raven's heart ripped from his chest the moment the heavenly light faded and Cole vanished into the darkness, along with the love of his fucking existence.

Chapter 37

Argh! White. Blinding white light shot through Tayla's irises, burning a hole in the back of her head. She squeezed her eyes shut, shielding them with her hand, but tiny red spots continued to flicker on the backs of her lids.

Where am I? The last thing she remembered was— *Oh my god.*

She tested the brightness by peeking open her lids and waited for the laser beams of light to dull before declaring it safe to open fully—

Tayla jumped back as a man appeared out of nowhere—no scrap that, not man, angel. Her gaze tracked past his large silvery-grey wings folded behind his back, all the way up, up, up to his square jaw with three-day growth and haunting eyes.

"I…died?" she whispered.

He gave a curt nod and motioned to one side with his open hand.

Tayla's breath hitched as she followed the direction of his outstretched arm. The landscape began to unveil, like thick white fog fading away to reveal a bright, sunny day. Two white iron gates appeared feet from her, and the more she stared, the more they came into focus.

She craned her neck, following the iron bars of the

gates all the way to the tip. They resembled gates commonly found enclosing those fancy estates for famous people, only these were white, and much more extravagant. The iron illuminated like it somehow glowed, and the center where the two gates joined, shimmered with a swirling pattern of jewels and—

Her eyes widened. *Are they diamonds?*

She closed her gaping mouth. "Are these the gates to…?"

"Yes. This is the mortal entrance to the Heavens," the angel replied.

She turned to face him. "What am I meant to do now?"

He arched a dark eyebrow. "You go through. Obviously."

She mentally rolled her eyes. Okay, maybe that was a stupid question. Her gaze drifted to the sides of the gates where there was…nothing. White vacant space. She turned around on the spot, taking in her surroundings, but it all appeared the same. The whiteness continued for as far as she could see, like they stood on a giant cloud. No, not on a cloud, more like in a cloud.

What the…?

She leaned to her left to peer around the gates; no oversized fence joined them, no wall, no visible intercom system. Not even a trench or moat filled with snapping crocodiles. Why have a big set of fancy gates when someone could just walk around them?

"The only way in is through the gates," the angel prompted.

She peered over her shoulder at him and raised an eyebrow. It appeared like it would be quicker to go around the gates.

He crossed his arms over his broad chest and the opening in his tunic revealed thick cords of muscles along his forearms. "Go ahead; try it."

Stepping forward, Tayla reached her palm toward the empty space beside the gates. The air rippled and shimmered around her fingertips, but her hand couldn't penetrate the invisible barrier.

She stretched forward further with both hands, forcing her palms harder against the space but again, nothing happened. As though she'd pressed her hands into a bottomless bowl of clear jelly.

Tayla stepped back and inspected her hands, rotating them this way and that. No marks, no left-over shimmering; absolutely nothing lingered on her skin. She turned to face the angel.

He half-shrugged. "Told you."

"How do they open, then?"

"Once you decide to go in, they will open for you."

An image appeared in her mind, and her chest tightened. *Raven.* No, how could she have left him?

She bit the inside of her lip. "What if I don't want to go in?"

The angel stepped closer and peered down at her. "Then you'll exist here, in Anahel, the in between. Outside the heavenly gates for the rest of eternity."

She grimaced. That didn't sound like much fun at all, but maybe Raven could...

"He can't reach you if you're out here. This is the mortal entrance. The mortal in between," the angel said, his tone slightly snappier than before.

Darn those mind-reading abilities.

Well, the decision was easy, wasn't it? If Raven

couldn't reach her out here, there was only one thing to do. Enter the fancy gates and wait for him on the other side.

The instant her thought formed, the gates slowly swung inward, revealing vibrant green grassy hills and brilliant clear blue skies.

Tayla crept forward a step. "Do I just, you know, walk through?"

"Yes. Farewell, Tayla."

She glanced over her shoulder. "Thank you...um?"

"Cole."

"Right. Thank you, Cole."

She turned back to the gates and took another step closer. A balmy breeze brushed her cheeks, and the possibility of seeing her parents again brought a smile to her face. One more step, and she could reunite with them. Would they be waiting on the other side for her?

The sweet scent of blooming jasmine and the tang of freshly cut grass filled her nose, while weightlessness drifted through her entire body. So peaceful...

Raven's face appeared in her mind, the image of him cradling her body in her final moments. Whispering in her ear, sweet words meant only for her...*made me whole...you were the key to my faith, this whole time.*

Her foot froze mid-step, hovering above the threshold to the gates.

She couldn't leave Raven. He needed her. If they weren't together, there was a huge chance her death would make him lose his faith again...then he'd turn into a Fallen...

She sucked in a breath and staggered back.

No, she had to get back to Raven before it was too late.

She spun to face Cole. "How do I get back?"

"Back to the mortal realm? Are you serious?" he scoffed.

She straightened her shoulders. "I can't stay here. Raven needs me."

Cole sighed heavily and glared at the sky above. *Is there sky above us?* "Tayla, you can't go back, you're dead."

Duh! "Yeah, I know. But how do I become undead? And not in a freaky zombie way."

His grey eyes locked with hers. "You'd need Fate on your side. And good luck with that," he almost spat the words at her.

"There has to be another way."

He shook his head.

Her shoulders slumped and her heart sank. She was left with no other choice than to enter the gates and wait for Raven, and hope like mad he maintained his faith long enough to complete his mission so he could return to her.

"Right. Well, thanks anyway, Cole." She trudged back to the threshold of the gates.

Think of her as you enter, the words whispered in her mind the moment blinding white light engulfed Cole's body and he disappeared.

Think of who?

Tayla peered at the picturesque landscape on the inside of the gates. Hopefully, Raven would hang on long enough to make it back.

She took a deep breath…*here I go.*

Chapter 38

Raven sagged in the armchair in the corner of his room, elbows on the chair's rounded arms, his head in his hands and fingers shoved through his tangled hair. He stared down at the .40-calibre Glock, a magazine full of Purah bullets, resting on his thigh as though waiting patiently for the command to fire.

One shot was all it would take. The heavenly water was powerful enough to kill any immortal, including him.

But each time he gripped the butt, her beautiful smiling face appeared in his mind; chestnut hair cascaded over her shoulders, hazel eyes lit with joy, and he'd release his hold again. Like she sent him some kind of message that she was okay.

But I'm not.

The hollowness in his chest expanded with each passing day and he found it more and more difficult to…

The dark stuffy room he'd become accustomed to suddenly exploded in light, power shimmered in the air before it gradually dulled.

Great, just what I need.

Raven lifted his head slightly and scowled at the unwelcome visitor. "What the fuck do you want?"

Cole glanced at the pistol on Raven's thigh and

Raven made no attempt to hide it. Instead, Raven glared back, daring Cole to judge. But Cole diverted his gaze and surveyed Raven's dump of a room before using his knee-high leather boots to clear a path and lean against the wall.

Cole inhaled deeply and screwed his nose up. "Thought you'd like to know Tayla arrived. She's gone through the gates."

Was that meant to make him feel better or some shit? All it did was make her death real. Final. He glanced at Tayla's burgundy leather jacket hanging on the back of his door, waiting for her to return.

The gaping hole in his chest expanded. If only he could see her one last…

The idea sprung in his mind and he stared hard at Cole. "Take me to her," he demanded.

Cole shook his head. "Don't you think if I could get past the gates, I would have done so by now?"

"Take me to the barrier then."

"So you can do what exactly? Sneak in?"

When Cole said it like that, of course, it sounded stupid. Raven lowered his head.

"Trust me, Raven, I have as much desire as you to get behind those gates. But you know I can only mist to the entrance and on that side, they only open for mortals." Cole stepped forward and softened his voice. "You need to let her go, brother."

Like hell he did.

Raven glared back at Cole in his ridiculous robe. "Is that what you've done?"

Cole's lips thinned.

"Didn't think so. For over three centuries, I've protected your soulmate on this earth, each and every time she's reborn. She's not my soulmate, nor a Chosen Fate assigns me. I keep her safe for you. Because that's what brothers do." He stared hard into Cole's grey eyes. "You owe me this."

Cole glanced through the window as the silence extended between them.

The ball was in his court. Raven needed an angel to mist him, and Cole had every reason to want Raven to stay alive.

Finally, Cole glanced back at him. "I'll take you there." He nodded toward the gun on Raven's lap. "But the handgun goes away. Permanently. Evie's due to be reborn any year now, and you're the only one I trust to protect her when I can't."

Raven glanced at the Glock. It meant giving up his ticket to end the crippling pain in his chest for a chance to see Tayla again. If that was what it took, then so be it. If all went according to his plan, he wouldn't be coming back anyway.

Raven placed the gun on the side table and nodded to Cole.

Cole crossed to him and placed his heavy hand on Raven's shoulder. The air around them shimmered as blinding light consumed them, instantly transporting their bodies across time and space to arrive at the gates. Not exactly the gates because they only appeared for mortals, but rather, arriving at the empty whiteness on the outside of the invisible barrier.

Raven took a moment for his stomach to settle and his head to stop spinning, his body unfamiliar with misting after so long.

Cole hung back when Raven stepped closer and placed his palms flat on the barrier, the white space rippled and shimmered. The power tingled his fingertips, now a foreign feeling

"Tayla!" he called out, turning his head slightly, listening for a reply.

Silence.

"Tayla!" he yelled louder but yielded the same result.

He glanced back at Cole who shrugged as if to say, "I told you." But Raven wasn't ready to give up yet. He'd gotten this far. He pressed his palms harder against the barrier, pushing with all his strength, but it wouldn't budge.

He would have to swallow his pride and call on the queen herself.

"Fate!" he roared at the top of his lungs.

Cole seized his wrist, gaping at him. "Don't bring her into this."

Raven clenched his jaw and yanked his wrist free. "Why the hell not? It's her fault I can't get in there in the first place."

Cole narrowed his eyes. "I know, but do you think she'll take kindly to you trying to sneak in? Or for me helping you? You know what she's like. Piss her off again and she'll probably exile Tayla to a different region from her parents just to spite you."

Goddamn it. His heart sank; he hadn't thought of that. No way would he risk preventing Tayla from reuniting with her parents. Cole was right. No telling what Fate might do.

"Argh!" he roared, stomping away. "Why does Fate keep punishing me?"

Cole held back. "I don't know, brother. We both know she works in strange ways."

Raven faced the impenetrable barrier, and his shoulders slumped in the defining silence that followed. Tayla was behind those gates somewhere, and he had no way to reach her.

He stepped forward and brushed his fingertips down the barrier. The air shimmered around them. "I will love you for the rest of eternity," he whispered.

Cole placed a palm on Raven's shoulder. "Let me take you back."

Raven waited several heartbeats of silence before he nodded.

****

Raven sagged onto the same armchair and dropped his head in his hands, he couldn't bring himself to glimpse the pity in Cole's eyes when he'd misted off the balcony.

His one and only plan had failed, and now he was stuck back in this empty room. This empty realm.

Without her.

Mortals said there were five stages of grief. Five stages one's body and soul staggered through before spitting out the other side all healed.

Well, fuck that.

He didn't want his soul healed. All he wanted was…her.

He didn't want to get through grief; grief equaled pain, and he'd cling to that until the very end. Because pain was all he had left.

He glanced at the pistol sitting on top of the dresser; the handgun he'd vowed to Cole he wouldn't use. Just as well, with his luck, the shitty move would send him in the opposite direction and he'd arrive at the fiery gates instead, and his chance to reunite with Tayla would be gone forever.

He wrapped his fingers around Tayla's peach-colored shirt and brought it to his nose once more, inhaling her lingering scent; the constant source of agony for his broken heart.

Correction, for the gaping hole where his heart once beat.

Chapter 39

The instant Tayla passed the threshold, the extravagant gates silently closed behind her and the gravity of her situation sank in.

How could she have been so careless? She should've let Raine drive the car. Raine would have had quicker reflexes, even with her lack of driving experience. Maybe if Raine drove, the car wouldn't have spun out of control. Or slid off the edge of the cliff.

Oh, god. Was Raine okay?

She rolled her eyes. Great to see her over-analyzing mind hadn't disappeared even though she was dead. Just perfect.

Tayla plonked down cross-legged on the softest green grass she'd ever felt. A light balmy breeze blew loose strands of hair across her face, and she tucked them behind her ear.

Now what?

She peered over her shoulder left and right. Manicured green hills scattered sporadically with flowering daisies stretched far into the distance in both directions.

Was she meant to just sit here on this cushiony grass for the rest of eternity waiting for Raven?

Raven.

If only she had the power to get back to him. If only she wasn't dead…

Wait! What had Cole said? *Think of her as you enter.* Did he mean there was an angel who had the power to change her fate? At this point, she'd try anything.

Tayla jumped off the grass and brought forward a mental image in her mind, of her and Raven reuniting. Her being no longer dead. Her fate changing…

Tayla gasped as the landscape around her shimmered, suddenly it swirled and changed before her eyes.

"*Tayla.*"

She sucked in a breath when Raven's voice boomed around her.

Spinning on her heels, she bolted toward the fading gates—and collided with an old rickety wooden park bench that appeared out of nowhere in front of her.

"No," she screamed. "Raven!"

Her heart raced as she frantically searched her new surroundings for the gates, but they'd disappeared. Gone. And so was Raven.

One moment she'd stood on a grassy mound, and the next, she'd been transported to some sort of secluded garden. Slowly, she turned on the spot and glanced around the space. Mature cherry blossoms surrounded a park bench; beautiful pastel pink and white flowers covered the extended branches and scattered on the grass below. The bench's wooden slats, faded and splintered on the edges, gave the impression of being built centuries ago. Ancient trees grew along the long narrow manicured lawn. She didn't know what type they were, but from the size and height of their trunks, they'd been there forever, probably longer than the bench. Brown fallen leaves and shrubs covered the ground underneath.

She started to wander down the never-ending lawn when a light shimmered out of the corner of her eye and an angel ducked out from under the cherry blossom branches.

The angel grinned. "You made it."

Tayla gaped at the breathtaking being standing before her. A slim figure dressed in an elegant white, lacy knee-length dress, her flawless skin on show between the intricately woven flowers. A narrow pastel pink satin sash tied around her middle, the ends hanging down to one side. The angel's golden blonde hair fell in waves over her shoulders, glowing in the sunlight streaming between the trees.

Tayla cleared her throat and closed her gaping mouth. "Ah, hi."

The angel folded her iridescent white wings behind her back and gracefully strolled toward her. No, more like glided, as though so light the ground wouldn't have realized she trod on it. A few steps from Tayla, the angel paused and tilted her head to one side, as though she'd heard a noise. For the briefest moment, her rose-pink lips thinned before she regained her composure and glanced at Tayla.

"How did I get here?" Tayla asked.

"You died, sweetie."

Why does everyone keep reminding me of that? "No, I mean, how did I get from behind the gates to here?"

The angel motioned toward the old rickety bench. Was it even safe to sit on? *It's not as if I could die if it collapsed.*

The wooden slats sagged and creaked as Tayla sat down and crossed her legs underneath the bench, not chancing any sudden movements. No need to test the bench collapsing theory. The seat didn't even groan as the petite angel folded her dress behind the back of her legs and gracefully sat at the opposite end, facing the majestic garden.

The situation couldn't get any weirder. Unless, a butler appeared and served them tea and cucumber sandwiches cut into tiny rectangles. Where the heck was she?

The angel glanced at Tayla. "Is this not where you wanted to be?"

Tayla peered at the majestic gardens and inhaled deeply. "Not exactly. I want to be with Raven, but everyone keeps reminding me that's no longer an option. Apparently, my path has ended."

"And what makes you think your path as a Chosen is complete?"

Tayla narrowed her eyes and raised an eyebrow. "Because I'm *dead*."

"And so, you thought to change your ending?"

"How did you...?" She shook her head. "Never mind. Yes, I'd hope to seek out an angel with the power to change my path. Make me undead." She chuckled. "Sounds silly, I know."

The angel smiled, lighting up her sapphire blue eyes. "Yet..." She motioned to their surroundings. "Here you are."

Tayla narrowed her eyes. "You're the angel who can change my path?"

"I am Fate," she replied with an air of authority.

What the…?

Tayla twisted around to face the angel, Fate, and the bench groaned underneath. *Please don't break.*

"Fate? As in…the Fate?"

"Mortals refer to me by many different names. Destiny, Chance, the Universe." She grinned. "I've always found that term amusing, how can I be the whole universe when I created it? Anyway, my true name is Fate."

Okaaaay. Now Tayla gave her mind permission to freak the heck out, and all at once, conversations she'd had with Raven made a whole lot more sense now.

"You…you set all this up? You brought Raven and I together to prevent him from becoming a Fallen?" She sucked in a breath. "Then you killed me."

"Technically, I didn't kill you."

"But I was so determined to drop my key off. I couldn't shake the feeling." Her eyes widened. "Did you compel me to go out, just so I would die?"

"You were mortal. How else would you arrive in the Heavens?"

"And I guess you compelled that Fallen to land right in front of the car?"

Fate pursed her lips. "No. I cannot see those shadows."

Whatever the heck that means.

Tayla threw her arms up. "Ugh! You took me from Raven, right when he needed me the most." Urgency laced her voice. "I have to get back to him. He needs my help."

Fate remained unaffected, staring at the gardens before her as though waiting patiently for those sandwiches to arrive. "And why would an immortal

Guardian as powerful as Raven need your help?"

"He said I'm the key to him maintaining his faith." She exhaled a long breath. "I love him, and I'm so worried my death will send him back down the Fallen path."

Fate smirked but continued to stare ahead. "And what would I get out of this bargain?" She turned her body to face Tayla. "Immortality is a big request, Tayla, even for a Chosen. Why should I grant it to you?"

Tayla froze. *Immortality?* She hadn't asked for immortality…had she? But now that Fate mentioned it, the chance to be with Raven for the rest of eternity sounded like a pretty darn good idea.

Think, Tayla, think! Come up with something, this may be your only chance. What could Fate possibly want enough to grant…

"You'll get your Guardians back." She stood, facing Fate. "If Raven maintains his faith, he'll no longer be at risk of becoming a Fallen. He can save Blaine and return him to the Heavens." She straightened her shoulders. "From what I understand, if Raven returns Blaine to the Heavens, he'll complete the mission you tasked him with, and he, too, can finally return. They all can. I'll ensure the light in Raven's soul burns bright."

Fate's sapphire eyes flickered with silver and after a slight pause, she nodded. "Very well."

What? That was easier than expected…

"Wait. Is there a catch?" Tayla asked.

Fate rose from the bench to stand, straightening her summer dress and brushed off imaginary dirt from the front. "Your immortality will be tied to Raven's. Where his path ends, so does yours." She peered over at her, staring straight into her soul. A prickle ran down Tayla's spine. "Last chance to change your mind. This deal means giving up the path to see your parents."

Her chest tightened. To see her parents after so long; to find out they were okay, to embrace them one more time. Could she give that up?

Of course, at the exact moment she needed her over-analyzing mind it refused to come out and play. Damn it.

Fate strolled—floated—to a cherry blossom tree and plucked a delicate petal from the branch. "Do we have a deal?" she asked.

Tayla took a deep breath. For Fate to mention them, her parents must be here somewhere, which meant they were okay. She'd always been in awe of the love they shared for one another, proof that soulmates truly did exist. They'd encouraged her to have faith in her destiny, which in the end, had led her to this very moment. She smiled to herself. Her parents would want her to choose love above everything else.

"Yes," Tayla breathed.

A sudden ache expanded in her chest. She would save the reunion with her parents until she and Raven returned together.

Fate turned back to Tayla. "Off you go then. That Guardian of yours is missing you. More than I expected," she muttered the last part to herself.

Fate tossed the pale pink blossom in the air toward Tayla. It hovered just out of reach, shimmering in slow motion, twisting and turning. A ripple formed in the air surrounding it. Suddenly, the landscape shimmered as well. A tingling sensation prickled over Tayla's skin and weightlessness filled her body from the inside out.

Tayla sucked in a breath. *What the heck is happening?*

Fate half-smiled, in a sad kind of way, and bid Tayla farewell with a flick of her hand.

A wave of dizziness washed over her as everything blurred, as if on a carnival ride spinning out of control, even with her feet planted firmly on the ground.

Nausea rose in the back of her throat.

Fate whispered in her mind, *Not all paths are destined to end here.*

And Tayla blacked out.

Chapter 40

Was it day, night, winter, summer? Raven didn't fucking know. And he didn't give a shit either.

Ever since Cole deserted him, dropped his ass back in the mortal realm, he'd been slumped in the same frickin' armchair, going through the motions of existing without actually living.

Is she okay? The question plagued him countless times a day, and each time it arrived in his head, his heart ripped open all over again.

He threw back another shot of tasteless bourbon, the alcohol having long ago lost its desired effect.

A shimmer of power rippled through Raven's bedroom and he turned his head to find Gabe standing on the balcony, facing the pine trees, his golden wings folding away.

Raven eased the empty glass down on the floor beside his feet; his knees and back creaked as he rose from the armchair. He rested his hand on the side table and stilled for a moment, waiting for the room to cease spinning.

He stumbled through the empty bourbon bottle obstacle course, shoving one aside with his bare foot, and pulled open the French doors. Crisp air caught his breath as he joined Gabe on the balcony. Bitter wind howled through the pine trees, their tops swaying like they too had been on one helluva bender.

Raven put his forearms on the chunky wood railing, squinting up at the deep purple and grey clouds.

"Good evening, my friend," Gabe sighed, staring out toward the forest.

"Is it? Good, I mean?"

Raven's gaze traveled over the snow dusted outer branches of the pine trees, down over the small powdery mounds scattered on the deserted garden beds. The remaining flowers were brown and droopy, suffering a slow and miserable death.

I know how they feel.

"How long has it been?" he croaked.

"Long enough, my friend. It is time."

"So everyone keeps saying." He peered at Gabe, who slung his navy checked blazer over the railing and used one hand to loosen the tie at his neck. "Have you seen her?" Raven asked.

Gabe's gaze lowered, and he shook his head.

Raven clenched his jaw. "You're an Archangel, Gabe, how could you not have seen her?"

"These things take time, Raven, you know that. And time itself moves differently there. Right now, it's as if she's only just arrived."

His ribs tightened, squeezing the air from his lungs. *Inhale…exhale…inhale.*

Gabe's firm hand squeezed Raven's shoulder and chased away the rage bubbling underneath his skin.

Nothing's going to fill the hole she left behind.

"Fate sent her for me, didn't she?" he choked. "To restore my faith."

Gabe slowly nodded. "As I understand, yes."

"Why didn't you tell me?"

"Raven, you know Fate's power doesn't work like that. You had to choose. She may pave a multitude of paths, but the individual must choose which direction to follow. You had to choose Tayla."

Raven shoved his fingers through his disheveled hair. "God. Why didn't I bloody listen to you in the beginning? I could have had more time with her." His voice broke, and he leaned his elbows back on the railing. "Why couldn't Fate have given me more time?"

"Each moment is a memory to cherish, my friend, however fleeting."

Raven scoffed. Gabe and his fucking positivity.

"I loved her more than she could ever know."

Gabe's shoulders dropped. "Which was the whole point."

Moments of silence past between them. Raven inhaled the bland air. The earthy fragrance from the pine trees and the smoky wood fire scent puffing from the chimney had vanished from the air, having died along with her.

Gabe turned toward Raven, leaning one elbow on the railing. "Why have you not cleared the air with Raine?"

Raven shook his head. "I know it wasn't her fault. I just can't. I'm not fit for company at the moment."

"She needs your guidance, Raven. Try not to forget your reason for being in this realm in the first place. Only you can lead this mission, and you must maintain the strength in your entire team."

Raven turned, pointing toward the armchair inside his room, the indent of his ass still creased in the seat. "I can't even bring myself to get out of that fucking chair. How do you expect me to lead them?"

The corner of Gabe's mouth twitched, and he straightened his shoulders. "Well, my friend." He motioned to Raven's bare feet. "You've just taken the first step. Now is time."

"How can you be so sure?"

"Because I have faith in your abilities as their leader. Faith you will complete the mission you set out to do all those centuries ago. I have faith in you, my friend." Gabe stepped beside Raven and peered into the trashed bedroom. "Don't let Tayla's Chosen path, and her resulting sacrifice, be for nothing."

Raven examined the shitty room through the open doors.

The vacant chair he'd parked in for so long. The Glock he'd vowed to Cole he wouldn't use rested on the side table, the empty bourbon bottles littered across the carpet, and the trays of uneaten food someone kept delivering.

Raven's chest tightened as his gaze lingered on the bed. The bed he'd shared with Tayla. Where they'd made love for the first time, which now felt like centuries ago.

Suddenly, something inside him, deep down, shifted. Clarity seeped in, like headlights in the distance slowly coming into focus on a foggy night.

He'd arrived at his metaphorical fork in the road; his destiny paving two paths for him again.

Thanks a fucking lot, Fate.

He could either continue on a bender of self-destruction and self-pity, drink himself into a stupor every day, and forget about the outside world. Forget any of that horror even happened, and forever live in the memories of her.

Or he could sober the hell up and get his shit together. Complete the mission he'd set out to do all those centuries ago—save Blaine and wipe all the Fallen from the face of this earth. Then, he could return to the Heavens. *No big deal.*

But when he stopped and considered his two paths, the one choice he could make to influence his own destiny, the decision was easy. Only one path reunited him with Tayla.

Straightening his shoulders, he faced Gabe. "What do you need me to do?"

The corners of Gabe's mouth lifted in a slow smile. "First, we need to get you showered and tidy that disaster you call your room."

Gabe meticulously rolled up the sleeves of his black, immaculately pressed business shirt, as if preparing for a long night of board meetings.

Raven took a deep breath and stepped across the threshold into his bedroom, sealing his decision.

He would not forget her. No fucking way. His heart would bleed for the rest of his existence. But right now, in that moment, he vowed to follow through with her final wish. He would save Blaine.

And after that, he would reunite with Tayla, his soulmate, and love her for the rest of eternity.

****

The legs on Raven's chair scraped against the wood floor as he pushed out from the table, the ear-piercing screech echoing in the silent room. He crossed the study to pause at the full-length window. Folding his arms across his chest, he peered out at the far side of the gardens.

In the distance, among the thick forest of pines, he

spotted a slim figure bolting through the trees. Raine. Dressed in all black, a silver weapon gleamed in her hand, she darted this way and that before she gripped a protruding branch and effortlessly swung herself up into the foliage, to nestle against a thick trunk.

She'd pulled that stealthy move on him a few times, too.

A few hundred feet behind her, a much larger figure in a black tee and jeans gave chase. Gaining. Aric, completely unaware of the pending ambush just up ahead.

Raven grinned. *Good luck with that, brother.*

Raven turned back to face the empty seats at the board table. The other Guardian's had departed maybe an hour or so before. Raine and Aric off to train, EJ headed to the gym and River intent on catching some rays.

It'd been one month, twenty-two days, nineteen hours and—glancing over at the antique clock on the side table—about thirty-four minutes, since he'd lost her, and today, he just wasn't into it. His body was physically here, but his mind, his soul, were absent, MIA on the search for its mate. It wasn't the first time he'd had a moment like this or a day. He wasn't about to send himself on another bender, he just needed some time alone.

He leaned against the wall and absently brushed his thumb over the fresh ink on his left pec; Tayla's name scripted across his heart.

His permanent reminder.

Each night, Raven had led patrols, being the first one to arrive at the agreed location and the last one to leave. He told the others it was to boost their numbers;

the more of them out there, the better protected they were. But, of course, that was a load of bullshit. Well, it was true, just not exactly the whole reason for his new found over-achieving enthusiasm to wipe the Fallen from the face of this earth.

Patrols were a helluva lot more productive than lying in his cold bed alone or wandering the halls to catch Tayla's lingering scent—which was fading too goddamn quickly.

Since the bonfire, Fallen sightings, even on the outskirts in the smaller, dodgier type clubs and bars, had decreased. Like they took a vacation or some shit and that was just his luck. The time he could use a fight, a distraction, anything, they were AWOL. He hadn't run into Blaine recently either, and considering he'd popped up almost fucking everywhere, his absence made Raven suspicious. The last time he'd sensed Blaine's presence was the night when…well, on that night.

Raven's ribcage closed in on his lungs as though someone decided to sit on his chest.

Pushing off the wall, he crossed to the mahogany board table to lean on the edge with both palms. Even if the Fallen were off sipping cocktails on a tropical island—no, skinny dipping in a pool of lava was probably more their style—he sensed the war between the two sides escalating. He and his brothers needed to use this little breather to their advantage, to get on the front foot for a change, rather than patrolling each night and reacting to whatever situation they found.

He studied the map of the Snowy Mountains spread open in the center of the table. It detailed Summit Creek Dam, the main town of Summit Creek, locations of various ski resorts, and the four major roads leading in and out. Aric marked Fallen sightings with a red circle, a cross through the center if they were taken out—which happened more often than not. Frequently visited places identified by the larger number of red circles.

Raven stood back with his arms crossed and studied it closer. There had to be something they were missing. He grabbed a pencil lying on the table and bent down, drawing a straight line from one red circle to the next until—

His mouth fell open. *No fucking way.*

"Rave!"

His head shot up to find EJ peeking around the door jamb, earphones dangling out the top of his charcoal hoodie, a bottle of water in his hand.

"You ready to have your world rocked?" EJ smirked.

"What?"

EJ winked before disappearing out of sight. "You'll see," he called out. "Any minute now…" His voice trailed off as he continued down the hallway.

What the hell was EJ talking about now?

Awareness shivered down Raven's spine and he jerked upright. The pencil fell from his hand and bounced on the floor.

He held his breath as a faint connection stirred inside, reignited, increasing in intensity and strength as it weaved itself back together. At the same time, the weight of his grief lifted.

No…it can't be.

He raced to the window and peered out toward the gardens as heavenly light faded, revealing a female sitting back on her knees in the center of the lawn. A soft glow encased her body. Her head lowered in her hands. Beautiful chestnut wavy hair tumbled over her shoulders, loose strands blowing across her face in the wind.

Raven's brain dissolved into mush. He couldn't think, couldn't process what happened.

His soul caught on first and screamed at him, as though it clued in light years before his head managed to connect the dots.

It looked so much like her. He sensed it was her. But how...

She lowered her hands into her lap and lifted her gaze toward the house, to the very window he stared from, like she somehow sensed him, too.

His knees weakened, and he steadied himself with his hand on the window sill to stop from falling on the floor. Then his head finally caught up.

Tayla.

Raven barreled out of the study and down the hall, leaping down the stairs, and throwing open the front door with such force it ripped off the hinges.

Should have jumped out the fucking window.

Crossing the entrance and gravel drive in a second flat, he raced over the dewy grass to her. His knees gave out, and he collapsed in front of her.

Her narrowed hazel eyes stared at him, her eyebrows knitted as though she had no clue where she was. Or who he was.

"Tayla?" he whispered, leaning forward, taking her hands in his.

A heartbeat later, her eyes widened. "Ra..." She cleared her croaky voice. "Raven?"

"Yes, honey, it's me." He tucked her windswept

hair behind her ear. Well, tried to, as the wind blew it back in her face a second later.

"She did it." Tayla squeezed his hands. "She actually did it."

"Who? Did what?"

She grinned, lighting up her clear hazel eyes, which were so much brighter than he remembered, more beautiful than the pictures in his head.

He brushed her cheek with his thumb.

"Fate. She sent me back to you."

His hand froze. No. Fucking. Way.

Tayla laid her warm palm on top of his. Warm hand. Not cold.

"She brought me back to you, Raven," she whispered.

His heart sank through the earth below his knees. Was this another one of Fate's sick jokes? He shook his head. "No. Tayla, please tell me you didn't bargain with Fate."

She chuckled. "I sure did."

He squeezed her shoulders to get her attention. "Tell me what she said. Exactly what she said. Every goddamn word."

"I'm immortal now, like you." She frowned. "Aren't you happy?"

"Of course, I am." He cradled her jaw in his palms and lightly brushed his thumbs over her cheeks. "It's just…Fate has a way of manipulating choices. Using them to her advantage."

"Well, if she uses returning me to you to her advantage, then so be it. I would choose you every single day. Who cares why she did it."

Raven exhaled a long breath. "Are you sure? What

about your parents? I can't ask you to give up being with them."

She smiled. "I'm going to save that reunion until we return together. They would have wanted me to follow my heart, and that's exactly what I did. Now stop talking and kiss me already."

He didn't know what the hell was going on, or how long it would last. What he did know was he had at least one more moment with his soulmate, and he would take Gabe's advice and cherish every second of it.

He lowered his voice. "I'm gonna do more than kiss you."

He rose to his feet and helped Tayla up. In one swift movement, he tucked one arm under her knees and the other across the back of her shoulders, lifting her. With his precious cargo cradled safely in his arms, he turned and beelined for the house. For his room. Their room.

Tayla giggled, "I can walk, you know."

"I know, but it seems right for me to carry you. You know, across the threshold into our new beginning."

Tayla touched his cheek with her hand. "Every choice I've made has led me to you. We were destined to be together."

He smiled down at her, unable to form a reply.

Out of the corner of his eye, he caught everyone standing on the edge of the lawn. Everyone, that is, except Raine. EJ casually stood beside the splintered front door, his hands stuffed in the pockets of his faded jeans, a mile-wide grin and a "ta-da" expression on his face.

Tayla glanced around his shoulder and waved to the others as he stalked past them; a chorus of "Hi" and "Welcome back" sang out. But they could wait for later tonight. Scrap that; they could wait until tomorrow. Or next week.

His shoes crunched along the gravel drive, coming to a halt at the far side of the house. He extended his wings and leaned his head down to take Tayla's lips in a fevered kiss as he shot up, landing with a heavy thud on his balcony. Their balcony.

Tayla leaned her head back and brushed her thumb along his lower lip. "Fate said you missed me," she teased.

His heart hammered against his chest. Every century in the mortal realm had led him to this moment. Tayla was the reason for his existence, the strength and source of his faith, and he planned to worship her every single day that followed.

For the first time in god knows how long, he looked forward to the future. Looking forward to the sun rising on a brand new day.

She made him whole.

"Honey, you have no idea," he murmured before kicking open the French doors, heading straight for their bed.

Epilogue

Raven wrapped his arms around Tayla and nestled her body closer to his. Her head rested on his shoulder as they lay naked, sprawled underneath a plush duvet, in the secluded spot on the side of the mountain that had quickly become theirs, rather than his.

And he was more than okay with that.

Tonight, the air was still. Clear skies exploded with an abundance of shimmering stars, sparkling in a kaleidoscope of colors. A perfect night. Well, except for the stupid stone underneath the rug, digging into his hip like a hundred miniature blades stabbing his flesh, shooting throbbing pain down his right leg.

His bad luck it pushed on a fucking nerve. Even so, he wouldn't move. No way would he disturb this moment for a measly rock.

Tayla sighed and snuggled in closer.

He kissed the top of her head. "You warm enough?"

"I don't feel the cold anymore, remember?"

"I know, but it's way more fun pretending you do."

Her chuckle vibrated against his chest and he grinned, lowering his head again.

The comfortable silence stretched between them. Raven lay content, listening to the steady beat of her heart in unison with his. It'd been a few short weeks since Fate returned her to Earth. Immortality agreed with her; she'd effortlessly become part of his thrown together family, fitting into the immortal world as though she'd always been there.

In a way, she had.

Tayla stretched her arm out and groaned. "My arms are killing me. I thought immortality would automatically come with immortal strength."

"It hasn't been that long; your body is still adjusting. Don't push it too hard."

"Can you put that in writing? Because I don't think Raine got the memo. I didn't realize self-defense lessons was code for learning to fight like a warrior."

Raven chuckled. "How are they going?"

It took a bit to accept Tayla was immortal like him and no longer a fragile Chosen needing his protection. At first, he'd rejected the request from Raine to teach her. He was all for Tayla learning to protect herself, but he preferred to be the teacher. Raine had insisted, though, and he didn't want to be an ass about it.

Tayla propped herself up on one elbow to look at him. "She's more protective than you, and I didn't think that was even possible. I keep telling her I'm not going to carry all those daggers she made for me, but she refuses to listen."

He absently pulled the duvet farther up her shoulder to protect her from the chill that no longer affected her. "I think she might carry a bit of guilt over what happened."

"I thought the same, which is why I agreed to the lessons. She keeps telling me a woman needs to be able to protect herself, which is fine, but seriously, I don't need to lead an army."

"I'll have a chat with her if you'd like."

"No, let her go. Maybe she just likes having another girl in the house." Tayla chortled. "She bought me a pair of shoes the other day, shiny red pointy ones with a gigantic heel. I can't even walk in them."

Raven's hand wandered down over Tayla's smooth skin to lightly squeeze her hip. "Maybe you could wear them for me," he rumbled.

She threw her head back and laughed. "As long as I don't have to walk anywhere."

"I'm sure that can be arranged."

He placed his palm around her nape and pulled her in for a feverish kiss—the only kind between them. New to immortality, Tayla had an insatiable desire in the bedroom. Which he wasn't complaining about.

She nestled in beside him once more, resting her head in the crook of his arm.

"Have you seen Blaine, yet?" she asked, circling her index finger around her name tattooed on his chest.

"No. But it's not unusual for him to disappear for months or years at a time. He possesses the ability to mist back and forth to different realms in Hell and I imagine the concept of time is similar to the Heavens. A week here might only be a minute there."

"I wonder what it's like there."

"Probably hot."

Tayla cocked an eyebrow. "Gee, you think?" Her finger paused for a second before continuing the lazy circles. "The Heavens were so beautiful," she said distantly. "The colors so vivid, bright lush green grass, clear blue sky. Is it always like that?"

It'd been so long since he'd been there, the memories had all but faded away. He inhaled a deep breath, expecting a heavy weight to fall on his chest as it did every time he thought of his home. But in this moment, it didn't.

"There are different regions in the Heavens with a variety of landscapes but yeah, they're all perfect. The soul gravitates to whichever region it desires the most, and that's where it stays. Almost like your soul chooses its favorite holiday destination to live out your eternity in."

She rose up on her elbow once more. "Is that the same for angels?"

"No, angels roam different regions depending on what role they have. Some of them have a region they call home, but others prefer to spend time in all of them."

"Seems my soul wanted a part in *The Sound of Music* until it disappeared and went to a garden filled with cherry blossoms."

"Fate's sanctuary," he muttered, propping himself up on his elbow. "Summoning Fate is no easy feat. I'm so proud of you. It takes an incredible amount of faith to pull it off." He paused for a second. "Unless, I guess, she's expecting you."

She smiled. "I did have a little help from Cole."

He nodded, but his gaze drifted to the pine trees behind her. He couldn't help but wonder what she'd seen, where she traveled, who she encountered, but he didn't want to rush her. Becoming an immortal was overwhelming enough without the added layer of comprehending the other realms outside Earth.

Tayla touched his cheek. "Hey, what's wrong? What are you thinking about?"

He met her gaze and tucked a strand of hair behind

her ear. "It's just…well, do you mind if I ask you something?"

"Of course not."

He paused for a moment to figure out the best way to approach the subject. "Aric asked the other day if you happened to see any other angels while you were there."

"Besides Cole, I only saw Fate. Why?"

He sighed. Even though he suspected that would be the answer, it still hit hard.

"He just…well, given you were able to enter Fate's sanctuary, he hoped you'd seen someone, or maybe someone had made a point of tracking you down."

Her smile dropped. "I wish I could say yes."

"Don't worry. It was a long shot anyway, and he knows that."

Tayla wriggled up to sit, wrapping half the duvet under her arms and across her chest.

Damn it, he shouldn't have asked. The last thing he wanted to do was ruin this moment between them. He sat up and let the duvet fall from his chest to his lap. "As much as I hate the idea, why don't we get dressed and rummage through that picnic basket full of goodies?"

"You mean we're actually going to eat something and not lie here naked all night?"

He laughed.

Tayla reached for her shirt but before she got the chance, he snatched it and tossed it behind him.

She smirked. "I thought we were getting dressed?"

He leaned in and paused just before touching her lips. "Nah, that was a stupid idea. The food can wait, it's not going anywhere."

Tayla's giggle turned into a moan as he took her mouth with his in a long, slow kiss, and lifted her onto his lap. He leaned back to admire her face, cupping her jaw between his palms. No longer did he possess the dire urge to return to the Heavens. No longer did he fear maintaining his faith. No longer did he doubt Fate's plan for him and his brothers. She had something up her sleeve, but only now he realized it wouldn't be another form of twisted punishment.

Only now he felt as though he and his brothers weren't entirely forsaken.

Everything he'd craved in his centuries on this earth was cradled in his arms. His soulmate. "God, I love you," he breathed.

A soft smile curved her lips. "I love you, too. Now, kiss me already."

He chuckled and took her mouth with his, tender at first before building to a slow burn that would keep them warm all night.

A word about the author...

Growing up in a military family, forever on the move, Cassie had a childhood filled with countless crazy adventures. Eventually, sunny Queensland stole her heart, and she now calls it home with her husband and their two BMX-crazy boys.

Borderline obsessed with the paranormal world, Cassie has a passion for crafting stories involving strong, otherworldly characters in need of redemption. She's a self-confessed book-a-holic and a sucker for a gut wrenching happily ever after.

When she isn't narrating imaginary characters, Cassie loves binging on TV shows, spending time at the beach, and curling up listening to the rain.

http://cassielaelyn.com